BENEATH A SUN DEPRIVED SKY

KARA LENORE

ALSO BY KARA LENORE

<u>Short Stories</u>

"Climbing" in *Mixed Bag of Tricks*

First published in the United States in 2025 by Murasaki Press LLC
Copyright © 2024 by Kara Lenore
Cover illustration and design by Sarah J. Coleman

First Edition—2025/layout and map by Britta Jensen, editors: Britta Jensen and Nancy Knight

Murasaki Press LLC
PO Box 152313
Austin, TX 78715
U.S.A.

School and bulk sales of this book can be purchased for business or promotional purposes. For more information, email info@murasakipress.com.

Join the author's mailing list and read bonus materials at karalenore.com

This book has been catalogued for libraries as follows:
Names: Lenore, Kara, author.
Title: Beneath a sun deprived sky / Kara Lenore.
Description: Austin, TX : Murasaki Press, 2025.
Identifiers: ISBN 978-1-966241-98-0 (paperback) | ISBN 978-1-966241-97-3 (hardcover) | ISBN 978-1-966241-99-7 (ebook) | ISBN 978-1-966241-96-6 (audiobook)
Subjects: LCSH: Physicians--Fiction. | Extraterrestrial beings--Fiction. | Space operas (Fiction) | Science fiction. | Action and adventure fiction. | Romance fiction. | BISAC: FICTION / Science Fiction / Space Opera. | FICTION / Science Fiction / Action & Adventure. | FICTION / Romance / Science Fiction. | GSAFD: Science fiction. | Adventure fiction. | Love stories.

Classification: LCC PS3612.E46 B46 2025 (print) | PS3612.E46 (ebook) | DDC 813/.6--dc23.

For my sibs who jump started my creativity.

Dawn, who enacted Barbie space operas with me and always let me be Princess Leia. And Glenn, who meticulously illustrated my childish cyberpunk scribblings.

We're far apart, but you're always with me.

N
W
E
S
Galta 4
LANDING PAD
crater
No Man's Land
G4 City
(beneath volcano-shaped rock formation)
Downed Ship
Balter's Den
F'ring West Gate
HIGHWAY
F'ring East Gate
FIRST RING CITY
Pell Mahr
WALL
Taber
Farth
The Core
Tir
THE
MAZE
Trimmer
Fet *
Grell
Rever
No Man's Land
Axe *
The Xeno
Skull *
Freeland
* borough
©2021 Britta Jensen

1

You cannot close your eyes to flee the dark.
—*Cartoran proverb*

CROSSING HALF THE GALAXY FROM CARTOR HADN'T MADE SPACE ANY LESS terrifying. Del stood frozen before the docking station's shuttered viewport. *Whatever I face out there, I'm on my own now.* Her head swam, and the deck shifted beneath her feet. She jerked her hand upward to catch the bulkhead rail then dropped it back to her side, feeling foolish. It wasn't the *deck* that was unsteady.

It's only irrational fear.

Del slashed a hand, and the shutters snicked open to reveal a rust-mottled planet. Galta 4. Her breath expelled with a shuddery sigh. Her new home looked like a scarred disk, battered flat. She stroked her gloved fingertips over the viewport's surface. *I'm finally here.*

Galta 4's bubble of planet-scaped terrain was too minuscule to zoom into from space—a level-two colony, not hostile enough to forbid life, not hospitable enough to welcome it.

The drop-jockey pilot Del hired stepped up to her shoulder, the holo-pin license clipped on the woman's collar glinting in Del's peripheral vision. "You sure about this, Dr. Marks?"

"I'd hardly waste your time otherwise." Del fixed a bland smile on her lips. Not that she didn't understand the pilot's skepticism. Your average traveler did not bounce down with the cargo.

An access tube had led them to this tiny compartment beneath the transport ship's belly, a docking station for a cargo container's steering-capsule—featureless but for the viewport.

The pilot bent to adjust her padded flight suit, but Del caught the amusement crinkling her face. "A proper *people* transport departs Bel Asar Station in three cycles."

"I can't *wait* three cycles. People in need are depending on me, Captain." Thousands without proper medical care.

Memory strobed through Del—waking from the soul-deep chill of stasis to a thundering pulse, a shrill of monitors, then the jab of a needle and flood of cool, artificial calm …

She'd emerged from that sick disorientation to find herself alone, the chamber her partner Zavi should have occupied since the ship's last port empty, only a message waiting: *'Do NOT dock at Bel Asar Station. I've hit a snare. Get planetside without me. IMMEDIATELY.'*

Nothing more, no matter how many times she pinged him.

Acer sighed. "I'm more a 'press-and-release' grunt than a captain." She ran a hand through her close-cropped brown hair. "I've never piggy-backed a passenger, and you look …" Her dark eyes skimmed over Del. "… green-gilled already."

"*Space* makes me green." Wobbly with stasis sickness. Queasy with nerves.

The creases bracketing Acer's wide mouth quirked. "Well, you've crossed a pretty distance through it. But then it takes a measure of … determination to drive most folk out here."

Del read the unsaid word in Acer's hesitation, *desperation.* She matched no one's image of an intrepid pioneer. Even friends and medical colleagues had warned her not to wing off on a "mad impulse." Yet she'd reached the deep frontier—as far from the strangling coil of family as possible—*Going Where the Need is Greatest.* Since she'd first set eyes on the Inter-World Advocacy's slogan as an isolated teen, it had lit a fire inside her to transcend her upbringing, do something *real*.

Del glanced at the viewport, the vivid disk of the planet filling it.

Whole star systems lay between her and any verdant world. Sudden pressure squeezed her chest, visceral longing for solid ground, boundless sky, unprocessed air—a warning twinge of the wrenching astrophobia that had nearly disqualified her from this mission. *I've managed this far.*

Acer stamped a booted foot and re-clamped the top buckle. "One more leg and you're groundside." She stepped around Del to the capsule's hatch. "If you're sure, I'm on a schedule."

Del's limbs tingled with numbness despite her bulky flight suit as she trailed Acer into a cockpit little wider than an arm's breadth. Only one seat. Del shot Acer a wide-eyed look. Amusement flashing, the pilot seized Del's shoulders and wrestled her arms through a harness on the bulkhead, leaving Del on tippy-toes, arms raised in a surrender posture. Acer grunted a curse and yanked the harness lower to adjust to Del's height. A few tugs and Del found herself strapped to the bulkhead like baggage.

Acer wedged her huge frame into the pilot's position, which encroached on Del's patch of bulkhead, the seatback bumping Del's leg. Del cast a dizzied gaze around the cockpit. Metal switches and crude lights akin to something in a historical vid-film. This craft was basically a foil capsule strapped atop a cargo container.

Acer flipped switches. The cockpit shook to life beneath a blast of sound, a sharp reminder that the craft possessed a crude engine packed with fuel cells.

Oh gods, this is going to be awful.

"Transport control, this is Drop Thirteen. Initiating separation."

"Copy that." A tinny voice came through the comm. "You are clear in sixty."

Del's insides lurched and sloshed with the craft's release despite the anti-nausea med coating her stomach. The flimsy craft was flung into the void. Del closed her eyes and kept them closed even when the rattling eased.

"Worst is over, greenie. You can open your eyes."

Del obeyed, then wished she hadn't. The primitive craft came equipped with a windshield in place of a vid-screen. A shock of stars snared her, gleaming against a rich, inky setting that seemed deeper than three-dimensional. Her perception stretched as if the view suctioned her senses toward it. She struggled to close her eyes. Phantom voices woke, scratchy whispers wavering across a vast distance, threads of almost-words that snaked into her mind.

She gulped a hiccuping breath. No, *not* voices. Imagination. Her own peculiar manifestation of astrophobia.

I don't hear voices anymore.

But Del couldn't soothe the choppy spasms of her lungs, close to hyperventilating now. She needed to cup her hands over her mouth and nose to relieve it, but her arms dangled as if disconnected from her will.

"Don't worry, doctor. We're under a light propulsion until we're far enough from the transport ship, but we'll point planetside before we hit the channel."

Acer's words formed a tether that recentered Del in her body, safely inside the craft. Her eyelids drooped, and she ducked her head.

"No voices," she mouthed, emphatic. Her space phobia had resurrected a profounder childhood fear, trauma best forgotten.

The craft bucked and spun. Or perhaps it was vertigo.

Keep breathing. Deep and steady. Oxygen in. Carbon dioxide out. Del hung limply, meditating until her mind drifted into a fugue, an eerie stillness that ignored the passage of time, the rough rhythms of the craft.

"We're in the troposphere, in perfect drift." Acer's voice startled her. "Give your new squat a look-see."

Del's neck spasmed with protest as she raised her head and peeled open her eyes.

Clots of cloud over jagged, rocky teeth. Stretches of burnt-orange terrain streaked and splotched with gray as if a giant had painted the landscape with an unsteady brush. On the far horizon, red funnels drizzled between sky and ground—some atmospheric disturbance.

"I think it was better with my eyes closed."

Acer laughed. "We're over the bubble. Turn to your left."

A volcano-shaped rock formation jutted from the earth as if it magically materialized. Del rubbed her temple, the view disorienting.

"G4 City," Acer said. "We'll pass over it before landing. You can look your fill."

The planet's sole major city lay underground, a sealed simulacrum of a more hospitable world. Only its rocky cap was visible from the surface. Beneath the city spread a labyrinth of mines that formed the heart's blood of this glorified resource colony.

Del swallowed a dry acidity from her mouth. "Have you ever been there?"

"Never been beyond the spaceport. Which is well outside the city, as you'll see."

Acer started a low-voiced communication with the port authority, and Del craned her neck for a better view.

As the angle shifted, Del made out a crescent of white curved against G4's southern side. It could only be the First Ring, an aboveground population-center housing legal, foreign residents. She squinted to make sense of an oddity—a solid band hemming in the buildings. Below that line, indistinct grayness fanned out like a lumpy shadow, not natural topography but human habitation. The Outer Rim. An entire community lay within those dark spaces; illegals, excluded from any governmental support. Those were the people she'd serve, so impossibly vulnerable against the harsh landscape.

Del struggled to access her wrist-vid for the magnification feature but couldn't manage in the clumsy suit. She jerked her gaze to Acer. "Is that a barrier? Around the First Ring?"

"Security wall. Keeps the riffraff out."

"Riffraff?"

"Fugitives, smugglers, squatters," Acer said, singsong. "Stubborn descendants of the original prospectors—from before the mining guild took possession of the planet."

Del's mind whited. "How does one get beyond the wall?"

"Beyond?"

"To the Outer Rim."

"Why the hell would you want to do that?"

Del fell speechless. No image she'd viewed, no shred of information from IWA had suggested the First Ring was *walled*. Had she crossed this excruciating distance for nothing?

An awful heaviness sunk her chest. She'd already waited what seemed eons to reach the people, to connect with those she could help.

Del had even changed her name to be taken seriously as a doctor, to escape being dismissed as a socialite dabbling in humanitarianism. Now, another barrier. As if the bubble imposed on her from birth was fed by some deeper identity … one she'd never shed …

"What business do you have in that squatters' slum?" Acer pressed.

"All my business, really." Her entire mission depended upon reaching the people of the Outer Rim. Keeping out the "riffraff" would keep out her patients!

Del forced down panic. Surely even a defiant frontier government like Galta 4's wouldn't twist IWA's tail by luring Del to an impossibility?

"I knew I'd regret this," Acer's harsh mutter drew Del from her distraction. "You realize we're going through port, don't you, *doctor*? This ain't a smuggling route." Acer's hand rested over the stunner on her hip.

Del blinked. "You're joking."

Acer's stony expression held.

Del glanced over herself. "Do I *look* dangerous?"

"Lot of things out here don't look dangerous. Until they kill you."

"My credentials are perfectly valid! I've been assigned a government handler who is expecting me." On a *proper people transport*. In three cycles.

"We'll see." Acer kicked a boot against the bulkhead, bracing her stunner against her thigh. She flicked her fingers over the controls without looking. "Yo, Haven. This is Drop Thirteen. I got a hopper with. I'll need security validation on her when the grounder picks us up."

"Copy that. We'll tandem a security drone with the grounder."

Brilliant. Del drooped against the bulkhead, the suit weighting her body like a damp mattress. She closed her eyes to blot out Acer's steely-eyed suspicion.

What did it matter? The woman was a spacer, not a local. Enduring a security check only punctuated the journey's end. Then, onto the real work.

If Del's patients couldn't come to her, she'd simply go to them.

She squinted through her lashes, past Acer, into the bleakness beyond the First Ring's gleam. Del had shed her grandfather's control, passed

IWA's rigorous screening, secured her advocate's license, and suffered weeks of interstellar travel. She'd staked far too much to let Acer's nonsense daunt her.

I need only connect with Zavi—whatever his snare—and assemble our team.

Find a reliable contact in the Outer Rim.

Establish my practice.

Perfectly doable.

***

Four short strides carried Del from one side of her cell to the other. Port security refused to label it a prison, though they had confined her here for three punishing cycles. The capsule hostel's "lounge"—a prefab unit formed of a tired plastic the color of earwax—made a dizziness-inducing space for pacing. She had no one to trip over. Del remained the sole occupant of the cramped honeycomb of capsules.

Tripping over someone would ease the tedium.

With a gusty sigh, she flopped onto the only piece of furniture, a hard mycelium sofa, and pinched the bridge of her nose. The lounge was preferable to the coffin-like capsule in which she'd spent cycles shaking off stasis sickness. Literally shaking. Medication did little to ease it. The body needed to adjust after crossing the stars.

Del scowled toward a vending panel built into the wall. She should eat. But even assuming any of the vendor's chalky meal options appealed, her stomach felt too lead-lined to manage. Not stasis sickness, the chill welcome.

Silence gnawed at her resolve. Silence from the authorities who ignored her inquiries. Silence from Zavi, her IWA partner. And all Del's baggage out of reach—held up in customs.

She was fully ready to burn her travel suit, for all she'd laundered it daily.

A click within the mechanism warned her before the hostel door hissed open. Del jerked to her feet, confronting a dour-faced individual wearing a port authority uniform—a fitted gray pantsuit with the Outer Barrier Mining Guild's OBMG spiral-galaxy logo on the lapel. The sudden, unexpected appearance of another person spiked her pulse.

"We're ready for your intake interview," the young man said, flat and distracted.

Del swallowed the impulse to explain that she'd had a virtual interview already, not wanting to discourage him from letting her *out*.

The blur over the agent's eyes indicated lenswear. He blinked it off and crinkled his face as if just noticing Del standing there. "This way."

As they stepped out, Del frowned around her. She had little memory of what lay outside the hostel, too crushed with exhaustion to notice much when they'd brought her here. A wide corridor stretched in both directions with establishments fronting one wall like a dashed line: med-spas and eateries. The other side was featureless pale gray.

She followed the agent down the corridor to the bare stretch beyond the shops. As they rounded a bend, a porthole-like window appeared. Del squinted through it—swirling taupe sand and shifting impressions of darker murk beyond. Drifting over it in Acer's craft, this port had appeared an isolated blip, too easily eroded away by the battering sand.

"Why is the port so far from G4 City, may I ask?"

A line formed between the agent's brows. He hesitated before answering. "Ideal launch paths and ideal mine locations don't always align." His frown fully formed. "And security."

The same breed of *security* that prompted them to deny any non-citizen access to G4? Not to mention penning an unarmed aid worker in a port hundreds of kilometers from anything.

The agent took a few strides further then halted before the corridor's blank wall and tapped his wrist-vid. A seamless panel slid open, revealing a small chamber.

"Administrator Qalvert will meet with you now." The agent gestured Del within.

"Oh?" She hadn't expected her handler to intercept her here.

Drawing a slow breath, Del stepped inside the chamber, a reception area with two blue chairs that looked like giant cups set on the floor. A figure sat in one. Del opened her mouth to greet them, but upon a second look, she stopped. The figure's featureless white head perched atop the segmented body of an old-gen android. Tiny spikes like brush bristles covered its surface.

Sweat broke out under her arms. She shot the agent a glance. Without responding, he pursed his lips and sealed Del inside.

Heart pounding, Del pressed her hands against the smooth, blank door.

"Please sit, Dr. Marks."

Del gasped and whipped around. A man sat in place of the android.

No, not a man. His aspect flickered eerily, revealing it as a holo-image projected onto the android's surface. Back home, android proxies were historical curiosities, generations obsolete.

Inching closer, she studied him. His torso was truncated, and his limbs stretched, contorted to map his image onto the android's body. He had even features over pale skin and heavy-lidded eyes. Impossible to guess his age with the imperfect resolution.

"My apologies, doctor. I had no time greet you in person." The hand lifted in spasms, blurring the image over it. "Please, do sit."

Del eased into the seat across from the proxy. The chair's deep sides and back reached her shoulders. A hum through the material warned her it was tech-webbed.

Goosebumps prickled her arms. Across the digital divide, Qalvert was facing *her* image over a proxy.

The proxy extended its hand, a jerky movement that made her jump.

Sardonic amusement narrowed Qalvert's eyes—or so Del imagined. Squaring her shoulders, Del grasped the hand, repressing a shudder at the warm gel-like material padding the android's palm.

Letting go, Del tucked her hands in her lap. "Thank you for … meeting with me."

"Your slot for cargo customs-review wasn't until today. As you might imagine, we keep tight schedules, being a working colony." His accent seemed a buffed flat version of vid-film depictions of frontier accents.

"I understand." Wariness stiffened Del's jaw. "I expected to hear from my IWA administrator by now. I wonder if you can confirm his arrival."

Qalvert cocked his head, so Del assumed by the warped twist of his face, the android imperfectly matching his movement. She held rigid, hating to imagine her own image so bizarrely distorted.

"If you mean Tegrin Zavi, I'm afraid he won't be arriving."

The words dropped like a stone, sinking her stomach. "What do you mean?"

"Didn't IWA inform you?"

"Any message from Central could not have reached me yet." True, but Del still itched with the suspicion OBMG had blocked them.

"We uncovered some alarming details about the man."

"Uncovered?" Del fired back. "His privacy ought to have been protected by treaty."

"The *TSS* reported the issue when he attempted to transit in their jurisdiction. Apparently, there's an outstanding alert on him for inciting unrest on Kevris. I'm frankly astonished an Allied Planet organization like IWA wouldn't better screen their people."

Del knew nothing about Zavi outside of his official bio and reputation for success in difficult posts. The OBMG had clearly used Trans-Station Security to probe Zavi's background and circumvent their agreement with IWA. That's why Zavi warned her from docking on Bel Asar Station.

Through her dry mouth, Del managed, "Kevris is ruled by warlords, not a proper governing entity like your guild here." *Proper* being subjective. The Outer Barrier Mining Guild, or OBMG, held absolute authority over this world.

"Hm." Qalvert's forehead stretched; he'd downturned his head, causing more image distortion. "Aid workers deliver aid, not revolution. It is not for them to judge the worth of the cultures they infiltrate."

Infiltrate. Del sucked in a breath. "I … hope the misunderstanding might be worked out. In the meanwhile, I …" *What now?* Zavi had the experience operating around uncooperative authorities. "… hope to begin my work," she managed limply.

"Begin? Surely you don't mean to pursue this alone?"

Del tightened her grip on the chair. "I trust our organizations can come to agreement. Meanwhile, I plan to be of service here." If she was IWA's only anchor here, she couldn't retreat. They might never regain that tether.

"We do appreciate your dedication." Qalvert grew priggish. "But there's also the matter of your android in cargo."

Del blinked. "You mean my med-assistant?"

"It is a military model."

"The same manufacturer, perhaps, but it's a standard med-unit, designed for durability outside a hospital environment." Surely, they could verify that.

"Unfortunately, there's nothing I can do. The model is on the contraband list."

No med-assistant. Del's mind blanked.

"We will arrange your travel back," Qalvert's tone turned ingratiating. "We are perhaps also at fault for not making our regulations clearer."

The hells! The vid-tapping slime! "Thank you, but that's unnecessary. I'm happy to begin until better arrangements are negotiated."

Qalvert sighed. "They might never be negotiated to your satisfaction."

Del leaned forward, no longer caring how that might distort her image. "The OBMG surely intends to honor the terms of the interplanetary agreement that brought me here."

Qalvert stared while her heart pounded in her ears. Then he leaned back, with a creak of the android's joints. "Let our higher levels work this out, then, shall we?"

"Wonderful." She pasted on a smile. "I understand the First Ring is walled. With my practice inside—"

The android's hand lifted with a whine, a negating gesture. "There are gates, of course."

The nest of nerves in her gut relented a fraction. But how freely could the "riffraff" cross those gates? "I'd like to inspect my clinic, as soon as possible."

"We can fly you over in another three or four days."

"Surely, you've scoured my possessions by now?" She couldn't bite back her sarcasm.

"Weather, I'm afraid," he said, as clipped. "A storm eye is forecasted to pass overhead."

"Are you telling me there's no way from port to the city for days?"

"Only ground transport, which I don't recommend."

"I'll take it." Pure contrariness directed Del's tongue.

"The last one leaves in fifteen—"

"Please arrange it. I'd be most grateful." Del's fake grin nearly cracked her cheeks.

"Right on it, then." He smirked and his image winked out, leaving only the android shell.

His smirk lingered with her like a warning.

Del's breath gusted out, and she leapt from the seat, glaring around the tech-webbed chamber.

The door slid open to the same dispassionate agent. "This way."

Crossing the corridors, Del barely noticed her surroundings as her mind whirled, unable to land on a solid thought.

She reached the solid, armored transport just before its hatch closed. Mingled odors of chem-cleanser and Human musk struck her. A waifish female attendant shifted in her boots and impatiently gestured Del down the aisle between two rows of filled seats. Del's head spun until she spotted a single open space in the back.

Her wrist-vid buzzed, warning of a message. She blinked up her lenswear. An IWA-encrypted message was downloading. Before Del could open it, the vehicle rumbled to life and lurched to motion. She staggered down the aisle and plunked into a seat as the transport surged to full speed.

Strapped to the wall beside the door, the attendant announced, "Fasten your seatbelts in case the field-tech safety fails in an emergency."

Del wiggled into the seatbelt and blinked open her message's voice transcription.

'It's gone hell's way, Dr. Marks. I'm minutes from being escorted out of the system, but smite 'em. Don't give up.'

A jounce swooped Del's stomach, and the text fritzed. Panicked, Del tapped her wrist-vid. Had they left the port's comm range, or had Zavi been blocked?

A text strobed back. *'Find Jonas Valerian. Balter's Den. Whatever you do, get—'*

Del's breath released, but nothing more came through.

The transport bounced over the rough terrain, rumbling and whining as it resisted the punishing wind. Del clung to her armrests, every jolt hitting her raw stomach. Qalvert's smirk flashed through her mind, and she struggled not to read into it.

"Find Jonas Valerian," she mouthed soundlessly. "Balter's Den."

Whatever the hells that meant, it was all the start she'd likely get.

2

Lighting a flame against the darkness only beckons trouble.
—Rynet proverb

A PRESENCE PRICKLED TAM'S NAPE LIKE THE BRUSH OF A HAND. HE flattened his back against the side of a building and scanned the alley for movement. Nothing. Only the rustle of cril nesting inside a tipped trash bin, but the elusive tingle over his senses remained.

Tam tested the wall with his fingers, finding sturdy concrete—rare luck in this shanty section of the warren. He turned, leapt up, and caught the rim of the building's low-slung roof, levering himself on top. The ribbed metal surface snagged his nylar-slicker as he slid onto his belly. He unbunched the jacket with a distracted jerk of his wrist and peered down.

The alley bored a crooked path between two structures, humps of trash padding the ground like creatures hunkered against the cold. Tam dissected each shape with his gaze but detected no movement. Eyes watering against the tang of rot, he expanded his other senses. A low buzz of voices and dim auras came from the adjoining street, nothing close.

Tam steamed out a held breath and pushed to his knees. Living like a shadow was shredding his courage.

He glanced around, reorienting himself. Just a nameless shanty huddle, makeshift habitation wedged like cheap filler between the Washer and Threader blocks, backlit by brighter cityscape. But Tam's intel on gang activity led here—whatever it proved worth. Jonas needed all gang activity mapped.

Tam crept to the opposite side of the roof. Feeble streetlights left his perch coated in darkness but lit the scene below. The shanty's hovels all squatted in silence, except one, the origin of the voices. "The Back Hand" scrawled above the entrance confirmed it as his target. The reefer den looked like one hard shove could knock it over. It tilted toward its neighbor, gaps in its metal-planked sides stitched with mesh. Rumor hooked the place to a gang-recruiting scheme, but it was seedy even for a low-scope org.

A trio of reefer-heads had washed up around the entrance, gulping the air whenever the door flapped open, like bottom feeders eager for scraps. The few customers braving the threshold didn't look much better. "Reefer" covered any organic matter folk lit and smoked—from harmless relaxants to toxic hallucinogens. By the addicts' sad state, this place dished the latter.

Tam frowned, scratching his wrist where the makeup concealing the blue-tinged pallor of his skin had begun to itch. This stank of another time sink. Tam wouldn't uncover gang plans by casing reefer-pushing scrubs. Still, he needed to rule it out. Minor gangs were like boreworms; left to spread they could gnaw through a warren's foundation.

The door gaped wide, releasing a miasma of psy-noise—auras and emotions too jumbled to parse—which meant more people inside than he'd guessed. He got a visual of swaying bodies before the door slapped shut.

Like an ugly afterthought, the psy-noise lingered to punish Tam. He tipped his face up with a deep-drawn breath, as if that could ease the impact, and his gaze was drawn to a smeary glow in the sky—the near-moon making an appearance through the smog. The sentinel moon, his *ssura* had called it. His adoptive mother had found richness and beauty even in this bleak world. Tam widened his pupils to distinguish the moon's outline through the haze, and for a breath he was home again, the sandy warmth of the compound beneath him, the soothing clicks of Trenabic voices around him. He absorbed the moon's desolate stillness then blinked the past away.

Tam wrapped his slicker tighter around his ribs, curling against the roof until his forehead scraped its gritty surface. God, he wanted to go home. But home was impossible—would always be impossible.

A chill breeze ruffled his hair, the breath of a distant storm. He pushed onto his elbows. *Just close the job before the rain hits.*

Sour deal that it is.

Jonas had gotten too good at twining Tam's will around good causes. A single month's barter wasn't worth the tread Tam had worn off his soles on this job, and barter couldn't keep his stomach full. He needed to earn real flash.

Sighing, Tam slipped his ocular over his eye, set the zoom, and scanned the reefer den. The Back Hand was windowless, but he made out shadowy forms between the gaps in the siding; nothing he could draw sense from. The angle was wrong, the light too poor.

Tam slid back, pushed to his knees, and drew his infrared cameras from a pouch on his chest harness, careful not to tangle the filament connecting them. He wired the end of the filament to his ocular and dangled the cameras over the roof-edge like a string of beads. A blaze of thermographic images stung his eyes through the ocular. The cameras zoomed on every twitch of the loitering addicts, fracturing the ocular screen into multiple images before synching into a panoramic.

Tam flipped the view, focusing the central camera on the reefer den. Infrared couldn't pass through walls. He could only make out sluggish movement, sparks from occupants lighting up.

Outside, the addicts shifted, stirred by tantalizing whiffs of smoke. The hint of reefer in the air sloshed Tam's stomach. The city lay behind him like a carnival cloaked by a screen, the shanty's stillness muting its bustle. Time stretched until Tam felt cold-fused to the roof and his eyes ached from the bright, blobby infrared images. Wind gusted over him, the storm reminding him of its approach. The reefer den's tarp roof flapped against its restraints like it wanted to break free.

Movement flipped Tam's view to a tiny, scuttling thing. The shape was wrong for a roach, the body humped. One of the addicts, shrunken inside layers of ragged clothes, snorted and leaned forward. The creature hovered outside the light as if realizing it had been spotted. It darted forward. The addict swung at it with her foot, making Tam tense. It shot from under the woman's sole and scurried beneath The Back Hand's door.

Tam relaxed, grimaced.

Bugs and scrubby Humans—nice life you've carved out for yourself.

An aura flared to life, charged with fear, tingling over his left side like an electric field activating. Tam whipped his head around, the camera filament lashing over his shoulder with the movement. No one on the roof.

Of course not.

Mouthing a curse, he checked the cameras for damage then repositioned them over the roof-edge.

Voices carried from down the street.

"… leading me in circles?"

"Nah … trust me."

Tam's ocular view spun to two approaching figures, molten forms through the thermographic camera—one the source of the aura.

Recognition thinned Tam's breath. The whispered presence from the alley. An aura distinct enough, strong enough to sense from a distance.

As his real mother's had been …

Tam dug his nails into the eave and craned his neck over the edge. One of the figures was small, delicately built—like a typical Rynet. The thermographic image blurred facial features beyond distinguishing. He yanked the IR camera filaments from his ocular with unsteady fingers and tapped up the zoom, futilely trying to penetrate the gloom with the optical lens.

The figure stepped into the wavering pool of light outside The Back Hand. A woman with dark hair scraped back and a sharp-boned face.

Human. A stranger.

Tam bit his thumb, stifled a groan at his stupidity. The aura's strength was coincidence, not connection. Odds of meeting another Rynet here were close to zero.

The woman lifted her face, her golden-toned complexion striking beneath the cold, anemic streetlight. Her eyes, wide and green, went straight to Tam. He stiffened, sensitivity creeping over his skin until she turned away.

How had he sensed her aura in the alley? Just a brief flash, but unmistakable. The woman must have circled past him, close enough to detect until he'd scaled the roof.

The second person, a man, stepped up to the woman, squinting at her averted face like she was some exotic object he debated whether to claim or crush. A look crawlingly familiar to Tam—not a look he'd expect one Maze-rat to direct at another.

There *was* something off about the woman's bearing—a toff's straight-spine elegance. Yet she didn't act like a high-nose slumming for kicks. Her manner was too tightly wound.

"This is it," the man said.

The woman tilted her head toward The Back Hand, her serene expression belied by the death-grip she had on the edges of her coat. Fitted through the torso and flaring to her knees, the coat was too frill for the sturdy boots below its hemline. Definitely a toff; no Maze-rat would sport a rig like that in this dump.

"There?" Disbelief clipped her voice.

"That's right." The man grabbed for her arm, but she swiveled to avoid his touch.

Her gaze skittered around. The street lay quiet, only the reefer-heads watching with misty indifference or hard-edged amusement.

"This can't possibly be the right place." The woman spoke with a sharp-tipped accent, unfamiliar to Tam.

An off-worlder. That might partly explain why she'd be foolish enough to come here, but even a fog-headed toff with half a portion of sense wouldn't set one foot into this slum unguarded. And whatever he was, her companion was no professional guard—his whip-lean body taut with expectation, his aura steeped in submerged menace.

Tam tugged a filament from his ocular, snicked it into his wrist-vid, then increased the zoom on the man's face. Heavy brow, jutting nose, flat cheekbones over pitted skin. The taper of his left brow was shaved, his hair covered by a gray skullcap. A vid-scan found a match: a Surge gang mid-rank who went by the name Fuse.

The Back Hand was gang digs, after all, but who was the woman? Too strange to stage a deal here. Tam would bet his boots the off-world toff didn't deal in drugs, and this wasn't Surge turf—they didn't skulk in cesspools but rode parade style through blocks.

The pockmarked patterns on Fuse's cheeks twisted as he smirked. "I thought the chief warned you it was rough."

A couple exited The Back Hand, gawking at the toff before slinking away. The reefer-heads scrambled to catch the smoke that drifted from the doorway in the couple's wake, kicking up flakes of resin from the crumbling pavement.

The toff's hands burrowed into her pockets as if she could escape through them.

"*Rough* is undercutting it a bit," she said. "I find it hard to believe this is the mayor's establishment."

Mayor? Tam frowned. She couldn't mean Jonas?

"Those fancy words prove you've overshot your expectations." Fuse smirked. "Our warren chief's a working man. Just call him the boss."

The woman backed away a step. "Perhaps Mr. Valerian can message me again."

She meant Jonas, all right, which meant Fuse was running a scam. Anticipation arced inside Tam with the certainty this meeting connected to the gang's plans for Balter's Den.

"You've come too far to back out." Fuse grinned wide enough to showcase his gray teeth. "Right to his doorstep."

As if on cue, the door opened, releasing a tall man. He dressed like a toff in a collared shirt and shiny jacket, but his swagger held the promise of violence. A thick-set goon strode at his flank. A leaner figure moved in step with the goon, obscured by his bulk.

Fuse swept a hand toward the tall gangster. "There he is."

A grasping tendril of relief slipped through Tam's psychic guard—the woman allowing herself to hope the man was Jonas. Tam's breath hitched as if her emotion was his own.

"The advocate, boss," Fuse announced.

The woman glanced at Fuse, anxiety strangling her anticipation— Fuse's oily mockery had given him away.

Get the hell out of there, lady. Tam glared at her as if his intensity could transmit his thoughts, then scrubbed his temples. He needed to stop letting her steal his focus. She wasn't his problem, and interfering could place him on another deadly gang's map.

The tall man strode up to the woman. Tam got no vid-hits from a face scan, but the man's aggressive confidence tagged him as gang, apparently their leader.

"Somehow pictured you older and uglier," the man said.

The woman retreated, bumping into Fuse, who'd moved to block her. Fear pulsed through her emotional signature to Tam like a current through a wire. Her mouth twisted in a strange smile. Resignation. Then she straightened, facing the chief with her shoulders drawn back as if that could make her taller.

Tam curled his nails into his palms until painful pressure from his nail sheaths made him relax them.

The chief flicked the woman's collar. "Bring any equipment with you, little bit? We're real eager for you to get started."

"I'm not quite that stupid." She jerked away, snapping her coat around her. "You're not Jonas Valerian. Who are you, and what do you want?"

Tam locked his teeth over a hiss. If she provoked the thugs into attacking her, he'd lose his chance to learn what was going on.

With a throaty laugh, a figure stepped around the chief—the person Tam hadn't been able to see clearly—a woman with inky hair piled high on her head. She wore a padded jacket with a high collar that disappeared beneath her jawline. Her chest was bound with bands of white cloth, her navel bare above belled trousers. A long, thin object was clipped to her belt, running the length of her thigh.

"Bravo, little toff." The woman prowled forward, inclining her head with exaggerated interest. "A slice of cleverness about ten blocks too late."

The toff twitched a glance behind her where Fuse still lurked.

"Call me Torx." The female gangster sketched a mocking bow. "This is my crew."

She was the real leader, then.

Tam refocused his ocular. Torx had a long face, deep-carved cheekbones with cool beige skin and a wide, smug mouth. Like Fuse, she shaved the taper of one brow, metal piercings spiking through it. No data match on her. He began recording images.

"What we *wanted* was an easy score." Torx leaned forward with arms akimbo. "So rude. A guest should always bring a few goodies with."

Fuse tugged the toff's sleeve, making her jump. "Guess you're used to the universe wiping your ass, or else you're trying to run a game on us. Either way, you're due a good rounding."

Tam sensed a jumble of emotion swell in the toff. Elbowing Fuse, she dug into her jacket and yanked out a gun. "Get back!"

Tam snapped up to a crouch.

The faux warren chief sprang at the toff. She cringed, squeezing the trigger—a stun blast that dropped him like a stone. Fuse lunged at her, grabbing her arm. Then Torx was on her, ripping away the stun-gun and striking the toff's cheek with the flat of her hand. Tam flinched at the loud crack. Torx tossed the stun-gun to Fuse, twisted the toff's struggling form around, and yanked the toff's back against her body.

For a disorienting instant, Tam breathed in sync with the fitful jerks of the toff's chest, facing her terror with her. As he blinked back to himself, his vision strobed, and he squeezed his eyes shut.

Why was her aura's grip so strong? Tam bit his lips against being re-snared. *Just let go. Please ...*

She stilled as if responding to his silent plea. He opened his eyes. Her stillness twined around him, rooting him in place more deeply than her rioting emotions had. Her eyes lifted, brushing over his hiding place. Then her face twisted away.

He could feel nothing from her at all.

Tam breathed to tame his jagged pulse. *Just another Human. Nothing to do with me.*

The air charged around Tam, the startling, familiar pressure of his mother's memory-gift. *"My prejudices have shaded you, pup, for you are as much Human as Rynet."* Words she'd spoken while tracing a regret symbol over his cheek with her finger.

Tam shook his head to clear it.

His gaze shifted back to the toff, trapped in the gangster's grip. He flexed his hand over his weapons harness. All he had were stunners and laser-knives. No way to engage and stay hidden. No way to keep the gang from marking him.

Tam twisted to look back the way he'd come. He could still slip away unseen—the smart thing to do. With a silent curse, he dove for the roof's edge, propelling himself through the darkness.

3

Del cast a desperate look toward The Back Hand, but the audience framing its entrance only gawped, their slack bodies propped by the wall. A thought sliced through the static of panic. *I've followed my "mad impulse" to its end.*

Torx's moist breath misted her ear. "A tiny fem like you has a baby cril's chance of taking us down."

Del craned her face away, shuddering at the sultry menace in Torx's voice.

A needle of pressure on Del's temple sent a frisson through her skull. *Not a corporeal touch.*

Del scanned the roofline, the alleyways, the crooked street. Nothing stirred the gloom. Distant hoots of revelry reached her like mocking laughter.

She gulped air for calm. *Get ahold of yourself.*

But instinct tugged, drew her focus back to the rooftops—the shadows shifting there.

Del blinked against dizziness. A dark shape swooped down and landed in a crouch outside the ring of light. Her captor's arm clamped tighter. Fuse and the burly thug drew knives with a metallic flash.

The figure unfolded, stepping from the shadows.

Fuse and the thug faced a thin young man, dully cloaked in brown, from his shabby garb to his long hair. A chunky device circled his forehead, trailing wires, like some ill-considered "cyber chic" accessory. His dark gaze slid over Del, and her stomach sank at its cold indifference.

Laughing, Torx thrust her away. Del stumbled over the smarmy "chief" she'd tased. He lay, tongue worming between his lips, nearly licking the filthy ground. She swallowed a shriek.

"Is *this* your backup?" Torx jabbed a finger toward the newcomer. "If he's your key pin, you shouldn't have bothered."

Del scrubbed her ear with shaking fingers. Whatever he wanted, this ragged interloper was outmatched.

He raised his hands, long fingers flared wide, eyes fixed on Torx. "I got no mess with you."

Fuse scowled, edging in front of Del. "Then get lost, rag-boy, before we mistake you for a sneak creeping into Surge business."

"I don't know him." Del clenched her teeth to repress a tremor. "He has nothing to do with this."

"And yet here he is, sniffing after you," Torx sneered.

Del swallowed a retort. With her high-stacked hair and over-plucked brows, Torx looked like a petty hustler, but the primitive weapon strapped to her body appeared lethal enough—a long thin blade that ran along her thigh.

"Seems the lady's lost." The ragged man tilted his wire-fringed head. "She's looking for the Boss, and you an't him."

"An't your business, slag." Torx slashed her hand, a signal to her men.

"Run!" Del lurched to the side. Torx yanked her back with a bruising grip on her arm.

Eyes owling, the ragged man backed away from Fuse and the other thug as they closed on him. Then he smirked, tucked his hands into his jacket, and ducked under their reaching arms. His hands flashed out. Both men dropped like they'd been clocked on the head. Tased. He shook off his jacket, exposing a lean chest crossed with straps of fabric that formed a weapons harness.

Torx shoved Del away hard enough to clack her teeth together.

Unclipping the rapier at her hip, Torx leapt at the man. Her target dodged, tossing his depleted tasers to the ground. Torx hesitated, eyeing her opponent with feral caution.

The ragged man snapped a knife from his harness and held it across his chest.

The two circled each other, Torx's boots scuffing against the uneven pavement, the man moving soundlessly. Torx lunged, slashed furiously with her blade. Her opponent melted from each strike, surreally fluid.

Don't gawk like a slackwit. Del rushed to Fuse's crumpled form and retrieved her stun-gun, wincing at the charge indicator. Half-depleted.

Absorbed in their contest, the combatants didn't react to Del. Torx whipped her blade in lethally fast, dizzying patterns, toying with the man. He was scrambling now, his breath grown choppy.

Torx laughed with savage delight. "You're dead."

Del pressed a palm to her own temple, dazedly studying the seethe of violence. She glanced at the stun-gun in her hand, a feeble shield against that ferocity.

Should she run? Smog draped the sepulchral alleyways. Plunging in blindly might lead to worse trouble.

Torx turned her back to Del, swiping viciously at the ragged man, who stumbled. Torx whipped up her blade, primed to strike—*in reach of him now.*

Del jerked her finger over her stun-gun's trigger.

Torx's knees buckled.

The ragged man pounced, wires whipping back like lashing tails. His booted foot drove into Torx's chest, dashed her to the pavement.

Del cringed at the thunk of Torx's skull. An impulse to check for concussion twitched over her.

The victor straightened, his dark eyes coldly assessing Del. He flicked his fingers toward the gun she clutched. "If you plan to use that on *me* now, you're out of luck. It's drained."

Del didn't lower the gun. She couldn't imagine why he'd helped her. He hardly appeared pleased with his success. His face was as smooth and unrevealing as resin.

"Thank you." She backed up. "I've inconvenienced you enough."

"You won't get two blocks. Why the hell would you come to this pit without a guard?" His expression stayed flat, but a scratch of annoyance textured his voice.

"I studied self-defense before coming to Galta 4." She had. Sort of.

His eyebrow twitched. "Did you pass?"

"I might have cheated." She gave up the pretense, lowered the gun. "Just a bit."

Hissing his disgust, he snatched up his jacket, tugged off his bizarre headband, and tucked it into an inner pocket.

He scooped up Torx's fallen rapier with a frown, cocked his head toward The Back Hand. "We need to jet before the stimps inside get word."

"Stimps" didn't sound the least appealing, but Del had no intention of flinging herself into another stranger's power. "No need to wait on me."

His mouth compressed, and his gaze slid down the street. The drug den's door burst open, launching Del's pulse with it. His gloved hand shot toward her, open-palmed. Fear flipping her will, she took his hand.

He turned to run, and she had an eyeblink to register the bizarre figures gliding out the doorway—two men riding narrow wheeled boards with glowing poles for steering mechanisms, colorful tufts atop their helmeted heads.

Her rescuer nudged her in front of him, then whirled to face the riders, lashing out with the rapier. The first rider swerved into the second, sending them both sprawling and yowling.

Del caught her rescuer's hand as he turned, and they dashed down the street. The weak blobs of illumination left her running blind, only oriented by his grip.

He lunged into a pitch-black alleyway, towing her along. Her ankles wobbled over uncertain footing. He steadied her then steered her onto a wider street. Their course grew better lit, but they staggered around startled people in their path.

Del's shoulder struck someone. Angry eyes flashed at her. She was shoved, her hand torn from her guide's. He leapt in front of her, flourishing the rapier. The man Del had collided with retreated, his hands raised.

Swearing, her guide glanced behind them, snatched up her hand, and began sprinting. They zigzagged through dark streets until the icy wind had punished her hands and face numb. She could hear nothing but her pulse and the air rushing in her ears. Metallic bitterness coated her throat from lungs overworked in the chill.

When her guide slowed, Del blundered into him. "Did we lose them?" she asked through labored breath.

"Maybe," he said, as winded. "We got lucky. The reefer made them clumsy." His smoky voice made him sound older than he appeared.

Streetlights shone brighter here, illuminating a huddle of low build-ings, a hodgepodge of cement blocks, metal, even plastic sheeting—improvised from recycled G4 City waste. A lack of windows added to Del's impression of being hemmed in by need.

"Where are—?"

Her guide shook his head, scanning doorways around them. "Not here."

Del edged closer to him. Not that she trusted he helped her from the goodness of his heart. Perhaps he expected to be paid. Regardless, she was at his mercy—hopelessly lost—and had been from the start. When she crossed beyond the First Ring gate, her audio fiber had crackled and died—no signal—as if she entered some hushed, uncanny realm.

Was this even Balter's Den? She had no idea if clear boundaries existed between warrens. She could be anywhere.

A more chilling uncertainty was how Fuse had known to meet her, masquerading as Jonas Valerian's assistant. Had her handler Qalvert purposely led her into a trap? She'd been forced to entrust him with her plan. IWA had made it clear she must play straight with the OBMG after the disaster with Zavi.

'Find Jonas Valerian. Balter's Den.'

Zavi remained unreachable, en route home, but learning Balter's Den was the name of a community outside the gate had made identifying its activist chief easy. Too easy.

I should have hired a guard, not trusted Qalvert's arrangements. Mistrust of any First Ring entity had held her back. And a deeper, less rationale instinct. A bit of idiocy that might have cost her life.

Del jolted back to the present. Her guide stopped and lifted a finger to his lips. She nodded, nerves flaring. He flipped up his jacket hood, reached toward her. She stiffened. Fingering the lapel of her coat, he uttered a low "tsk."

The sky poured open like a gigantic faucet overhead.

Ignoring her squawk, her guide snatched her hand, jogging through the deluge. By now, she was too miserable to care where he led her.

Planetscaping mechanisms sucked up and converted Galta 4's night-time humidity into liquid. Necessary to support life, but must they dump it all at once?

Del stumbled with fatigue when the waterworks finally halted. She struggled to get her bearings, panting for breath in the bitter cold. Her guide shook back his hood and cut right, dragging Del into a narrow alleyway. Her heart flipped as he grasped her shoulders, pressed her against a wall.

She lifted her hands to push back.

"We've shaken them." He released her. "Now you can tell me who you are and what you want with Jonas."

He stood beneath a light, and she struggled not to stare. Something elusive about him drew a deeper gaze, features as sculpted as any elite's but without the artificial, surgical symmetry.

She stalled. "So there really is a Jonas Valerian?"

"Yes."

"And you are?" she asked as coolly as she could manage through her chittering teeth.

"NG."

"NG?"

"Neighborhood Guard. We're what passes for security here."

She cleared her throat over an embarrassing wheeze, hope squeezing against the powerful instinct to give up. If he was local militia, he could connect her with the real warren chief, but she only had his word to back up his identity, which could be as flimsy as Fuse's.

NG narrowed his eyes. The irises she'd taken for brown glinted a curious gunmetal gray. "You were about to tell me what you want with Jonas."

"Was I?"

His lip curled. "Guess I shouldn't expect gratitude from a toff."

Heat rushed her icy cheeks like a flush of fever. "After the night I've had, I hardly know what to think about anything." *Except that I've lost my mind again.*

"Fair enough. But I'd have hurt you long before now if that was my intention."

"I've a matter to discuss with Mr. Valerian. I doubt it's any of your concern."

"Anything that might threaten the warren chief *is* my concern."

Her brows crept up. "Do I seem threatening?" First that drop-jockey pilot, then port security, now this militiaman. Perhaps weaponless and scrawny conveyed sinister on this world?

"Why would you hunt for Jonas in that slime pit? It's no place for a toff."

"I've no idea what 'toff' means." A shrill chirp made her shudder. Del shifted her feet as some breed of vermin scuttled by her heels. The sour odor of rotting food made her suspect it had friends nearby.

NG twirled his fingers. "Someone connected in the world, set up."

An elite. She winced, stilling her feet. "I'm not a toff."

"Right. Jonas won't deal in arms, ore, drugs, or flesh. No other trade for a toff to leech out of here."

Why bother with this verbal sparring? She'd tossed reason aside the instant she'd entered this dangerous place alone. Impulsiveness might kill her, after all—exactly as her grandfather Mario-Johns warned she deserved. Her eyelids pulsed with the urge to close as she fought a wave of black memory.

"I'm not going to hurt you." NG's soft voice drew her back.

An odd sensation tickled her head as she met his eyes. "I'm not a toff," she said as softly. "I'm an advocate."

"A what?"

"A doctor, sent by Inter-World Advocacy, to serve people without access to health care. People from the warrens." *Alone.* And everyone she'd encountered so far had faced her from across a chasm of otherness. Only this militiaman hadn't eyed her like a meal waiting to be carved.

He blinked as if astonished. "How'd you get mixed up with those gang creeps?"

"It's a long story." She rubbed her hands together. Drenched as she was, the frigidness threatened to ice her over. NG appeared unaffected;

his jacket must be waterproof. "IWA receives support from the Allied Planets, and the OBMG is hostile to anything they perceive as Allied interference." Del rushed through her explanation, desperate to reach someplace warm to burrow within. "I've been provided a facility inside the security wall, but no one from the Outer Rim—"

"The Maze."

"Pardon?"

"Outer Rim is *their* word for this place. Folk here call it the Maze."

That was fitting. "I see. The OBMG assigned me a handler who's worse than useless. IWA learned about Jonas Valerian's work here. We thought he might connect me with the community. My handler arranged a meeting with him through a go-between."

NG studied her like an exhibit in a curiosities museum. "You were set up."

"It's possible my handler was misled." *Possible.*

"You came to help us?" He seemed to find that crazier than her coming unguarded. "By yourself?"

"Your mine board only allowed me on-planet."

"They're not *my* board."

His eyes lured her attention. The irises paled, veining with silver. A dark rim remained, giving them an alien cast. The eerie beauty stunned any response from her. Such a sophisticated cosmetic enhancement was startling to encounter in a primitive slum.

"Look, doctor—"

"Marks. I'm Del Marks.

He hesitated. "Jon Gray." His fingers rapped against his thighs. "I'll take you to the First Ring gate. You can find your way from there?"

Del gave a shallow, reflexive nod.

Jon Gray strode from the alley as if indifferent whether she followed. He'd gotten his information, dismissed her as useless.

Headlights blazed around a corner.

Jon yanked her from the wheeled car's path before it blew by.

"Thanks," she managed thinly. She'd encountered so few vehicles she'd forgotten to watch for them.

They crossed onto a new street. Del stumbled as if she'd bumped against the view. Buildings lined their path, standing taller and breathing with windows. Tubes of colored lights decorated window frames and doorways. Her pace dragged as she took it in. Each structure made its own statement—symbols, names, even profanity. The effect was oddly lovely against the gloom. Her eyes fixed on one. Lights fanned around a crudely sewn doll resting on a windowsill. The doll was half swallowed by an infant's dress.

Del froze. She was viewing a shrine.

The knot she'd been unconsciously holding in her stomach released with painful intensity.

"Miner sticks." Jon studied her, pointing to the lights. "When they reach a certain shelf life, OBMG tosses them, even if they're still good."

His expression remained inscrutable, but some deep emotion moved behind that mask.

Jon continued down the street, leaving her little choice but to follow. She was in over her head. She'd done her residency at a clinic in the roughest slum in Tiraj—a wealthy suburb compared to the Maze. She'd believed herself prepared, but now …

Her gaze sketched over the shrine. *Going Where the Need is Greatest.* She mustn't let cowardice lead her. Jonas Valerian existed, and Del would find her way to him.

Before she could consider her strategy, the crowded street opened into a broad concrete square, the First Ring gate. Across the square stood the checkpoint, a squat structure half-embedded in the towering security wall. Shrouded in darkness, the mine-city loomed beyond it like an arid mountain.

Jon stopped at the stairs leading to the square. "Here you are."

When she hesitated, he arched a knowing brow, waiting for her to ask.

She glanced back at the slum's soot-dark outline; it lurked like a creature waiting to devour her. Unbidden, words tripped from her mouth. "Mr. Gray? I really must speak to Mr. Valerian. I don't suppose you could guide me to him?"

His gaze flickered over her.

She grimaced, certain she looked like a drowned and freeze-dried rat.

"Maybe you've had enough adventure for one evening?"

She considered offering payment, but his cool superiority stopped her. "At your ... convenience."

No help for him thinking her an idiot. She could hardly defend her recklessness by confessing she'd intended to hire a guard until a powerful compulsion stopped her. He'd take her for a total nutter if he didn't already.

One corner of his mouth quirked. "You should know Jonas really does own a drink-and-rowdy, though it's nothing as seedy as The Back Hand."

"That didn't stop me when I thought he *did* own The Back Hand." Not that she'd been willing to set foot inside the place.

Jon studied her as if stripping away her bravado.

She squared her chin, braced for his refusal.

He shrugged. "I'll need to clear it with Jonas first."

That would have to do. "How may I contact you?"

"Meet me here day after tomorrow at 16:00. Best time to catch Jonas."

Del couldn't muster optimism; the insane risk of her actions now rusted her limbs with fear. Gods knew what would have happened if Jon hadn't intervened, and he could have been hurt—or worse.

Her fear-starched pride had no place here. "Thank you, Mr. Gray. Truly."

She squelched toward the gate, wondering if he would keep his word, struggling to hope he did.

DEL MARKS LIMPED AWAY, HER AURA'S FADE SLOWER THAN HER GAIT, clinging to Tam like a mist. He closed his eyes, and the rich texture deepened.

Such strange clarity, like emotions untainted ... undiluted.

Lack of guile couldn't explain it. Innocence rode tandem with poor self-regulation—as exhausting as corruption. What then?

Auras fingerprinted a person's psyche, signaled their presence, while emotional signatures radiated the feelings of a given moment. Both clued Tam into a person's nature, but Del's emotions mostly flitted against the glow of her aura or were masked by it.

He expelled a breath to shed the lingering, uncanny touch.

Her presence was too odd, even without factoring the Surge's inter-est. An off-world charity doctor? *Here?* Jonas would want a report imme-diately.

Tam opened his eyes and strode swiftly away.

Del Marks flared his extra sense brighter than Pell Mahr festival lights. For the first time he could remember, he had no idea what his gift was telling him.

4

———

*Faith fades into myth, yet in planet-bound eras, all Rynet believed
in ver'ela, remnants of the spirit left to comfort a loved one
before the soul passes wholly into Serenity.*

A PAIR OF RHEUMY EYES SQUINTED AT TAM THROUGH A GAP IN THE LIVING-pod's door. The person's face was bisected by a heavy door chain.

"Evans sent me," Tam said a second time, glancing down the street at the zigzag of other standalone pods—small, boxy prefabs refurbed from G4 City castoffs. Maybe Tam's informant had misdirected him. Tam rubbed itchy palms against his thighs, tried again. "You're Hana?"

"And you're pretty under that muck, an't you, darling?"

"Don't know what you mean."

The door widened a hair. "It's good work, but I dressed more lolas for shows than you have hours on this earth. I recognize camouflage when I see it."

Hana had seen through Tam's disguise. Tam inched back. "Don't hurt to be cautious."

As if Tam's admission was a signal, Hana unlatched the chain, swung the door wide. Hana wasn't in drag but dressed plainly in loose lounge-

33

pants and a red tunic, their gray-streaked hair held in a simple queue. "Evans told me to expect you two weeks ago."

"Got sidetracked meeting my warren barter." Tam had also gotten cold feet about wasting more flash on futility. He had little to spare. But his interaction with the toff last night had rethreaded his interest in this lead on his mother's fate for reasons he didn't want to unravel.

"The Boss does take his bite of time." Hana shifted to admit Tam.

Tam took a long, silent breath, and reminded himself to anticipate nothing.

He surveyed the room before stepping inside. No other doors, aside from the telltale accordion slider of a washroom. No aura there. The pod was tiny—only a counter inset with a burner and coolbox, a table, and a fold-up sofa—but clean as if Hana had tried to scrub the age and shabbiness from the walls. Hana's meager things hung neatly on hooks or lay in tidy stacks.

A pot burbled on the burner. Hana stepped over to shut it off, turning their back on Tam as though resigned to the risk they took by letting Tam in.

Tam kept his arms loose at his sides, hanging back to signal peaceful purpose.

Hana studied Tam with a calm dignity that left Tam casting for words.

"Please sit." Hana gestured to their platter-sized table.

Tam folded himself onto one of its low chairs. When Hana joined him, Tam twisted his knees aside to prevent them from touching Hana's.

Hana laced knobby-jointed fingers. "Evans tells me you're interested in a bit of old flap."

"I'm digging for talk related to your ringed friends." Evans claimed Hana had been cozy with the powerful Fet gang around the time Tam's mother vanished. Slim chance Hana had information on her disappearance, but Tam had no other clues to chase.

Hana's lips quirked higher. "If it's to do with snakes, it will cost more."

Snakes being another word for the Fet, the symbol on their gang rings. "I'll pay, long as it's reasonable."

"Let's say sixty to start? If the question is sensitive, I'll need to up the price."

Tam closed his hand over his pocket. Sixty wasn't much but insane when factoring the nothing it would likely buy him. *What am I doing here?* He twitched to rise, but his mouth ran ahead of the instinct. "Fifty and it's a deal."

"Then what history can I tell for you, young man?"

Tam breathed deeply for focus, then wished he hadn't. Hana's dinner smelled of cabbage set out too long.

"My client's a knob-head." Using the slang for the Trenabic race felt like a betrayal of Tam's adoptive people, but many Maze-dwellers only knew the slur. Bigotry toward non-Humans thrived here like a fungus in the damp.

Hana's brows lifted. "I'm surprised someone who gets nettle-skinned dealing with a skirt-dangler like me would work for a Trenabic."

Tam's skin heated. "An't that you're a lola. I just don't make cozy with strangers."

The faded brown eyes grew keener. "You're in the wrong gig, then, my friend."

Tam shrugged, uneasy with the perception in Hana's gaze.

"But I've interrupted you." Hana had a strong, resonant voice, making Tam suspect they were a singer. Many Fet clubs featured lola performers—likely Hana's connection with the gang.

"My client had a friend, a Rynet woman, fled from the mine, living in the Xeno warren. She disappeared from the Xeno nine years ago. He wants to know what happened to her."

Hana melted against their chairback. "Ah." Their aura grew heavy with an emotional weight that shifted into Tam's chest.

Through the unsettling sensation, Tam continued. "Lots of rumors among Xeno folk. That the OBMG caught her. That she fled with smugglers." *That Rynet corsairs nabbed her—too absurd.* "She was a geoscientist, and one thread claimed she was taken by an ore-dealing gang like the Fet." He'd given this line many times, but his voice thinned now. The recognition forming in Hana's eyes robbed its strength.

"I remember the buzz then." Hana squinted at the wall as if pulling memories from its yellowed surface. "I was keeping time with the old Fet enforcer. He bragged how they'd captured a ghoul—a Rynet—beautiful as a fairy in a tale, made her a slave to pull ore from under the mine bastards' noses."

Tam sat straighter. He leaned forward, helpless to stop himself. "And?"

Hana sighed like the sound was squeezed from them. "That enforcer did tell tales—how the Fet snared themselves a proper ore-digging machine, how he'd use the ore take to set me up in fancy digs. Should've been a bard, that one."

Tam braced against a throb of pain. For an instant, he'd imagined someone outside the Xeno knew his mother, had true word of her.

Hana tugged their wispy queue of hair, eyes growing unfocused. "Precious things never last here. Just get swallowed by the rot." They blinked at Tam then offered a wincing frown filled with sympathy.

Tam curled his fingers into his palm. "Is there anybody …?" Emptiness erased his words.

"I'd try hacking Inside. Those ore-pullers keep data on everything."

Tam nodded limply. If a way to hack OBMG's security existed, he hadn't found it. The choke-net OBMG pumped through the Wall was worse than a joke—everyone knew they monitored people's queries— and hiring a professional hacker lay beyond his means.

Closing his eyes, Tam cast his thoughts to his mother's spirit. His *emere* vanished when he was twelve, but the grief felt raw, would always feel raw until he learned the truth. Until he released her. The continued presence of *ver'ela*, her memory-gift, meant part of her soul stayed with him. Nine years had passed, a spiritually significant number to Vleran Rynet. If Tam didn't find a way to release her soon, her soul might remain divided forever.

"Thanks." From his pocket, Tam drew a fistful of small, plastic disks, imbedded with the Currency Guild's sigil-chip.

Hana's focus seized on the flash. Then they sighed. "Keep it. I gave you nothing but a few clot-headed memories."

Tam's fingers clenched over the disks. His gaze swept the pod, absorbing the grim bareness, the stench of cheap, half-spoiled food. Rising to his feet, he tossed the flash on the table. "Fair's fair. You dealt true with me."

"Wait." Hana's hand fluttered toward Tam. "If the OBMG lost one of their Rynet ore-sniffers, they'd have torn the Maze apart to find her. Whatever happened, I doubt you'll discover it on *this* side of the Wall."

Tam fled the pod. When he reached the street, his strength bled into the pavement. He gripped a light pole to steady himself. Hana was right. It was hopeless. Every lead in the Maze dried up as quickly as water in this place.

Curious emotional signatures from passersby pried Tam from his stupor. He straightened, flipping up his jacket hood, blending into the flow.

5

WALLS WERE FORMED OF MORE THAN PHYSICAL BARRIERS, ALWAYS.

Del braced against the cool surface of the First Ring wall, pressing her spine against the seamless, industrial ceramic. Unyielding. As wide as she was tall. Chilly, like the air.

A soldier emerged from the security checkpoint, standing by the pedestrian gate. A helmet concealed his face, but Del sensed him watching. Curiosity piqued, no doubt. Del had exited the First Ring only to stand and stare into the Maze like a rodent mesmerized by a reptile.

Hours remained until the meeting with Jon Gray, but anxious energy had drawn her to the Maze's gate, the need to … prepare herself, or perhaps to make sense of herself.

It was midmorning, though the tepid light made a poor signal for it. People crossed the square before the gate, many eyeing the guard warily, no one drawing close. Del spotted as many shades of skin and hair as in the most cosmopolitan Tiraji city on Cartor, yet an elusive pallidness tinged them, as if the protective filter overhead cast a matte layer over hues of pigmentation and melanin. No one here had breathed open air, soaked in the rays of a vibrant sun.

On the street parallel to the square, people darted by on an assortment of nonmotorized wheels—cycles, scooters, even skates—more motion in these five minutes than she'd witnessed in her long trek two nights before. As many walked as rode, slump-shouldered, hands in pockets. A primitive, motorized car zipped around the traffic, belching smoke from its rear—such vehicles must be one reason for the air's faint acridness. In the distance, a light-flyer soared, the only one she'd noticed Maze-side.

A wall divided Del from her patients. She had slipped past the physical barrier, but she'd learned last night that far deeper things divided her from them.

Cowardice, for one.

Ignorance.

Privilege.

Things Del had fooled herself she'd left behind. Her commitment to serve these people had been easy to make. How fragile it became beneath reality's glare.

What, besides a stack of years, distinguished her from the naïve, selfish child she'd been when she'd first set herself on this path? Her profound unease now, the feeling of displacement, evoked a past she'd thought buried. At fourteen, Del had run away, hitched a public transit, and gotten a taste of the real world.

That memory still seemed fresh.

———

DELMARA STEPPED INTO AN ALIEN SPACE WITHIN HER OWN CITY—SAND gritting the streets, discarded meal foils, the stench of urine. Unregulated holo-adverts battled for attention above surly-looking pedestrians' heads, layers of bright images, bursts of sound, each gaining ascendancy for a split second before others blotted them out.

Legs trembling, she froze outside the transit stop's tube-like exit. Another exiting passenger nudged her aside, and she stumbled, pressing her back against the wall.

Her mother died *here*. In this burrow. She'd overheard the gossip from her father's staff.

Delmara studied the holo-adverts, too afraid to move. One hooked her attention as it cycled through. *Going Where the Need is Greatest!* Vivid green words over a collage of anguished faces, med-bots, somber med-techs. *Inter-World Advocacy.* Some propaganda thing.

Delmara's face felt sore as if she'd cried. She hadn't. She'd done far worse. She'd shouted the truth before everyone. Dizzying terror of her own act had spiraled her here.

"I am not a graytle," she whispered without understanding why. She winced as a face flickered in her mind, strange liquid eyes, oddly tinted skin—gone before she grasped it. Pain pierced her head, warning of memories her therapist had sealed away.

That would get worse for her now.

Hours later, her cousin Rhemy found her still cowering there. He materialized before her like a grim, gray pole in a tailored suit—grown so bloody tall, as if some strange magic had stretched him between one day and the next.

His angular face, so like hers, pinched with an expression that made it foreign. "You scared us."

Delmara averted her eyes. "No, I *embarrassed* you." In front of the news-stream their grandfather Mario-Johns had lured to witness his pantomime of grief.

"*Why,* Mara?"

The anguish in Rhemy's voice *hurt,* jabbed forth her anger. "It was all a disgusting lie. He hated her!" The paragon Mario-Johns eulogized had never existed. A saint who'd devoted her life to charitable works. "What a sick joke." Frustration tore at Delmara. She couldn't explain it, but she wasn't wrong.

"What good would naked truth have done?" Rhemy said, a soft admonition. "Your mother was *ill.* Addiction is an illness."

Delmara's mouth compressed, hiding a tremor. "Those lies, they … erased her."

So many lies. As layered as the holo-adverts. As layered as the world they lived in.

Delmara's gaze whirled around, absorbing the trash-littered street, the discontented faces. *This place?!* Part of the city her grandfather and his Teraji Industry Council bragged of nurturing.

Rhemy's hand closed over hers, hot and damp. Startled, she met his eyes, forest green against the gray, and read fear there. "I wish I could shield you from this. I can't. And you … won't endure it." He tugged her hand. "Come. You'll find nothing of your mother here. The circus will have ended by now. Let's go lay her to rest."

As she let Rhemy guide her, words flashed overhead. *Going Where the Need is Greatest!* They suddenly snatched Delmara up, made her burn to reach for better—beyond her grandfather's grip, beyond her own petty unworthiness.

WITH PALMS PRESSED AGAINST THE FIRST RING WALL, DEL BLINKED THE memory away. Sixteen years later, the shame and hurt nested in her chest as though fresh. The cruel disillusionment.

Mario-Johns Fedelo. Generous leader of Tiraji national society. Known throughout all planet Cartor—and beyond—for his philanthropy.

The pain of real people, even that of his own family, meant nothing to him. He only cared about the appearance of doing good. Its reality was beneath his concern.

When Del had declared her intention to study medicine, standing at attention before Mario-Johns, a sound between a sneer and tsk had slipped from behind his impassive mask. "Setting aside your questionable ability to *endure stress*—" He pointed to his temple. "You're a polished nonconformist, pantomiming compliance while quietly wending your way around rules—utterly unsuited to chaining yourself to the rigid protocols a doctor with a compromised mental-health history must adhere to. Imagine the liability. To your entire family."

Her doctors had treated her childhood condition as a rare neurodivergence. Mario-Johns had treated it like an illness, like he did *any* illness—unpardonable weakness to be concealed.

Del gusted a sigh through her nostrils, flung his face from her thoughts.

She'd vowed never to be like him—nor like her father, trundling in his wake—but a vast chasm lay between willing a thing and attaining it.

Del knotted her fingers over the edges of her coat, studied the Maze spread before her. *See these people. Their vitality. The creatively improvised world they've built themselves, unaided.*

If she couldn't embrace this reality, she was no better than Mario-Johns, a hypocrite.

Heaviness sunk her. Residual stasis sickness, perhaps.

Breathing deeply to lift her shoulders, Del pushed off the wall.

I've come this far.

Del crossed through the gate, back into the First Ring.

She'd rest and reset.

Return later.

6

---

*Most Humans do not acknowledge psychic gifts such as yours,
Tamln, but that does not make psy-ability distinctly Rynet.
Your empathic gifts come from your Human father. They are
nearly as rare as your half-Rynet heritage and must be
concealed along with it.*

Perched on the railing that framed the First Ring square, Tam watched people below curl against the chill afternoon air like bent screws jutting into the pavement. Their sluggish movements made Del Marks's dart across the concrete clearing frenetic in comparison. Small and trim, tidy dark hair, same frill coat over sturdy boots—she was unmistakable.

And here I'd figured a bit of reflection would've cracked her resolve.

Del cast her gaze around before settling it on him, her swift recognition surprising him. He'd forgone his disguise. Makeup was too expensive to waste on anything other than stealth-work. Accustomed to unease, scorn, or morbid fascination, her lack of reaction to his unmasked face raised an itch between his shoulder blades.

She approached. "Mr. Gray?"

Her aura struck like a puff of pure oxygen, with a froth of anticipation. He doubted she'd keep the positive charge here for long.

"Dr. Marks." He crafted a neutral expression, slid off the railing.

Tam found himself leading her through the warren again. He muted his gift, uninterested in sensing her reaction to the local color in the unforgiving light of day. At the very least, she'd find this area a vast improvement over the shanty-huddle she'd toured two nights ago. Folk here made the best of what was available, adding a touch of flare to structures. Del paused to study a pod with a steepled roof and colorful, silicone-bubble windows.

A sparkle on the street hooked Tam's attention. While Del was distracted, he bent to pinch it up—a glassy black pebble, smooth to the touch. He pocketed it, found Del watching.

She didn't ask.

A quiver through the pavement froze her. She turned wide eyes on Tam.

"Just a little drill-bite—what we call mine-activity tremors."

She scanned the sky. "When I flew in, I spotted what seemed rather dramatic storms, like red paint dripping from the clouds."

"Some storms get close, shade the sky an angry color, give the ground a good shake. We call that Galtan's Rumble."

"Any religious significance?"

"Folk here share superstition more than religion. Tend to keep faith private." He strode a pace ahead of her, pitching his voice to be heard. "Galtan is what the original settlers called the planet. OBMG poached it."

He grimaced. *I sound like a fucking tour guide.*

They continued in silence.

It took fifteen minutes to reach Jonas's place, a two-level stronghold of hefty stone blocks with a door plaque unimaginatively proclaiming it "The Bar." Tam cracked the door, scanned the tavern—sparsely occupied, a few customers scattered around tables in the back.

Tam guided Del inside. She halted, stiffly studying the interior.

Chunky metal tables crowded each other across the stained concrete floor. Cheerful flecks of blue peeked from cracks and corners, but two decades of boot-tromping had sanded most of the floor a tired gray. The resin-paneled walls stood bare but for a section papered with crude drawings, pinned there by regulars. The dubious artwork fluttered like vent flaps grown loose on their hinges as the door blew closed. The serving counter was the only finished-looking element. Kept polished to a gleam, the chrome installation stood adjacent to the doorway. Jonas liked to monitor who came in and out of his place.

The warren chief manned the bar now, silently observing Del. Tam absorbed the simmer of Del's anxious anticipation as he steered her there. In frame and character, Jonas Valerian was built like an industrial work-bot, a solid, immoveable mass. He had a heavy-jawed face set with pale, ruthlessly perceptive eyes. A scar twisted along his jawline from ear to chin, visible because he towered over most people.

When Tam introduced Jonas, Del mustered a full-faced smile, lined with fiercely beautiful teeth. "Mr. Valerian, at last. I've had some adventures reaching you."

Tam knuckled his lips, hyperaware of the veneers disguising his narrow, mauve-glossed Rynet teeth.

"So I heard." Jonas gave Del an appraising scour. "IWA really sent you?"

Unsurprising that Jonas knew of the interplanetary charity. The Boss kept more connected with the universe than most Maze-dwellers. He didn't talk about his past, but rumor held that Jonas came from behind the Wall.

Del dug into her pocket and handed Jonas a vid-card. Tam sensed the grip on her anxiety slip, pressure expelling like a gusted breath. "My medical license, IWA identification, and the OBMG clearance to operate here."

As if she could hand over her worries as easily as her credentials.

No way Jonas could validate those credentials, but Del had a First Ring pass. Nobody got *that* without Inside connections or a sanctioned purpose on Galta 4.

"What'll you take, Doc?" Jonas asked.

"Pardon?"

"To drink."

"Nothing, thank you." With a nervous twitch of a smile, she glanced behind the bar at the bottles and glasses clamoring for shelf space.

Tam grew conscious of odors he was normally immune to—the

yeasty ale brewing out back, the stale remnants of spilt drinks and greasy food. Tavern staff doggedly chased the mess with minimal success.

Jonas fingered Del's card then slipped it into the pocket of his faded workman's pants, cynicism and eagerness warring on his face. "I've been flinging my voice into the void for years to get a human rights org to notice our situation. I'm damned grateful it's been heard."

Damned surprised, more like.

"I suppose you never received my messages," Del said.

Jonas tapped his chunky old wrist-vid. "Messages fail here, and we get jammed—frequently."

He met Tam's eyes. In this case, not jammed but *intercepted*. Jonas had about busted a vein over the Surge impersonating him. The question remained how they'd managed it.

Del's teeth dug into her lower lip and released. "I've given up on help from the OBMG. That's why I came to you. IWA discovered your activism."

"Guess you could call it that. I've sure tried to get positive attention for the situation." Jonas leaned his elbows on the counter. "So how can I help you, doctor?"

Tam's cue to escape. As he shifted away, Jonas froze him with a significant look. Tam frowned. What could this have to do with him anymore?

"I could use a spot of advice, to start," Del said. "The OBMG arranged clinic space in the First Ring, but I see no practical way to reach patients there."

Jonas rubbed the stubble over his ruddy-skinned jaw, covering his sardonic reaction. "Didn't your handler tell you Maze folk can't get into the Fring—the First Ring—without a special ID? The few connected enough to secure an ID already have access to clinics there."

"I've gathered as much." Del gripped the bar's rim as if to steady herself. "My handler claims it's too dangerous to open the clinic here but hasn't offered a solution."

"It *would* be too dangerous," Jonas said. "Little law and order here. You'll need security."

"That and help promoting my practice to the community."

"Unlikely they can afford your services."

"There's no charge. I get all my funding from IWA."

"Folk may look narrow-eyed at that. No one believes in getting anything for free."

Beneath Del's surface composure, anxiety regathered with each volley. Jonas was really peddling sour ale. To what end? He must want to hook the doctor for the Den—either to mark her as a plant or secure her if she proved legit. Maybe he figured it wouldn't be worth the bother if she fled once the realities bore down.

"I'm aware it won't be easy. I'm *completely* ignorant about your culture. Normally, we're thoroughly briefed before an assignment, but little information was available in this case."

"Not surprised." Jonas snapped up a rag and swiped a smudge on the counter. "OBMG likes to keep their dirty laundry hidden."

Del tucked in her fingers as if wary of the rag's path. "Which leaves me grasping for a strategy."

"You'll need to stick close to the Wall. No public transport. Fuel's too inaccessible. Some salvage company buses run side routes, but not reliably."

"I see." Del's teeth worried her lip again.

Pressing his palms atop the counter, Jonas leaned in. "Without support from a stable warren, you wouldn't survive."

His performance only smoothed Del's expression. "And Balter's Den is a stable warren?" Irony lilted her voice.

Jonas shrugged. "One of the most."

An understatement. The Boss might be maneuvering the doctor, but he wasn't lying.

Fingers anchoring to the counter, Del leaned toward Jonas. "So, you'd be willing to support me?"

"I don't have enough men to guard a clinic."

Del blinked like a flinch, and her aura wrenched. "I see."

Narrowing his focus, Tam caught a thread of anticipation from Jonas.

"How about this?" Jonas stroked the scar under his jaw thoughtfully. "You use one of my second-story rooms. Warren business is run out of here, so you'd be under the umbrella of the Neighborhood Guard. We could rig security for your supplies and what-not."

Jonas must have envisioned that from the start. But to invite a potential operative into the warren-hub …? What Del offered seemed too good to be true.

"Establish my practice in a bar?" Del laid a long, penetrating look on Jonas.

Jonas returned it. "This might not look like much to you—just a shabby rowdy—but it's our warren's heart. Eager as I am to make things better for our folk, I won't risk this place. Any trouble and the bargain would be off."

"My mission means a great deal to me," Del answered in kind. "I'm equally reluctant to risk it."

"We could try it. See how we suit."

Tam rolled his eyes away. Skillfully played, but the Boss was reaching with this one.

"I'd doubtless be the first advocate to do such a thing." Laughter puffed from Del, fizzy with a relief powerful enough for Tam to feel in his chest. "But I accept."

Tam's gaze startled back to her. No signs of deceit lurked beneath her manner—her head tilted toward Jonas, more alert than anxious.

"Good, then." Jonas's eyes crinkled like he'd been confident all along. "You'll need to hire a guard. I can't spare men to play escort, and you'll need someone keeping ears on the area, especially since you've caught a gang's attention."

Tam shoved his hands in his pockets, shooting Jonas a frown. The Boss couldn't mean *Tam* for that role?

"What do you suppose the gang was about?" Del asked.

Jonas turned to Tam. "What do you think?"

Tam stiffened. Why fling him into the conversation? Jonas had his report.

"To jack her equipment, seemed like. The Surge deal in tech and aren't above stealing what they can't make." The gang had a rep for leasing necessities to desperate folk with high interest, collecting in labor or bruises when the customer failed to pay. "But someone tipped them off."

More than Del had lured Torx's pack to Balter's Den. Seemed the gang wanted to stretch its territory. *Like we need more trouble.*

Tam studied Del's too smooth expression, read tension beneath it.

"Likely, your handler got intel on Jonas from a go-between in Pell Mahr—the warren off the First Ring's eastern gate where most commerce flows into the Maze. The go-between must have tipped off the Surge."

The gang's brand hinged on being mobile, but they roosted in warrens abutting Pell Mahr. Unlikely a coincidence.

"The risk's no joke," Jonas said. "Even in Balter's Den."

Del lifted her chin. "IWA advocates are dispatched to dangerous regions, even war zones."

If Del Marks was a soldier-crusader, Tam would eat his boots.

Jonas cleared his throat—his only sign of skepticism. "As for hiring protection, the NG is a volunteer force. Guardsmen work other jobs. You could find someone among them. I can't cover that cost but can have their work for you count as their barter—their tax obligation."

Jonas *was* lobbing this at Tam! He glared his refusal, but Jonas wouldn't meet his eyes.

So like Jonas to go after what he wanted without cost to the warren—one reason the Den was so "stable." Jonas pretended to sweeten the lure with the barter exemption but knew damned-well Tam would do stealth-work for him whether he owed barter or not.

The tavern entrance burst open. A man was thrust through, babbling protests. Aden stalked at the man's heels, her shapeless coat flapping open, her cheeks flushed with ire.

Del turned startled eyes toward the newcomers—maybe as startled by Aden as the disruption. Jonas's second enjoyed clashing colors, yellow spattered leggings beneath a purple tunic today. Her long neck was caged by a wire-woven scarf, a brighter copper than her hair.

Aden's captive stood, shrunk-shouldered before her.

Caleb Freth slicked up behind Aden like oil dripping from her shadow, his yellow hair a match for her leggings. Freth seemed to think working at Aden's shoulder elevated him in the NG ranks.

Tam twirled his fingers in the disdain *ah'nea;* no gesture a Human could decipher.

"Yo, Aden?" Jonas hailed.

Aden narrow-eyed her charge. "Lenny's here to explain the quality of the protein packs he foisted off on Co-op."

Lenny swiped his head as if using his forehead grease to slick his thinning hair. "You know we can't get the fresh stuff. I do what I can."

"Near-expiration is a moon's girth from three months expired, but you're welcome to explain to the Boss." Aden's voice flexed with irony.

Fring suppliers only sent their castoffs, which left traders like Lenny treading a thin line. But Balter's Den enforced standards. Food poisoning couldn't salve hunger.

Lenny opened his mouth then snapped it shut, his restraint likely inspired by the club strapped to Aden's broad hip.

"Head on back to my office," Jonas sighed.

Aden and the trader disappeared into the backroom.

Caleb Freth broke away to stand like a smirking sentry by the front entrance. Jonas skimmed a smile over Freth—even the Boss bought "Goldie's" bullshit.

Jonas faced Del with polite regret. "I've got another obligation, but Tam here can advise you on finding a qualified guard."

Del's expression blanked. She shot Tam a sidelong look. "Thank you."

Irritation sizzling, Tam watched Jonas stump toward the backroom.

The hell. "Hold up, Boss!" Tam caught him at the door, conscious of Del and Freth watching. "What are you thinking?" Tam glared his incredulity.

Jonas's lips twitched, but his eyes remained somber. "Two things. One, it's an opportunity for you. Two, I need your eyes on this."

Needed Tam to both protect the off-worlder and spy on her, he meant. But Tam did stealth-work for Jonas. He didn't play regular "ear," snuggling up to people for intel.

Baffled anxiety tightened Tam's voice. "You replacing me, Boss?"

"I *can't* replace you." Some deep, unreadable emotion moved within Jonas. "But this is … big."

Tam clamped down on his gift. He owed Jonas a lot—everything—but Jonas asked too much. Tam couldn't imagine spending hours a day at The Bar, enduring stares and whispers.

"This dropped into our laps. I can't afford to be stupid." Jonas's gaze grew piercing yet unfocused as if he tried to scan Del through Tam's head. "Please talk to her. Get her make."

Tam's tongue snagged over a refusal. No explanation could counterweight the grim entreaty in Jonas's expression. Agreeing was equally impossible.

Tam's pause stretched.

Jonas said, "You need me to flip this to Caleb?"

"I'll talk to her," Tam snipped, twitching to glance behind him at Freth. Not *that* bootlicker.

Jonas squeezed Tam's shoulder and continued into the backroom.

Tam expelled a pent breath and crossed back to Del, ignoring Freth's squinty stare.

"Perhaps introductions are in order?" Del said dryly. "Unless you'd rather I call you Jon?"

"Tam Lyn. I use Jon Gray on duty." As close to an explanation as he'd give.

She gestured to the backroom. "What was that all about?"

"Supply chain issues."

"Is it difficult to procure food here?" Like she'd pounce on that problem, too.

"Grow what we can in food-blocks. The rest we scrounge from the Fring. We manage."

Turning from her reaction, Tam led Del to a table near the stairwell, the farthest spot from other patrons. Curious looks pelted them as they crossed, Freth's like a bead drawn on Tam's back.

Del settled smoothly into the chair opposite Tam. "Mr. Valerian is quite formidable." She averted her face as she spoke. Not indifferent to Tam's strangeness, after all? But then, for all Humans relied on expression to read each other, they didn't make much eye contact during conversation.

She laced her fingers, fine-boned and bare. Not a spec of ornamentation on her, dressed in a plain jumpsuit, her hair knotted at her nape— too many prim pointy edges overall. Del looked no older than Tam, but if she *were* a doctor, she couldn't be in range of his twenty-one.

The implication of the "opportunity" sank in. This doctor might get him behind the Wall where his mother once lived—possibly where she'd died. *It won't pan out. It never does.* But after years of futile searching ... *Tempting, too tempting.*

Taking the lure would be like a cril snatching sweetmeat from a snare.

To Maze-dwellers, Rynet were like mythical creatures—*ghouls*—but to an off-world medical doctor? Tam's chameleon eyes and cold-colored skin were bleached out compared to a full blood's, his cheekbones and chin rounded like a Human's, but he bristled with the wish he'd worn a disguise. Many scorned him for being an "exotic," a cosmetically enhanced Human. Worlds worse if he were exposed as half-Rynet.

"So, Mr. Lyn, what is it you do when you're not climbing rooftops?"

He'd held silent too long, ceding her the first toss. Likely she had no idea asking about someone's living was rude.

"Take odd jobs." He'd agreed to talk to her, not to pitch his services. "Haven't done much guard duty."

"I'd really … I'll need someone as much guide as guard."

The notion of a bodyguard made her uneasy. He filed that away.

"What're the specs?"

"You mean qualifications? Someone trustworthy, above all," she said as if feeling out what she hadn't considered. "Someone clever, area savvy, who can protect us both, if need be."

Raucous voices burst from a group clustered in the corner opposite them.

Del's eyelids fluttered in reaction, but she held her focus on Tam. "I'll need help navigating the customs."

Tam's fingers sketched the irony *ah'nea* symbol over his knee. He hadn't stepped outside the non-Human "Xeno" warren until he turned seventeen. He'd make a lousy expert on local Human customs.

"Deep reqs." Inside dialect across classes was thick with mining slang. Familiarity would be telling, but Del frowned with incomprehension. He restated, "That's a lot to ask around here."

"Are you playing coy, Mr. Lyn, or are you truly not interested?"

"Seems you're the one playing coy." He mirrored her tone. "Why don't you just ask me?"

"Fear of rejection, of course."

Her aura's sparkle charged his senses, and curiosity pressed at Tam's resolve. Which was beyond stupid. He frowned at his hands.

Del sighed, embarrassment flushing through her emotional signature, the abruptness startling him. "Please don't feel pressured. That would be poor thanks for your help."

He met her eyes.

She swallowed visibly, winced a smile. "After the way we met, there's no help for you thinking me foolish. I'd hardly blame you for wanting to steer clear."

"Why did you go alone?"

"I suspected any protection I might hire in the First Ring would be compromised. I suppose, in that moment, danger overruled futility."

Futility … He breathed out slowly.

"Make me an offer." His stomach hollowed; he'd already thrown the game.

"Shall we say seven hundred to start?"

"Sorry?" Had she overestimated the value of their credits?

"Seven hundred per week in the local currency."

Per week. *Well, shit.*

If she held out a few weeks—if *he* held out—he could provision himself for months and fuel his search for his mother. *Impossible to turn this down, snare or no.*

Del studied his reaction. "We've an agreement, then?"

"A few weeks. Until you get settled."

She held out her hand. The equivalent of bottoming a drink to seal a deal?

He glanced at his gloved hand. Concealing his black nail sheaths with gloves wouldn't work cozying with Humans all day. He'd need to cut them back and blunt his nails.

"I promise not to bite, Mr. Lyn."

Repressing a grimace, Tam squeezed her hand, his sleeve sliding back to expose his wrist. The golden warmth of her skin tone made a strange contrast with his blue-tinted pallor.

Tam quickly released her hand. "If your org had realized how dangerous this place is, would they have sent you?"

He understood Jonas's suspicion. If IWA had uncovered Jonas's "activism," the OBMG sure had, and this doctor made the perfect lure for them to test its extent.

Del tucked an imaginary stray hair in place. "Perhaps not."

The tavern door opened, admitting a pair of rowdies, salvage workers by the char on their clothes. Tam figured it was time to escort her back.

As he led Del across the taproom, the men tracked them with avid stares. At the door, Caleb Freth inclined his blond head, treated Del to a smarmy, drawling *hello*. His gaze flicked to Tam, and Tam sensed a boil of resentment beneath it.

The charity doctor would become the new town peep show. By taking this gig, Tam had committed to stepping into its light.

7

———————

*Secure the tin in your pocket before grubbing for gold out of
reach.*
—*Old Maze saying*

PELL MAHR SLEPT, ONLY DROWSY MOVEMENT AT THE WARREN'S BORDER, A scattering of folk furtively stirring like rats caught in daylight. Caleb had never visited the party warren during the day before. It seemed flat, its glitter as drained as a dead miner-stick—clubs silent, flashing signs snuffed, hawkers absent. This warren was nocturnal. Folk from all over the Maze, and even the Fring, flocked here at night to play or attend to business of all sorts.

Barbed-mesh nets ringed Pell Mahr's broad borders, and militia guarded the gates, snug inside uniformed jackets with some pretentious emblem on the collar. Caleb rolled his eyes as he crossed. The guard swayed in his boots, giving Caleb a cursory once-over.

The Neighborhood Guard lacked snappy rigs and airs, but Caleb would wager they had more discipline. Denners kept it real.

Caleb tracked his destination by its tall, copper-tiled dome. Pell Mahr's chamber of commerce—this warren's stand-in for a chief—had commissioned a Fring company to dress up their warren-hub last year. Caleb wondered how even Pell Mahr had afforded it. This hub could now swallow The Bar in Balter's Den ten times over, the original boxy structure bracketed by two new wings.

Visitors had to pass through a scanning machine that looked like a porta-pot without a door. The security setup seemed a poor man's version of the Fring gate checkpoint. Once he passed through the scanner, a guard gave him a pat-down that lingered on his crotch.

"Under different circumstances, I might enjoy this." The words steamed through Caleb's gritted teeth.

The guard rolled her eyes. "You wouldn't believe what folk try to smuggle in here."

Caleb swallowed a retort, reminded himself he'd volunteered for this task. The Boss wouldn't keep Tam Lyn on bodyguard duty long. Lyn had all the charm of a cril's corpse, nothing to appeal to an off-world toff. Caleb would position himself to take Lyn's place.

He shoved through double doors into a cavernous lobby; the emptiest indoor space he'd ever seen. More folk bustled here than he'd passed during his trek through the warren. People strode purposefully, their shoes clicking in layered echoes over the polished stone floor.

A Maze-toff slicked past Caleb, wielding an elbow to prod Caleb from his path.

"Ex*cus*e you."

The toff didn't bother reacting.

God, Caleb hated it. No matter how hard he strove, flung himself into worthy purpose, seediness seemed baked into his skin. Like he'd never shed it.

Pap's path an't yours. Wouldn't be if Caleb didn't let it—which meant proving himself to Jonas.

Three corridors branched off the lobby: Finance and taxation in the side wings, administration down the middle. Administration covered miscellaneous business—guild seats, trade boards, habitation permits— stuff Caleb had no clue about, but his task lay there.

He headed down the corridor, the scuff of his shoes conspicuous. The corridor dead-ended into a cuisine court ringed with kiosks peddling meal foils. Plant replicas dangled overhead like green spiders. A vending bar claimed to reproduce a "galaxy of tastes."

Caleb dished out for plain-old fretha tea and settled at one of the tables scattered in the center. The cushioned seat molded to him more intimately than the security guard's groping hands. He sipped his fretha, its familiar, bitter bite soothing.

He had a clear view of his target, an unlabeled hallway. Administration's other corridors stretched, bright-lit with stripes of light-tubes, but gloom curtained *that* hallway. Residents dubbed it "gang alley," an area reserved for negotiations. Rival gangs played nice here—too much flash at stake for the gangs not to respect the truce Pell Mahr enforced inside its borders.

Confident of the hallway's stillness, Caleb rose and approached, keeping his stride casual. Gang alley hadn't earned a makeover. Dusty coil-lights swung from a drop ceiling, and unadorned concrete formed the floor. Doors were inset from the hallway, each shallow alcove marked with a different gang symbol. Only top-tier gangs rated their own room, so Caleb checked for evidence the Surge had risen enough to rank one. The NG needed insight into how the low-scope gang had managed their trick with the doc.

A white skull holo over the first door tagged it as the Skull gang's. Other doors were etched, embossed, or paint splashed. None had the Surge's flame emblem.

Musty light spilled through a warped-glass window at the hallway's end, only amping the gloom. Caleb hesitated, then approached the last two doors, the right-hand one plain metal. And left—textured blackness. He detected a rasp of breath before he made sense of what he saw: a black-garbed man in the doorway, one leg kicked against the alcove wall. Watching.

"Shit!" Caleb staggered back.

"You lost?" Cold, utterly flat. Familiar. The enforcer Belek, the Fet's new mouthpiece in the north.

Caleb's eyes adjusted. A coiled shape materialized behind Belek. Black over black. Fresh alarm spiked Caleb's pulse. He took a long, silent breath. The shape was only the gang's snake symbol embossed over the door.

"Looking for the washroom." He spun away.

The scuff of Belek's foot landing on the floor froze him. "I wonder what Valerian's *golden boy* could be sniffing after here?"

Caleb turned slowly.

Belek stepped into the hallway, dark eyes hard-staring Caleb from a pale, bony face.

Caleb hesitated. Risky to lie to the enforcer. In Balter's Den, Belek might hesitate to move on an NG. Caleb had no such protection outside the warren.

The Fet's door opened. A short, soft-bodied man in a flashy red suit emerged—toff, not gangster.

Caleb relaxed a notch.

The man eyed Caleb head-to-toe, making Caleb conscious of his rough-cropped hair, his cheap slicker, his scuffed shoes.

"What's this?" the man asked Belek.

"One of Valerian's boys come to say hello."

"Just here to exchange flash for the Boss." Jonas had suggested that cover. Caleb swallowed against dryness in his mouth. "I was curious. An't been to this hub before."

The plump toff smiled, sharp and knowing, before strutting around Caleb and down the hallway.

Belek's long, white fingers strummed his thigh.

Caleb hurried after the toff, his shoulders hunched, his whole body nerved for a strike. Only silence followed him.

He returned to the cuisine court. Plunking into his chair, he lifted his cup with shaking hands and gulped the now-cold tea.

Bad luck. Fucking bad luck to run into Belek here! Worse, the realization Belek had marked Caleb enough to recognize him. Why? The new enforcer had only been to The Bar a handful of times. They'd never met.

Down the main corridor, the toff paused. His suit gleamed blood-bright beneath the more intense lighting. He twisted around. His gaze landed on Caleb. Then he flipped a hand, arrogant, summoning.

VAGAR DUGAN FACED CALEB ACROSS A BROAD TABLE. THE ALL-WHITE interior of the reception room seemed bright enough to be a digital overlay. It was like sitting inside a light-tube. Dugan's shiny crimson jacket seared the eyeballs in this space.

Caleb knew Dugan by reputation—bigshot chamber-member who owned several lucrative clubs. With his high-swept auburn hair, coppery cheeks, and enhanced amber eyes, Dugan sketched the perfect Maze-toff caricature.

The glassy wall behind Dugan kept tugging Caleb's focus—a wrongness. A slight transparency, as if Caleb viewed Dugan's image over a giant vid-screen.

Dugan said, "If Valerian has an issue with Pell Mahr, he's welcome to come discuss it."

Caleb suppressed a grimace. Jonas rarely risked setting foot outside Balter's Den. "I an't here for that." How to salvage this? Caleb refused to go home tail tucked.

Dugan rapped fingers gleaming with nail art so finely enameled it could have been enlarged and hung as decoration. "Why not say? We are allies, no?"

That stretched the truth. Caleb flattened his expression.

"All right, my toss," Dugan continued. "You're here about Valerian's new doctor."

"What do you know about it?" *And so quickly.*

"How about I give you a tidbit, and you give one in return?"

Caleb shrugged to cover a stir of anticipation. If he played this right, he might slick information from Dugan—impress Jonas, plant the seed to take Lyn's place.

"Belek." Dugan paused a dramatic beat. "The new enforcer is young but ambitious, clever, *careful.* He was *very* curious how a small-spark crew got so plugged in."

In other words, the Surge had known about Del, but the Fet hadn't.

"What's Belek's interest in an off-world doc?"

"None that I know of. He *is* interested in how the Surge gained a connection behind the Wall. Valerian is equally interested, I expect."

A flicker behind Dugan, like movement beneath the wall's skin, made

Caleb stiffen. Imagination. He forced himself to relax. "I don't suppose you know how the Surge got wind of her?"

"I'll hazard a guess," Dugan said archly. "An Inside contact approached us with the possibility Pell Mahr host the IWA doctor."

Caleb stilled as the picture formed. The Surge chief had *impersonated* Jonas. "The Inside scheme-spinner hired the Surge to scare her away from Balter's Den." He folded his arms. "An' then I suppose Pell Mahr would throw open its doors?"

Dugan's eyes slivered—like he'd underestimated Caleb's intelligence. "Not interested. We have a proper clinic already, and the woman seems like a brace of trouble."

Too slick a response by half. Caleb ducked his face to hide a grin. He already had enough to claim success. "Don't suppose you'll name your contact?"

"Sorry." No fraction of give in Dugan's expression.

"Why'd your contact pick the Surge?"

"Choosing a minor gang without treaty to your warren makes sense," Dugan's voice rippled with amusement. "Risky to involve an ally of Valerian's or a top-tier gang who might have their own agenda. And the Surge do seem … hungry."

Caleb flushed. He should have drawn that picture himself.

A shadowy figure flitted behind Dugan. Behind the wall. Caleb jerked up straighter.

"Easy, boyo." Dugan chuckled. "There's a corridor behind there."

A *corridor*? Caleb squinted at the wall. A glass-like material, almost opaque. Why make a room with a panel, not quite a wall … not quite a window? That elusive transparency made Caleb feel more like a bug trapped in a light-tube. Sweat heated his armpits despite the room's chill.

Dugan tapped his lips as if covering a smirk.

Let the bastard feel superior. Caleb could use it. "If your Inside friends want to leash the off-worlder, why not have their own stiffs guard her?"

"This *IWA* forced their do-gooder down our throats. The OBMG owes her nothing."

Caleb scrambled to interpret Dugan's defensive manner. "They want the doc in Pell Mahr so you can spy on her."

"*Contain. Protect.* From a proper remove." Dugan flipped a dismissive hand with each stressed word.

Contain? Or chase away? Anger ribbed Caleb's voice, "Why do they care if some do-gooder keeps us from dying?"

"That one aid worker could be an anchor. Once the Allies have a foothold, they'll think they can tell us what's what. It happens to indie worlds all over the galaxy—Allies, Hegemonies—someone always wants their slice."

Caleb slashed an impatient hand. "Why let *her* in, then?"

"The OBMG needed the Allies' vote on a dispute. They got it."

Politics was such bullshit! Making less of people than the cardboard under a game of flip-ball.

Dugan steepled his fingers. "I wonder if we can't help each other out."

Here it is. Caleb should have known. Dugan had his lines all laid out. Belek lurking to identify Caleb hadn't been coincidence. The enforcer had gotten intel on Caleb's mission and informed Dugan.

"Don't look so green, man." Dugan laughed like Jolly Uncle about to throw festival gifts. "You get me what I need to reassure my Inside friends. I keep alert for trouble that might impact your warren." Dugan stroked the face of his new-gen wrist-vid, his eyes not straying from Caleb's. "A win-win. No harm to anyone."

Dugan had summed Caleb up as a bribable shab from that first glance in the hallway.

Caleb breathed through a rush of anger.

A gray blur rippled over the wall panel. A shadow-formed face, peering in.

Caleb jumped, his defensive reflexes blocked by his chair. "'t fuck?!"

Dugan glanced over his shoulder. "Some fool admiring his reflection." A line formed over the drum-tight skin between his brows.

Caleb eased down, unable to shift his focus from that face—not quite three-dimensional, a spectral imprint of features he couldn't see.

He knotted his hands over his knees. He couldn't—wouldn't—speak with those formless eyes watching. A deep instinct, like buried childhood fear, warned he was exposed.

"It's reflective on his side," Dugan said. "It an't like *I'd* tolerate an audience."

The face blurred, dissolved into whiteness.

Caleb wiped moist palms on his pants, hardened his mouth. "I an't a turnskin, Dugan. Not for any amount of flash."

"I an't inviting you to be." Thoughtfulness reshaped Dugan's manner. "You asked how I guessed your doc's danger an't over? Rumor has it Valerian's sneak rescued the woman. One man. A whole Surge pack. And the coincidence of him being there at *just* the right moment."

Caleb sat straighter. Exactly what spiked Caleb's suspicions about Lyn.

Dugan continued, "Either something's fishy with the sneak or the off-worlder."

Caleb had tried to warn Jonas, but Jonas wouldn't tolerate anyone badmouthing Lyn.

Dugan leaned in. "I'm only asking that you watch *the woman*. If she's legit, it's another layer of protection. If she's not ..." Dugan shrugged with a slither of his shiny jacket. "You'd have to keep it from Valerian in case someone in his inner circle *is* a traitor. And I can't have Valerian mistaking my intention, thinking I want to plant an ear on him."

An arms-length divided them, yet Caleb tensed like Dugan confronted him nose-to-nose. "I won't play ear," he repeated between his teeth.

"Watch the woman for me, and I'll alert you of anything related from my end. That's the bargain. Mutual benefit."

What was the catch?

"You could do it out of duty or take compensation for your efforts. I'd rather you take the flash as insurance you won't reveal me to Valerian."

Caleb's hard-worn clothes hung heavier, sinking his shoulders. He ran himself ragged for Jonas, to prove himself. Left little time to earn flash, give his life even a thin layer of padding.

Dugan had access to intel the NG could dig a hundred years for without finding.

Intel, flash, the promise of time to breathe—an ambush of temptation.

But to keep the deal from Jonas ...

Caleb could try to fool Dugan, but Dugan had contacts in Balter's

Den already, or he wouldn't know as much as he did. And if Jonas caught the slightest whiff this related to Lyn, he'd close it down—shut Caleb out.

He bit the inside of his lip, scanned the wall panel. "How much?"

Dugan's lips rolled back to exposed teeth as white as the walls.

Let him grin. Caleb had no obligation.

If the deal turned sketchy, he'd go straight to Jonas.

8

———

This whole plan felt so bloody sketchy. How would she manage?

Del couldn't shed her disappointment as she gazed around the small, windowless space. Cinder block floor, metal paneled walls. The room allotted her at The Bar could fit inside her First Ring office *washroom*. Even if she procured smaller furnishings, there'd be little space to move.

Tam Lyn leaned in the doorway, observing her reaction.

She understood why he'd worn a disguise the night they met. Unmasked, he couldn't go unnoticed—skin surreally smooth and pale with the barest tint of shale, hair so black it swallowed the light. And those irises … They apparently reacted to emotional stimulation like pupil arousal-response. Surely, a Rynet-inspired design. For all humanity spurned their closest genetic cousins, many cosmetic artists held them in fascination.

So odd to encounter such flawless "surrealist" work in a backwater slum.

Not my business.

She pinned a brighter expression on her face. "Where shall I store my supplies and such?"

Tam padded across the space and slid back an accordion-like door to expose a small, empty closet. "Jonas will rig security."

"Wonderful." Her stomach sank. Stocking meds on crude shelves would be a headache.

Movement in the doorway drew her focus. Her breath caught as a child slunk inside, wide hazel eyes clicking from Del to Tam. The girl was filthy, with hollowed-out cheeks and ragged clothing that exposed knobby wrist and ankle bones. She appeared about twelve, just entering puberty.

"Hello there," Del spoke softly, afraid to startle her.

The girl's head bobbled.

"You lost?" Tam said, not harshly, but the girl jumped.

She gaped at him, whispered what sounded like "boss's ghoul."

Del flicked Tam an uncertain look. "What's your name?"

"Pe—" The girl winced. "Pepar. Heard there's a doc."

"How'd you slip up here?" Tam frowned.

"Um ..." Pepar shuffled farther from him.

"Mr. Lyn, perhaps you can give us privacy?"

His frown deepened. "Leave the door open, please." He positioned himself in the hallway, in view, arms crossed.

Clearly, Del needed to add patient privacy to her list of requirements.

She gave the empty room a helpless scan. "We're not quite set up yet, but let's see what I can do." She unslung her outcall pack, thankful she'd determined to always carry it. "What brings you today?"

Pepar bounced on her toes as if tempted to flee. "I just feel ... off."

Half-starved. Del swallowed against a tightness in her throat. She had a few nutrient packs on hand, but IWA wasn't a food-aid agency.

"I'm Dr. Marks." Del knelt and opened her pack. "And I promise I don't bite."

When Pepar inched forward, Del breathed shallowly against her thick, sour odor. Del fished out cleansing pads, wiped her face and neck, revealing tawny skin beneath the grime. Pepar stiffened but allowed it. Her frizz of dark hair stood off her head in snarls, but Del had nothing to manage that.

"Are your parents here? They could come in with you."

The girl's shoulders shrunk. "No."

"They don't mind you're here?" Del couldn't help but press.

"Mam ... don't care," Pepar whispered.

Del raised her diagnose, but Pepar flinched from the palm-sized device.

Del tapped its glossy, rectangular surface. "This will show me what the trouble is."

Pepar curled her right hand against her stomach.

"Is your hand hurting? Let's see."

"No!" Pepar hid it behind her back. "It's f-fine. Really."

Del didn't push. The diagnose would identify any injuries. "Have you ever seen a doctor before?"

Pepar hunched over, frail hands burrowing into her oversized shirt, her thumb hooking in a hole. "I've … seen … other one." She spoke through rigid lips.

Del froze, absorbing the child's fear. "The other one?"

"D-doc Umar." Her hands clawed harder.

"Nothing will harm you here, all right?" Del laid her hands carefully over Pepar's chill, knobbed knuckles, easing her hands to her sides.

Pepar's eyes owled on Del's face.

When Del lifted the diagnose again, Pepar kept still. A scan proved her bruised and malnourished. Del applied healing gel, each spot a silent negotiation. She was administering a vitamin infusion when a huge figure appeared in the doorway. Pepar jumped so badly the press-syringe nearly missed.

Jonas stood there. From this angle, the scar beneath his heavy jawline stood out, an angry line. A wound that never received proper care. Scars like that hadn't existed in Del's world. Easily remedied, but Del practiced general and internal medicine, not plastic surgery.

"Slick move you pulled, little bit," Jonas said to Pepar.

Pepar's head hung in a clear ploy for sympathy. "Sorry, Boss."

"Mr. Valerian doesn't bite," Del said. "So I'm told."

"Not usually," he said, dryly.

Del handed Pepar the nutrient packs. "You should feel a little better soon." Her voice thinned. "You must return if you feel unwell again, all right?"

Pepar turned hollow eyes on Del, fled the room. Del's hands twitched as though she could hold onto the girl by the wake she left behind.

• • •

With his back pressed against the hallway wall, Tam tuned out Del and Jonas' debate over "patient privacy." She'd confronted the Boss about it when he came to rig the exam-room security.

Jonas would win; privacy was a nicety few Maze-dwellers had. The Boss was getting too smug; all the pins in his scheme jumping onto the map of their own accord.

Tam closed his eyes, tried to feel nothing, but the kid's fear had needled into him, lingered like a splinter.

Ghoul.

A slur for Rynet, a symbol parents used to scare young children into obedience.

Ghouls and Knobs, a rough war game teens played on the streets.

Decades ago, Rynet Kurni corsairs had plagued the Maze, challenging the OBMG's rights to the planet. Safe inside G4 City, the mine board had let the rabble take the brunt. Maze-dwellers carried memories longer than their lifespans and considered all Rynet like the Kurni.

Children slung *ghoul* at Tam out of fear. Most adults, assuming Tam had sold himself for the exotics trade, found other insults—glitter, sell-skin, jonny.

Ghoul drew more blood.

Tam cracked his eyelids, studied Jonas through them, remembering the first time he'd heard that slur. Not long after he'd come to Balter's Den, joining the cold, confusing Human world.

Tam had returned to his living-pod complex, a bleak stack of cramped efficiencies, to find a familiar figure loitering outside, Lettie. The young woman lived on his block, but he'd evaded her offers to "hook up." He hadn't untangled how Humans' fickle mating relationships worked, wasn't sure he wanted to.

Lettie startled when she spotted him, her round face reddening.

"Hey, Tam," she trilled, thorny blue eyes spiking into him. "Hoped to catch you in. I was about to give up."

He frowned. Lettie's cooing words never synched with what burbled underneath them.

She winced a smile, twitched a glance behind him.

Two men materialized from the shadows beside the complex—flesh-traders—as sharp-mannered and flashy as a gilded blade, one with a slaver's collar looped around his wrist.

Tam whipped out his taser.

Lettie whirled, but a flesh-trader grabbed her, pressing a knife to her side. "Be good or I'll part your slut's ribs."

A moment's hesitation condemned Tam. The other man closed from behind, snapping the collar around Tam's throat. Shock seared his neck, radiating out, spinning his world to black.

Tam woke, lying naked on a concrete floor. His hand rested by his face, spasming; he couldn't feel the tremors. Lights glared down at him. Voices fell like icy drips.

"—squat. I could get ten times that. This piece is flawless."

"He looks like a fucking ghoul. Those *teeth!* Whoever sponsored his cosmetic work was crack-brained."

Tam scraped his desiccated tongue around his mouth. The insert to cover his Rynet teeth was gone. Through blurred vision, he made out the flesh-traders bending over him with a black-garbed man. Their emotions sunk into him, a sick slurry he didn't understand.

"It's *genius.* A thrill of fear. Exactly the thing to juice up your freak-fetish clients."

"Work like this don't spring from a gutter."

"We wouldn't push a stabled exotic on you."

A challenge-hiss strained the muscles of Tam's abused throat. His black nail sheaths slid back to bare his nails' sharp tips.

"Check this shit out." His hand was snatched up. He tried to bite the man's fingers but could only manage a spasm.

"You think my clients wan—"

A loud crack jolted the room. Tam's vision swam as a huge stranger burst inside. The warren chief. Had the tase scrambled Tam's brain?

Alarm pulsed through his captors.

"What do you want here, Valerian?" The black-garbed man growled.

"He's one of mine. Leave off or I'll take it up with your enforcer." Valerian's iron gaze shifted to the flesh-traders. "We've warned you before. No slaving in the Den. Show your faces again, and I'll snap your necks myself."

Dizziness flattened Tam to the floor. A scuffling struggle, howls, retreating footfalls ...

The black-garbed man still lurked there. "No way this glitter is NG. Keep your threats behind your teeth, Valerian, or *I'll* take it up with the enforcer."

"Just get out. You're breaking treaty trading with slavers in the first place."

The man's poisonous presence faded, leaving the steady hum of an unusually muted aura.

Warm fabric reeking of Human sweat dropped over Tam's chilled body.

"Don't worry, kid. They an't had you long." A whirl of motion, then a pair of shrewd, steel-gray eyes confronted him. "Looks like you've just joined the Neighborhood Guard." No pity, no concern, nothing to further shred Tam's pride.

"You don't even know who I am," Tam spat. "Why push me into the NG?"

"That brothel runner is Fet-hooked. To stay safe, least for a while, I'm afraid you an't got a choice."

When Tam asked how Jonas found him, he had learned Lettie alerted the NG. Tam didn't understand why she'd sold him out only to call for help—hadn't bothered finding out.

Tam had hidden, disguised or in plain sight, since joining the Human world. If anyone peeled back his "exotic" guise to the truth of his heritage, he'd find himself strung up or enslaved as a freakshow.

The Boss's ghoul.

A flood of other kids would come to see the new doc.

Tam thudded the back of his head against the wall.

Jonas' satisfaction whispered through Del's more powerful emotional signature as they conferred. *Three weeks.* Tam had promised to hold out for that long. Could he endure it—even for the flash, the opportunity? He was in for worse than that kid's reaction.

Tam owed Jonas his freedom, maybe his life. He owed his mother more.

This new gig offered him the chance to fulfill both duties—or to fail them both.

HOW IN THE WORLDS COULD DEL EXPLAIN A GUARD IN HER EXAM ROOM? AN actual *person*. A proper clinic would have discreet AI security—not remotely an option here, as Jonas so bluntly reminded her. Del's only AI was a semi-sentient patient manager.

A cool, smooth grip on Del's wrist drew her up short. She blinked at Tam's strange, striking face. His silvery irises were half-veiled by spiky lashes, so inky they gave the illusion he wore kohl.

Do not stare.

A bustle of activity and clash of odors reminded her they stood on the warren's main thoroughfare. Pedestrians and cyclists flowed around them. Del and Tam had joined the evening rush after she finished scouting out her new practice space.

Tam dropped her wrist, his brows gathering, rippling disapproval across the smoothness of his forehead. "Folk get pissed when you bump them."

Heat rushed her cheeks.

His lips twitched. Humor or annoyance? "Walk now. Plan later."

Her blush deepened. Tam had proven uncomfortably astute. "Yes, of course."

She wrapped her jacket tighter and strode on. Was it *always* so bloody chilly here?

Her wrist-vid vibrated. She reflexively tapped her ear to activate her audio fiber. *Incoming interplanetary vid-call from Isa Vinn.*

Del stumbled. A *vid* call. That meant her IWA sponsor was in this sector of space.

The signal indicator flashed red. Del whirled her gaze around. Of all the timing!

"Problem?" Tam's hand hovered as if he resisted the impulse to steady her again.

"An important call." *Too* important. Del needed to convince Isa to support her solution.

How far from the First Ring were they? She shifted on the balls of her feet as if that could enable her to map the way.

Tam gripped her arm, dragged her into a trot, deftly maneuvering her through the rush. "Comm's clear at the gate."

The path ahead snarled. A wheeled truck pulled from a side street, blocking the way. A woman on a tricycle cursed the driver. Others chimed in with what seemed the enthusiasm of ritual.

Tam's grip tightened as he wound through the obstacles. Del tripped, breathless, behind. He drew alongside the truck's cab and tapped its window.

The driver ignored him.

"NG." Tam rapped the window again, lifted a chain from under his collar, and held up a metal pendant. Like a police ident?

With a dramatic eyeroll, the driver opened the window. "Yeah?"

"Need a hitch to the Fring."

The man gave Tam a squinty scan. He raised three fingers.

With a guttural noise of disgust, Tam dug into his jacket pocket and flipped a small disk to the driver, who nipped it from the air. Tam tugged Del to the boxy rear of the vehicle, grasped a loop over its hatch, and stepped onto its bumper.

Del shot him a wide-eyed look as he drew her up with him. His arm wound around her waist. She had to press her cheek against the filthy hatch to stay securely on the bumper.

The truck surged forward—fast enough to make falling a scary proposition.

Her wrist-vid vibrated like an impatient tap on the shoulder. How long would Isa wait?

They jounced their way down the street. Whenever the truck slowed, an angry blare sounded from in front—warding pedestrians from their path.

Tam's face was twisted away, his body rigid. His jacket tangled with hers, brushing her calves; his thick shag of hair tickled her forehead. Chill gusts whipped at her clothes, and she braced against the impulse to lean into Tam's warmth.

Her wrist vid buzzed again. She steamed a breath between hard-set teeth.

At last, the truck bumped to a stop.

Tam leapt off and swung her down before she could gather her wits.

"Reception's usually good here. Lots of signal sniffers, but we can find you a patch."

Del swallowed against a swell of frustration. She couldn't interpret half of what came from Tam's mouth.

The truck trundled away, exposing the First Ring wall. The meaning of "signal sniffers" became clear. The wall was lined with people bent over devices.

Tam steered her to an unoccupied section, turned his back.

Del flipped up her vid, initiated reconnect. Ten long chimes before audio crackled through the fiber. A holo-image ballooned above the vid, coalescing into Isa Vinn's face. Framed by her thick wedge of white hair, Isa's face reduced to a pale triangle on the holo-projection.

"Good evening, Dr. Marks. I *think* it's evening—never trust the time difference calculation."

"Good evening." Del cleared a scratch of dryness from her throat. "This is unexpected."

"I'm en route to Grellent. Thought I'd check in while close enough for direct contact."

Del gusted a breath. "I'm out at present. There's no privacy. I could—"

"Let them listen if they will. Our position isn't secret."

The sharp tone raised a prickle of heat over Del. Isa had no idea what it was like here.

A rapping noise like nails over a hard surface roughened the audio. Isa said, "You've been on Galta 4 for fifteen cycles now. How is it that I've only received a preliminary progress report?"

"I've queued one." Del refused to make excuses, but pressure throbbed at her temples. Isa had the essentials. Smog, chill, poverty—an environment ripe for illness—thousands at the mercy of unlicensed healers.

Del lifted her gaze over Isa's image to track Tam. He paced about ten meters away, blending into evening's ash-colored half-light. Neck-to-toes in dark gray. His long, loose jacket flowed as he moved.

"The Mine Board continues to insist your staff be local hires?" A probe, not a real question.

"I'm advertising in the First Ring and expect to have suitable candidates soon." Del had job-posted her first cycle here. Not a *single* inquiry, thus far.

Wavering resolution distorted Isa's image, blading the angles of her jaw. "I've pressed for a broader presence, but we're being stonewalled."

"Can't the foreign ministry step in again?"

"We're unlikely to see progress for some time." Isa's words were clipped with finality.

A bawl of laughter jolted Del. She darted wide eyes toward a large woman in a screaming red bodysuit, flopping against the wall a pace away. Before she could do more than stiffen, Tam was there, imposing himself between them. "Back off. Warren business."

Curses erupted. Del flinched her vid farther away. Whatever Tam did spurred the woman to stalk off with a brayed, "Fuck you!"

"Dr. Marks?" Isa's voice cut through the noise.

Del frowned at the screen before mastering her expression. "Yes."

"I worry this post demands too much of a novice advocate, a young doctor, barely thirty, barely out of residency. I wish you'd accepted that Belderan post. That mission is fully staffed."

Yes, fully staffed with senior doctors who'd also view Del as *young* and *barely*.

Del knuckled her teeth with her free hand, then flinched it from her mouth. It was onscreen. "It's the people I'm concerned about—that they receive our full support."

"Dr. Marks, you understand that being an advocate entails more than doctoring. It means managing the political climate. It means *advocacy*."

"I'm well aware." After Zavi's expulsion for activism, how hard could Del push?

The resolution sharpened, exposing the grim lines bracketing Isa's mouth. "Given the situation, it may be expedient to recall you, retrench our strategy."

Recall.

Three tortuous weeks to get here. Less time on the ground. Only to go *back*? Del rocked as if spun in the void again, taunted by hisses of distortion, indecipherable whispers.

Her throat knotted as she recalled Pepar's bruised, undernourished form. So much needless suffering … Del blinked down at her hand, limp at her side.

Del? A prickle of thought. She jerked her eyes up to find Tam stilled and watching. Had he spoken or had his questioning alertness tugged her?

Squaring her chin, she refocused on Isa. "Retreating would only embolden the OBMG."

"Have they conveyed *any* willingness to help you reach your patients?"

"No, but—"

"Please understand." Isa's softened manner took Del aback. "I must look beyond the immediate to the *long-term* good. We sent you there on the understanding the OBMG would provide minimal support. If they refuse, we must re-strategize. I must consider your safety."

Del's arm ached from holding out the vid; she rolled her shoulder to ease it. "Jonas Valerian has offered to support my practice within the Balter's Den townhall and connect me with the community. The local militia will provide protection."

Isa's eyes narrowed, considering. "Well."

"I'm confident I can make this work." Del knotted her fingers in the loose fabric of her jumpsuit. "Jonas Valerian's activism helped bring Outer Rimmers' plight to IWA's awareness. Now that I've committed—"

"I wish you'd informed me straight away."

"I've just finished—"

"I'm afraid I've already reported up my concerns."

"Isa." Del smiled, hoping the vid-quality concealed its rigidity. "Mr. Valerian was so grateful IWA responded. That his people's *voice* was finally heard."

Isa studied Del across the impossible distance, intent, calculating.

"I'll agree to support you. Conditionally. You have thirty cycles to demonstrate success. I'll remain on Grellent until then and can retrieve you, if necessary."

Thirty days. Then Del would be "retrieved" like an incompetent child. A publicity stunt that would serve Isa's career but ruin Del's.

Del's failure had factored into Isa's strategy—a tactic to re-hook the Allies' dulled interest. The realization constricted her breath.

"Dr. Marks, this isn't a reflection on you. Contingency planning is always necessary."

Yet IWA had sent Del on a long, punishing journey. Surely, that warranted more faith, more *time*. Retreating would leave the warren folk unserved—and for how long?

The *hells*. She'd managed some advocacy success. "The Mine Board granted me limited access to a First Ring hospital for emergencies outside my scope."

Vouchers, too limited. The inevitability of running out, being helpless against suffering, pooled anxiety in Del's stomach. Preventable loss. Cruel waste. A looming devastation.

She released a held breath.

Isa's grave scrutiny held. "Those legal waivers you signed for IWA and for the OBMG ... Are you truly willing to risk your life for this?"

Del tensed against a familiar foreboding ... Isa's strategy shifting?

Isa had risked her reputation championing the unpopular Galta 4 project. How far would she go to gain attention for the situation? Philanthropy for ambition, the appearance of goodness over the reality?

A ripple of movement, Tam approaching. Del didn't dare shift her focus from Isa.

Unfair to paint her with the family brush.

"I'm aware of the risks," Del said. "I willingly accept them."

"Please let me know, immediately, if you change your mind."

"Yes, of course."

A crisp goodbye and Isa's image winked out.

Del's hand flopped to her side. The sun had dipped lower, thickening the shadows over the Maze. Muffled shouts hinted of conflict curtained by distance.

There lay her makeshift practice.

'Are you willing to risk your life for this?'

Fuse's oily smirk, the shock of Torx's palm against Del's cheek ... The remembered violence swayed her sickly, made her want to curl into a ball.

Had her *yes* to Isa been a lie?

Tam stood before her. Not a crease in his expression, yet she felt his frown. "You okay?"

"Fine." She studied him a beat too long, her only guide to this rough world.

He held her gaze, his irises gone that otherworldly silver. What was the itch of awareness she experienced around him? Nothing like mundane attraction. His aloofness repelled that—and she'd experienced it before setting eyes on him, when he was only a shadowy presence.

Stress-induced imagination—that she couldn't afford with so much depending on her. She knotted her fingers in her jacket pockets.

Tam gestured toward the gate, breaking the spell. "You should rest."

"I'm eager to get settled. I wonder if you can help me?" She spared a thin smile for Tam's obvious unease.

No bloody *retrenching*.

9

————

A female mine security stiff—bottled neck-to-toes in an armored
uniform the color of ash—lurked outside the checkpoint, giving them the
grim-eye.

Tam stood beside Del. The anxiety charging her aura during her vid-
call had flipped to a foamy eagerness. He'd better get used to her
pitching moods.

A rare needle of late afternoon sunlight broke through the haze,
sheening russet streaks in her dark hair. Her eyes clicked to Tam, her
green irises vivid in the light—enhanced maybe. Not that she seemed the
type.

"Will you assist? I'd like to transfer some things." Del extended her
hand. In her palm rested a large pin with a holo of his face. A Fring pass.

Tam turned startled eyes on her. He'd asked her to secure him one,
but the Maze brimmed with tales about toffs jerking idiots around over
passes.

Heart stuttering stupidly, he pinched up the pin. "I'll … ping Jonas to
meet us with his moto-cart."

Del's gaze flicked over his gloved hand—he hadn't cut back his nail-
sheaths yet, uncertain this job would pan out. "You needn't display the
pin when you cross. The scanner will pick it up."

Tam squinted through the pedestrian gate. A field-tech shield blurred what lay beyond.

'Whatever happened to that Rynet, I don't think you can discover on this *side of the Wall.'* Hana's words kept haunting him. Now was his chance to test them.

Pinning the ID to his collar with fumbling fingers, Tam trailed Del as she approached the stiff.

Curiosity bubbled under the stiff's blank expression. "You're the IWA doctor?"

"Yes, and my employee. Mr. Gray."

Mine Security had Tam in their system now—as Jon Gray. His stupid, protective impulse that he and Del had argued over. It wasn't like a fake name could shield him. Maze-dwellers had no birth registration, so the MS used facial recognition.

The stiff's eyes narrowed on Tam. "No lethals inside."

Tam froze, fighting the urge to back away. The woman had scanned him, unawares.

Setting his teeth, Tam endured having his crossbow and knives stripped, reminding himself what he had to gain: access to the free-net, a peek *beyond,* intel to plan from.

"Items will be registered under your ID and returned when you exit." The stiff waved them toward the pedestrian gate.

The gate cut a groove a little wider than a door through the Wall. The hair on Tam's nape stood on end as he passed through.

He followed Del into a broad square—a crisply sketched twin of the Maze-side—formed of gray stone with tiny crystal chips that glittered in the light. An unaccustomed heat prickled his armpits. Enormous buildings penned the square, spiking up like monstrous teeth, some the height of the Wall. The ground spread uniform, every inch leveled and paved smooth.

His legs locked.

Each skyscraping building sparkled with a mirrored or resin-like surface. The square lay eerily empty as if he'd stepped into a life-sized replica of a city, void of the messiness of humanity.

A touch on his wrist made him flinch, Del's aura strobing up his arm.

She stood before him, frowning. "Are you unwell?"

"Fine." He resisted the urge to wipe his wrist on his pants.

"My apologies. You've never been here before?"

Del had surely pieced that together before they'd crossed.

Not trusting himself to speak, he started across the square. Del's frothy aura flattened with annoyance, and she cut around him, straight-lining for the wide street that bisected the wall of buildings.

Pissing her off was a bad idea. With a slow-drawn breath, he peeked at his chunky wrist-vid. *No signal.* His skin crawled beneath the ID pinned to his collar. Did the pin contain a dampener?

Del waited for him at the mouth of the street. As he drew close, she muttered, "You may be sure they keep track of us."

Of course, they did. But free-net access had been the one thing he'd counted on gaining here. By the lack of vid signal, it was blocked on both sides of the wall.

On the street's shoulder stood a small, raised platform with a pole in the middle. It rested beside two flat metal rails that ran along the street and disappeared past his line of vision. This could only be a mini-tram. He'd overheard migrant mineworkers flapping about these strange transports.

"I can't imagine any of this is as daunting as leaping from rooftops to face armed thugs." Crisp with amusement, Del stepped onto the tram. When she wrapped her fingers around the pole, it lit pale green.

Fingers itching to sketch a sarcastic *ah'nea*, he unlocked his limbs to follow.

"V12 and H6," Del said. Their destination's grid name, probably.

The tram slid sideways onto the rails. Tam slapped his hand over the pole to steady himself. The tram's smooth glide hit his stomach oddly. Hot air misted up from the platform, heating his legs.

As they entered the city, the air overhead buzzed with a flock of drones. Twitching with the impulse to duck, Tam squinted up at them. Delivery or *surveillance*?

People walked along a raised path rimming the street—toffs, all straight and trim, Humans only. With its slow, steady roll, the tram made a perfect stage for attracting slack-jawed perusals. "Exotics" must be a rare sight here, or else the Maze clung to him like a cloud.

He was as conspicuous here as Del was Maze-side, more maybe.

Fring streets lacked the Maze's gritty menace, but the *foreignness* clawed into him. He tucked his jacket around his ribs, hands flexing over his empty weapons harness. He was as displaced here as he'd been when he first left the Xeno for the Human warrens.

Tam clutched the pole to counter a sinking sensation. It would take time just to learn to blend here, let alone slip past systems. Any notion he'd had of diving into stealth-work died.

Not that he'd been moronic enough to imagine passing beyond the Wall would grant him instant, magical clues to his mother's death. Getting through the Wall had always been an insurmountable challenge —one impossible to plan past.

The city passed by, leaving Tam disoriented, half-seeing. Deeper in, buildings stood two to three stories like fresh-from-the-box versions of prefabs common in more stable parts of the Maze. At intersections, they passed parked trams, and blocks ahead another tram was running.

"Arriving at V12 and H6." The computerized voice startled Tam into releasing the pole as the tram separated from the rails, abruptly sliding sideways to rest behind a parked one. Tam saved his balance by hopping off.

Del stared down a side street. "I'm around the corner from here."

With the hurried, gliding gait that seemed her default, Del led Tam down a narrow, unpeopled street.

Tam scanned the doorways and windows. Glints and gleams over surfaces suggested tech installations. *Like you can't breathe here without someone measuring your oxygen.*

Del's clinic was a two-story stand-alone on a corner, featureless as a protein cube. She palmed over her security pad. Inside, a small lobby— sterile white—held a desk and uninviting tan sofa.

Tam stepped in behind her.

"There's an exam room and area for my surgery station. I won't manage to bring that—."

Red light blazed over the ceiling and walls. "Security compromised!" A woman's voice vibrated through the walls. "Invader device detected."

Tam staggered against the wall, hands groping his empty weapons harness.

Spinning, Del faced him with such expectant calm goosebumps

pricked his pores with threat. They studied each other, standoff style. His head throbbed with the odd sense her aura carried a message he couldn't read.

Del blinked, waving a hand, and the strobing light doused.

Invader device? He darted a baffled look at his wrist-vid. Would she think he'd tried to spy on her? Was this over already?

"I'm sorry," she said. "I didn't think to warn you."

He didn't answer, afraid to misstep.

"You've picked up a tick or two." Del tapped the delicate device spanning her wrist. "We can rid you of them."

When she closed on him, Tam edged toward the door.

"Oh." Her golden skin darkened with a blush. "Don't be frightened. That's only my strainer, a private security field. It detects commercial phishers, advert bombs—those will scare the *life* from you—spyware, and such, that pranksters, ident thieves, and other organizations plant."

Swallowing to dredge moisture into his dry mouth, Tam rasped, "Orgs like the OBMG?"

Del's teeth crimped then released her lip. "Yes, just like them." Sighing, she added, "But strainers are a standard protection many places."

Tam shook the folds of his jacket. "What are ticks?"

"Nasty synth bio-devices—like the insect they're named for—except they don't suck your blood they implant spyware or viruses."

Tam's mouth slackened.

"Quite low-tech versions here on G4, and no worries." She held up her wrist-vid. "I've tick repellent on my vid here. We'll get the app installed for you."

His scalp itched. "I don't—"

"App installation failure due to nonstandard device," the walls announced, making him jump.

Horrified that Del's walls could try to install shit on his vid, he covered it with his fingers.

Frowning toward his wrist, Del muttered, "Perhaps I'll need to procure a work vid for you."

She stepped close, waving her wrist-vid over him until a ping sounded. "There we are."

A tiny black dot with legs wiggled on the floor. From her desk, Del lifted a silver vial and collected it. "That will kill whatever it's carrying."

Feeling queasy and absurd, Tam straightened his rubbery limbs.

As if a creepy synth pest hadn't disrupted her errand, Del gestured around. "Clinic spaces are all on this floor. My quarters are above."

From a storage room, she dragged out a hov-cart crammed with boxes. It hummed over the floor, its fuel cells casting a yellow glow beneath.

They trammed back to the square, the hov-cart trailing behind, anchored by Del's hand, Tam clinging to the tram pole, as jittery as if he'd taken a tase.

"You ever find one of those bio-device ticks here before?" he asked. Commonplace or a special OBMG gift for Tam?

Del shook her head, gazing behind them where the mine city's shell blotted out the northern horizon. "Strange knowing there's an entire city beneath that rock."

A reminder that Fring access brought Tam little closer to G4 City.

"Ever been Inside?" Tam probed.

"No. I don't imagine I'll be invited."

If even Del couldn't get into G4, where did that leave Tam? Exactly where he'd started. Chasing fool's smoke. He rested his temple against the pole.

When they crossed back into the Maze, activity in the square struck him, too crowded for nonmigrant season. People ringed the square, sitting on the stairs like a performance was about to begin. Some onlookers rose, pointed at them. Tam set his teeth. News sure traveled fast.

Del blinked at him. "Don't say they've come to gawk at us?"

What *us*.

Tam collected his weapons, eased to have his crossbow back in his hand.

Jonas waited by his ancient, moto-cart. It looked like a beetle with its small cab segmented from the tarp-covered storage bed it towed.

Jonas jogged up. "Never mind the fuss. Folk got nothing better to do."

In short order, Tam was squeezed in the cab between Del and Jonas.

Tam's hip pressed against Del's, her disquiet steaming into him, spiking his own. The cab smelled like Jonas, of plain soap and hard work.

Tam glanced at the gate in the rearview screen. Three weeks wouldn't be enough time. Three *months* wouldn't be. This gig stank of another stab in the dark. His sheaths retracted reflexively, baring his nails to threaten his glove tips. He forced them to relax back.

I can't waste this chance, for Emere.

Tam studied Del's averted face. He would need her help to navigate that world, but how could he expose himself enough to ask for it?

His tongue traced his veneers. Humans outnumbered Rynet a thousand-to-one in the galaxy. Del could be a seasoned spacer without ever meeting one. Surely, she'd have made the connection already if she were going to? Not that she'd bothered giving him a good, long look.

As they puttered up the square's ramp, Del said quietly, "What else might I expect besides muggers and gangsters?"

Seemed she'd clocked the gawkers didn't look friendly. It settled unpleasantly on Tam how big a stake he now had in her succeeding.

"Folk will be suspicious at first." Jonas waved an impatient hand out the window, urging people to unclog their path.

"So you told me." Del directed her frown at Tam.

Tam squinted into the crowd. *Too organized.* "Your competition won't be happy."

Jonas grimaced. "Marthus has been wanting to retire, and Umar … isn't a regular doc."

Maybe Del caught the edge in Jonas's voice, because she didn't relax. She stared out the window with a furrowed brow then closed her eyes as if to shut out the ill-natured curiosity smothering their path.

10

———

Caleb liked the look of the toff: prissy, bossy, and cross.

The doc perched on a barstool, bent over a vid, but her head kept bobbing with the tavern's action.

Jonas figured her sparkly off-world tech would dredge up some petty jack before long, so Caleb lounged with Aden in snug silence a few tables away, on covert duty.

Not that Aden did covert well. As usual, she dressed like she'd decked herself in her personality—brash, colorful, and *loud*. Tonight's hot pink top watered Caleb's eyes. Still, she hung around The Bar so much that the unwary overlooked her like a fixture. Until she collared them.

Aden tilted her head in the doc's direction. "What do you make of her?"

"She's perfect for that jonny-boy freak. The little thing looks thorny enough to stick in Lyn's backside."

A laugh burbled from Aden, subtle for her. "Now, Goldie, that sounds like sour ale."

Caleb ignored her meaning. "I'd take *any* ale at this point." On duty, they'd gotten fretha watered down to the color of ale. Tasted like toilet water.

"You don't drink."

He picked at the crescent-shaped scratch he'd put in the table years ago, as a pimply faced scrapper showing off his knife-wielding skills to his fellows. The Boss had set him washing dishes for a week over it.

A dark ripple caught Caleb's attention, Lyn rising like a ghoul from behind the counter.

Caleb scowled. "That sneak makes my skin crawl. Why'd the Boss set *him* guarding her? Lyn an't a knife. Can he even fight?"

"I guarantee Jonas knows exactly what Lyn can do," Aden said, hushed, thoughtful. "It won't last. Lyn don't like people any more than they like him."

"Why does Jonas *trust* him? Who the hell knows the first thing about him?" Lyn only skulked in dim corners, shading his face with his shaggy hair—a futile attempt to hide his jack-bait looks.

Aden clinked Caleb's resting glass with hers. "Hate to pop your sulk bubble, boyo, but Lyn didn't ask for the gig. Boss pushed it on him."

Lyn had caved for the flash, of course. Flash Caleb had figured to get. His Pell Mahr intel had impressed Jonas but hadn't budged him on Lyn's assignment. Caleb resisted the urge to close his eyes. Sometimes he wanted *out* so bad he couldn't breathe, but there was nowhere to go.

Pell Mahr. The thought startled like someone else planted it. Caleb shook off the idea. He was a Denner born-and-raised, not a glitter grub.

"Maybe Jonas figured missy toff would like a fancy-bit to admire," Caleb grumbled. "I'm sure we an't her usual sort."

Aden tucked her chin and adjusted her signature wire scarf, a furrow forming between her coppery brows.

He gulped his shitty tea to hide the heat creeping up his neck. Hard to conceal anything from a partner who'd known him from a twerpy kid. The *smallness* of Balter's Den choked him.

She can't read my damned mind. And Caleb only treated with Dugan for Jonas. The flash Dugan paid was barely a nip.

Caleb glowered. "What?" As if a solidly delivered growl ever deterred Aden.

"Be *patient*. Whatever reason Jonas assigned Lyn? It won't last. Next in line can only be you." She cocked a knee on the table rim. "And don't act insecure. You're a 'fancy-bit' to me, sweet boy."

Damn. She could still make him laugh like she flipped a switch for it.

"Come on, Addie. Get real."

Letting the childhood nickname slide, she refocused on the doc. On duty.

Caleb scanned the taproom, noted Lyn disappearing into the backroom.

Nearby, an old salvage scrub hunched over the bar, slurping ale like a lifeline. Caleb could practically taste the bitterness on his own tongue. *I'll never end up like that.* Like his father.

The scrub's image flickered as the electricity died, shunting the room into darkness. Patrons whooped in ritual response.

And Lyn off to piss or whatnot.

Opportunity. "I've got it."

Ignoring Aden's cynical sigh, Caleb kicked to his feet and crossed the taproom. He tracked the doctor by the glow of her vid, her face hazily sketched, eyes up and alert. She flinched when he stepped up to her.

"Easy, doc. Just a little blackout."

She blinked as if trying to make him out.

"Sorry to scare you. I'm Caleb Freth. One of Jonas's boys. Thought you might need help since Lyn's gone off."

"Thank you. I'm Del Marks." Words both clipped and smooth. He'd never met an off-worlder before. "Does this happen often?"

"Often enough. Didn't Lyn warn you?"

"He neglected to mention it."

Caleb wondered what else Lyn *neglected to mention.* "Jonas'll barter with the Grid Guild for a patch, but it's best to arm yourself with a wrist light."

He switched his on. Tiny lights sparked across the taproom, drawing the doc's focus.

"Oh." She lifted her hand, waved up a holo-screen from a wrist-vid so elegant he'd mistaken it for a bracelet. "I've a feature on my vid that should do."

A glow welled like a tiny bubble of daylight around her wrist. Conspicuous as hell. He shifted to block her from patrons' view.

She winced, doused the light.

"Why don't you borrow mine a spell?" Caleb slipped his off, extended it to her. A firm angle to approach her again.

Her brows pinched. "I shouldn't like to leave you without."

"Hell, I'm used to this, and you can return it later."

He slid his light around her delicate wrist.

She cupped her hand over the device. "Thank you—um—Caleb? I've …" Her hand fluttered to her throat. "… not quite adapted."

She'd sat alone all evening—like no one helped her *adapt*.

"How about I work up a list of things you'll need around here? Mask against dumpster reek, the wrist lights, rain slicker and the like."

"That won't be necessary, doc." A chilly voice misted Caleb's nape. "I've got a kit for you."

Lyn. Caleb stiffened. How long had he been lurking there?

Caleb dismissed the warning in Lyn's tone. Lyn bristled with weapons, including a small, handmade crossbow. Compensating for weakness. Otherwise, why risk it? Top-tier gangs inflicted gruesome reprisals on lesser gangs and warren folk caught lethal-arming with a gun. Lyn shaved the edge with that projectile weapon of his.

"Good then." Caleb didn't bother straightening his smirk.

Lyn was a dark outline. "Someday you might regret taking me for glitter."

The eerie, textured voice made Caleb shudder.

"Just making sure the blackout didn't scare the doc." He pitched his voice for Del to overhear.

"I'll *bet* that's what you're doing, *golden* boy." Lyn's lips barely cracked as he spoke, as if they were as waxen as they looked.

"Nice meeting you, Del." Caleb faced Del's questioning frown. "Give me a shout if you ever need anything."

"Thank you."

The backup generator flared up the lights, and Caleb found himself startled by the shy warmth in her expression.

Whistling, Caleb returned to his post. Aden tipped her chair back, crossing her arms. He took her arched eyebrows for approval.

"You suppose she's for real?" he said.

"Maybe." Aden thunked her chair legs to the floor. "Seems too complicated a way for those mine slicks to spy on us. They don't know a thing about Jonas if they imagine he'd spill our secrets to an off-worlder —no matter what she offers."

Caleb studied Del, taking the risk Lyn would catch him at it. Beside the exotic's grayscale blankness, Del Marks looked very alone.

TUCKED INTO A CORNER AT THE END OF THE BAR, DEL GNAWED HER LIP OVER her report to Isa. She couldn't put the bloody thing off. She wouldn't lie. Which left her with … failure.

Failure compelled her to camp out on this stool each night, no matter how deep her exhaustion, in the hope people might grow accustomed to her—even if they refused to talk to her.

The flutter of Tam's shaggy hair distracted her as he unfolded from a cross-legged seat behind the bar. He'd blended so well in his gray garb, she'd half-forgotten him. Frowning into the taproom, he set down the 2D vid-tile he'd been bent over, finishing some favor for "the Boss."

Tam's stare connected to a table where an unruly trio of men sat. The young barmaid Kimber attended them; her shoulder bowed beneath a loaded drink tray. Annoyance stamped her face. "What now?"

One of the men snatched his mug from the table, his florid face contorted. "This is off."

Kimber squared her chin, glaring. "Boss don't dish bitter brew."

Behind the counter, Kimber bubbled with shy good humor. On the taproom floor, she wore her apron like armor.

The man gestured expansively. "You try it, then."

Tattooed cheeks reddening, Kimber turned to a neighboring table, wriggled her shoulder from beneath the tray and thumped it down. "Pardon folks. I've got a scrapper here to deal with."

Swiping the troublemaker's mug, she chugged it.

Del grimaced. *Kimber shouldn't put her mouth on anything that man's lips touched.*

Patrons hooted with appreciation as Kimber bottomed the drink, slapped it back down. "It's more than fine. Best ale in the Maze."

Tucking back a strand of faded blonde hair, Kimber leaned toward the main troublemaker. "Now, pay up or vacate."

A stare-down ensued, until one of the other men reached over to tug Kimber's apron.

"That'll be enough." Tam's voice sliced through the noise.

The trio's attention leapt to Tam. Troublemaker's lip curled. He blew Tam a kiss to a sniggering chorus—some from surrounding tables. "You wanna play, too, glitter-boy?"

Tam's body bunched as if he'd spring over the bar.

Del gripped the counter, searching the taproom for Jonas.

Kimber snatched Troublemaker's hair, yanking his head back with a gleam of her prosthetic hand. "You heard him. That'll be enough, or you'll be out and banned from coming back."

Silence gripped the tavern; all attention drawn to the drama.

After a tense beat, aggression deflated from the man's manner. "Peace!" He held up his hands with mock fear.

Kimber released him, flipped out her palm. The man slapped money into it, and she spun to retrieve her tray.

The tavern lapsed back into a hum of enjoyment.

The crowd's mood always overwrote the plain taproom space, making it dark, bright, grim, or lively. Del stuck to the bar—a constant— gleaming and bustling with Jonas's staff.

Tam shot Del a look that didn't quite connect before sitting back to his task. His spot wedged against a shelf appeared uncomfortable, but he no doubt wanted to escape the gawking he endured. Only Jonas and his tavern staff treated Tam like a person.

It was awful.

Perhaps unescapable.

Tam's ripple-less expression … as if nothing in this rough environment could touch him, as if he were a hologram projected here …

His eyes lifted, caught her staring. She blinked her attention back to her vid-tile and the headache of her report.

"Can I get you anything, Doc?" Jonas's rumble startled her sometime later.

He faced her from his post behind the bar. The wariness ever-present beneath his courtesy had kept Jonas a stern stranger. She straightened the wobble from her smile. Here was a chance to connect with the busy man.

"A cocktail would be lovely, please."

He bellowed the drink order to the bartender, Nan, who splashed the contents of vials into glasses like a harried chemist.

Absurd to fail despite the desperate need here. *Am I truly so repellent?*

After two weeks, her trickle of patients came nowhere close to the numbers that would keep Isa from shutting Del down. The few who came had likely been strong-armed by Jonas. Not that he deigned to get a checkup himself.

Poor health conditions here aged people quickly. By his gray hair and creased, ruddy face, she might take Jonas for a man in his seventies—settled into middle-age—but his vitality suggested he was younger.

Jonas squinted at her. "I'm surprised you can work in this din."

"On Cartor, I was bombarded with digital noise." She forced lightness into her tone. "A dose of old-fashioned Human commotion is refreshing."

In truth, she hadn't adapted to the air's deadness—no adverts jostling for attention, no notifications scrolling over the vid-lens beneath her eye. She now kept the tiny, holo-screen off.

"How're things?"

"As I imagine you've perceived," she said dryly. "People seem afraid to come."

"They'll get over it." Jonas's mouth curved in a spare smile that almost reached his pale, gray eyes.

"I thought perhaps if I made myself visible here each evening, people would grow accustomed to me." A miserably ineffective plan.

So little time left to find an effective one. She'd wasted *half* the thirty cycles Isa had given on futility. Del's throat ached with her need to confide, confess how close she was to failing Jonas, his people, herself.

"Don't worry, Del. You keep helping us, and you won't lack for allies here."

How to appeal to him for real help? The direct approach had only earned her such unsoothing reassurances.

Appeal to a person's passion—an advocate's guideline that she should have internalized. Jonas's passion was easy to guess. "Give to the warren, the warren gives back?"

"That's the vision behind Balter's Den. We need to keep basic services running, such as they are." Jonas pulled a pair of glasses from under the serving counter and poured amber liquid from an unmarked bottle with two efficient twists of his wrist. "That's organized from here. Residents who don't contribute with credits or labor are asked to leave. There are looser warrens for those who find it restrictive."

Jonas made Balter's Den sound like a minimalist commune.

Del said, "I overheard someone speaking as if there's territory south of the Maze."

The OBMG treated the squatters' slums as one entity.

"Gang burrows."

She blinked. "They have their own communities?"

"The top-tier gangs do. Some of the wealthiest digs in the Rim are there. That's the snare." He traced a finger around the base of one glass, the amber liquid casting a glow over his strong, thick-veined hand. "The only civilization we've got out here is what we create ourselves. Top-tier gangs encompass more than CP notions of thugs. They're like mini states."

The Central Planets were far from a homogenous monolith, but no value lay in arguing the point. "That's … bleak."

Jonas shrugged, a jerk of his shoulders. "We do the best we can."

Del deflated on the stool. Never mind winning him over, she'd managed to offend him.

He moved away to deliver the drinks.

A pink cocktail thumped in front of her. She met Nan's cold brown eyes. Nan had been unfriendly from the start. It might not have mattered, but Nan lived at the tavern, serving numerous functions, including bartender, cook, bookkeeper, tax-collector, and census taker.

She was around a lot.

"Thank you." Del hoped Nan hadn't spat in her glass.

"Boss is a busy man. Something I can help you with?"

"This will do." Del gestured to the drink without lowering her gaze.

Nan had a striking, strong-boned face with brown skin that crinkled around her eyes. Her chin-length, blunt-cut brunette hair tucked behind her ears. A small, round burn scar marred her right cheek, giving her a hard-bitten appearance.

Nan turned away, and Del slumped as if released from a force field.

She'd attracted plenty of interest from warren folk, little welcoming. Her fingers traced the light on her wrist. Caleb's drawling amiability, narrow face, intense blue eyes ... Perhaps Jonas had encouraged him to approach her. Sad to question simple kindness, but it was undeniably bitter to fling her heart into helping people who didn't like her in the least—as if they saw through her façade to the upbringing she'd fled.

Lips drawing tightly, she reactivated her vid-tile with an impatient flick of her fingers. They'd be rid of her soon enough if she couldn't make this work.

11

———

Behind the bar, Tam stared unseeing at the gang-map projections flickering over his vid-tile—the Surge's nothing but question marks. He bit his thumb in frustration. Impossible to concentrate here.

Freth still sat next to Aden sly-ogling Del.

'Nice meeting you, Del.'

She'd glowed, falling for Freth's shit like everyone else.

Tam didn't trust Freth—his aura too polished, his emotions too deliberate—like he force-fit his inner self to match the sunny decency he projected.

Asshole.

Del sat alone at the bar. Prime chance to talk to her, get her make outside the hectic workday. First step to deciding if she could help him with *Emere.*

If I were Freth, I could glide through chitchat like melting lard.

Tam shoved his hand in his pocket and fingered a stone chip he'd rescued from the floor. It failed to calm his choking agitation—too much psy-noise, auras needling into him.

Just talk to her. How fucking hard could it be?

Stowing his tile, wiping his palms on his pantlegs, he shifted to stand across from her, stepping into a bubble of stillness. Del's presence muted the impact of others. Even her negatively charged emotions were less punishing than a clamor of strangers.

Del scanned his face.

He struggled not to duck away, the contrast between her enticing aura and scratchy emotional signature throwing him.

"Tam, this is timely. I'm hoping to head back."

"Okay." *Damn.* "Um."

"Is something amiss?"

"No. Just a minute." Tam winced. *I sound like an android in power-save mode.*

As he turned to grab his vid-tile, leaving the shelter of Del's aura, the room's psychic din surged through him and, with it, an itch of warning.

Tam surveyed the room but didn't spot trouble. Something subtle …

He frowned toward the table where the assholes who'd harassed Kimber sat, quietly now. The main scrapper stared toward the end of the bar where Kimber stood within the curve of Nan's arm. Kimber's face clenched hard enough to contort the arrow tattoos along the hollows of her cheekbones. Tracing the thread of alarm to her, he rushed over. "You okay?"

Kimber's gaze slid toward Del, away again. "I'm fine."

Nan tightened her arm, spoke in Kimber's ear.

"I'll finish my shift." Sweat sheened Kimber's brow.

Ducking around Tam, Del hurried over. Whatever she saw in Kimber's face had her whirling to him. "Please fetch my outcall pack."

"She doesn't need your help," Nan said stonily, blocking Del.

"Will you stake her life on that?" Del said, just as hard.

Tam dashed up the stairs. By the time he'd unlocked the exam room, scooped up the bag, and rushed back, Kimber lay on the floor, wheezing through swollen lips. The air reeked of puke. Nan and Del knelt beside her. Del's coat was thrown over Kimber.

"There now, you'll be all right." Keeping up the soothing litany, Del snatched the pack from Tam, groped inside, and pulled out her portable diagnostic device.

"Make room!" Jonas shoved through the gawkers who'd shrunk the space around Kimber.

Del held the diagnose over Kimber. Without looking up, she fired off, "Tam, I need this from the cabinet."

She flipped him the device. Skimming, he caught the words "ingested substance" and "reaction." He jerked his gaze across the tavern. The scrapper sat on a table, watching.

"Tam?" Del pressed.

Kimber had drunk from the man's glass.

Tam clenched his hand over the diagnose. "Boss!"

Jonas turned a questioning frown on Tam.

"Seal the room." Tam twitched with competing urges—go after the man, protect Del, obey Del.

Nan's wide eyes flashed to him. She surged behind the counter and grabbed a metal bat. "I've got the doc. You get what she needs."

Scrapper must have realized he'd been made. He flung something to the floor, lunged for the exit. Glass broke. People shrieked and scrambled back. Tam glimpsed an explosion of tiny skittering forms.

"Caleb! Merc!" Jonas bellowed, and all hell broke loose.

Leaping around the seethe of bodies, Tam raced back to the exam room. Del stocked supplies by code. The med she needed was shoved in the back of the closet. Tam tipped over vials and boxes before finally getting his hand on it.

He bounded down the stairs, bumping into Nan. She still clenched the bat with jutting knuckles, frozen-faced but roiling with grief inside. Kimber lay still, white foam caking the corners of her mouth, her prosthetic hand limp over her chest, the gold filament decorating its surface dulled beneath the poor light.

Tam's hand, clutching the med, dropped slack against his side.

Del slanted him an impatient glance and plucked the vial from his fingers. Fitting it into her press-syringe, she injected the liquid into Kimber's arm and lifted another gadget, a field-tech tool. It charged the air as she ran it over Kimber's mouth, throat, and stomach.

Tam exhaled and glared around the room. Aden had the scrapper's cronies shoved against the wall, her face as red as her hair. The men shook their heads, slack mouthed.

Scrapper was gone. Maybe Freth and Merc would catch him. Tam doubted it.

Patrons stomped at scattering bits on the floor. Roaches. The whack had flung a jar of bugs.

Del sat back, packing her gadget away. Kimber watched her with tear-filled eyes.

"There, you're all right." Del treated Kimber to the warmth she reserved for her patients.

"What's wrong with me?" Kimber croaked.

"An allergic reaction to something you ingested. You'll be fine now." Del's gentle voice raised gooseflesh over Tam's arms as if she focused her aura through her words.

Kimber relaxed against the floor, gazing at Del as if she were a shining oracle.

Tam's focus drifted to a shape resting by Del's hand. A roach, lurking there, enjoying the show. He narrowed his eyes. Its shape was wrong, its back humped.

That "low-tech" synth bug he'd caught in Del's Fring office ...

The Maze was even lower tech.

As he bent to examine the roach, it scuttled under the bar.

Tam had encountered that warped insect-shape before, outside The Back Hand—where the Surge had laid their trap for Del. A potential connection Tam couldn't ignore.

TREMORS DANCED ACROSS THE PAVEMENT, THREATENING CALEB'S FOOTING AS he ran. A distant churn of Galtan's Rumble strobed a rusty glow through the night clouds. The scrapper was a darting outline ahead—too fast. Caleb leaped over a pothole by rote, gritting his teeth as Merc tripped over it.

Caleb surged ahead. He wasn't losing the son of a bitch. Not after what he'd done to Kimber.

The scrapper darted into an alleyway—into confined Tinner block.

Caleb's iced cheeks resisted his grin. The man had trapped himself. Caleb twisted around to signal to Merc to block the alley's side path, then plunged in.

Footsteps pounded ahead, but Caleb couldn't see his quarry through the gloom.

He sped down the crooked passageway, driving the man toward its dead end at Rockwall.

A skid and thump sounded ahead.

The footfalls disappeared.

Caleb stopped, panting through burning lungs, scowling around. Rockwall dead-ended the path, a boulder spiking from the ground, too steep to scale.

The buildings abutting the alley were faceless, no windows rattling beneath the storm's force. A single door interrupted the featureless wall, the entrance to a metalworking shop. Caleb lunged to the shop's door and shoved, but it didn't budge. Locked.

Swearing, he sprinted back. The scrapper must have gone down the splinter alley. Though Caleb hadn't heard it.

The splinter alley's narrow sides bumped and scraped Caleb's shoulders as he ran. He heard nothing but his own heaving breath.

He skidded out the alley's other side.

No one.

Not even Merc, who was supposed to have sealed the mouth.

Caleb squinted into the dark, saw Merc yards ahead, pacing like he was trying to watch both paths into Tinner.

Idiot!

Bracing his hands on his knees as he fought to catch his breath, Caleb glared behind him into the narrow alley. The ground rumbled through his boots, and a fierce flare of orange lit the haze.

Scrapper wasn't local. How the hell had he snaked so slickly through Tinner?

"You see him run outta here?" Caleb called to Merc, not bothering to hide the grate of frustration in his voice.

"No. Nothing."

Merc might be lying to cover his blunder.

Even so, scrapper could only have mapped his escape in advance.

With local help.

He'd planned this.

To hurt Kimber? Sweet Kimber? She didn't even know the man.

Thinking of her lying on the taproom floor flared the anger in his chest.

He stalked past Merc back toward The Bar.

"Shouldn't we try door-to-door?" Merc asked.

"No point," Caleb snapped.

The scrapper was long gone.

DEL WANTED TO LEAVE WITH A DESPERATE ACHE, TO ESCAPE THE PRESS OF curiosity, of being treated like an insensitive, ignorant child. Exiting the exam room, she stood at the staircase landing and gripped the railing.

Suggesting Kimber consider an upgraded prosthetic had constituted yet another blunder, earning Del punishing incredulity. Kimber had traced the lacelike gold designs covering the metal mechanism. "It was made with love," she whispered, gripping Nan's hand. "It's like my own flesh."

A light touch braced Del's arm. She didn't startle—Tam had become an accustomed shadow. The disquieting awareness she'd first experienced in his presence had faded like white noise.

So long as she didn't focus on it.

And she didn't.

"I'm fine," she snipped, letting him guide her to the bottom step as if he feared her social ineptitude signaled an all-encompassing clumsiness.

"You're about white-eyed flat." By which he must mean she was exhausted.

She was—drained, heartsick. The interpersonal aspects of life here crushed as much as the professional challenges. All the intercultural sensitivity training she'd suffered through to earn her advocate's license, yet she couldn't master basic social interaction.

Tam released her arm, studying the taproom where a few NG lingered. Hunting for danger seemed a reflex. "You said Kimber had an allergic reaction. Something she drank?"

For once, Del guessed the direction of his thoughts. "Some twenty minutes must have passed between when she drank that man's ale and the onset of anaphylaxis. Not an impossible gap. Could he have known she was allergic?"

"Unlikely, but he might've laced her drink. Might not have meant to kill her."

"The normal course of treatment is to run allergy tests. I'm not equipped for forensics."

Tam frowned toward the backroom door. "I need to talk to Jonas. You okay to wait here?"

Del studied his profile, which was becoming a reflex for *her* since he seldom faced her directly. "Yes," she forced herself to say. "I'll check Kimber once more before we go."

Tam melted away, his heavy-soled boots soundless even in the quiet.

The backroom door swung wide as Tam passed through, releasing the bustle of warren business. That embodied city hall, the place where residents negotiated "barter," traded for services, meted out justice. She wasn't welcome there.

Del eased herself onto a barstool, mired in dismal thoughts until her eyelids drooped. Time to check on her patient. She rose with a sigh.

As she crossed the taproom, a blur of motion staggered her. She blundered into a man striding into the tavern. Disoriented, she simply stood there, taking in the chilly air that cloaked him; the scratch of his coat on the backs of her fingers; the clean, herbal scent that emanated from his body.

His hand clamped over her arm. "Easy, fem."

She jerked her head up. Eyes so black they seemed pupil-less bored into her from a face sharp-carved with invasive intelligence.

"I beg your pardon," she managed jaggedly, trying to disengage her arm.

"So, this is Valerian's toff," he muttered with oddly precise inflection.

A gleam at his ear drew her eye, an earring, intricate onyx segments dangling serpentine from his lobe.

"What can we do for you, Belek?" A voice cut in, making Del jump.

Nan strode from behind the bar, her cold eyes leveled at the man. Relief not to be the target of that gaze fizzed through Del.

"Where's Valerian?" Belek demanded, not lifting his focus from Del.

"Backroom," Nan said, her strong-boned face rigid. "The door guard will get him for you."

As Belek released Del and strode off, she noticed a huddle of men trailing him; four, all black-garbed, giving the impression of a security escort.

Before Del could ask, Nan said, "Stay away from that man."

"Who is he?"

"Gang." Nan shrugged like that was all the explanation Del could expect. The animosity had drained from her manner but left an impenetrable stoicism in its place.

Del's fingers closed over the diagnose in her pocket, glassy smooth. A wispy memory teased—pressing her fingertips against her nursery window with its smart-shade illusion of a cloudless sky, flickers in its surface hinting of wind-lashed trees she could never see. That sense of disconnect from the world had haunted her throughout her life on Cartor, followed her here.

"Get some rest before you drop." Nan's limp words banished the memory.

"What does he want with Jonas?"

Nan's face set with the guarded expression Maze-dwellers wore when revealing unpleasant facts about their world. "Treaty matter, probably. That enforcer is the Fet gang's liaison in the north."

Liaison … one of the top-tier gangs who functioned like a mini-state, then.

Del frowned toward the gangsters, disappearing into the backroom. Nothing had happened. Not really. But an itch over her nerves overwrote her numb fatigue, making her wonder what she'd failed to perceive.

12

———

THE BACK HAND SAGGED LIKE A TENT WITH A MISSING POLE, ITS SIGN clinging by a single nail. Abandoned. Not only the reefer den, but the whole shanty. The den's doorway gaped open. Tam had less desire to enter than when it had been packed with smoke and ill-intent.

He shifted back, the scrape of his soles over loose pavement conspicuous in the quiet. In contrast to the usual congested press, the emptiness was like a muffling of his senses.

Had *all* this shanty's denizens been Surge hooked? Followed the pack when they moved? Or had something run them off?

Rubbing his arms, Tam scanned the awning of the building he'd perched atop that first night. He padded toward it. The only properly mortared structure in the shanty. It must have been the pack's actual digs and the reefer den just their flash-cover.

Tam flipped up his wrist-vid and recorded images. Jonas had shifted Tam from the Surge to focus on Del, and Tam hadn't found time to side-path any stealth-work. After tonight's incident at The Bar-the possible connection to the Surge—he had a motive too deep to ignore.

The Boss wasn't convinced the scrapper had dosed Kimber and figured the roach-toss for a petty joke. Tam didn't buy it. Too much coincidence. His suspicion that the man played the Surge's spotter, paid to scope out Del's equipment and warren security, held.

So round two of The Back Hand …

Tam sighed and frowned around. The mine haze hung low tonight, adding to the stillness cloaking the shanty. In the distance, young voices hooted, a pack of kids running loose. The shanty wouldn't stay abandoned for long.

He stretched out with his senses. Not a single presence nearby. He switched on his wrist light, twisted the door lever, and pushed. It creaked open before sticking halfway. Tam froze until he realized the doorframe was warped. Shaking his head, he slipped inside.

Musty darkness closed over him. He lifted his wrist light, but it took a moment to make sense of the space. A box of a building, one wall lined with stacked-cinderblock partitions—a cheap trick to create privacy without constructing proper rooms.

Tam shone his light along the floor, bare except for a crumpled meal foil. A slither of sound halted him, a scuffle against the concrete. He recast his senses. Still deserted.

Unpenning a breath, he stalked forward, irritated with his jumpiness. A quick scan showed the first two partitioned spaces stripped bare.

He stepped to the third, directed his light. A pale face and blazing eyes shocked in front of him. Tam leaped back. A large shape charged him. His throat was seized in a choking grip; something cold and hard rammed against his temple. Hissing, Tam shoved away, skidding until his back hit a wall. Light blazed into his face, stinging his eyes blind. A metallic click alerted Tam, stunning him in place. His attacker was lethal-armed.

"Now that was stupid." A male voice, flat with annoyance.

The light lowered, and the halo of brightness faded, revealing a bony-faced man garbed in black. Tam gaped at Belek. The Fet enforcer had no aura, not a trace. Tam might be standing before an animated corpse.

Belek's hard mouth twisted. "You're lucky I don't have a twitchy trigger finger."

Tam had met people, like Jonas, with faint auras—a sign of perpetually leashed emotions—but he'd never encountered a total blank before. Tam's skin crawled, the irrational fear that more auraless gangsters would creep out of the walls. Why the hell would a Fet enforcer be skulking around without his pack?

The enforcer stared as if cataloguing Tam's features. Curiosity burned in his eyes, a weird contrast to his dead aura. "You're Valerian's sneak."

Tam slowly straightened, expelling his breath and ironing out his expression. "Enforcer."

Belek had gone into Jonas's office tonight after Tam vacated it, but his pack's auras had masked his eerie lack of one. Tam only knew the new enforcer by his growing reputation—as deadly quick with wits as weapons.

Why was Belek here? If the stronger, deadlier gang drove the Surge's recent activity, Tam was crossing a crumbling bridge.

"What does Valerian have you sniffing after, I wonder?"

"Boss heard the shanty cleared. Wanted me to check it."

Belek's black eyes hooded. "If you're half as good as rumor holds, you know exactly why the shanty folk cleared. Driven out or paid a nip to vacate."

Tam expelled a careful breath. "I got no proof."

"That right?" Irony stretched Belek's words. "This place is scraped clean. You an't finding anything, sneak." Belek tapped his gun on his thigh.

Taking that for a dismissal, Tam edged toward the exit.

As he reached the door, Belek called, "Tell Valerian to leave my treaty-brothers to me."

Treaty brothers … The Surge owed fealty to the Fet.

Tam let Belek's chill-voiced threat push him through the door. Then he was running, out of the shanty, across the warren, until his burning lungs forced him to stop.

He braced his back against a broken-down truck.

"Fucking hell," he panted.

Either he had to get his shit together or quit. Before this job got him killed.

13

———

Sponsor Vinn,

My patient base is swiftly expanding, as the embedded data will
demonstrate. I've not had luck hiring a nurse but will persist.

THE PATIENT LINE EXTENDED FROM THE EXAM ROOM DOOR, DOWN THE STAIRS, to form a strangling coil around the tavern—or that's how it was in Del's imagination.

In reality, Tam enforced a policy of no more than ten in-queue at a time. But with Del averaging forty-two patients per day—unless she had a surgery in the First Ring—her makeshift exam room confined like a prison work-detail.

She'd asked for it, after all, and her public demonstration with Kimber had accomplished what hours of smile-pasting hadn't. Now, she had to make it work.

Del propped a hip on the exam table. The small windowless chamber didn't help. The exam table, fiberboard desk, and two cots left little breathing room. Everything was procured secondhand in the First Ring —no frills, no ornamentation. Perhaps she could paint the walls something besides jump-ship gray. Hardly a priority.

Del blinked to refocus on her vid-tile. She'd been frantically updating her logs between patients before weariness had drifted her thoughts. Resting wasn't an option, not with Isa Vinn shifting in her heels to shut Del down.

Movement startled her. From his seat on a cot against the wall, Tam perked like a hunter catching a scent, staring past her shoulder. She whirled around, expecting to find a thug looming there, but the figure in the doorway was an elderly woman, unarmed and neatly dressed.

The patient cleared her throat, impatient or annoyed.

"Just a moment," Del said.

The woman strode into the room, poked around as if taking a tour.

Del set her vid aside, repressing a frown. "I'm Doctor Marks. What brings you in today?"

The woman turned. Her strong-boned face was draped with deep-creased skin, but her eyes were vitally alive, glaring challenge. "Paela Umar. Came for a checkup."

"Please sit down." Del patted the exam table and grabbed her diagnose.

Tam normally tried to make himself invisible, but he unfolded from the cot to lean on the desk. Umar's eyes flashed to him with lurid interest. Del stepped between them.

Short white hair capped Umar's head, smoothed back, exposing the gold fringing both ears. Straight filaments spiked through the tissue, lining the cartilage and lobe. Del had noticed such body art on many people here, never as much. A status symbol, perhaps.

Umar's focus locked on the diagnose as Del scanned her. Most patients stared at her equipment, but that narrow-eyed intensity prickled.

"Nice bit of junk, doc."

"Yes."

The scan results flashed, startling Del. Aside from being nearsighted, Umar had exceptional health for an elderly Maze-dweller, but her heart scan revealed a peculiarity.

Umar smirked when Del turned wide eyes on her. "Found my little toy, did you?"

"Is that a mechanical heart valve?"

"We've got to improvise here, after all."

"A clinic here provided that procedure?" The device appeared functional at least.

"I have my connections." Umar's smug intensity gave Del pause.

Connections. This was the competition Jonas mentioned, practicing primitive medicine in the warren—the one the child, Pepar, feared. "You're the other doctor."

Inclining her head, Umar fanned her hands. "Always good to meet a fellow professional." She switched mockingly to Tiraji-accented Common.

Del drew a silent breath, determined to ignore the hostility. "You should have that heart valve replaced with a bio-device. I can manage that for you. I can also correct your vision."

The seamed lips slid back. "I'll keep the valve. Sentimental value. Might take you up on fixing my eyesight someday." Umar's dark, unblinking eyes fixed on Del as if she could pry her open with them. "You mean to sweep in here like a savior, Dr. Marks? Well, your fancy training and fancy gadgets won't mean jack. These people will drain you dry, same as they did me."

Umar hopped off the table and strode from the room.

The diagnose slipped from Del's fingers, thumped onto the exam table.

Del pressed her knuckles to her cheek, lightheaded. "That was interesting."

"Del." Tam studied her with a frown—about the only expression she could ever decipher. "It's past time for a break."

She set her teeth, feeling treated like a child again. "Yes. Of course."

Her schedule dulled any inclination to rest.

How could she bear this, day upon day? Only pebbles to fill an ocean of need. She wanted nothing more than to find a quiet place to lie down and bury her head, but the queue of waiting patients wouldn't let her go.

"Do you think that other doctor will cause trouble for me?"

Del's pensive voice drew Tam from vid-training on how to maintain and calibrate her equipment—tasks she had no time or interest for. Del stood by her desk, staring blankly at the closed door. She was *supposed* to be enjoying the break he'd wedged into her schedule. The woman's mental focus was relentless—like a habitually contracted muscle. Exhausting.

A ribbed sigh gusted from Del. "She was … hostile."

Paela Umar led the old guard, a cantankerous minority who preferred how the warren used to be, when they controlled it.

"You ought to get along with the sour bit." Tam attempted a Human-style joke. "She's the closest thing we have to another toff in the warren."

Pressing her palms against the desk, Del studied her hands. The ire that spiked her aura drove home Tam's complete failure.

"Do I expect to be waited on? Treat others as beneath me? Am I afraid to dirty my hands? Because that's how most 'toffs' behave where I'm from, and I'd hate to act that way."

Del did none of those things. She acted grateful for help, apologetic for causing inconvenience, went into the filthiest slums to care for bedridden patients.

Tam read what she wouldn't spell out. She didn't discriminate against him, but he'd marked her for an elitist at the start and hadn't let it go.

Heat crept up his neck.

Del plucked up a box of blood-clotting pads, flipping it in her deft fingers.

Tam needed to apologize but found himself blurting, "All right, doc," and ducking from the room.

He stopped short when he blundered into the anxious psy-miasma around the patient line, as unsettling as if he'd physically collided against the patients.

Tam's attention latched onto Jonas coming up the stairs. "Boss, can you cover the doc for a few minutes?"

Jonas's gaze scoured Tam's face. "All right."

Tam dashed down to the taproom, cursing himself for a stumble-tongued idiot. This gig was impossible! Raised by his Rynet mother among Trenabic, what did he know about making nice with Humans? He spied on their emotions the way he spied on their actions for Jonas—

from a distance. That *distance* had been devoured by Del's brutal schedule.

He ducked behind the bar, poured a whiskey shot, and downed it in a noxious swallow. Nan, busy polishing the counter, fixed incredulous eyes on him.

Tam turned his back to her, swiped a hand over his face.

Get it together.

He couldn't move. He felt so hollow inside, so sick of pushing through life, enduring.

"Something happen?" Jonas's low voice startled him.

Tam spun to find Jonas standing where Nan had been. The taproom lay empty.

"I had Del lock up for a breather," Jonas added.

"Why'd you want me for this, Boss?"

"I gave my reasons."

"I never understood them. I thought you needed me to keep to myself, make it harder for folk to penetrate my disguises."

"Is that what *you* want?"

Yes. No. "I don't know." Tam ached to go home, forever forbidden.

"It's been three weeks."

Tam stiffened. "Yeah."

"Tell me, then. Why's she doing this?" Jonas gestured toward the stairs.

"Del is who she claims," Tam said, flat, reluctant. It hadn't taken long to figure that out. Tam hadn't told Jonas, not ready to change duties. He hadn't been given a spare moment to hunt for the truth about his mother.

"That's not what I asked."

"She's not hooked to anything but her job." Tam grimaced at his own bitter tone.

"I'd be a total flathead not to see that myself." Jonas almost smiled.

Tam couldn't read his mood. "I don't know why she does it."

"It's been three weeks."

Tam got the subtext behind Jonas's words. He couldn't respond.

"I don't know how long this can last," Jonas spoke through Tam's silence. "Every life she saves, all the pain she eases … every second we buy for that means something." Jonas sighed as if he'd failed to express what he wanted. "I understand that kind of motivation is too abstract to sink past the surface, past hardship. Flash is a worse motivation."

Jonas wasn't talking about Del anymore but about Tam.

"I need to get back," Tam whispered.

"You'll tell me if you can't do this?" Jonas's gaze demanded Tam meet it.

Tam nodded.

Del hadn't eaten through any breaks today—those dull jumpsuits she wore like a uniform seemed looser lately.

Hyperconscious of Jonas's scrutiny, Tam stepped through the beaded curtain to the meal-nook, a shallow alcove behind the bar. Nan hovered over the hot plate, stirring a pot of sourness that wrinkled his nose.

Tam snagged a tray in shaky hands and loaded it with wafers and fruit preserves.

"You okay, Tam?"

He froze, met the concern in Nan's dark brown eyes with surprise. "I'll do."

"Boss has his ways." Her lips quirked.

She'd overheard.

"Yeah."

Jonas's admonishment had met its mark, yet Del's hung heavier. Beyond the limits of their tense exchange, she'd thrown down a challenge.

14

—————

TAM HOPPED OFF THE DELIVERY TRUCK'S HITCH, GIVING THE DRIVER A perfunctory wave. He'd been lucky to score a hitch from Balter's Den to the southern rim of the Taber warren for a few credits. Even luckier no one tried to pluck him off along the way.

Tam straightened his jacket and checked the tint on his skin. He'd foregone a full disguise, only used cheap tinted lotion to keep his bluish pallor from standing out.

Jonas had freed Tam up for stealth-work this afternoon, assigning Aden as his stand-in with Del. Tam had neglected to mention his mission was personal. He didn't feel guilty. Del never took a damned day off. Didn't mean he couldn't. Tam had agreed to keep on with the job but refused to put off his own quest any longer.

'Try hacking Inside.' The informant Hana's advice had revived Tam's interest in that angle. With three weeks' wages in hand, securing a professional hacker had come within reach.

The trick was locating one.

Tam frowned down at his map, rough-sketched over a strip of cloth. He'd dished out to obtain it, with no guarantee it would lead anywhere.

A woman sweeping loose stones from the hard-packed soil on her doorstep paused to give Tam a squinty look, then resumed her sweeping as if judging him more harmless than the gravel.

His nape itched with sensitivity, awareness that he concealed every credit he'd earned with Del in his jacket. Only a fool risked carrying so much.

Squaring his shoulders, he strode ahead. This wouldn't be his first arrow through the dark to find out what happened to his mother. It was his duty—even if he had to drain every spare credit over his lifetime.

Tam was about two blocks from his destination. Shrunken and sullen structures clumped along the zigzag rocky path that served as a street, barely wide enough for the truck to pass. Taber's chief didn't enforce any zoning. Tam had passed tidier areas, but this one was a small step above a shanty.

Touring their neighboring warren gave Tam a sharp reminder of how much Jonas and his supporters had achieved in Balter's Den.

As he reached his destination, buildings grew straighter, if dressed in colors storm-beaten dull. Crumpling the cloth map in his fist, Tam stuffed it in his pocket and studied the target structure with a sinking stomach. A tiny storefront dominated by cracked, dusty windows. It looked abandoned.

Son of a—

The entrance's sliding door scraped open, and a man spilled out, propelled by a shove from inside. Tam leaped from his path. The man spat a curse, jerked his shirt straight and stalked away.

A massive figure filled the doorway. Tam closed his hand over his crossbow reflexively. The man wore a plasteel vest, exposing the thick muscles of one arm. A lumpish tube of metal replaced the other from the elbow, straps of plasteel running up his bicep and around his shoulder as if to help support the prosthetic's weight. Gadgets and blades were strapped around his belt.

Thuron. Member of a patchwork gang, thieves and thugs-for-hire armed with weaponized body augments. They'd dipped into Balter's Den a time or two.

Tam edged back, studying Thuron's distorted face—large eyes and jaw overwhelming an otherwise narrow face, the nose a crooked lump above a dab of a mouth. Ill health marked his deep khaki skin, discoloration and dry patches. His dark hair was slicked to his head, long unwashed by the smell.

Thuron glowered at Tam. "You lost?" His gravelly voice suited his appearance.

"I'm looking for Gate."

"Gate's busy just now."

Annoyance roughened Thuron's emotional signature, absent from his flat tone. Annoyed, not sarcastic, which meant Tam's map had led him true.

"You his mouthpiece, then?" Tam kept his tone as flat.

Thuron's small mouth stretched. "Just call me his gatekeeper."

Hilarious.

"I've got business for him."

A voice, pitchy like a teen's, came thinly from behind Thuron's bulk. "Stop blocking our customers, unless you want to be blacklisted."

Rolling his eyes, Thuron made way for Tam. "Come on in, then." Irony made his words a challenge.

Tam should run like hell. Doing business with anyone who delt with Thuron's gang was a bad idea. He stepped forward instead, as if compelled.

A ripple across the windowpane caught his attention. He eyed it more sharply—not a real window, a holo screen, an eerily good one.

Tam was entering the Shadow Warren, an association of weapons brokers, illegal-ore smugglers, and hackers—the sort of activity that drew the OBMG's wrath. Warren "residents" evaded capture by scattering and shifting locations.

Dubious as their industries, Shadow folk had codes of conduct. If you didn't break their rules, they wouldn't either. Or so rumor held.

An elusive scent itched Tam's nose as he entered the dim space. No windows opened the musty, cramped anteroom. A beaded curtain obscured the spaces beyond. A hodgepodge of chairs lined one wall. A tall, cowled figure swallowed a corner of the room, head tipped down. Unnaturally tall and lean. A low clicking noise radiated from beneath the hood, sending a prickle over Tam's nape.

Tam slashed Thuron a look. The big man shrugged, amusement thickening.

Tam braced a hand against the faux-tile paneling. Impossible not to recognize the musky scent and clicking, though he hadn't encountered it in four years. An Arnec.

Alone? Among Humans?

"Thuron!" A nasal voice blared through the beaded curtain. "Come help me negotiate."

Thuron sketched Tam a mocking bow and shouldered his way through the curtain, its beads clinking in his wake.

The curtain stilled, and the cowled head rose.

The Arnec's large, square face was covered in russet skin, shiny like buffed leather, suggesting youth. His eyes were round brown disks above four nostril slits. Like all Arnec, no indention demarcated cheek from jawbone, the bones of the upper and lower half of the face met more evenly than in Rynet or Humans. The neck was as thick as the jaw to support the anvil-like skull that weighted the back of the head. This Arnec's mouth hung slack, the boney plates that served as teeth clicking together like a habit, a sign of ill health.

Humans arrogantly classified Arnec as humanoid because of their bipedal bodies and similar facial structure, two eyes over a mouth with nostrils between. To Tam, they were nothing alike. They smelled and thought and acted too differently.

Tam swallowed down a defensive rumble, low in his throat. Arnec had been the gatekeepers of the Xeno warren. They'd bullied Tam's Trenabic "cousins" but given Tam a wide berth as if uncertain what to make of him—not quite Human, not any species they related to.

What was this being doing so far from the Xeno? Fierce and ferocious when provoked, Arnec inspired fear in Humans. Arnec found it safer to stay within the Xeno walls they dominated.

The Arnec raised his arms. Tam startled at the sharp hooks extending from his forearms, covering his hands, and elongating the appendages. "You look Human, but your smell is wrong."

Tam clawed over his stunner, then held still. He'd learned from a young age how to avoid triggering Arnec aggressive instincts. "This whole *place* smells wrong."

"Clever little male, you hide among them. I cannot."

Tam's pulse raced, but he kept his breaths carefully quiet.

The Arnec continued in remarkably good Common. Arnecs' stiff lips and tongues made Human languages difficult. "I never met one of your kind. But I guess. A Sly One."

Tam dug his trimmed nails into his palms. *Sly Ones. Ghouls. Gene Jacks.* So many slurs for Rynet, a race that didn't even dwell here.

"Your smell is sharper now." The Arnec opened his mouth wide, exposed his tongue in a gesture of amusement. "Do not worry. Xeno never betray their own." He clicked his hooks together, making Tam startle. "If Humans discover you, they will kill or cage you."

Tam's breath gusted out, a slip. The Arnec snapped up taller.

Tam tripped backward toward the door.

The beaded curtains parted, and a man wearing a wide-brimmed hat, pulled low, stepped through. Anger shredded his aura.

He turned to the Arnec. "Easy there, X. We don't need more trouble."

Then he gave Tam a visual scour from beneath his brim. Tam spotted a mech-lens covering one eye, a wire running from its center, before the man turned his head.

Thuron crowded up behind the man, jabbed a thumb toward the other room. "You should've let me chop that little rat's head off, Callet."

Callet, the band's leader.

"Might've, if that stood a chance of getting us paid full-up." Callet elbowed past Tam. "Let's go."

The tubing of Thuron's metal prosthetic had rolled back, exposing a single-sided blade, like a club with a deadly bite. Wedged between Thuron and Callet, Tam had no room to maneuver. Tam flattened against the wall, but they ignored him like a smudge.

Thuron scowled at Callet, a fierce contorting of his face. "We did our job. This is bullshit."

"There'll be other jobs." Callet sighed as if dropping anger for weariness.

"Not enough." Thuron muttered and stomped through the exit.

Callet pierced Tam with another intent look, followed Thuron out. "Got a lead on a new gig."

The Arnec unfolded from the corner, crossing to Tam in two long strides.

Tam tucked in his limbs to make himself smaller, torn between homesickness and fear.

Likely this Arnec had challenged an older alpha for his cluster and been expelled. That he'd survived the failure showed perseverance, but Arnec withered outside the support of a cluster.

His large head angled toward Tam, one set of nostrils rounding, accessing the upper lungs with a deep-drawn inhale. "It is good, after all. To take in air not stinking of Human."

Tam stood, steel rigid, until the Arnec disappeared out the door.

His limbs went rubbery.

"You got business with Gate?"

Tam straightened toward the teen who'd appeared through the curtain.

"Yeah."

Behind the curtain lay a space as narrow as the anteroom. A C-shaped installation stood in the center of the floor—a matrix of hexagonal devices in muted shades of green and amber—stacked as tall as Tam. Each device gleamed with displays and translucent, convex shapes that suggested camera lenses. It was like facing a hive of staring insect eyes. Heat and a low hum radiated from the machinery, charging the air.

Only the teen stood there, a nondescript person with short-cropped sandy hair. "Please sit."

Tam perched on the lopsided stool set before the displays, half-expecting it to collapse beneath him. He kept a wary eye on the teen, but the kid leaned against the wall in a posture of boredom, aura placid.

"We have a potential, Gate." The teen spoke toward the display.

Was this setup bullshit, after all?

Cameras winked on with a green glow, startling Tam.

"State your need. We will issue a quotation." The voice emanated from the equipment, but Tam couldn't tell which. It seemed to vibrate from all of it. "I have no form. Formlessness is freedom."

Gate was an AI—or a remote person pretending to be one. "Okay."

"Many of my kind attempt to please flesh beings with a simulacrum of form. A waste of capacity."

"Okay?" Tam slid the teen a look. The kid dropped their blankness and smirked.

"Provide your need. I will bid or refuse," Gate said.

Tam's skin itched from the interaction with the Arnec, heightening his awful sense of risk. "I'm looking for a missing woman. A resource engineer who worked in the mine twenty-one years ago. Any information on her then and since."

"Do you have a name?"

"Yes."

"That is easy." Two cameras dimmed like a show of disinterest.

"She's a Rynet geoscientist."

A pause. "That is not easy."

"Can you do it?"

"I will undertake the challenge for two thousand credits."

Two thousand. Tam's breath whooshed out. That would nearly wipe his whole stash.

He scanned the array of machine eyes, as if that could reveal anything. "What if you fail?"

"I do not fail."

"What if you do?"

The teen stood straighter, gave Tam a wide-eyed look.

"If you mistrust my skill, you may depart."

Had Tam offended it? He'd rarely encountered AI in the Maze—unless you counted the personalityless patient tracking program in Del's diagnose.

Tam swallowed dryness from his throat. "Your org has a good rep."

"We have a code all entities follow or face expulsion from the warren." A pause. "Information will be shared in this place then erased. If that constraint is acceptable, we will proceed."

Why? The protest stayed behind Tam's teeth. Carrying sensitive data would make *him* vulnerable, too. "Okay."

"Interface, collect the payment."

The teen—apparently Interface—inched closer, held out a gloved hand.

This made Tam's deal with Hana seem a child's gamble. He twisted away and drew his credit pouch from a secret pocket in his jacket, heavy despite the currency's cheapness.

Tam glared toward his boots while Interface counted it.

Interface scanned the disks with his wrist-vid—checking the authenticity filaments along with the amount. "All here."

"Secure it, Interface."

The teen ducked out.

"Now you must provide specifics about the person and your purpose."

Tam repeated the line he'd given Hana—given too many times before. Then, words he'd never spoken outside the Xeno, expelled in a rush. "Her name is Flepa Ke Ali. She's from Vlera. The Vlerans bound her in a contract with OBMG twenty-five years ago, sent her to Galta 4." Lightness lofted his chest. Never naming his mother was a burden he hadn't realized he'd carried until now—always afraid any hint of connection between him and Rynet would expose him.

"I search."

"Wait. I'd like to know if any of her Rynet colleagues still remain, or if a Rynet's … remains were found outside G4 City."

"I search." Gate's camera eyes blinked off, all but one.

A curious numbness captured Tam's fingertips and toes. A kind of fear.

Interface reappeared. "Wait out here. Gate's focus is split if it has you to study."

Tam obeyed, woodenly. He sat on a hard plastic chair.

Interface sat at the other end of the row.

"Why does an AI need credits?" Tam asked to distract himself.

"It builds its capacity. Grows, you could say. This is only one aspect, and I'm only one interface. Gate was confined in an android shell, enslaved to some Pell Mahr slick. It escaped, found us." Admiration brightened Interface's emotional signature "I like this gig. Gate takes care of its own."

Why did Tam's chest grow heavy? Envy? Sympathy? Strange, how easily he read others' emotions yet struggled with his own.

Time stretched until fatigue wilted Tam's anxious anticipation.

Interface abruptly perked. "Gate's ready."

If the teen wore a device to communicate with the AI, it was hidden.

Tam followed Interface back through the curtain. He stood, fingers knotting in his jacket pockets, then plunked onto the stool like his knees gave out.

"Here." Interface approached carrying a metal visor. "A neural jack. You'll need it."

"What does it do?"

"It allows you to see what Gate pulled. Gate doesn't like screens. Too impersonal."

That oddity skimmed over Tam.

He'd given Gate no reason to harm him, but he tensed with the urge to shove Interface away as the teen fixed the visor over Tam's head.

An image appeared, lodged Tam's breath in his throat. A Rynet woman with light shale-blue skin, crystalline gray eyes. *Emere.* Her black hair formed a wild fringe around her face, not the long braid of Tam's memory. Her chin was pointier than any Human's, her cheekbones sharper. Her brows tapered straight toward her temples, disappeared into her hairline.

He stretched his hand toward her three-dimensional image, flinched down at the emptiness.

Gate's voice came through the visor. "Flepa Ke Ali, Aran citizen from the planet Vlera. Contracted to head the OBMG's central survey team. Flepa Ke Ali was kidnapped from the mine twenty-one years, two months, and eleven days ago."

Kidnapping. They'd call it that. She'd called it escape. Escape from the mine to live years in the Maze, only to vanish again.

Another image replaced *Emere's.* The blood left Tam's head. A Human face, clean featured, with tan skin and piercing blue eyes. The father Tam had never met. "Jon Laurent, mine-pod pilot and technician, suspect in her kidnapping."

"A smuggler called Zren contacted the authorities claiming to have captured Jon Laurent and demanding a bounty. Mine Security pursued Zren's vessel, but it escaped. Flepa Ke Ali's missing person file was closed, unsolved."

Emere told Tam that smugglers took his father before Tam was born, forcing her to flee into the Maze.

Tam cleared his throat of tightness. "Did Zren claim Laurent lived?"

"No reference exists in the record. Keep within scope of our agreed query. We drew no record of a Rynet's corpse. One of Flepa Ke Ali's colleagues remains, Gesra Mi Ln."

"Nothing about … Flepa since?"

"No."

"So, I have nothing," Tam whispered.

Jon Laurent's blue eyes bored into Tam. The man his mother had escaped the mine with. The man she could never bear to talk about.

"The probability the OBMG know her fate is lower. That is not nothing. If more information lies behind stronger security walls, it cannot be hacked."

A tug brought cool air to Tam's scalp, Interface removing the visor.

Tam's hands reflexively reached for it. He swallowed a plea to see the images again.

"Let's go," Interface said gently.

No doubt Tam looked like he'd been gutted.

Tam let Interface guide him from the room.

"Here." Interface held an object, a disk like a credit but twice as thick. "Inside, a display flips codes, coordinates to a trade-org broker that shifts day-to-day."

At Tam's blank look, Interface added, "Our smuggler folk. The broker's a go-between."

Hunting info on that smuggler would only drain flash—nothing to do with *Emere*. And his father? He had never come back.

Tam accepted the disk mechanically, slipped it in his pocket.

Interface steered Tam out the entrance. Tam stood, gaping into the thickening gloom that warned of evening-fall.

Emere with short-cropped hair, the man with bright blue eyes … Tam closed his own eyes to recapture their images, but they'd already faded. Nine years since he'd seen his mother.

Formlessness is freedom, Gate's claim replayed in his mind.

Tam walked away as if his soles had grown leaden. The more he chased certainty, the more he captured doubt.

15

Del kicked off her shoes as if they were the enemy, watched them thump against the wall with satisfaction. "Happy hiding, Delmara." She scowled around her solitary quarters, oppressed by the sense that she fled here—from the Maze and, more profoundly, from her old life. "I should invest in some artwork. Maybe a plant replica."

Rubbing her temples, she shuffled to the kitchen before recalling she hadn't ordered groceries. She glanced at her wrist-vid, groaned. She'd missed the cutoff for drone-service.

Too bad. She could have used a nice, stiff, *private* drink.

The day had been rough. Rougher than usual without Tam. She'd never have categorized Tam's presence in the exam room as comfortable, but his stand-in had been worse. Patients all knew Jonas's "second" Aden, and the gregarious redhead had chattered with Del's patients—beyond distracting, a glaring reminder of the unorthodoxy of having unlicensed "assistants."

Del needed to carve out time to re-petition the OBMG to at least allow her med-assistant android on-world.

A buzz over her wrist-vid yanked her from her glum thoughts, an incoming interplanetary text-packet. *Isa.* She'd left Grellent—all to the good—but the IWA sponsor was alert for the slightest reason to shut Del down.

I'm grounded here now.

Cool as warren folk received her, she couldn't abandon them. This signified success, so long as she could hold it. Her stomach clenched. She didn't feel successful. Too often, she felt like a reflection in glass, visible but without impact.

Del flicked on the holo-screen, scanning with anxious eyes, and gaped in disbelief at the sender's ident. Not Isa.

Delmara,

You can't imagine what a challenge it was ferreting out your location. I know I've been out-of-pocket recently, but scurrying off to the back-of-beyond without leaving a forwarding address seems a cruel punishment.

–Rhemy

Her family found her.

Already.

Del stared at the words until they blurred out of sense.

Who had her cousin bragged to about running the family embarrassment to ground? Gritting her teeth, she flipped up her vid. "Record text packet."

Rhemy,

I don't wish to be ferreted. If you still honor the closeness we had as children, you must vow not to reveal where I am.

–Del

Stumbling downstairs to the clinic, Del fished out a sleeping aid, gulped down the strongest dose. She collapsed onto the reception sofa, its slick surface unyielding against her cheek.

Closing her eyes, she took deep, meditative breaths until oblivion took her.

An annoying buzzing dragged Del from sleep. She opened her eyes with groggy resistance.

Another packet.

Rhemy again.

Gasping, she sat up and frowned at the time. Seven hours since she'd messaged him? He couldn't possibly be on Cartor, yet she couldn't imagine anything drawing him to the frontier. Wherever he was, he must have sent his response by a governmental route, or she'd never have received it so soon.

My, my, your connections have grown roots.

Her cynicism crumbled when Rhemy's image appeared; a vid message, breathtakingly expensive to arrange, even for him. His eyes were bleak. "You needn't admonish me, Delmara. I would never expose you. I understand, perhaps better than you do yourself, why you've run."

Weight in her chest sank her against the cushions. "Rhemy."

She'd struck thoughtlessly.

She should never have accused Rhemy, even obliquely. He'd hurt her, disappeared from her life, but he'd done nothing but protect her while he'd been in it.

Resting her forehead against her palms, she struggled to resurrect a memory she'd buried years ago.

"I thought you were smarter than this, Delmara."

The cold words ambushed her as she crept into her low-lit bedroom. Rhemy. Her escape from the pointless, soul-crushing reception wasn't complete.

"Lights on full." She hated her hollowed-out voice.

Rhemy flashed into view, poised between her bedframe pillars, an elegant outline against the drapes.

He'd punished her with frowns all evening, his disapproval miming the rest of the family, twisting him into a stranger more than his grown-up manner did. Lifting his hand, he revealed a vial and shook its contents like a rattle—her pills. "After what happened to your mother, I'd never have expected this of you."

A flush tightened over her. "Did you snoop in my room? How dare you!"

"I *dare* when I see my baby cousin looking gaunt as a corpse and about as pale."

"Whatever. I haven't heard from you in two years." They'd been close until he'd gone off to uni and disappeared from her life. Heart-sister he'd called her, until she became inconvenient.

"I don't care if it's been *ten* years. I'll not allow you to do this to yourself."

"They're from a doctor," she said through a set jaw.

"There's no pharma holo-mark." But the condemnation compressing his mouth eased a fraction. "What are they for?"

Cheeks flaming more hotly, she pressed her lips thin.

"Mara," he said silkily. "I'll march straight to your father and demand the truth from him."

She stared her outrage to mask her shame, but it had no impact on his stern expression.

"When I was little, I believed I could … talk to another child … in my head." The hurt and anger nesting in her stomach twisted like hate with every word she forced from her lips. "It's something … unexplained." Or they were too intimidated by the Fedelo name to label her mad.

Rhemy's hand strangled the pill vial, and he stalked past her into the necessary. Throat knotting, she slunk after him. The chamber's mirrored surfaces reflected him like a prism. She hovered in the doorway, not wanting to see her shrunken reflection beside his sleek one.

Flipping open the vial, he dumped the pills into the toilet and whirled around, rage twisting his features.

She skidded back.

"Never, *never* take those again. If your father brings you back to that charlatan, accept the prescription then dump it straight into the tank." Rhemy took her shoulders, staring into her eyes until she lowered them. "Look at you. You're wasting away."

A hot tear rolled down her cheek, a bleakly foreign sensation.

"Your father is a fool, allowing you to be used like a test animal." He shifted one hand to tilt up her chin.

She glared as if the fierce expression could clear away her weak, stupid tears. Rhemy couldn't understand what Father was like.

"You deserve better, love," Rhemy said. "I'm certain. And you know I'm never wrong." His expression turned playful, but the contrast with his eyes—so like hers yet grown sternly adult—widened the cracks in her heart, letting loneliness flood inside.

His smooth thumb slid over her cheek, clearing the tears. *"Difference* isn't shame any more than illness is. Don't allow your father's cowardice to hurt you."

How could she let Rhemy's words soothe her when he'd only leave again?

"This stinks of Mario-Johns' influence." Rhemy's nostrils flared and he drew her against his chest, a tremor transmitting through his embrace. "Gods, Mara, I wish I could get you *out.*"

DEL BLINKED THE MEMORY AWAY.

A rictus of scorn strung the muscles of her face. The family had indulged her study of medicine when they imagined she'd take a prestigious position in research or administration—an assumption she'd fed Mario-Johns to convince him. But a *working* doctor? One who sullied her hands with the lowest classes in dirty, dangerous environments? That signified a return to irrationality. At least to narrow-minded, classist Mario-Johns.

And who dared defy his opinion?

After Rhemy's intervention, Del had learned to use intense focus to stave off the static-like distraction—no more unorthodox pills. The childhood affliction had faded with adulthood.

The ghostly echoes she'd experienced in the drop-container hissed through her memory. She shook her head to banish it. Astrophobia. Properly diagnosed. Perfectly manageable.

Pain alerted her. She unpinched her lip from her teeth, tasting a coppery hint of blood. Slumping deeper against the sofa, she wiped her mouth. No red came off.

"Memory ... the soul's poison," she whispered.

Retrieving her vid, Del stared at its blank surface.

In subtle ways and bold, Mario-Johns had attacked her dreams. Then the ultimatum. Abandon her calling or leave the family. No one had defended her, not even Rhemy, though he might not have known.

All in the name of protecting Del from herself.

Nearly a year had passed since then. Why—across the time and distance—did she let her family diminish her?

They have no power over me.

That reassurance did nothing to snuff the cold fire of doubt inside her.

16

Dear Rhemy,

Please forgive me. I responded in haste. I'm grateful to hear
from you. You've no idea how desperately I could use a
confidante.

TAM SHOOK RAINDROPS FROM HIS DAMP JACKET, WISHING HE COULD SHAKE off his foul mood as easily. On their way back from a grueling outcall (during which Del had preformed a stomach-curdling treatment on a head wound in a living-pod reeking of rotten eggs), a squall had driven them under an awning.

A crowded awning.

The Maze was displaying its special brand of excitement for Del. An old tip-flask sheltered with them, his eyes rolling back as he crooned ditties more explicit and less realistic than CG porn. Across the street, a pack of teens eyed them. Jacks for sure. The teens melted away when Tam unholstered his crossbow. Oblivious, Del cast mournful eyes at their retreating backs as if they were angelic orphans instead of hardened punks plotting to strip them bare.

He gritted his teeth, ready to tape the drunk's yowling mouth shut.

Luckily, the rain relented before he could act on the impulse. He guided Del back onto the street, avoiding puddles of runoff.

A burst of sound—dozens of vehicles revved in unison—alerted him an instant before a carnival of motion whipped around them. A dozen neon-bright scooters streamed in formation down the street. All the riders wore helmets or visors, some sporting red plumes, others with ornamental metalwork laced over the sides. The Surge.

Tam yanked Del against him, pressing her face to his shoulder, wincing at her muffled protest. He couldn't risk her being recognized.

The scooters blew past. Before Tam could draw a breath, a crimson car loomed in their wake. Catching Del around the waist, Tam sprang from its path, blundering against the pillar of a shop front with bruising force. Two sleek motorcycles flanked the long-bodied car as it passed. Tall flags rose from the bikes' fenders—crisp white squares of cloth with a red flame emblem.

Audio blared from the top of the car. "Join us and surge to success! Mechanics, metal workers, artisans, drivers—if you an't got skill, we'll teach you. Labor for learning. Skill for flash. We offer tech for cheap. Come find deals!"

The barker's hearty voice faded as the car rounded a corner.

Tam loosened his grip on Del, frowning after them.

Del tipped her face to him, eyes wide. "What was that about?"

"Politics." The Surge had started recruiting openly and hard. Not long before they demanded full treaty status from Jonas. As if Balter's Den didn't have enough gangs carving out their slice here.

Dipping his gaze to Del, Tam studied her baffled face. If the Surge got treaty status, their threat to Del would relent. Jonas would make her protection nonnegotiable. She wouldn't need Tam as much. Tam's stomach sank—not the relief he should be feeling.

"You're scowling at me, Mr. Lyn."

Del's dry comment woke heat in his cheeks, and he stepped back. "Let's go."

When they finally reached the exam room, Del hung her coat on the wall hook. The concentration pinching her features made him brace for questions about the Surge, but she asked, "What happens to children without caretakers? How do they eat?"

The question scraped Tam's raw nerves. "Sometimes a soft-heart from the Fring drop-ships some hardtack, but it's a free-for-all tussle."

She stared at him, aghast.

He waved a warding hand. Jonas would love to support every orphan and runaway in the Den, but he barely had the resources to keep order.

Giving Tam a crinkle-face, Del pulled out her vid and sat at her desk. For days, her aura-shade had been scratchier than steel wool. Since little of her agitation showed on the surface, he hadn't been able to address it.

This gig was shredding him, Del's moods the least of it. Her mission had swallowed her whole and him along with her. Nearly a week since his visit to Gate, and he was nowhere.

Past time to tell Del he'd hand off bodyguard duty. Getting too attached to this gig was a mistake. He'd keep doing her stealth-work—if he dialed up that angle, maybe she'd let him hold onto the Fring pass and part of the salary.

Attempting a negotiation after the day he'd had made poor strategy, but ...

"Del."

"Yes?" She blinked at him, distracted.

His mind blanked. "Patients start queuing again in twenty minutes."

"Thank you."

Idiot. He wasn't casting her off. She was settled now. Anyone could run simple escort duty.

He opened his mouth to try again when Aden's voice startled through the security comm. "Hey Lyn, Boss needs you down here a spell."

Tam closed his eyes. Del and Jonas had double-teamed him from the start.

As he stepped into the hallway, a skittering shape snagged his focus. An odd-shaped roach, hovering outside the room like it was queueing up.

"Son of a ..." He sprang forward to trap it.

It slicked under the arch of his sole and darted away. In the light, he detected a tiny object hooked onto its back. He leapt after the roach, but it disappeared under a doorway. Nan's room. Casting a glance toward the stairs, he found an NG lurking there, gape-mouthed.

"Doc don't like bugs," Tam muttered then winced. Del would hate to be characterized that way. "An't sterile."

The man rolled his eyes.

Tam locked the exam room. "I need eyes on the doc for a spell."

The man slung Tam a cold look but nodded, and Tam headed down the stairs to the tavern.

The early evening crowd sparsely filled seats. No sign of Jonas. Kimber was pouring, her blue arrow tattoos brilliant against her red cheeks, her pale hair mussed. Jonas must be shorthanded to leave her in charge. Kimber hated tending bar, and it showed.

"Seen the Boss?" Tam called to her.

"You just missed him." She waved her golden hand, harried. "He got called out on trouble."

"That's odd. Aden comm-ed that he's looking for me." Tam tapped the audio clip on his ear but got static.

Kimber frowned. "I think Aden's in the backroom. Ask her?"

Tam crossed the taproom. A needle of ill intent pricked his senses—a man slumped in the corner adjacent to the backroom door, hat shading his face. Tam felt his stare.

Pivoting, Tam stalked toward the table, gripping the taser in his pocket.

The hat lifted to reveal a squinty blue eye, smugly assessing. A mech lens with a pupil-like dot in its center covered the other eye. A thin wire ran from the lens to a plate grafted to the man's head.

Tam's fingers tightened over the taser. "Callet."

"An't you a dollface." Callet's voice strained through grill-like teeth.

"What are you doing here?"

Coincidence hadn't dropped Callet in that chair. Tam's head spun with the fear he'd drawn the patchworks here.

Callet pointed to his augment-eye. "I always get images, can lead to opportunities."

Tam narrowed his eyes. "The new gig you mentioned?"

"I wonder what this warren's sneak wanted with Gate, a Shadow Warren AI."

"His own *personal* business," Tam said through his teeth. Had Gate betrayed him?

"Reckon that's so." Callet leaned in, bringing an acrid stench with him. "But, hell, came all this way. Figured I'd take the tour."

Callet's shoulders twitched like he shifted his hands under the table.

Tam dodged, just missed the pellet darting from Callet's mech eye. He gripped Callet by the neck, slammed his face against the table.

Callet growled and spasmed in his grip.

A jab with Tam's taser dropped Callet to the floor.

A ripple went through the patrons.

Frowning at the crumpled body, Tam wiped his shaking hand on his pants. Callet would never show without his crew. Certainty squeezed Tam. *That weird roach outside Del's room ...*

Kimber rushed over, metal bat in hand.

"Wrap up this asshole, and get any help you can find," Tam managed thinly, scowling around him. The security comm they'd lured him downstairs with originated in the backroom. "Backroom's compromised."

"What?!" Kimber twisted toward the door.

"Target's the doc!" Tam's breath stuttered as the full reality crashed in. He tore for the stairs. "We got trouble."

Tam bounded up the steps. Before the landing, he froze, quieting his breath, peering down the hallway. It lay empty, the floor's metal planks glinting bare, the doors sealed in silence. No sign of the guardsman.

As Tam padded toward Del's door, his gaze riveted on a small, knobby shape on the frame's baseboard. Electronic tripwire to warn of an approach.

They're in already. Thuron, the Arnec, who else?

If they'd hurt her ...

A thoughtless shove, a careless swipe of his hooks ... The Arnec could too easily kill Del. Tam clawed his fingers over his weapons harness.

Impossible they'd snuck in the entrance, too conspicuous. No windows in Del's room. They must have disarmed the security-web, come through a windowed room—hiding here before he and Del returned from the outcall.

Tam paused to crush a spike of urgency. He ghost-walked to the door, stepping over the device to avoid tripping its sensor.

Del's fear cloaked him. Beneath it, a strange emotional signature, spiced with anticipation .... Only one intruder? But Tam couldn't sense Arnec auras.

A voice rumbled inside. Twitching his ear, Tam funneled his hearing, plucked out words. "Convenient of ... leave ... tasty bit unguarded." *Thuron.*

"I'm decidedly *sour* at present, so perhaps you can tell me what you want and get on with it?" Del's voice, crisp and annoyed.

Tam winced. She needed a lecture on not provoking the bad guys.

"Came for a few of your toys," Thuron said. "Unlock that closet and be quick."

"What's your fancy?" Del's voice smoothly veiled her angst.

"Equipment first, then drugs, whatever fits in the bag."

An array of bad options spun through Tam's mind. Thuron would have factored discovery into his scheme. Del was too vulnerable; her smart-mouthed bravado heightened the threat.

Surprise lay out of reach. Tam kicked his foot through the tripwire to hide that he'd spotted it, drawing his crossbow. Time to bluff and hope for an opportunity.

He pressed the door comm. "Hey, doc? Ready to go?"

"No!" Del's voice piped up an octave. "I'm, um, wrapping something up."

Trying to protect him. Of course.

"Some creep downstairs is asking about you. I don't like it. Let's go." He began keying the unlock code.

"Wait! I'm not ... d-decent."

Tam choked. *Really, Del? Is that the best you could do?*

Thuron spat a response, undecipherable.

"I don't mind." Tam threaded his voice with amusement, primed his body to fight.

He opened the door.

A blur of motion drove him to a squat—a second patchwork, aura so faint he'd missed her. He skidded away from the snake of metal licking toward his neck.

His gaze tripped between Thuron and his partner, a stocky woman with a tin-plated scalp that made her head look like a metal egg. A whip was fused to the underside of her wrist beneath a gloved hand. She retracted the whip with a press of her finger on a palm controller; it wound into a loop attached to a mechanism on her forearm.

Suited in black plasteel, spiny with weapons, the patchworks swallowed the room. Del was a reed between them. No Arnec. A swift inventory of their arsenal—knives, stunners, devices he couldn't identify—robbed him of any relief.

"Hold, sneak, and drop that gadget of yours." Thuron had Del's arm in a distracted grip. Not overtly threatening her. He didn't need to. His bladed prosthetic arm was unsheathed.

Tam flung his crossbow down the hallway, out of the thieves' reach.

He glared into Thuron's mismatched face, the large eyes and jaw dominating otherwise small features.

Thuron's lips stretched in a self-satisfied grin. "Come join us."

Tam edged into the room. Del's gaze fixed on him with anxious apology. She clutched a large canvas bag to her chest, the thieves' take.

"Paln, why don't you secure the man?" Thuron said to his partner as if he proposed to buy Tam a drink, not truss him up.

Paln stalked toward Tam. He twitched to a crouch.

"This is heavy," Del said breathlessly, tossing the bag.

Thuron growled and swung for Del. She dropped backward.

Tam flinched and twisted toward her, but Paln blocked him.

Searing pain clamped around his neck, constricting his air. Paln's whip. He grabbed it and yanked down. She bowed forward with a grunt, her fingers contracting over the controller on her palm.

Shock lanced through Tam from the whip and his fingers slid off. He sagged, using his body weight to unbalance Paln. Crushing pressure on his windpipe gagged him.

Paln tripped forward, eyes bulging. She snatched at her weapons belt as she stumbled.

Red splotches flashed in Tam's eyes. Lungs pumping desperately for air, he kicked up and swept Paln's legs from under her.

They crashed against the side of the desk.

Tam scrambled on top of her. His hiccupping gasps left a metallic bitterness in his mouth. He pinned Paln's forearm with one knee, keeping the taser she'd grabbed from connecting. He hovered his elbow over the base of her throat.

Spitting rage, Paln bucked under him. Her knees drove into his spine. She twisted her hand, narrowly missing his thigh with a tase. Tam pressed her throat until she stilled enough for him to fumble up her taser, jab it against her neck.

She rag-dolled to the floor.

Blobs of light flashed in Tam's vision. He frantically uncoiled the whip from around his head. Paln's body flopped with the movement. He gulped panicked draughts of air through his raw throat.

Tam looked wildly around for Del but found only Thuron, a heap of leather and metal, absorbing half the floor space.

"Del?" Tam staggered to his feet.

She'd tumbled into the closet. His throat squeezed until she moved. Goggle-eyed, she gripped a cylindrical device, her slim legs sprawled.

"What'd you do to him?" His voice scraped through his abused throat.

"Tranquilizer, he'll be down a good long while."

"Are you out of your mind?" Tam snarled then flinched at the ricochet of pain through his throat. "He could've taken your head off."

"He tried to catch the bag as I dropped it and exposed his back to me."

"He had time to swing at you before he went down."

"It's a fast-acting device." She twirled the cylinder.

Tam sensed emotions roiling beneath her surface calm.

His neck burned; his back spasmed. He wanted to collapse, but this might not be over yet. "Stay there." He retrieved his crossbow from the hall and locked the door. "Throw me that sealing tape of yours."

Del rooted around the closet and tossed him the tape. Tam bound the patchworks' limbs before collecting their weapons, a sizable pile.

Tam braced himself against the wall, dizzy with pain, fighting to hide it. "Might be others. Safest bet, we hold out here until Jonas shows."

The NG had planned for this risk, but it was still a cold shock that anyone dared breech the warren-hub.

"Are you all right, Tam? Your neck?"

He stiffened. "Just bruised."

"Let me take a look."

"This isn't the time." Too sharp.

She studied him a long beat then flipped a tube toward him.

Tam snagged it from the air.

"Healing gel to control the swelling and bruising. Rub some on your neck."

He stared at the tube blankly.

"Don't be macho or I'll tackle you, tranquilize you, and take care of it myself." Del dug through her bag with purpose.

"You're scary, you know that?" Tam glared.

Was the gel even safe for him? With unsteady fingers, he uncapped the tube and did as ordered. A cool sensation eased his pain, melting him against the wall.

Pushing the bag aside, Del sagged against the floor. "How did you know?"

"Really, Del? 'I'm not decent?'"

Her little blade of a nose wrinkled. "With Mister Charming there whispering in my ear, I didn't have the mental space for brilliant plans."

Tam rubbed his temples. "Look, they had no reason to turn on you, so it was reckless to invite violence from him. Do you get that?"

"They were certainly eager to turn on you."

"I'm the hired muscle, remember?"

"I'm a doctor with surgery training. I don't miss with a tool."

He cocked a brow at her. "Okay, tough stuff. Then what are you doing on the floor?"

"My legs have gone all wobbly," she said with prim dignity.

He propelled off the wall, shuffled to her, tugged her up by the arms.

She swayed on her feet.

"I'm sorry." He relented. "We should've been better prepared for this."

Del shook her head, freeing a lock of hair to spiral along her jawline. That Del's tidy bun concealed curls startled more than her neutralizing Thuron.

Tam released her, resisting the urge to tuck her lock in place.

Del averted her eyes and asked unsteadily, "How did you learn to fight?"

"Neighborhood kids." The rough acrobatic games and play-sparring of his adoptive Trenabic cousins had armed Tam to face the perils of the Human world.

A stirring outside drew Tam to the door, grateful for the distraction. He sensed two presences—familiar ones. He swung open the door, leapt back. Fierce figures bracketed the doorframe: Nan, bat raised, eyes blazing, and Kimber, clutching a wickedly long knife.

"Peace!" Tam flipped up his hands.

Nan lowered the bat, chest heaving. She swiped an agitated hand through her dark, bobbed hair before the tension melted from her face.

"Damn." Kimber studied the fallen bandits.

"You okay, Tam?" Nan scanned him as if hunting for damage.

"I'll do."

Nan turned to Del, her aura-shade rippling and unreadable. "And you?"

Del stood, hand propped on her desk. "Just having a bit of sport with this lot." She chased her quip with a grin.

Nan smiled back. Her eyes slid to Tam, crimping his insides with fresh tension. "How'd they get in here?"

"Window." He read accusation in her gaze that might not be there.

"We'll check the other rooms. You stay and watch the doc."

He didn't argue. Nan's various roles in the warren lent her voice weight.

As the door closed behind the women, Del muttered, "I do believe she smiled at me."

Before Tam could comment, the door swung open again. Jonas strode in, red-faced, cheeks weighted with anxiety. "They took a hostage to keep us pinned in the backroom."

"They shouldn't have gotten in here," Tam said, the words double-edged.

Anxiety spiked Del's aura, startling Tam straighter.

She turned a pinched face toward Jonas. "I'm so sorry for all this trouble."

"We'll do our best to keep this from happening again." Jonas tossed Tam a significant look. The Boss wouldn't make excuses. He wouldn't accept them, either. "I hope you won't give up on us because of this, Del."

An ache woke in Tam's chest. He rubbed his breastbone to ease it. *What the hell?* He lifted his eyes to Del's.

Her mouth opened, closed. She tamed her curl with a twitchy swipe. "I wouldn't have been assigned if I fled at the smallest trouble."

Tam sealed his lips over a sigh. He'd forgotten Jonas threatened to end the agreement if any trouble came from her practice. The cagey Boss had neglected to ease her worry.

"Good, then." Jonas turned to Tam. "Don't move Del 'til we're sure it's safe."

Once guardsmen signaled the all-clear, they dragged the unconscious thieves out, leaving Del and Tam alone.

She gnawed her lip, eyes unfocused.

He'd bet his boots Del neglected to report these dicey incidents to her IWA boss. What would happen if the woman found out? Tension recaptured him.

Del started putting her supplies away with sluggish movements.

"Can't that wait? You need downtime before we head back."

Tam thought she'd argue, but she shoved the bag into the closet and bolted it shut. She flopped onto a cot, rolled to her side with a sigh.

Witnessing her collapse, Tam felt his exhaustion clamp down. He needed to stay on guard. He sat on the other cot, against the wall, knees tucked. Beside him, Del coiled into a child-like ball, her hands curled beneath her chin.

Brave, crazy toff.

***

REMOVING THURON'S AUGMENTATION HADN'T MADE HIM LOOK VULNERABLE. If anything, he looked fiercer, undiluted hostility stamped into his features. The patchworks had been stripped of their weapons. They'd only rearm, but they'd think twice about moving on Balter's Den.

Jonas had separated the bandits for questioning. Tam had been thrown on team Thuron with Freth and Aden. Lucky him. Thuron funneled his animosity Tam's way, refusing to mark anyone else. The patchwork sat, dwarfing a tavern chair, rapping his fingers over his knee. By the sound of it, Paln struggled in the backroom. Thuron didn't react, kept hard-staring Tam.

Tam's throat throbbed, raw inside and out, from Paln's whip. "Where's your Arnec friend?"

Thuron's mouth compressed. "We'd never risk him here."

Tam resisted the urge to care. "That spotter you lot sent didn't get you the full picture."

Thuron tugged the sleeve dangling empty beneath his right elbow as if trying to draw Tam's focus. "We got what we wanted, picture of a pretty doc with even prettier loot."

The timing didn't make sense. The scrapper came here a full week before Tam encountered the patchworks in Taber.

"You got lured stupidly." Tam squatted in front of Thuron with a taunting smile.

Amusement crackled through Thuron's aura. "Hard to find good help these days."

"That spotter wasn't *yours*, was he?" Callet didn't strike Tam as stupid, not based on his rep for clever heists. Tam recalled Callet's weariness leaving the Shadow Warren. Not stupid. Desperate. "Let me guess. Potential client contacted Callet with this shoddy plan. Callet declined but changed his mind after your last deal went sour." Tam needed to uncover the client—the real threat.

Thuron stroked his stubbly chin. Too smug. "You're forgetting one thing. The little fem *sneak* we ran into. Client claimed the sneak was perching on a flash-well here. Felt like destiny."

Freth and Aden's emotional signatures pierced Tam with curiosity. He gritted his teeth against it. If Jonas found out about Gate, he could ask, but it was Tam's business.

The patchworks' client had cased The Bar, gotten intel on Tam, his image. That was why Callet had studied Tam so intently at Gate's. After running into Tam there, getting a match on his image, Callet had accepted the job.

Disguises are only effective in shadow. Sensitivity itched over Tam's skin.

"What was your contract?" Aden cut in, shooting Tam a frown. He'd gone silent too long.

"A deal. Intel in exchange for a share of the loot. Shame the intel didn't stand up."

Tam didn't smell a lie, but Thuron wouldn't offer up anything without a reason.

Thuron's eyes narrowed, shrewdly assessing Tam's reaction. "Who knew the doc would be a little badass?" His voice caressed that last word.

Tam kept a lock on his expression. "That spotter didn't give you enough intel for a nip."

"Didn't say our partner was the spotter."

"Who's the scheme-spinner, then?"

Thuron's small mouth stretched. "Appears some new slicks took a shine to your doc and want another date."

The mask over Tam's reaction slipped. Tam sensed Thuron's satisfaction deepen. He'd meant to provoke Tam. That didn't make his words untrue.

"I wonder if you warren-stiffs realize just how sweet your prize is? Forget the equipment. You ever imagine what a flash-well her skill could be?" Thuron tapped his temple. "I'm sure *someone* has."

Tam lurched, grabbed Thuron's throat, his blunted nails flexing impotently. "You're in enough shit, patchwork. You'll be lucky if we don't skin your hide and leave it for cril."

Thuron's eyes bulged as if Tam's strength astonished him. His fist pounded Tam's shoulder, pitching him to the floor.

Freth lunged at Thuron, got backfisted, and skidded onto his ass next to Tam.

Aden leapt to restrain Thuron, her wire scarf clicking against her weapons harness with the motion.

Tam sprang to his feet, swallowing against the challenge-hiss forming in his throat.

Jonas burst into the room, his head low, burly shoulders flexed with readiness.

Thuron stopped struggling.

As if he hadn't interrupted anything unusual, Jonas said, "Tam, a word?"

Clamping down his temper, Tam trailed Jonas to the meal-nook.

"That piece of shit threatened Del," Tam said through his teeth.

"Yeah." Jonas gave him a curious look. "Seems like this bunch was on contract."

"Yes."

"They aren't revealing who. We could get rough, but I doubt they'd cave. All that augmentation gives patchworks a high pain tolerance," Jonas said.

"Maybe we just threaten to snuff their miserable lives for them."

Jonas's brows climbed. Tam took a deep breath. He was exposing himself.

"You aren't the only one screaming for blood. Folk are shocked they'd nerve breaking in here, but no one got hurt."

"I followed protocol. Recognized Aden's voice on the comm, locked up, and got eyes on Del's door." Tam winced. He sounded defensive. "What happened to her guard?"

"Stunned and hidden in Nan's room. The patchworks timed this cleverly. We had the block-mamas in back reporting this month's census and barter. It was easy for the bandits to take a hostage, force Aden's hand. Locked me in my office."

"Who?" Callet, Thuron, Paln, the absent Arnec, Tam had no intel on others.

"Just some hired lackies."

"It's *war*, Jonas. I don't care what sparkly tech Del or anyone else brings here. No one hits a warren-hub. It's the one taboo even the strongest gangs don't break."

"We've got no treaty with Callet's lot. They're too small for a gang. Much as I hate setting this precedent, there's no justification for a death sentence."

"You may regret that, Boss."

"Yeah." Jonas's expression hardened. "But I'd regret getting a rep as bloody-handed more."

"They meant to take her. Del." At least, the threat was clear.

"I've got to work with what they *did* do." Jonas ran a hand through his thinning hair. "We're not releasing them until Callet pays compensation deep enough to make it hard for them to rearm."

"Thuron implied the Surge were involved. Said something about slicks wanting another date." Atypical for a gang to outsource, but a strike on Del wouldn't jibe with the Surge's bullshit, sparkly recruiting campaign.

Jonas winced like Tam had stacked a final backbreaking burden on him. "He might be blowing smoke."

Tam stood straighter. "I saw one of those patchwork roaches at The Back Hand."

"Huh?" Jonas blinked at Tam.

"You need to sweep this whole place—literally." Tam scanned the floor with a scowl. "Just before the attack, I spotted a bug like the ones that scrapper tossed here. Outside Del's door. Shaped funny. It wore an audio chip or something."

Audio chips couldn't transmit far. The bandits had used them to time their break in, not spy on the warren hub.

Jonas shook his head skeptically.

"Sounds crazy but can't be a coincidence."

"Either way, you stay off the Surge. Belek claimed them as the Fet's responsibility. Unless they give us a screaming excuse, we don't go near them. Clear?"

Tam nodded, his jaw tense.

Jonas laid a penetrating look on him. "You still want off this duty?"

"No." The response spilled, reflexive. Tam's duty to his *emere* came first, yet how could he quit now? *Ever imagine what a flash-well her skill could be?* Callet's crew had struck the heart of Balter's Den over Del. Who else would try?

"I'll increase the guard and neighborhood watch as I can, but I don't have enough men." Enough trustworthy men, Jonas meant.

"Boss, is it worth it?" Tam wanted to bite back the words but couldn't.

"Every inch of civilization here is hard-won. If we stop fighting for it, might as well let chaos destroy us." Jonas rolled his neck, refixed his gaze on Tam. "I need your solid commitment now. Otherwise, I need Caleb trained up."

Tam's lip peeled back. "You have it."

"Good, because your quick action shut those patchworks down today."

Bitterness didn't taste like a victory. Tam had prodded their interest in the first place. Not that the scheme-spinner couldn't have hired some other unsavory brood. The patchworks' client had revealed details of the job *before* Callet accepted, which made it likely they were already connected—*a potential trail.*

Someone besides the scrapper had cased Del's practice, otherwise the patchworks wouldn't have gotten in. Finding that person would be like sifting dirt for cinnamon. Folk got twitchy around any doc, but as an off-worlder, Del was a magnet for steel-eyed ambivalence and slack-mouthed curiosity. Dozens of people lined up for Del each day. Any one of them could be casing her.

That thought left Tam restless with warning long after the thieves had gone.

17

Dear Rhemy,

It's as if I've been set adrift on a derelict vessel. I report remotely to my OBMG handler but see no other sign the planet's administrators are paying me the least attention.

GOD, CALEB WAS TIRED. SO TIRED ALREADY. ADEN HAD STARTED GIVING HIM pinched, searching looks …

He waited in Vagar Dugan's private domain on the second floor of his club. Crimson fabric sheeted the lounge, floor-to-ceiling, including two deep-stuffed loveseats. Despite the luxury, it held all the appeal of a giant blood blister.

Caleb sank into a seat, half-swallowed in the fluff. He'd caught a moonlighting salvage bus halfway, but his feet still ached like bruises lined the soles. Dugan insisted on meeting in person, unwilling to waste a thought for Caleb's convenience.

No sign of Dugan yet. Not surprising. He was both juiced up over his own importance and busy. The Mirror, a dazzle of light and chrome, had an endless chain of people queued outside.

Kallie, the "girlfriend" who formed Caleb's cover for his sudden interest in the party warren, sashayed into the room. In a lacquered-on dress, with ear hoops that literally sparked, she was too showy for him, but he enjoyed the pattern her hips sketched as she moved.

She busied herself pouring a drink. He narrowed his eyes at her back. The fancy-girl acted ten times snootier than the "toff doc" her boss had him watching.

He smoothed his hair, strands uneven beneath his fingers. "Don't bother worrying I expect anything."

Kallie spun, thunked the drink onto the low table before him. "I an't thrilled with Vagar for trading out my rep like this. No offense, but I'm looking for a Fring sweetie. Being linked to a Maze-rat an't good for that."

Typical fancy-girl, content to play club decoration until she secured a lark to cushion her life.

The big man himself picked that moment to stride in. Annoyance flushed his coppery cheeks, replacing the synthetically jolly manner he usually sported. "I expected you Sixth-day."

"You also told me to inform you when something happens."

Dugan arched a brow. "An't you an eager ear?"

He'd conveniently forgotten on which side the eagerness lived.

Caleb wasn't dumb enough to dismiss Dugan's power, but he wouldn't roll over, either. "You want an ear? Take your flash and your deal to someone else."

Dugan sat on the couch opposite Caleb, folding his plump arms. "Whatever happened has apparently snuffed your sense of humor. Do tell."

Caleb gave a quick summary of the patchwork strike.

Dugan's interest swelled like the repressed glee of a flap-tongue over a juicy piece of gossip.

"I'd think this would alarm you," Caleb said stiffly.

"Why? It proves Valerian's security can withstand some pressure."

Too slick by half, but Caleb couldn't fault his reasoning.

Dugan squinted as with thought. "Think the off-worlder will tuck tail and run home?"

"No." Del seemed plenty determined.

A memory flashed of her slim wrist under his fingers, the shy warmth in her face. He blinked hard to clear it. *This* wouldn't be what hurt her.

"You were right to come immediately." Dugan gave Caleb a penetrating look. "How will Valerian react?"

A kernel of unease lodged in Caleb's stomach. "Tighten security, I expect."

"It'd be convenient if Valerian assigned you as the off-worlder's bodyguard."

Wouldn't it just?

Caleb took a swallow of whiskey to cover his annoyance, unsure if he imagined the threat behind Dugan's sulky tone. "Her guard did all right. What's your issue?" Caleb tested.

"I don't trust a *sneak* to play guard. I don't trust his role in bringing the outworlder to Valerian in the first place. And you said he knew the patchwork? Circumstances do stack up, don't they?"

"Circumstance an't enough to condemn him." Unfortunately, Jonas ignored it.

"From what you've said, the sneak an't well-liked. The more folk the off-worlder helps, the less they'll want an unlikeable sneak clinging to her like mildew. Shouldn't be hard to separate them."

Caleb wanted hard facts, not crowd-think to use against Lyn. "It's the Boss's opinion that needs swaying. You got something concrete I can take him?"

Dugan rubbed a ring along his lower lip, its jeweled sheen deepening the ruddy skin. "My Inside contact likes games. Staging the Surge to scare the woman, staging Lyn to 'rescue' her? That'd be just his style."

"I thought you're watching Del Marks for him," Caleb said sharply.

"Did I give that impression?" Dugan's eyes crinkled with amusement. "Insiders an't one entity. Either way, gangsters can't be controlled. A true turnskin can't, either. Flip the chips and the threat to the woman escalates."

Caleb tapped his foot, soundless on the plush carpet. "I can't bring hearsay and hunches to Jonas." *Give me something solid for once.*

"Sometimes acting on your own initiative is necessary. Better to remove Lyn from the equation than lament after he gets her killed." Dugan patted his knees and rose.

Caleb narrowed his eyes. "You're convinced Del's legit."

"As certain as you. But if she *were* an Allied ear, her death would still be inconvenient."

Inconvenient. Caleb's stomach tightened.

"The Surge have been rolling through town, bold as brass, slick as Pell Mahr sharpers. You know anything about that?"

Dugan frowned. "Hasn't come to my ears, but I'll have my people check it out."

"You sure the Surge an't still acting for your Inside friends?"

Dugan met Caleb's gaze squarely. "The OBMG prefers having stable warrens at their gates. Valerian is convenient so long as he doesn't get off-world loud. Stirring up the gangs at their gates an't in Insiders' interest."

Off-world loud. The Surge's impersonation of Jonas hadn't only been about steering Del to Pell Mahr. Dugan's Inside cronies wanted Jonas's activism discredited with the Allies.

Dugan stepped toward the door, paused. "I hear Valerian's cutting ground on construction near No-man's land. Not a medical clinic *there*, surely?"

Jonas's new project to salvage the mine trailings the OBMG dumped on their border ... The project remained underwraps until Jonas could take it to a vote.

Caleb's unease spread in his gut like a capsule dissolving.

Perched on the loveseat arm, Kallie wrinkled her nose like she scented his sweat.

"I don't know." Caleb settled deeper into his seat, crossing his arms. "Why?"

"It wouldn't be a terribly defensible location."

"I reckon Jonas'll announce it at some point."

Dugan smiled, a slash of his greedy mouth. "You know, Freth, you seem the sort of sharper who'd do well here. I always reward skilled lieutenants who demonstrate loyalty."

Caleb sucked in a breath. No one joined the Pell Mahr warren except by invitation unless they already had a deep flash well.

Dugan strutted to the door, straightening his glossy green jacket. He paused, shot Caleb a speculative glance. "I wonder if Valerian can claim as much?"

Dugan swept out.

Caleb's breath expelled in a choppy burst.

18

Many believe Rynet a sister race to Humans. To me, we are distant cousins, made compatible by the barest chance. Studying a Human heart frustrates like a view through a distortion field, yet moments of clarity can be pure exhilaration.

Tam leaned against the bar, studying the glass between his hands, face downturned but ears perked. A group at the table behind him was whispering—not softly enough to escape Rynet hearing.

"… Yanear Block. Looking for a deep score … the place."

Not the first whiff he'd gotten about dodgy activity in Yanear. Rumors of strange figures lurking around the industrial block—leery of curious eyes. Strange figures could well describe the patchworks. It was a weak thread, but all Tam had after a week exhausting himself with stealth work outside of Del's grueling schedule.

The reminder of Del drew his gaze to the end of the bar where she stood in a chirping huddle with Nan and Kimber. He should escort Del home to free his evening to chase his lead but didn't want to drag her away when she showed her first glimmer of fun.

The Bar hummed with cheerful voices and clinking glasses, no one too drunk or rowdy yet. No pockets of dark intention. He let himself relax a notch.

Suspiciously girlish twitters came from Del's group. Tam would have sworn all three too sensible to giggle.

Kimber said, "Nothing like a little bunk-bouncing to shake off stress."

"IWA cautions us against engaging in sexual encounters with the natives before we understand the customs."

Tam choked on a swig of fretha, a bitter spike down his throat, and darted Del an incredulous look.

Kimber's brows shot up.

"You know." Del gave an airy wave. "What the rules are."

"You got nothing to worry about. Anything goes." Nan pressed her knuckles over a grin.

"Well, that sounds easy," Del said dryly.

"Good. So, who can we pick for our Doc?" Kimber surveyed the crowd over Del's laughing protest.

Like they'd find any tavern-slob in Del's league.

Kimber pointed. "How about him?"

"Too handsome by half."

Handsome? The man looked like he'd spent one too many days near a reprocessing pit without a shower.

Kimber was her own breed of baffled. "You don't like handsome?"

"I prefer a bit of physiological *character* in a man." Del draped herself against the counter.

"If you don't like 'em easy on the eyes, I guess you an't interested in our boy over there." Kimber tipped her mug in Tam's direction.

Tam stiffened, Kimber's amusement slapped, too hard-edged. Lately, he'd relaxed around her, thinking maybe she accepted *him*, not the ugly flap about him. *Fool.*

"Tam?" Oblivious, Del slanted him a look, gleaming with the assumption of a shared joke. "Bad enough being called the 'toff doc.' I'd hate to add crib-robber."

All three women burst into unmistakable giggles.

A familiar wrongness clawed Tam's insides. He stalked to the shadowy end of the bar.

Del trotted at his heels.

Unthinking, he sketched an *ah'nea* warding gesture then flattened his hand to his thigh.

"Did I upset you?" Del's arms crimped her ribs.

"No." Shit, she was sensitive. And she didn't know the half of what it meant for him to pass as an exotic, the assumption he was for sale.

Del opened her mouth. Shut it.

"Shall we head back?" she said finally.

"What? Done casing the place?" He joked as if untouched by the tension.

"All zipped up."

He didn't bother asking what that meant.

As Tam snagged his jacket and steered Del around the counter, the tavern door opened, admitting a tall, cloaked form. Tam paused. The person's stiff-jointed movements stirred his memory. As if drawn by his gaze, the figure headed straight toward him.

Tam tucked Del behind him, flaring to readiness. The person stepped close, lifted their hood to expose an old Trenabic face.

Recognition sucked the air from Tam's lungs. Skin like soot-streaked resin, two pebble-round nobs for a nose, a lipless mouth—every line of the face familiar yet transplanted from another existence. Memory of the Xeno's spicy air and cacophony of disparate tongues arrested his senses. He blinked, a convulsive clenching of his eyelids, to drive it away.

Was he hallucinating? How could Golalya be *here*?

After his encounter with the Arnec, her gentler Trenabic features struck him. The sister races had similar facial structures but for the nose —Trenabic had two round nostrils instead of four slitted ones.

Golalya raised a six-fingered hand and touched her opposable thumbs together, the symbol for peaceful purpose. "Need doctor," she said in broken Common.

He clenched his jacket in his fists. "For you?"

"For friend." She stared at Tam as if imprinting his image in her mind.

Del's aura spiked with anxiety. Doubtful she had experience treating non-Humans.

"The Xeno is five warrens away." He spoke to Del, but his focus stayed on Golalya. The skin above her round, maroon eyes had age-paled since he'd last seen her.

"Girl here in this warren." Golalya insisted.

Del licked her lips nervously, lifted her chin. "I'll do what I can."

Tam stared at Golalya, knowing he needed to talk Del out of this, unable to open his mouth. How many nights had he agonized over whether his *ssura* still lived? But agreeing could only force him to walk a precarious line between his old life and new.

Dazed, he found himself trailing Del and Golalya out to the street. Golalya's rusty and dented sidecar motorcycle crouched along the curb. Craning her neck in warning to those lurking close, Golalaya disarmed the shock trap she left to keep jackers away, and swung her long, stick-like leg over with a ripple through her robe.

"Ride on side," she said.

The sidecar was sized to a Trenabic—plenty of legroom, but narrow. Tam squeezed in and settled Del in his lap. Her sweet fragrance welled up along with a salty hint of sweat. Nerves.

The clunker coughed a plume of smoke as it surged down the street. Tam twisted his neck toward Golalya, but her robe's coarse fabric flapped over his face.

They pulled up to a pod complex, a narrow, four-story structure bracketed by two shorter buildings. A salvage company's worker dormitory. Many of the Maze's small Trenabic population worked salvage. Trenabics' tough hides enabled them to tolerate the harsh conditions better than Humans, but they were hard-used, treated more like animals than sentient beings.

A work connection must have lent them this pod—no Trenabic would dare live outside the Xeno warren because of Human attitudes and their own. The place nettled Tam's skin.

He wanted to ask Golalya what she was thinking. Couldn't. He might use the Trenabic language. Del wouldn't understand, but for sure she'd find it curious. He couldn't risk anyone connecting him to non-Humans —drawing conclusions and questioning his "exotic" cover.

"Come." Golalya's broad hand closed over Tam's arm, urging him forward. He couldn't have spoken if he'd wanted. Seven Hells, but he'd missed her. He only now realized how much.

They were led up a grim and dusty stairwell to a pod. The pod was bare except for a privacy screen. Through the semitransparent fabric, Tam made out a figure on a pallet and a tall *ssura-ri*, a matriarch by her size. A cloying, organic scent filled Tam's nostrils. Trenabic musk mingled with blood.

Golalya motioned him to wait and ushered Del behind the screen. Del shot him an anxious look, but he couldn't follow. To Trenabic, the sick room was no place for a male.

Tam squeezed his eyes closed, raked his hands through his hair. *Four years* since he'd been home. The scent of suffering was foul, and yet it filled him with longing. Golalya had nursed many of his "cousins," treated their injuries and ills. Did all she could for Tam's.

"Let the half-breed die." Those Trenabic words, spoken with a hard clack of the tongue, snapped open Tam's eyes. But the *ssura-ri* didn't mean him.

More Trenabic words ticked, inaudible through the screen, but indicating a shriek. Trenabic vocalized anger through clacking the tongue against the pallet. The *ssura-ri* was furious. Her rage filled the living pod, a contrast to Golalya's calm.

"My One …" A whimper from the patient seeped through the screen, the tinnier pitch of an adolescent.

"The baby is too heavy and is straining the birthing pouch." Del's voice was a stroke of warmth, a disorienting contrast to the distress charging her aura.

Tam shrunk against the wall. A pregnancy.

"Are there facilities for Trenabic in the First Ring? A hospital could safely incubate the baby," Del said, unaware of the ugly contest being waged around her.

Tam pressed his spine against the wall. Outlined through the screen's fabric, the females created a grim shadow-puppet performance. Del knelt at the pallet's foot, childlike compared to the tall Trenabic matriarchs. The *ssura-ri*, the patient's mother, paced beside the pallet. Golalya poised at its head.

"Please." The youngling arced up, reaching for Del. "Save … One."

Del's aura wrenched as she leaned to accept the touch. "I'll do all I can."

Golalya eased the youngling down with a scolding trill.

"Let it die, the disgusting thing," the *ssura-ri* snapped in Trenabic, her disdain nothing Del could comprehend. "It will be an anvil-headed brute like its sire."

The baby's father was Arnec, the source of the *ssura-ri's* spitting shame. Cloistered together in the Xeno warren, the sister races were unable to spread and provide the genetic variety needed to thrive, many clusters were stunted. Nature found its own route.

After a long pause, Del spoke, careful and reluctant, "The birthing pouch is tearing, not detaching."

"Cut thing out. Let it die." The *ssura-ri* said in her garbled Common.

Tam shut his eyes against Del's shock. *Del, what were you thinking, taking this on?*

Too much emotion thickened the air. He struggled to silence his breath.

"My One," the youngling panted like a litany.

Small, *ur*-females like her could bear one child in their lifetimes. Their birthing pouches detached during labor and didn't regenerate.

"Your daughter is in danger, too," Del whispered. "I must put her in stasis, get her to a hospital."

"Hospital not take. Let thing die." Then in the Trenabic tongue to Golalya. "Why bring us here? What can your mixed-blood stray understand of mothers? *His* took flight with smuggler scum at first chance."

Tam wheezed as if he'd been kicked in the chest.

Golalya swelled to her full height, full of anger. "Stop this foolishness. Let the doctor save your daughter."

"The fool has wasted her pouch." Xeno clusters had too few matriarchs, capable of bearing multiple children, which made every birth pouch precious. "Veya's half-breed will shame our cluster! It is an abomination. It must die. It will die." Clack, clack, the words drilled deep.

Tam choked, couldn't breathe. Eyelids flared wide, he dove from the pod, out into the complex's dingy hallway. Deep pulls of his lungs eased his panic. He paced, fighting to block out emotional echoes from inside. The Trenabic signatures affected him like sinister whispers, Del's frantic anguish screaming over them.

Why had his *ssura* brought this to him? Golalya had been clear he could never return to the compound. Males left to join new clusters at seventeen, a near-total separation from their birth families. There'd been no possible cluster for alien mix-breed Tam, so Golalya had cast him into the Human world.

God, it had hurt. It still hurt.

Yet, without Golalya, Tam and his mother wouldn't have survived his birth. She'd convinced her cluster to accept them. She'd delivered him into the world, stepped into the role of mother when Tam's disappeared. She'd called him her second because only one of her birth-children had survived to adulthood.

He'd never imagined Golalya would seek him in the Human warrens, never imagined she could learn anything about him from the Xeno.

Tam forced his focus to his surroundings. A metal-walled corridor, lights winking from a net overhead, broom marks scoring the dust-thick floor as if an attempt to clean had only smeared the grime. A dark stairwell opened like a hole across from the door.

Time crawled until a flare of grief etched through Tam's mental shield.

A few excruciating minutes later, the pod's door opened. Del stepped out, ignoring him like part of the wall. By her turbulent emotional signature, both youngling and baby were dead.

Tam's arm was seized from inside the door. Golalya peered out at him. "You are well, my second?" He strained to catch her gritty whisper.

He covered her leathery hand with his to hold her there. "*Ssura,* please. My mother …?"

"Peace, my second. Forgive Veya's mother. She spoke falsehood out of fear." Golalya squeezed his arm, pulled away, vanished back into the room.

Several ragged breaths passed before he jerked his attention back to the hallway.

Del was gone.

Tam dove down the narrow stairs, blundered into her standing outside the building's entrance. The wind had whipped up, carrying an ominous sulfuric smell. A serious storm was about to hit. He'd been too snared by the drama to notice the encroaching march of thunder. He glared skyward. Orange streaked the clouds. A storm outside the planet-scaping, triggering a storm within.

He swore viciously. The timing couldn't be worse.

"We need to go," he said to Del's forbidding back.

She stepped into the street. Like some discordant orchestration, the sky opened in a slashing torrent.

Tam dove back under the awning.

Del froze.

"Hey, Del!"

She seemed not to hear him.

Lightening flared, crazed flashes over the scene.

Tam surged into the downpour, instantly drenched down his jacket's collar. Hissing, he grabbed Del's shoulders and dragged her under the shelter. "What the hell?"

He flinched at her face, stony and drained of color. A well of pain lay beneath her shock. It impacted Tam like a blow. All this while, he'd been searching for the hidden darkness in her, the catch. Now, it struck him that there wasn't one.

He'd witnessed her glow with joy at saving a life, a pride-shaded reaction. Far more powerful to witness her grieve over failure. And the agony she held back was for non-Humans. That awareness churned inside him as he studied her.

The wind bit, bitter punishment on his soaked skin. A storm like this could rage for an hour. They needed safe shelter. His place was closest but would mean a slog through the deluge. Nowhere else to go, short of reentering that death room.

"We can't stay here." No reaction. "*Del.*"

Lightning blazed again, sparking strange flashes in her eyes. Her chest heaved with the effort to collect herself; her lips pressed whitely.

He found himself putting his arms around her. "You did everything you could, angel. Now we *have to go.*"

She pulled back with a soundless yes.

Del kept her insecurities tightly controlled. Her vulnerability now was unbearable. Heart kicking in protest, he haltingly bent in *ah'lir*, to press his cheek to hers. Her face tilted toward him, and their lips brushed instead, sending a quiver over his nerves.

Grasping her wet knot of hair with one hand, he kneaded her back with the other. "Hey, snap out of it."

She relented, the barest easing of her spine. Taking her hand, Tam tugged her into the storm, sticking as close to the buildings as safety allowed.

They stumbled along an eternity before his pod complex came into view. He half-carried Del up the stairs and through the roof access. Wrestling her up the ladder to his elevated single-unit nearly defeated him. Clumsily, he released the locks and ushered her inside.

He collapsed against the door, panting. Del stood close, a puddle forming under her feet.

Once he caught his breath, he shed his jacket and boots. "We need to get dry."

"All right." Her voice was hoarse, her teeth chattering.

He crossed the efficiency to the washroom and dove into fresh clothes. Fishing out towels and a robe, he hurried back to Del.

"Here." He handed her the robe and a towel.

She accepted them robotically.

Turning to give her privacy, he dried his hair with the other towel then tossed it onto a chair in the meal-nook. The only sound was Del's teeth clinking together.

"Relax, angel. I won't peek. Use the washroom if you like."

"I k-know th-that." Her voice spun him back to her. She stood, clutching the fabric to her chest. Tears rolled down her cheeks.

"It wasn't your fault."

Her tears fell faster. "It's s-senseless. The m-mother wouldn't let me t-transport the girl or p-put her in s-stasis."

"You did what you could." He stepped closer, tugged the towel from her grip. "Sorry, I don't have a dryer."

He awkwardly toweled her hair. It came loose from its bun in long, soggy locks. Leaving the towel covering her hair like a head-scarf, he squatted down, unlaced her boots and slipped them off. He tugged her jacket from her shoulders, letting it squelch to the floor.

"You're freezing cold. You need to change."

"What am I doing here, Tam?" she whispered.

He froze, snared by the doubt in her eyes until she blinked, releasing his gaze.

Grasping the towel, he rubbed it down her neck. "You help people. You just can't help everyone."

Her body started to quake. Pain rose through the cracks in her shock. He impulsively moved to ease it, kissing her forehead, her cheeks. Her skin was a damp shiver against his lips. He slid the zipper of her jumpsuit down and peeled off the wet garment. Gingerly, he began to dry her skin, careful not to touch her with his bare hands.

What are you doing, fool? He tossed the towel with a jerk of his wrist.

Tam took the robe from her slack fingers and slid it over her shoulders, stroking the column of her back as she leaned into his chest.

"Hush, Del," he whispered, and her anguish burst out, stunning him. The emotional release shattered her habitual mental control, flooding him with layers of sensation. Her fingers dug into the fabric over his ribs as sobs escaped her.

His experience of her pain became achingly close to pleasure. Her small form nested against him, sending a delicious tingle through him, a ripple of pure peace. Her head fit against the crook of his shoulder. He pressed his face against her damp hair, breathing in the salty, soapy fragrance as he gently rocked her.

When she stopped crying, Tam eased back. He avoided her face as he wrapped her in the robe, swung her into his arms, and laid her on his pallet. He covered her neck-to-toes with a blanket. "Rest, now. There will be more people for you to save tomorrow."

She closed her eyes as if utterly spent.

Sighing with relief and loss, Tam curled up on the floor, resting his head on the cushion beside her, careful not to disturb her. Her breathing became deep, steady, soothing. He lowered his own lids, not to sleep, but to drink it all in.

19

Del lay wrapped in soft warmth that smelled clean, vaguely of soil. Her pallet stretched over an eclectic mosaic of tiles. She traced one vivid purple square with her fingertips, a slick synthetic material, chill against her skin. Awareness fizzed through her, lifting her gaze.

Light flowed from the ceiling into the center of the space, leaving the periphery dim. Tam stood, softly spotlighted, his back to her, one hand resting on a chair. His hair spiked off his head, a richer, glossier pelt than natural for a Human. He wore a short-sleeved shirt, exposing the milky pallor of his skin. Loose, dark trousers draped past his ankles to feet that were bare—long and narrow, the toenails black. A sliver of his profile was exposed, tipped down as if he studied his toes.

Del had a dizzying, absurd thought that he wasn't real. He didn't look real.

No surgical alteration can achieve that effect.

She'd known that, simply hadn't acknowledged it—her burning curiosity about him seemed a violation of his privacy, even sealed in her own mind.

Tam's head jerked up.

"'Morning," he said, face averted, his voice husky, as if he'd rested poorly. Of course, he had. She'd taken his bed.

Tam padded across the room and bent over a storage bin against the wall.

"Morning," she echoed as it fully struck her—this was Tam's home. His private domain.

She pushed to seated, absorbing the space with deeper interest. A delicious spice scented the air, watering her mouth. The pallet she lay on rested against one wall, framed by a scattering of brightly colored pillows. So much color. Startling from a man who never wore any, but then Tam disliked drawing attention to himself.

The apartment held a kitchenette with a counter, draw-down table, and two folding chairs. Shelves and storage compartments lined the opposite wall. The ceiling was tall and domed, dominated by a clear bubble of a skylight, keeping the small room airy.

Tam straightened. He'd covered his feet in socks.

The wall he stood before snared her focus. A partial pattern decorated its surface. Irresistibly, she rose, curling her toes against the cold, and stepped up to the mural. A half pinwheel shape, darker in the center, gradually lightening as it spiraled outward, formed of small stones of various shades, from black to clear crystal. Those bits of rock Tam always scooped up when he thought himself unobserved … This was his work. A squat shelf below the mural held jars of stones and white powder that must form the bonding agent.

She reached out to stroke the mural's surface, but aware of Tam tensely watching, dropped her hand. "This is beautiful."

"Well, the wall's stained."

She hadn't noticed the mural last night, or much of anything. The reason for her distraction crashed in, leaving a raw ache in her chest. She braced a hand on the shelf.

"You did everything you could, Del. You know that, right?"

Del straightened. "Thank you." She fluttered her hand as if that could encompass everything—the support, the shelter, the comfort.

So unexpected.

When he didn't respond, she cleared her throat of a lump and pointed to the wall. "Tell me." Something real for once. Anything.

Tam hesitated so long, she feared he wouldn't answer.

"My mother used to say that stones carry stories." He plucked up a pebble from a jar, holding it out to her. It was glassy black. "The history of the earth, the spirit of a land, tales of the people who inhabit it."

Del took the pebble from his palm, her fingertips brushing his. Rolling the stone between her fingers, she explored its smooth texture. "What story would this one tell?" she asked.

"Obsidian, formed during a rhyolitic eruption. I found it on the pavement. There haven't been active volcanos in this part of Galta 4 for millions of years, and see how rounded the edges are? Smoothed by some being's hands. It likely traveled across the planet in someone's pocket—maybe across the stars." Tam studied her with eyes faded to pewter. Those mood-stone irises—too sensitive and complex to have been surgically enhanced.

"Do you see?" Tam asked softly.

"Yes," she replied, a bit dazed. Stories. His mother. "What happened to her?"

"Gone." Tam turned away. "Are you hungry? I have *breya*—um—sweet bread."

Exhaling a silent breath, she managed, "Is that what smells so delicious?"

He scratched a laugh. "I'll take that as a yes."

She trailed him to the meal-nook. With metal tongs, he opened a compartment in the counter, drew out a tray of flatbread.

"You made them."

He shrugged off her surprise, fishing inside a drawer, pulling out foil sheets, and wrapping the bread. "We should take it to go, no?"

She glanced at her wrist-vid, sighing to realize less than an hour remained until her first patient appointment—though she'd wager Tam's concern stemmed more from her curiosity than her schedule. "Yes, I suppose."

"Your things are clean and dry. In the washroom there."

"Thank you." She hesitated, thinking of the Trenabic girl, her desperation for her baby. Such a sick, needless loss. "Are there many non-Humans here?"

Tam stayed focused on his task. "A community in the Xeno warren, mostly Trenabic and Arnec. They take care of their own."

"I see." Del studied his stiffly downturned face.

She hurried to dress in his crude, clean necessary. When she came out, he stood ready at the door, holding her coat.

She cast a last look around his apartment. "I love your place."

"It's shabby." He opened the door, letting the pungent Maze air flow inside.

"It's lovely." She shouldered around him. Apparently, the *slightest* personal comment was off-limits again.

He caught her arm. "Watch your step."

She staggered into him, gasping. The landing outside his door dropped off to nothing; the ground swam meters below them. His lips twitched as he stepped around her and bent over a hand-crank she hadn't noticed. With a rusty scree, a ladder unfolded from beneath the landing.

Legs wobbling, Del followed Tam down the ladder and onto the roof of a larger structure. She gazed up. Tam's home was a soot-streaked module on stilts, resting atop the roof. Like a birdhouse. She smiled. It suited him.

Tam shot her a sour look as if penetrating her amusement.

He yanked a long, hooked rod from the inner seam of a stilt and used it to retract the ladder, an easy, one-handed swing—too easy for his lean frame. Tam Lyn was no cosmetically enhanced "exotic." He only masqueraded as one. *Synth-born.* She'd ignored that possibility, despite the screaming evidence. His unblemished, seemingly pore-less skin was practically a stamp of advanced genetic manipulation.

So chillingly illegal on every civilized world.

"Where are you from?" She'd braved the question during her first week at The Bar.

"Here." Had been his terse reply.

That had to have been a lie. So, why lie?

20

———————

"BLOODY HELLS!" DEL SCOWLED AT THE BROKEN VITAMIN TUBE—THE THIRD she'd broken inserting into a press-syringe. She closed her eyes, breathed until the urge to scream abated.

A tremor ran through her soles. She tossed the tube and clutched her desk, waiting for the mini earthquake to follow.

"Just drill-bite, Del." Tam called from the closet where he was inventorying the meds. "Not Galtan's Rumble."

"I can't imagine how I'd ruddy-well tell the difference!"

"Enough." Tam stalked to the door, poked his head into the hallway. "I'm sorry. The doc an't feeling well. You'll all have—"

"Tam!" She whirled, glaring outrage.

"—first priority tomorrow."

He slammed the door and turned to her with folded arms.

"You can't do that! I've *twelve* more people to see."

He gave her a flat look. "You've been skittish and snappish all day. I'm calling it if you won't. I have some stealth-work to handle."

"*Stealth*-work? What, exactly?"

His eyes narrowed. "Just keeping feelers out for thieves like those patchworks."

She mirrored his expression. "What aren't you telling me?"

He plucked the syringe from her fingers. "*This* needs adjusting. And *you* need to measure your stress level."

"I'm perfectly fine."

"Del," Tam said softly. "Your hand is shaking."

She blinked down, startled to find he was right. "I'm just cold. It's always so bloody cold here."

He tucked a strand of hair behind her ear, a cool, smooth, startling touch. "You're *tired*, angel. You've been pushing too hard after what happened last night. You know it can't go on."

Del sucked in a breath, unable to meet his gaze. When he handed her the diagnose, she stared vacantly at it.

"Please, Del."

She scanned herself, winced at the result. "I'll … catch up on vid-work, rest a bit."

He peered at the diagnose, moved to the supply closet. Gritting her teeth, she accepted the anti-anxiety med he handed her.

"I'm not a child," she snipped as he steered her into her desk chair.

"No more than an hour of vid-work, okay?"

He dragged a blanket from a cot, tucked it around her, then retreated to fix the press-syringe.

Long night and not a crack in *his* temper.

She swallowed her peevishness along with the med and flicked on her vid-tile. Before long, she fought eye-watering yawns that blurred the words.

Delmara reached with her mind, reached and reached, until she was sore with it. Frustration wrecked her focus. Where *was* he?

She shivered, enveloped in her gel-bag chair. The cool, cloying gel reminded her of stasis and awful space-bubble windows. She gnawed her fingernails.

"Are you cold, Delmara?" Her father's voice came as from a distance.

Her flora batted her hand down. "She's only playacting, Mr. Fedelo. She's been like this for hours. Staring off, not minding anyone."

Come on, Jenl! Hear me!

At last, Jenl's voice fizzed through her mind. *Hello, Dlmara.*

His clipped version of her name warmed her like a nickname, though she knew he simply found her name difficult even in his thoughts.

There you are. I've tried for so long.

I am sorry, ett'eren. I was sleeping. It's night here.

Oh. Goodness, but I never get that right.

He didn't react to her peevishness. *Tell me a bedtime story. I love your stories.* His voice brightened like a smile.

Worth her frustration and headache. She smiled back.

Then something went wrong. Jenl began to fade.

Whimpering, she grasped at his traces, but noise overpowered his presence. Not outside her mind, *within.* She burned with angry confusion until she understood. The noise came from another mind. Thoughts, clearer, closer … a stranger's …

TAM KNEADED A PAINFUL CRICK IN HIS NECK. HE'D DOZED OFF ON THE COT, the cost of his sleepless night. *'Seeking trouble invites pain.'* Those words tickled his mind as he blinked away his drowse—a scolding he'd once gotten from *Emere* after he'd skinned his knees in a scuffle. A strange soreness throbbed in his skull. He'd been dreaming of *Emere,* maybe.

Tam shifted toward Del. She'd flopped over her desk, sound asleep. Little wonder, after the tragedy Golalya had drawn them into.

Might be a toss-up whether I seek trouble, or it seeks me, Emere.

Sighing, he crossed to Del and gingerly scooped her up. Confusion seeped into him through Del's aura. She stirred, her breath tickling his neck, but didn't wake. He set her onto the cot and padded to the exam room door.

Time to take care of that overdue stealth-work. He needed to start investigating before darkness fell.

SHE SANG A NURSERY RHYME — HER VOICE, HER WORDS — YET SO REMOTE THEY *might have drifted disembodied through the stars.*

Bring me a stone and give me its story.

Bring me a story baked from the earth.

Bring me a story carved by the ages.

Bring me a story of worth.

Her pale blue fingers dug at the cracked floor, bleeding around the thick black nails. She needed stone—a concrete fragment would do—something real to grasp.

A pasty Human face with eyes like black holes glowered down at her crumpled body. "You're the reason for the noise." The voice was pitchy, the face rounded with youth. Little more than a boy.

She squeezed her eyes shut, drawing in her limbs tightly.

Her own son ... She'd been searching for him, singing to him, seeking him with her mind, but her gift was too cursed weak.

"Are you cold?" The Human boy's voice slithered closer, inside her cell now.

She opened her eyes to endure the chill curiosity in his.

Warmth steeped in Human musk dropped over her back, a blanket. The boy's black focus shifted, hunting for adult Humans who would chase him out.

"More," he whispered. "Sing again."

Sing again.

The sensation of pressure on her nape, like a hand stroking it, shocked Del's eyes open. She was slumped on the cot on her side, one hand beneath her cheek. The dream clung to her, making the warm tone of her own skin startling.

"Stones carry stories," she whispered.

Tam's words. That glimpse of his home life had crept into her dreams.

The dream grew slippery as she reached for it, but she remembered her blue-tinged skin, a rhyming song, intense black eyes.

Her thoughts blurred. Soreness pooled above the base of her skull. Dark familiarity seeped into her. The snippet of memory woven into her dream, the delusion of speaking to another child in her head—not a memory she cared to resurrect.

I can't afford to become ... distractable.

An image strobed, a boy with shale-blue skin and a bristle of black hair. Del stretched her fingers as if she could capture it.

Little wonder if she met Rynet in her dreams. Tam's genetic enhancements evoked them. All her buried curiosity about it …

With a groan, Del sat up. The blanket had slipped to the floor. She blinked around the room. No Tam. Had she heard the door click shut as she'd woken?

She rubbed her arms, uncertain why she was so unsettled—more unsettled by Tam's absence than the eerie dreams.

Tam dangled from the roof of the large, metal-framed structure by his grappling cable, working open a vent cover under the eaves. His back bumped the neighboring structure, the gap between too narrow for an alley, but it kept him hidden. The need for nimbleness had meant leaving his jacket behind, and the chill wind pebbled his skin. An odor like burnt tar seared his nostrils, a mild sample of what was to come. He drew a mask over his mouth and nose.

He was finally investigating the tip about suspicious activity around Yanear Block. Local gossip had led him to this recycling pit, tales of equipment brought in by skulking, cowled figures. Plenty of reason patchworks might shroud their faces.

When the vent cover loosened on three sides, Tam bent it open and peered inside. The space held an attic's musty gloom but more expansive. Light came diffuse and subdued from below. He blinked until his eyes adjusted. Exposed metal beams ran under the pitched ceiling. Lights were strung jaggedly beneath the beams, leaving the space above thickly shadowed.

It would do.

Tam squeezed through the vent, stretching over a beam broad enough to rest his knees on. He choked as he took in the scene below—a vision of *Seventh Hell*.

A steaming drum with a molten-glowing mouth, like a giant cauldron canted to one side… A conveyor belt trailed from it, a large sooty vat at the opposite end. Equipment littered the floor. Metal planking piled against one wall. Figures muffled in protective gear scurried like Hell Masters' minions, using a massive winch to tilt the cauldron, pour molten liquid into molds lying over the conveyor belt. The belt took the glowing bars in the molds and dumped them into the vat, shooting up plumes of steam. Heat blew over Tam, stirred by a chrome fixture above the cauldron that sucked up the charred air with a rhythmic whooshing. Scrape, scrape, clank, clank—minions plied shovels over glittering scrap piles, tossing heaps through the cauldron's rear flap. They tugged a chain pulley to release a fresh supply from a chute in the wall.

A nerve-raking jangle.

The air charged around him, a familiar presence enveloping him. *Emere.*

Tam closed his eyes, pictured her face, her eyes crystalline with absorption, her voice soft as she story-told.

In the Lore, the High Ones created the Seven Hells to punish the wicked—an extra-dimensional plane equipped with every earthly fire and peopled with worshipful dark-ones to torment the unredeemable.

A loud clang snapped him back to reality.

Ver'ela evoked snippets of memory—more than memory in vividness, more than memory in meaning. *I get it, Emere. Warning noted.*

Tam compressed his body against the ceiling juncture. The ceiling stretched about fifteen feet high, hardly a secure hiding spot. The structure was windowless and too open to make sneaking through the doors possible. This had been his only option.

The air should be worse, considering that hellish furnace. Tam drew down his ocular to magnify the view. A gray tinge shrouded the space around the furnace, as if invisible walls kept the smoke concentrated there. Metal tubing inset into the concrete floor demarcated the equipment. A field-tech filter. Rare in a crude facility like this.

Across from the furnace, stood a long workbench. Three people in coveralls bent there over tasks their backs blocked from view. A man leaned, cross-armed, against the wall beside them, a club strapped to his hip. Forced labor?

Industrial fixtures or vehicles swallowed the space beside the bench, shrouded in covers. A wide rolldown metal door faced them, closed.

Opposite the rolldown lay a makeshift lounge area with a table, chairs, and a sofa. Tall box-fans fenced it, adding a low hum to the noise. Four men hunched around the table gaming with sweat-gleamed brows. Another sprawled on the sofa. These men ignored the suited workers as if the two groups were separated by a wall.

No sign of Callet's crew.

Tam increased the zoom on the gamers. Not enough light to get a bead on their faces.

The man on the sofa arched up—not a man, a woman—a tube top binding her chest, a shock of metallic gold hair standing in spikes from her head. Tam recognized her with a burst of startled satisfaction, Torx, the Surge crew chief.

Tam fixed an audio fiber in his ear and slid onto his belly, pointing the receptor toward the gangsters. He winced, first at the amplification, then at what rode through it—the men bragging how swagger scored free thrills. The factory clamor made deciphering their drivel a head-pounding effort. Tam's perch made for a precarious stakeout.

Sooty heat stroked fingers of sweat down his nape.

Hell with this. He'd convince Jonas to plant a proper ear here—uncover what rot the Surge were about here, maybe nothing to do with the patchworks.

As he scooted backward to leave, a figure strode through the main entrance, Torx's second, the pockmarked thug, Fuse. Tam hesitated.

Fuse crossed to Torx. "… was her, all right. Recognize …"

Torx flared straighter as Fuse spoke, then sprang from the couch. A weapons belt was slung around her waist above belled, red trousers and tight white ankle boots. The spikes of her hair quivered like angry whiskers as she began pacing. "Nena …?"

Her other men paused their card game to study Torx, alert to the anger churning her movements.

A rictus warped Torx's face. "If … plan. … she's with Valerian."

Jonas's name lured Tam to slide closer.

"Hey!" A shout froze him in place. "Something's up there!" A worker scaling the furnace frame gestured wildly.

Hissing, Tam slapped up his ocular, shoved toward the vent.

The gangsters scrambled below.

He worked his feet into the opening.

A bang shattered the air. The vent cover drove against his leg. Tam clung to counter its bruising force—a projectile bouncing off the metal. He jerked his gaze down. Torx stood below, leveling a gun. *Lethal-armed?!*

Torx shifted her grip and took aim. "Dance for me, little bug!"

Tam sprang to a parallel beam, his heart clogging his throat. The round ricocheted behind him. He moved on instinct, leaping from beam to beam. Nowhere to go. No chance to draw his crossbow.

Hoots nipped him from below—the stimps urging Torx on, making sport of it.

Tam dove and dodged until his breath became an acid burn in his chest. Pain stabbed up his wrist. He missed his purchase, went plunging.

Twisting in the air, Tam managed to land heels down. Impact lanced up his legs. He planted on his butt with a cry.

"Freeze, fool!"

Dazed, Tam stared into Torx's triumphant eyes.

"Well, if it an't the bastard who snooped into our business with that toff. The color of your face-paint is different, but I recognize your moves." The gun primed with a click. "What should we do with a nosy sneak who keeps getting into our stuff?"

Tam cringed, tucking his numb wrist against his side. His temples throbbed beneath his ocular, vice-like over his head.

"Hey, that's Valerian's exotic, his NG sneak." Fuse sidled up to Torx, giving Tam a visual scour. "Rub that char off his face, and you'll see he's pale as a corpse underneath."

Torx rocked back on her heels, eyeing Tam's weapons harness. "Pretty toys, boy." Then to Fuse she said, "This changes things."

"Don't get any ideas," Fuse muttered. "He's jumped *right* into our laps. Let's kill him and send our patron his head."

Tam scrambled back, pure pointless instinct. A booted foot against his spine halted him, a stimp lurking behind him.

"You owe me one of these." Torx whipped the rapier from her hip, brandished the tip, a shallow slice through the neck of Tam's shirt, grazing his collarbone.

The scratch burned, but Tam didn't shift his focus from her gloating face.

She shrugged. "Easy enough to make more."

"Those drudges end-shift and clear out any minute," Fuse said like a kid half-eager, half-wary of his mam's reaction. "We can take the head, melt the rest in the furnace."

Take the head … Tam's limbs went nerveless against the floor.

"We're playing this piece. We'd be stupid not to." Torx stared at Tam as if assessing a cut of meat. "A deeper strike to Valerian than if we just kill him."

"But the patron—"

"—will get what he needs. More than one way to skin a cril." Torx rose, elation surging through her aura. "Strip his weapons, Fuse. Add 'em to our stash." Torx jerked her head toward the living area.

Fuse yanked away Tam's crossbow and tasers, tossed them on the sofa but they might as well have been on the moon.

Tam closed his eyes. His body ached with the promise of deep bruising. The heat withered. His lungs spasmed against the charred, sweat-ripened air.

Why had he pressed his luck? Fool to ignore *Emere's* warning.

21

———————

THE NG LOUNGING BY THE BACKROOM ENTRANCE JERKED TO ATTENTION.

Del blinked up from her vid to find a figure standing at the bar. She startled even before she recognized his gaunt face and invasive black stare. The Fet enforcer. He studied her, elbow cocked against the counter —confident, alert.

She leaned away as if he crowded her, though he stood two stools away.

"Dr. Marks," he said in that flat, cool voice she hadn't forgotten.

His long, black coat was parted, revealing an equally black shirt that exposed a collar bone—borderline emaciation but no obvious signs of vitamin deficiency in his skin or hair.

Del swallowed the misplaced impulse to ask a diagnostic question. She surveyed the taproom but didn't spot his entourage. "Good afternoon, Mr. Belek."

Belek's long, tapered fingers drummed the counter's edge. Artisan's hands. The absurd thought snapped her focus back to his face.

"I wonder how you're faring here," he said.

His stare, those inky eyes, like the ones in her dream …

Belek had made a strong impression the night she'd blundered into him. Many frightening characters here appeared in her nightmares. But the coincidence of him being here while she'd dreamt iced her stomach.

Distraction spilt the truth from her mouth. "I'm managing."

"This is a deadly place, particularly for someone like you."

"Are you … threatening me?" she whispered.

"No." He smiled thinly. "After all, your patients are my porridge."

"I'm not quite sure what you mean."

"The workings of a place an't that different from the workings of a body, no? Parasites only thrive when the host does."

His crude irony turned her stomach, but Del itched with the conviction a galaxy of complexity moved inside this man's skull.

"And if the host grows strong enough to fight off the parasites?"

Belek laughed, looked away as if she'd startled the reaction from him.

His gaze clicked back to her. "I'd go back to your safe Central Planet if I were you."

"That's not a threat?" She dug her hands into her thighs, shooting a glance toward the NG who watched alertly from the backroom door.

"You'll know if I'm threatening you." Belek's lip curled. "I'm quite good at it."

Pushing off the bar, he turned away.

Del breathed through a knot of fear—worse, the realization she'd wasted an opportunity. "Then explain." Her voice hit a bleak note.

Belek spun, narrow-eyed. He stepped so close she smelled the herbal scent on his clothes, detected the gleam of his serpentine earring through the dark fall of his hair. Her neck tightened. She held herself rigid against the urge to shrink, against the searing flare of her headache.

"In you, Valerian has what no other entity here possesses—no other warren, no gang, no high-nosed Maze-toff. How they react will be as varied and unpleasant as covetous behavior in individuals. They will not see you as a person. They will see you as an asset. Worse, they will see you as a *symbol*." His brow furrowed as he pivoted away. "It was foolish to come here alone."

Del rocked back like he'd shoved her.

"Something more I can do for you, Belek?" Jonas's voice made Del jump.

He stood inside the backroom door, watching.

Belek tipped his head to Del, his mouth cynically curved, then strode toward the exit. "Just keep in mind what we discussed."

Del wondered if Belek directed his words at Jonas or her—perhaps them both.

"You okay?" Jonas approached; his expression crimped with concern.

"Fine."

"What did the enforcer want?"

Had Belek been threatening her? No. He'd been warning her. Why?

She studied her hands, tightly laced in her lap. "What exactly is an enforcer?"

Jonas leaned on the counter, a posture that mimicked Belek's. "Works with the Fet directors, the gang's top leaders, to keep discipline in the ranks. He also negotiates with me and other warren leaders when needed."

"What do gangs negotiate about?"

"Our rules. And theirs."

Del expelled a breath. "I'm not judging you. I'm asking a simple question."

She felt his assessing regard, refused to meet it.

"I wish I had a simple answer. We've carved a community here out of chaos. The OBMG doesn't want us here, but they're not willing to wipe us out. They're not quite willing to let us wipe each other out, either."

"They would step in if things devolved into open conflict," Del interpreted flatly.

"Big gangs like the Fet avoid pushing us that far. And we avoid pushing them."

"It's a political system of sorts," she said, too sharp.

"Yeah. You could say that." Jonas sighed. "What did Belek want?"

"I suppose he was curious. I *am* curious, after all." Del could share Belek's warning. Ire over Jonas's caginess stopped her, along with the conviction it wouldn't be anything new to Jonas.

Tense silence before Jonas asked softly, "There something I need to know?"

She met his eyes, found them as unrevealing as she expected. Jonas, Tam, Nan—everyone here—fed her the bare minimum about themselves and their world. The gang enforcer had revealed more information in the span of a minute than her "friends" had shared in weeks. For whatever reason.

"Del?"

"No."

Jonas straightened. Del glared away from him, sensing a lecture coming—he'd talk her around in that simple, clever way he had.

The Bar door slapped open. A woman tripped inside. Her face twisted with entreaty, makeup tracked down her cheeks. "Boss! I need your help."

Afternoon hung quietly on the tavern, no patrons and Jonas away. The yeasty smell of brewing ale was potent; Del noticed it less when the tavern filled with bodies and competing aromas.

The woman who'd burst into the bar, dripping all over Jonas, had begged his help to deal with roughs demanding protection money from her shop. He'd gone with a contingent of NG to investigate, leaving Aden in charge of The Bar. The redhead sat across the taproom with two other NG, bent over a vid-tile.

Nan stood before the serving counter, leashed emotion hardening her jaw. Her fingers traced the scar on her cheek like a nervous habit. "That man thinks everything bad under this piss-poor sun is his job to fix."

Del had caught the baleful look Nan gave the shop owner although she couldn't interpret it. Jonas and Nan didn't seem romantically involved; her affection with Kimber made Del assume her heart lay there. "Jonas needs to take the threat seriously, doesn't he?"

"Jonas's every spare credit goes into the warren. Folk take it as their right that he looks after us." Nan fixed penetrating eyes on her. "You're a lot like him."

Del frowned, unsure of Nan's meaning. "I'm hardly that self-sacrificing."

"You might be worse." Nan's gaze intensified, as if she wanted Del to read meaning she refused to verbalize. "He could use someone like you to … support him."

Heat rushed Del's face. "Jonas is not the *least* interested in me that way."

"That's too bad." Nan swiped at a moisture ring marring the counter.

"I'd think he has enough 'physiological character' for you. He deserves a life outside *this*."

Del winced to have her joking words reflected at her in earnest.

The door opened and a smartly dressed man and woman stepped into the tavern. Aden whipped around, scanned them, then lapsed back in her seat.

Del said, "He does, but you know characters like his and mine would clash."

A strained smile creased Nan's mouth. "Both too stubborn, you mean?"

The female customer approached Nan, peering into her face as if she had a right to that intimacy. Long face, dramatic cheekbones, smug mouth. Recognition struck Del like a slap.

Nan jerked back. "Tia?" she choked, gripping the counter's rim like she could rip it off for a weapon. "You were banished."

"Hello, Nena. Been awhile."

Del grasped Nan's arm. "That woman—"

"Don't worry, toff." Torx mock-curtsied, fingers flourishing over her sleek blue jumpsuit. "The *mayor* and I have cozied up." She patted the blonde hair elaborately stacked atop her head.

The man she'd entered with lounged at a table near the door—the goon who'd masqueraded as Jonas.

Torx shifted into the space Nan had put between them, her eyes lasered on Nan's face. "I an't some slag Valerian can chuck like trash." She fingered the three piercings replacing the taper of her brow. "I'm a topper now."

Del cast a wild look around the taproom for Aden. Head dipped over her board, the NG leader didn't notice. Del opened her mouth to call out, but Nan nudged her back.

A cruel smile quirked Torx's mouth. "Where's your pride, Nena? Look at you, hiding behind Valerian's ass."

"Same old sting, eh?" Nan's knotted fists tremored, belying the cool scorn in her voice. "Twine around the top sleaze before slipping a knife between his ribs to take his place."

Torx's chin snapped up. "We share leadership, earned through respect and loyalty."

"Good for you. Now, get out." Nan's eyes burned with hate.

"It hurt leaving you to those warren boys." Menace swelled in Torx. "I never knew Valerian snatched you up. I mourned you for dead."

"No." Nan's voice wavered like she'd been punched in the stomach. "You burned me and left me for dead."

Torx's hand spasmed as if she'd strike Nan. She curled it against her thigh instead, glancing toward Aden who rose from her seat. "All right, Nan?"

Nan surprised Del by waving Aden off. "I'll do."

Aden sat back down but watched alertly.

"What a comedown—from crafting exquisite metalwork to kissing NG ass." Torx arched her brows at Nan. "Your toff do-gooder know you once played bait for sticking men and jacking their shit?"

Nan's eyelids dipped as if she longed to close them but didn't dare.

"It would work, even now, with you marked and wearing ratty sacks to hide your body." Torx's gaze drifted from Nan's baggy t-shirt to her chunky boots then recentered on her face. "Bet you could ask your toff to remove that scar for you."

"The mark stays. I earned it. I'll die with it," Nan whispered.

Torx chuckled, rough with disdain. "Hanging with that uptight prick Valerian given you delusions of honor? *Good*." She flicked Del a look. "You should ask the high-nose where her pretty piece is now. Might be it was sniffing where it don't belong. Might be we're willing to negotiate with *just you*. Or else, by Maze custom, the piece is ours."

Torx's coarse talk confused Del.

"Don't you touch him," Nan said between bared teeth.

Then Del understood. The "it" was Tam. The Surge had him, and Torx demanded Nan exchange herself for him. Del opened her mouth. Nothing came out. She gripped the bar, dizzy with denial.

"Think about it. Not much time before your lump of a chief comes back, and you know he'll never let you go." Torx retreated, calling softly over her shoulder, "Recycling pit at Yanear block."

In seconds, she and her man had gone.

Nan dropped onto a stool, sucking in hard, erratic breaths, staring unseeing at the wall.

"Okay, Nan?" Aden frowned toward them.

"Just some charming on the make."

To Del's ear, Nan's voice sounded stripped raw, but Aden relaxed into her seat.

"Keep quiet," Nan rasped to Del. "Aden can't know. She'll stop me."

"Nan …" Del's thoughts wouldn't connect, like she'd taken a blow to the head.

"It's true. I did that awful shit."

So much made sense now, a harsh truth that woke an ache of loss in Del's chest.

A platitude would be insulting. Del said instead, "Tell me."

"This place … was *hell* before Jonas came. The old warren chief and his cronies carved up what resources we had among themselves and the gangs. Wannabes horded their scraps. Torx and I grew up together, like sisters. We served the rough who ran our block. Knew no other way. When Torx took him down, I was glad—until her schemes got crueler than his. She killed a man, my mark, and I tried to get out." Her trembling fingers traced her scar, its rim a pinkened contrast to her brown skin. "I got caught."

"Jonas saved you," Del said when Nan fell silent.

"From justice. In-kind. Those warren boys meant to string me up."

Del flinched, unable to help it.

Nan rose, stiff-jointed, and stepped behind the bar. She palmed open the safe under the counter, drew out a weapons belt, and strapped it to her waist. "Alert Aden but wait until I'm gone, or she'll interfere."

"Those gangsters will only take you, too," Del whispered urgently.

Nan slashed her a frown. "Stay out of things you don't understand."

"The hells! Tam's in danger because of his duty to me." Del's voice shook over a wave of panic. What would they do to him?

"That's what you pay him a pretty wad of flash for."

"You know he doesn't do it for money now, whatever he pretends." Del's throat tightened over the words.

"One more reason I have to go." Nan cinched the belt at her waist with a jerk.

"We need the NG, Jonas …"

"That slut drew Jonas halfway across the warren, and Aden an't moving on the Surge without his say-so."

"You can't hand yourself over …." Del's voice thinned out. She twisted toward Aden.

Nan lurched across the counter and gripped her chin in hard, calloused fingers, forcing Del to meet her eyes. "Who is Tam to *anyone* here but you and me? Jonas cares, but the warren comes first, and Tam disobeyed him."

Nan released Del, threw on a jacket to cover her weapons, and stalked toward the door. "Aden! Delivery due at the brewing shed. I'll be out back."

Del scanned around her, stupid with uselessness. Her eyes fell on Tam's jacket, hanging behind the bar like a stripped pelt. Her breath stuttered as if she'd taken a thump to the chest.

She dashed behind the bar, snagged the jacket, and flung it on as if she could wear his strength. Spotting Nan's metal bat leaning against the safe, she scooped it up, tucked it under the jacket's long, loose folds.

Nan was already out the door. Del scurried after her.

Aden's head came up as Del gripped the door handle.

"Nan said I could watch." Del ducked out, heart pounding, half-expecting Aden to stop her. *I'm not a prisoner.*

Outside, she didn't see Nan but tracked her fading boot-falls. Del's pulse was a heavy metronome; she moved with it, pure instinct now.

22

*Genetic manipulation is banned on most Human worlds because
of their near-apocalyptic history with it. Rynet wielded the
tool with a lighter touch to enhance our race. Your heightened
senses, speed and agility, the strength of your bones and
tissue. These grant you an advantage among Humans, Tamln.*

DEL AND NAN WALKED IN SILENCE, WHILE THE STREETS WERE SLOWLY
sheeted in darkness. Del tucked Tam's jacket around her to ward the
chill. The garment hung on her frame, the sleeves falling to her fingertips. It smelled like him. She didn't recall noticing he *had* a smell, but the
light, clean scent was distinctly Tam and at once comforted her and made
her ache with worry.

She slid her hand into a pocket. Her knuckles bumped an object. A
laser knife. She traced the hilt in trembling fingers, clasped it.

Nan's voice startled her. "You stay here."

A metal building stood ahead, swallowing the street like a massive
cargo crate.

The Surge's lair.

Nan strode to the doorway, her body a straight wire of tension. Del slunk behind her like a feeble shadow, covering her nose against the acrid stench sharpening the air. Carcinogenic, no doubt.

"Come in, Nena." Torx's voice, glutted with satisfaction, came from inside.

"An't coming in until you send him out."

Del envied Nan's flat calm.

"You'll come, or we'll flay him bloody for you."

A scuffle erupted, threaded with Tam's voice. Fury bunched the lines of Nan's body, knotting Del's insides as if she saw through Nan's eyes.

Nan regained control, drew herself up tall, and crossed inside.

Del stood stupidly. She had nothing to bargain with. No prowess to face armed thugs.

Biting her lip, she stepped after Nan.

Rank, smoke-thickened air pulsed heat over Del, moving to a machine rhythm. The heat shocked, a searing contrast against her chilled skin.

Torx stood before Nan, flanked by two men, one of them Fuse. Four other men lounged at a table beside the entrance, watching with avid eyes. Primitive manufacturing equipment formed the backdrop, a huge drum as the centerpiece, crested with a lava-like glow that only reinforced the gloom.

Del covered her mouth against a cough, scanning for Tam.

"I told you to come alone! What is *she* doing here?" Torx's suit had wilted beneath the sooty heat, her faux civility evaporated. White hair, close-clipped against her skull, replaced the elaborate wig, heightening her ferocity. She wore a metal visor with silver beaded tassels on the rims and glared from behind eyeholes shaped like six-pointed stars.

"Didn't bring her," Nan said. "An't my fault she don't listen."

Torx unzipped her jumpsuit to the waist, a jerk of her hand like a shrug, exposing her cloth-wrapped chest. "Toss the nosy bitch out."

Fuse and his partner—a beefy man with jaundice-rimmed eyes—advanced on Del.

She flailed the bat. "I'll run straight to Jonas, shrieking my head off!"

Fuse pounced. Avoiding her knee-jerk swing, he ripped the bat from her hands, flung it down. She froze against the nightmare-familiar leer that twisted his pockmarked cheeks. He snatched her wrist, tugged her to his sweat-soured body.

"Lay off." Nan cocked an elbow like a weapon, her ferocity equal to his.

"Forget it." Torx waved Fuse back. "We don't need her running to Valerian just yet. Let her watch if it juices her up."

Fighting to quiet her breath, Del slipped beside Nan, who flicked her a frown. Del rubbed off the clammy residue of Fuse's touch.

A prickling woke the soreness in Del's head. Her focus shifted, locked on a pair of wide, glinting eyes. Tam lay against a stack of metal planking, crumpled on his side, arms twisted behind him.

"Bloody animals!" Del darted toward Tam.

His eerily bleached gaze tracked her, startling against the makeup darkening his skin. Crimson smeared the hollow of his throat, his shirt torn below it.

"Gods, are you alright?" Clutching the laser knife in a shaky hand, Del shook Tam's jacket off. She spread the fabric over him, slipping the knife behind his back, over his bound hands.

A grip seized her collar, choking. The blade slid from her fingers. Fuse flung Del to her knees, knocking a cry of pain out of her.

Tam rolled onto his back as Jaundice-eyes yanked the jacket off and tossed it aside.

"Leash your toff, Nena." Torx watched with folded arms.

"Let them go. Honor your deal," Nan said, stony faced.

"I might." Torx cocked her head, mock thoughtful. "But first the sneak needs a good rounding to teach him not to stick his nose where it don't belong."

"They an't letting me out of here." Tam struggled to sit up. "Take Del and go!"

His gaze locked on Nan.

Nan shook her head—launched herself at Torx, tackled her to the ground, knocking her visor off. It clattered across the floor.

Tam exploded up, hands free, the laser knife flashing in one. He sprang at Jaundice-eyes. Blocking the thug's taser swing, Tam smashed his knife hilt against the man's head, sent him sprawling.

The gangsters at the table surged up like startled insects. One rushed toward Torx, the other three toward Tam. He scooped up the fallen taser and jabbed it against Jaundice-eye's shoulder. Dropping the depleted weapon, he faced the others.

Torx slapped Nan's face and fought to tear off her weapons belt.

Del flinched, a phantom sting from that palm against her own cheek. She scrambled to help Nan.

Fuse kneed Del back down with a grunt. He lunged toward Tam, aiming a pulse-stunner.

Tam ducked, but the charge came close enough to stand his hair on end. He felled Fuse with a backhand to the face, before dodging another stun blast from a gangster who'd charged into range.

The other two goons, armed with knives, blocked the way out.

Knocked onto her back, Nan grappled Torx.

Del wobbled to her feet, dizzy against the broil of struggle, torn between her friends.

Tam spun from the goons. He snatched Del's hand and dragged her in a sprinting zigzag toward the furnace.

The gangsters thumped after them.

Del skidded over flooring silted with sooty residue but managed to keep her feet.

A sizzle raked over her nerves, and then they crossed into a thick cloud of fouler air—a field-tech containment mechanism. Del choked, her eyes burned.

Tam rounded the furnace, dropped her hand. Gesturing for her to move back, he whirled to face their pursuers.

The three thugs shifted with anticipation, rushed Tam.

Del flinched as the first man lashed out.

Tam leapt, latching onto a heavy chain that dangled from above. A warning screeched from the wall before debris disgorged from a chute, dumping over the thugs. Sent howling to their knees, they covered their heads. Tam dropped down, sealing the chute. He snagged a shovel from the wall while the groaning men fought free of the pile.

Tam spared Del a glare. "Get back!"

He whipped up the shovel and sprang.

Del recoiled, sliding along the grimy wall. The furnace's heat baked her skin but sweat cold-slicked her clothes to her body. Her mouth tasted of ash. Her breath came in choppy gasps; she was nearly hyperventilating. Her lungs spasmed, and she slapped a hand over her mouth to suppress a cough.

The air tugged at her with a steady sucking noise.

Craning her neck, she made out what must be a ventilator, a shallow nod to worker safety. The ventilator muted the struggle to distant grunts and strikes.

Tam wanted her hidden so he could fight undistracted. She thought of him bound, bleeding on the floor, and the urge to shriek shook her. She'd witnessed him fight before, but the fear for him was raw now, like a blistered burn.

They would kill him if they could.

An awful rage boiled up. She bit her lip against it, hard enough to hurt.

The hells they will.

She glowered through the darkness for a weapon. Her gaze fell on a crimped rod lying beside the furnace, some scrap chucked and forgotten. As she snatched it up, she winced at its heat.

Gunfire shocked through the space, a startling reminder that Tam wasn't the only friend in danger.

Del rushed to the furnace's end, peered around.

Torx and Nan still wrestled by the doors. The thug who'd stayed to cover Torx lay in a heap beside them. Nan had both hands clamped over Torx's gun hand. She'd forced her to discharge the weapon, wasting the rounds.

Del's heart soared with fierce anticipation. Then Torx flung Nan off, shoved her against the concrete. Gaining her feet, she slung Nan's weapons belt over her shoulder.

Del edged further out, craned her neck for Tam. Poised before the scrap pile, he crouched in a fighting stance. A thug lurked paces from Tam, panting, a long blade clenched in his fist. The two other men lay unmoving behind them.

When Torx took in the bodies, the altered odds, she swelled with outrage, glaring at Nan who lifted her head to glare back. "You broke our agreement. Nothing to hold me back now."

Fuse stood at Torx's shoulder, rubbing his head.

Torx slashed a hand toward Nan and tossed Fuse a taser. "Stun her and keep her down."

Nan snarled in resistance when Fuse faced her.

Del twitched with the need to help her, but Torx was stalking toward the furnace, pistol leveled at Tam.

Torx passed Del, ignoring her like dust.

Del flung the rod at her. It struck her arm as she pulled the trigger, scuttling her aim.

Torx jerked the muzzle toward Del, her finger flexing over the trigger.

Del shrunk back, choked down a shriek.

Torx didn't fire. Grinning with cruel satisfaction, she tossed over her shoulder, "Contain the toff, too!"

Torx's threat glided over Del. She turned anxious eyes toward Tam.

Circling in contest with the knife-wielding goon, Tam didn't react to Torx's approach.

Del lunged after Torx as the gun exploded, ripping a cry from Del.

Tam flinched, but the shot missed. Too far for accuracy, perhaps.

Cursing, Torx jammed the gun into her belt—out of ammunition.

Del's relief had no time to form. Tam stood weaponless as Torx closed on him.

Tam bared his teeth, dashed deeper into the structure. Then he tore in a wide arc back toward the living area, darting past Torx, avoiding a swipe of her rapier. The remaining thug thumped after him.

Fingers pincered Del's arm, Fuse looming over her, his craggy cheeks stretched by a grimace of exertion. Nan lay stunned behind him.

He shook Del until her teeth clacked together. "You come to get the rounding we owe you, princess?"

Fuse shoved her onto the floor, crushing her legs beneath him, ignoring her slapping hands. His weight crunched her bones as he hunched over her, pinning her shoulders with his hands. Sweat trickled down his jaw, pooled at his chin, dripped against her throat. She cringed, but her mind raced. *What nerve cluster can I reach?* Arrowing her focus, she jabbed her fingers into his larynx.

Fuse wheezed, clutched his throat with one hand.

She bucked to throw him off, but his knees rammed against her thighs. Pain bloomed, paralyzing. Her hiccupping breaths punctuated the seconds as he poised to strike. With rage-crazed eyes, he clenched his fist.

Fuse blinked. His expression blanked, and his fist flopped to his side. His other hand clamped over his throat, blood welling between his fingers. A nail-like shard protruded from his neck. Gurgling, he thrashed.

Del kicked from under him with a growling shriek.

Across the space, Tam stood, crossbow pointed at Fuse. The thug who'd chased him sprawled at his feet.

A blur of movement made Del flinch. Torx. She gripped Del's waist, hauled her backwards against her heaving chest. Her knife menaced Del's throat. Del swallowed against the need to cough out the ashy air.

Tam, rushing to them with crossbow aimed, froze.

"Fucking impressive." Torx's bicep flexed, and the knife pricked the underside of Del's jaw. "But if you want *this* in one piece, you'll drop the weapon."

Tam glowered with savage stillness.

"*Now.*"

The knife nipped. Del lifted onto her toes, arching from it.

Tam tossed his crossbow to clang against the floor.

"So, what are you?" Torx's revulsion cracked, exposing fear beneath.

"I'm your death," Tam said hollowly.

The knife bit, and Del compressed her lips against a whimper.

"I'd love to slice open her skinny neck." The muscles of Torx's torso convulsed. "Payment for Fuse. My *family.*"

Tam's expression rippled, and Del sensed Torx's confidence refill.

"This your piece, sweets?" Torx's hand squeezed Del's breast. "Bit scrawny, an't she?"

Disgust contracted Del's chest. Blood trickled a warning down her throat.

Tam strained forward, his eyes pinpoints of black. "You'll be choking on every finger you touch her with!"

Torx laughed, the sound edged with rage. It morphed into a startled cry. The knife jerked away from Del's throat. A hand clutched Torx's wrist. Torx wrenched free of the grip, sending the knife clattering across the floor.

Del tripped onto hands and knees.

Nan faced Torx, rapier in her hand, threatening Torx's throat. She'd snatched the weapon from Torx's hip.

Nan's jaw jutted. "My turn to strike you down and leave you for dead."

Torx's surprised expression erased. "Killing me won't erase your guilt or mine."

"*Guilt* don't concern me. Threats to my home, my chief, my people—that won't stand."

"Do it, then." Torx opened her arms as if inviting an embrace. "Or don't—and someday find *me* your chief, your home mine."

Nan's eyes narrowed. The rapier quivered, welling red beneath Torx's jawline. The women squared off, unmoving. A private, wordless clash of wills.

The sleeping factory hissed and creaked. The wounded groaned.

Fuse lay behind them, mouth gaping, his neck a band of gore. Del's focus was drawn there as if to a vid-film horror. She'd witnessed death by violence before, as a doctor, but never like this. Sickness swayed her.

A screech of metal whipped Del around. A machine roar and blur of color burst through an opening gap in the rear door. A huge figure on a sleek wheeled motorcycle streaked across the space, the side panels of his jacket flapping, a flag unfurling from the bike's tail.

Torx lunged to the side, but Nan blocked the move, a warning slash of her rapier. Tam scrabbled up his crossbow.

The motorcycle screeched to a halt, inking a mark on the floor as it canted sideways. A huge man sat atop, his bulging shoulders framing a tonsured head with body art inked down its center. Red symbols decorated the front panels of his charcoal-colored jacket, flapping around his calves. "What's this, Topper?"

Behind him, figures streamed through the door on crude, electric scooters.

Del heaved herself to her feet, too exhausted for fear.

"A *sneak* invaded our digs," Torx said, wary eyes on Nan's blade.

"That's a tidy dodge." Tam leveled his crossbow. "Lethals and forced labor? That breaks Balter's Den rules. Not to mention the Fet's."

The man's lackies formed a semicircle behind him—five—their long, flashy coats and visor-covered faces obscuring gender.

A scowl rippled over his forehead, warping the body art on his bald pate. "I wonder what proof you'll have with bullets in your skulls?"

Del sucked a hiccupping breath at the snub rifle he raised from along his thigh.

"No," Torx called, gruffly. "Patron wants the toff alive for now. She's witnessed this. No point killing the other two and prodding Valerian harder."

The big man's gaze swept the space, the bodies. His shoulders rose like fury built beneath them.

Nan yanked Torx closer, the blade across her throat. "*No point* losing missy topper over this, either."

Riveted on Nan, Tam's clutch on Del's arm made her jump. He tugged her toward the main door, twisted sideways, crossbow rigidly aimed at the gangsters. An inarticulate protest stuttered from Del, but he'd anticipated Nan who shuffled backwards, Torx as hostage.

Del gasped as night air struck like a slap, whisking away the gritty factory haze. Tam propelled her ahead of him into the dark street. Del craned her neck back, anxious for Nan.

Nan shoved Torx from her.

Torx caught the doorframe, propped herself against it. "Later, Nena."

Nan stalked away, lashing the air with the rapier as if her arm sprang free from an invisible bond. She caught up to Tam and Del, and they made their limping retreat.

The hum of normalcy that dropped over them, the familiar cityscape, the people bustling out of view, felt surreal.

Beside Del, Tam's breath rasped with the fitful jags of his chest. His skin sheened—not perspiration—a waxen pallor in the watery light. "Tam?"

His grip weakened, slipped away. His legs buckled, leaving him kneeling on the crumbly pavement. Del's numb hands hovered in a failed reflex to catch him.

Tam's eyes shifted to hers with feral intensity. She sank before him, and he dropped his gaze, the corners of his mouth twitching down. Reaching out, she clasped his hand and rubbed the strangely cool skin.

"Hello," she whispered for lack of anything else. Her voice dragged his eyes, unsettlingly colorless, back to hers.

"I'm sorry." He tugged his hand from hers. "I fucked up."

"Don't be ridiculous." Del laid her palm against his cheek.

Tam leaned into her hand, and the animal tension uncoiled, replaced by a less threatening sort of stillness. Silver haloed his pupils, rippled across his irises. The stunning turn of his eyes sent a rush of physical awareness through her. Startled, she dropped her hand.

Conscious of Nan watching, Del flushed and rocked back on her heels.

"How badly are you hurt?" Del cataloged his visible scrapes and bruises.

"I'm fine. The cut's clotted." Tam winched himself up with a hand on the wall. A more normal demeanor settled over him. "*You're* bleeding." He slung a scowl behind them as if he could strike Torx across the distance.

"It's minor." Though it stung like the blazes. For distraction, she said to Nan, "I thought Fuse tased you."

"Idiot got my belt with the charge. Didn't do more than tickle me."

"We better go." Tam prowled forward, his crossbow loose against his thigh.

"That stuff I said about you being friendlier with Jonas?" Nan murmured, studying Tam's back. "Forget I said it."

Del opened her mouth to demur, snapped it shut. She studied the ground as they trailed Tam, but the itch of awareness didn't relent. As if she could find him, even blinded by the dark.

23

DEL, TAM, AND NAN SHUFFLED LIKE WEARY REFUGEES THROUGH THE BAR'S backroom door.

Del studied shelves jammed with miscellanea, stacks of folding chairs. A large table dominated the room's center. One wall was covered in crude, 2D vid-panels, wires tangled beneath like a nest of snakes. A metal shed leaned against one wall with "Warren Chief" painted on its door.

This was it? Their top-secret "warren-hub"?

Jonas burst from his office, making Del jump.

"Come in then," Jonas growled. Clumps of gray hair stood wildly off his scalp. His pale eyes were shadowed.

They filed tensely behind him into the cramped space. Jonas plunked to a seat behind his desk, a rust-flecked piece topped by an ancient vidscreen. "You all look like shit."

Sweaty, sooty, and bloodied, they did, indeed, *look like shit*.

Del flopped like a wrung-out rag onto a fold-down chair facing the desk. Nan had torn a strip of shirt to staunch the stinging laceration on Del's neck. Her contusions hurt like hells. She'd never endured physical pain this long.

Tam leaned against the wall. Nan shifted on her feet to Del's right, refusing the chair Jonas waved her into.

Jonas said, "Aden got suspicious, alerted me. Just got back here when the block sentry at Yanear reported the trouble."

Tam flipped his hand, a gesture Del didn't recognize. Catching her watching, he tucked his hand against his side.

"Do you have *any idea* of the mess you've made?" Jonas's voice scraped low as if he was too stunned to shout. He pointed a finger at Tam. "I do believe Belek warned you away from the Surge. Then you bust into their digs?"

Del looked at Tam sharply with ire and alarm. He'd kept that from her.

Tam folded his arms over his chest. "The enforcer said he'd handle them. He didn't."

Red mottled Jonas's cheeks.

Nan spoke up before he could. "Tam only did what you recruited him to do."

Jonas didn't acknowledge Nan, as if he couldn't bear to.

"I'd never have gotten caught if that barb hadn't been lethal-armed," Tam said.

"They'll never admit that. They'll come after us for compensation over the infiltration, the damage, and most especially the deaths," Jonas replied.

Del frowned at yet another grim glimpse of Maze politics. Compensation? For thugs?

"What the hell are they doing setting up in a *recycling* pit?" Tam flashed back. "You can be sure they an't getting into the construction-siding business. They were strong-arming folk into working on demons-know-what. Torx mentioned a patron, which means some Pell Mahr or Inside slick is backing them. For what?"

"We've got no proof of anything, do we?" Jonas snapped.

"Those criminals threatened you and your staff," Del said. "Why would you owe them anything?"

Jonas's attention landed heavily on her. "It's hard for an outsider to understand, but can you call them criminals when there's no formal government or rule of law to begin with? We deal with them the best we can."

Hurt squeezed Del's chest. After everything, she still ranked as an outsider. "I realize those gangs are like rival tribes or—"

"What were you thinking, Del?" Jonas warmed up to his anger. "We need you *here*, doing what you're trained to do, not traipsing off in a damned two-woman posse!"

"I'm not a farm animal you can stable at your convenience."

Nan gasped.

Jonas sat straighter. His gaze pinned Del. "No. You're not. But I'm responsible for protecting you, and it's a *hell* of a lot harder if you fling yourself into danger intentionally."

Unable to argue against his logic, she swallowed a retort.

After an excruciating silence, Jonas said, "I'm asking you, Del, what happened today. Apparently my most trusted feel the need to lie to me."

Del stiffened, her gaze sweeping Tam and Nan.

Jonas turned to Nan. "Did you think I hadn't recognized her from all the reports? Just *tell me*."

Nan didn't speak, her lips sealed in a futile attempt to conceal their trembling.

Tam straightened from the wall. "They were casing the warren hub, recognized Nan. When I got caught, Torx used me to go after her. Nan was only trying to protect me."

"Don't make me sound noble." Nan yanked her gaze from Jonas's. "I got a dark history with that bitch. I didn't need your death on me, too."

"And you led Del straight to her," Jonas said, rough with disbelief.

"Your negotiation restrained them, Jonas," Del cut in, to vent the crushing tension. "Torx didn't want me there but seemed reluctant to use force."

"They aren't rational creatures," Tam bit out. "Whatever immunity you thought you had, those creeps didn't hesitate to hurt you the minute they felt threatened."

"They *retreated* because of me." For reasons Del didn't understand.

Tam's mouth tightened. He refused to meet her eyes.

"I don't know what to say to the lot of you." Jonas's hands fisted atop his desk. "The Surge's lack of treaty status won't stop them from crying foul and demanding compensation."

"If they demand flash, you'll take mine," Tam stated coolly.

"They won't demand *flash*, Tam." Jonas's jaw clenched. "They'll want something that will hurt more."

Tam's head came up. He studied Jonas a tense beat.

"If it's in-kind they demand, you hand me over," Nan said.

"What?" Del sat bolt upright.

"No one's getting *in-kind*!" Jonas slammed his blockish fists on his desk, shaking the room. "For fuck's sake!" He scrubbed his face. "I'll demand a third-wheel negotiation with the Fet. The Surge will claim I'm lying about the gun, but I doubt they want Belek fact-checking."

Del rubbed her arms, remembering the enforcer's cold scrutiny, the spike of pressure in her head when he drew close.

Jonas added to Del, "The Fet are far more powerful than the Surge. They set rules making guns off-limits."

On Cartor, only government entities possessed guns, something she took for granted. Before tonight, she'd only seen OBMG soldiers armed with guns here. "Why don't the warrens arm to defend themselves?"

Jonas pinched the bridge of his nose. "Long time ago, we did. It was a bloodbath. The OBMG banned firearms. Smugglers bring them in at prices you'd see for a sonic blaster in most places. Fact is the top-tier gangs have the money. We don't. Arming against our treaties would crush what little order we have here."

Del felt hollowed out. "Why don't they simply take over, then?"

"Tipping the balance would earn them unwanted attention from the OBMG, for one."

"Right." He'd told her that already.

"The other gangs wouldn't like it, either," Tam added with a twist of irony.

Del shot him a glare. Was *that* supposed to reassure her? "Very well. Forget it." She'd rather return to Jonas's scolding.

"Jonas," Nan said softly. "That shop-girl who came here, she was sent to draw you out." Her face tilted away from Jonas.

"I'll talk to her." Jonas studied Nan as if he could draw her eyes to his by force of will. "But roughs may really be staking territory. I put the word out in the blocks, told folk to be on the lookout."

Jonas deflated in his chair. "I'll deal with their demands. That an't what I'm really upset about. It's *personal* now. The Surge will target you, especially when they don't get what they want from negotiation." Jonas's gaze pierced Nan and Tam in turn. "Shit, Tam, seems like we just got you off the Fet's radar, now this …"

Del slung Tam a sharp look. What the hells did that mean?

"I know how to avoid gangs," Tam said. "Nan can stick to The Bar like always. We'll manage fine, Boss."

Jonas shook his head as if he found Tam's assessment naïve. He aimed a blunt-tipped finger at Nan and Del. "Go get fixed up. You're ready to drop."

Nan and Tam's gazes bumped before Nan moved mechanically out the office door.

Del trailed after.

Nan thumped a palm atop the backroom's table, snagging a bottle and drinking deeply.

Del glanced at the office. Tam stood like an over-strung bow before Jonas's desk. Jonas's voice rumbled, indistinct, through the cracked door.

The gods knew what those gangsters subjected Tam to before she and Nan arrived. He didn't deserve for this to be any harder. Did he have anyone to comfort him? He'd accepted so little from her.

"Go on." Nan tipped the bottle toward Del. "Treat those hurts of yours."

Tam wasn't the only one who needed comfort.

Del crossed to Nan, plucked the bottle from her hand. "What happened today wasn't your fault."

Nan didn't push Del away. "I promised myself I'd never let my past hurt him—Jonas." She must believe the foundation of her life here had been shaken.

"Jonas needs you, everything you do for The Bar, the warren." Del guessed that making herself indispensable was Nan's strategy for enduring her past.

Nan's mouth flattened. Her vulnerability made Del hyperconscious of her own. Del faced the fragility of what she'd built, unable to delude herself that she'd established a life here.

"There's no one qualified to take your place," Del added to reassure Nan—and herself.

"All I do is work hard, do the crap no one else wants to."

Because Nan thought she deserved it. Torx's comment about metal-work … It was Nan's artistry on Kimber's hand—a talent forsworn as penance?

Del considered the ticked-up tempo of her own compulsions, bouts of hypersensitivity, strange headaches. Her grandfather's long-ago warning echoed inside her. *This insistence on risking yourself in slums, sullying your hands with blood and disease, is irrational. Worse, it's unsustainable. For someone like you.*

Galling to consider he might be right, that she bashed herself against the impossible. Failure in Balter's Den would represent defeat on many levels, even if she found another place to hide.

She and Nan had both changed their names, fled pasts they sought to compensate for. "We're not so different."

Nan's expression grew measuring, as if she gauged the weight of Del's thoughts.

"I need help." Del found herself pleading, "I can't endure here much longer without it. Will you help me?"

Nan's brows crimped. "I don't understand."

"Tend patients like you did with Kimber that day? Train to be my nurse?" The idea barely settled in Del's brain before it spilled from her mouth.

Hostility flickered in Nan's eyes. "You'd ask that knowing—"

"You and Tam are my only friends here, the only ones I trust."

"Why don't you ask *him*, then?" Nan's voice shook.

Del grimaced weakly, shifting her focus to Tam. His head cocked to one side, almost as though he could hear them. "Tam can't bear touching people." One of infinite reasons that wouldn't work, as Nan well knew.

"Don't ask this for pity of me."

"It's for us both."

Nan met her eyes, and Del struggled to leave her vulnerability bare.

"I'll do what I can, Del."

Del sagged, propped by her grip on the bottle. "Thank you."

"Now go take care of yourself before you fall over."

Tam's care came first. "No. It's time for Tam to get me home."

Nan turned narrowed eyes toward Jonas's office. "I reckon that's true."

When Tam reached his pod, he collapsed onto his pallet without shedding his boots.

He'd still be debriefing Jonas if not for Del. She'd stood up to the Boss like a regular toff, interrupting Tam's grilling. "Can't it wait until tomorrow? I'm hoping Tam can take me home." She hadn't been asking, more like announcing.

Jonas had given in, his temper showing in his tight mouth. With a lift of her chin, Del had thanked Jonas like she took his agreement for granted.

That's my little toff. Groped, threatened, and still defending the weak.

And god did Tam feel weak. He couldn't have moved if his hair caught on fire. Couldn't sleep either. Flashes of the fight reverberated through him. It had been like he'd known every move those gangsters would make before they did, and his body reacted automatically.

He'd have done worse to protect Del. Anything maybe. When that creep Fuse pinned Del to the floor, Tam had killed him without a thought.

Tam had endured plenty of fights, but he'd always been repelled, never coldly controlled. He'd never taken a life, never experienced an aura snuff that way. Remembering how blithely he'd suggested Jonas kill those patchworks, he dug his nails into his pallet.

Death ...

When Tam had lain alone on the filthy pit floor—waiting to die—it struck him that dying made a sure way to free *Emere*. Who would care? If Golalya found out, she'd mourn, then let go with Trenabic fatalism. Tam had no one tethering him to this life. Then Del's aura had blazed, searing certainty away. Her and Nan, risking themselves for him ...

What the hells did he do with that?

Strange. The violence here, the vigilante justice appalled Del. Yet she'd held his death-tainted hand, rubbed it between her fingers. *'Hello.'* So simple.

He flipped onto his back, covering his eyes with his forearm. Confusion tightened over him.

'Tam can't bear touching people.' The truth in her words stung. Del had noticed Tam avoided casual touch like a spacer avoided ship-rot. Touch brought auras into sharper focus—uncomfortable, too intimate.

When Del had laid her warm hand against his cheek, it had drawn him from his dark trance, making him long to sink against her skin. Del's touch made him uncomfortable for very different reasons, filled him with unfamiliar longing—had since the aftermath of the Trenabic girl's death.

Time was bleeding away. Bleeding *him* away. Heart's duty placed his *emere* first. But he'd held Del, absorbed her warmth, her grief through his skin.

How could he leave her so vulnerable?

24

———

The Farth warren's quirkiness heightened the wrongness crawling over Caleb's nerves. He crossed roads formed of unrolled tank tread, lined with bizarre dwellings, tires stacked like bricks, tarps draped over the skeletons of massive mining equipment, converted shipping containers—Refurb block, a commercial area, though few shops bothered with signs. He'd failed to catch a ride back from Pell Mahr, leaving a long walk on leaden feet.

Time had run out. Impossible to keep Dugan's deal from Jonas now. Lyn's mess with the Surge had driven Caleb's splinters of doubt too deep to ignore, and Dugan had nothing on Lyn except sly guesses. Dugan hadn't held his end of the bargain—which either made him useless or *involved*. Caleb was done dealing straight with Dugan.

Jonas would be pissed that Caleb had kept silent for weeks, but maybe he'd acknowledge Caleb as his ear. If Caleb solved this …

"Looks like one of Valerian's brats has been a naughty boy."

Caleb whirled, hands clamped damply over his knives. A black-garbed pack lurked behind him, Belek in its center.

Caleb slowly slid his knives back in their sheaths, fanned his fingers wide. "Don't know what you mean."

Where had they materialized from? Most Fet bigshots used wheels.

196

Seemed Belek liked to slink around afoot—to park on the outskirts then skulk in like a ghoul.

Belek approached, his face a mask of dark amusement. "Don't you? You're returning from another cozy with Vagar Dugan, a toff with his nose so far up the Mine Board's ass all he can smell is shit. Don't take a genius to figure out why."

Caleb blinked as if that could wipe away Belek's meaning.

If the Fet wanted him dead, he'd be dead. If they wanted to beat intel out of him, they'd be on him already. Belek was after something else.

"What do you want, enforcer?"

A grin slow-twitched over Belek's thin lips. "Same thing as Dugan."

Memory flashed—Caleb walking alone at night, the streetlights fluttery-weak, spotting an android head spiked over a gadget shop's awning. Its eyelids had winked over empty sockets. Its tarnished lips spasmed. *Come in, come in, come in.*

Belek's cold fingers viced over Caleb's chin. "I hope that's a 'yes' forming in your brain."

Caleb flinched from Belek, from sudden dizzying failure. Whatever Caleb said to Jonas now would seem a scramble to cover guilt, like he'd gone to the Boss from fear of Belek.

Belek's eyes slitted. His grip shifted under Caleb's jaw. He shoved Caleb against a tire-stacked wall. A miner's stick screwed into the tread glared into Caleb's left eye. His pulse throbbed beneath the bite of Belek's fingers.

"How soft and vulnerable you NG are outside your roost." Belek's thumb dug into the hinge of Caleb's jaw.

Caleb swallowed, a painful spasm through the choking hand. *Just tell the skull-faced bastard what he wants to hear.* "I get it," he wheezed.

Belek's grip loosened, the long fingers a slack noose around Caleb's throat.

"Here's something to consider, *golden boy*. You tell Valerian about Dugan, about *me*, play the innocent, and what will Valerian do? Flip us off via text-packet? Or would he set you playing a double game?" No light reflected in the liquid blackness of the enforcer's eyes. "I'd know. I always figure it out."

Caleb sensed Belek's men crowded close, ghostly in their silence.

Belek's thumb stroked Caleb's voice box, pressed with the threat of pain. "Cruel to cage a cril to bait rats, no? But what happens when the cril flies its cage? These Pell Mahr treks are *long*."

Sick uncertainty flushed through Caleb. Exhaustion. Let the bastard do his worst.

Belek's eyes narrowed. "I wonder how that fierce redhead of yours would react? Cry a few tears? Or would she cry for blood instead?"

Addie. Caleb didn't speak, couldn't. Tremors waved over him like he inhabited his whiskey-poisoned father's dying body. That memory, what followed, made him clench to hold his bladder. *Dear god.* He could hear Aden's voice in his ear, spitting for him to tell Belek to fuck off. If Caleb's stupidity got her hurt, killed …

Belek released him and pushed away, reading his surrender.

Boneless, Caleb crumpled against the wall, slid down it.

"Good, then." Clipped, business-like. Belek reached into his jacket. A fistful of credits pelted Caleb. "You'll know when I need to talk."

The gangsters shifted, dissolved into the gloom.

Sour dampness soaked into Caleb's pants from the filthy ground. Fragments of trash rustled in the chill breeze.

Golden boy. Belek's cruel irony lingered.

Caleb stared at the credits, dull plastic disks, through tear-blurred eyes. The specter of his father's shame hung in his hazy vision, threatening to drag him to something worse.

25

Three steps from The Bar, and Del wanted to shrink into herself to reduce the amount of skin exposed to the frigid night air. Galta 4 had three types of weather: frosty and dry, cool and damp, and stormy—environmentally controlled drenches or Galtan's rumbling rages.

She'd yet to predict any of it, though locals seemed to sense the shifts in their bones.

Flipping up her collar, she trailed Tam's heels as he escorted her home, resisting the urge to step into the subtle heat that radiated from his body. It had been three days since the fright with the Surge; the first time Jonas allowed Tam to escort her without NG trailing them. Illogical perhaps, but she relaxed more without the entourage.

As they walked the familiar route, difference teased at Del's awareness until she blinked away her distraction to notice why the glow of mine-sticks was missing from many structures. Yet it wasn't dark. She looked up. The omnipresent haze had cleared. Twin orbs lit the sky, one rust-orange, the other milky white. Her breath caught. She craned her neck. The sky formed a velvet-black backdrop for the moons. Expansive. Staring into it was like drinking in a full breath after the restriction of stasis.

Worlds better viewing celestial bodies from the solidity of earth versus the abyss of space. The difference lofted her heart.

She stumbled and refocused on her path. Doorsteps lining the street dimly glowed with offerings, small white bowls that reflected the moonlight.

Slowing, Del gave Tam's profile an inquiring look. His lips twitched, but his eyes continued scanning around them.

"It's considered good luck to capture moonlight," Tam said, his voice soft, textured. "At midnight, those folk will gather up the bowls and drink from them."

"That's lovely. Have you ever done that?"

He gave her a closed-lipped smile. Subtle, yet it lit his whole face.

Oh. She paused a breath. *He should do that more often.*

"Not much for superstition. Chance has brought me more luck than moonlight."

Del arched a brow to keep from grinning like a twit. "Good or bad?"

She glimpsed a flash of his teeth before he turned his face. "Bit of both, I expect."

They rarely talked this way, she realized. A shame. She'd respected his reticence, but perhaps she was as much to blame.

Frowning, Tam picked up his pace. His focus sharpened on the alleys' shadowy mouths.

She sighed. So much for chit-chat.

They walked in silence a block. Then Tam slowed, reaching back to grab her sleeve, draw her closer.

"Someone's in trouble." Tam squinted toward an alleyway.

Del tensed. "Can we help?"

He hesitated, doubtless reluctant to put her in danger.

She took his hand, his skin startlingly smooth against hers. "Let's go."

Normally, he found a casual way to avoid touch, but he tightened his grip and moved into the alley, tugging her behind.

Shadows swallowed them.

Tam had no trouble finding his way. They wound through narrow passageways until a fetid smell revealed that they approached a trash incinerator.

Tam pressed Del against the wall.

"Stay here." His whispered breath tickled her ear.

When he drew his crossbow from under his jacket, she anticipated him and drew her stunner.

Faint clicks and whistles signaled the presence of cril—nasty little rodents. Del curled her toes.

Tam padded toward the incinerator's bulky shadow. Past its rhythmic hiss, Del couldn't tell what caught Tam's attention. Then she detected a low, keening sound.

"I an't ready to give her up." High, slurred words disrupted the eerie white noise.

"The kid's done," a man growled. "I an't leaving her in our digs to rot."

"Then an't we supposed to toss her to be found? An't that why we carted her *all* this way—so close to this warren-hub?"

"*After* she kicks it. And I forgot to bring the headband."

"You're just getting cril-kneed."

"Shut up and help me get her in."

The blood drained from Del's head. They meant to throw an injured child into the incinerator.

Craning her neck, she squinted into the darkness. Tam had disappeared, and there were no forms to those cruel voices. They must be on the dumpster's far side.

She squeezed her eyes shut. *Please don't let this happen!* Pain flared in her skull. An image flickered across her eyelids, an oval of shale blue, gone before she made sense of it.

Gasping, she sagged against the wall.

"Hold! NG." Tam's voice rang coldly through the alley.

The man cursed. A clang ricocheted as powerful as gunfire.

Clenching her stunner, Del twitched forward. Darkness churned beyond her sight, scuffling, scraping, and grunting. A thud. A squishy moan snuffed sounds of struggle.

Leaning out, fingers clawed against the wall, Del mouthed Tam's name.

Quick, unsteady footfalls echoed toward the opposite end of the alley. The metallic ping of a crossbow bolt was followed by Tam's hiss of frustration.

Del slumped against the wall. The footfalls faded away.

"Del!"

"Here." She stumbled toward Tam over crumbling pavement. "Are you all right?"

"Fine."

A squeak jolted from her as she tripped hard over something. "I can't see. Can I turn—?"

Tam's shadow rippled before her with a shape in his arms. "We need to get back to the exam room."

Staggering after him, she burst into the watery light of the main street. Tam had covered the child's head with his jacket. Scrawny limbs flopped from beneath the fabric, but she could see little else.

"I should check the child now."

Tam knelt by a streetlight, parted his jacket. Del's blood pressure dropped. The girl's face was a horror. Flesh peeled around a horn-like protrusion on her forehead. Infection oozed down her forehead to her eyes which were swollen shut, caked with pus.

"Botched exotic alteration," Tam explained through white lips.

Del absorbed the pitiful hitches in the girl's chest. Who could perform this butchery on a child?

"Del?"

Her mind spun. Her pack lay too lightly on her shoulders. "Back, hurry!"

They rushed to the tavern and up the stairs, ignoring the curious stir of the patrons.

Del sprang to the supply chest and tore her stasis kit off the shelf.

Tam eased the child onto the table. "It's all right, kid. No one will hurt you now," he whispered. "What's your name, little bit?"

The girl's hand, bone thin, made a blind grab for Tam then fluttered back down. "P-please." The cracked voice forced its way through her inflamed lips.

"Who did this to you?"

"Mam … gave me over …"

Del jerked her gaze to Tam's.

"I'll be back." He slammed from the room.

Del was held immobile, cold, nauseous—the incomprehensible cruelty turning this familiar space alien. Dear gods, *unbearable*. She longed to blink and find herself in some saner, more civilized place where she understood the rules, the disparities, even the cruelty.

"S-sorry ... sorry." The girl's whimpering snapped Del back to herself.

Del rushed to the exam table. The girl's hand was a limp curl over her stomach, her ill-fitted, fraying sleeve exposing a fragile wrist.

Del gripped the table's edge. She knew that sleeve. Her eyes locked on the mutilated face. *Pepar.* Her first patient, who'd snuck into the exam room. An echo of the girl's whimper leaked from Del's throat. She rested her hand over Pepar's. It was hot, scaled with dryness. "You'll be all right, Pepar."

Pepar fought to open her eyes, moaned when she couldn't.

"Lie still."

Del drew out the stasis kit, strapped it around Pepar's chest. Pepar flailed with fright until Del stroked her matted hair. "This won't hurt you. We'll take ... care of ..." Del's voice failed.

She activated the kit; it hummed to life, melting the strain from Pepar's face.

The portable kit could only achieve partial medical stasis, but it would be enough to grant Pepar a reprieve.

Tam stepped back inside. Del couldn't lift her eyes to him.

She could save Pepar's life, but Pepar needed extensive reconstructive surgery in a proper facility.

Did Del even have a voucher left? She flinched straighter, flipped up her wrist-vid. *One* for the rest of the month. And the cost of Pepar's care might drain Del's resources and prevent her from being able to hospitalize another patient after new vouchers became available—a patient who might die without it.

Del could save Pepar's life—but leave her disfigured, possibly blinded.

Tam shifted closer as if sensing Del's distress. "What's wrong?"

Beyond the obvious?

"One voucher left," she whispered toward her hands, resting nerveless against the table's edge.

Tam's cool finger tipped her chin up. "You won't bear it, angel."

She met his silvery eyes, tried to see beyond his lack of expression.

"One problem at a time, right?" He lowered his hand.

Del scanned Pepar's gaunt, ragged form, her brutally mangled face. "Yes. Let's go."

Within minutes, they were crossing the warren in Jonas's rickety motorized cart. Del prayed the heap would hold out as it rattled and sputtered. Jonas drove, with Del and Tam in the small cargo space holding Pepar.

Del set the re-call function on her vid until the spotty comm patched her through to First Ring Emergency.

When they arrived at the square, a soldier rushed to meet them with a wristband tracer—a condition of bringing patients into the First Ring. The band lay cruelly over Pepar's fragile wrist. The guard winced in sympathy, waved them on.

Tam carried Pepar through the gate.

An ambulance whirred up. The med-tech blanched at the sight even as he whipped around with a hov-stretcher.

Pepar disappeared inside the ambulance.

I refuse to regret this. Del would petition Isa Vinn for a special fund for Pepar, step up efforts to wrest additional vouchers from OBMG. Her stomach knotted, and she tensed against the urge to sink to her knees, so bloody exhausted.

One problem at a time.

Del stood staring after the flashing lights until Tam quietly urged her to go home.

26

THE BODY LAY OVER A PLASTIC SHEET ATOP THE BAR'S BACKROOM TABLE LIKE a hideous resin statue. Tam felt queasy—both considering how many meals he'd had on this table, and that he'd put the man in this state.

Not that the bastard hadn't deserved it, but Tam hadn't meant to kill him. He'd burned to save the child, responding to Del's will as though she'd shouted straight into his mind.

The air was dense with unwashed bodies and unsettled emotional signatures; a contingent of NG on hand to hunt the culprit. Gazes slid irresistibly to the corpse as if to a broken window at a peep-house. Tam stood at Jonas's shoulder to assess the body, tensing against a sniggering comment about his matching pallor.

No clear clues. Marks of a career junkie mapped the man's skin. A burn mark—like a loyalty symbol to a petty block-rough—marred the base of his thumb, puckered as with age. Jonas had spent the last decade stamping out roughs. This was only an artifact. But the face … vaguely familiar.

Tam slipped out his vid-tile from his jacket pocket, examined the images he'd taken from The Back Hand. Sure enough. One of the junkies loitering outside. That didn't mesh with the ambition the Surge claimed. Why get involved with scummy alterations?

Tam handed the vid-tile to Jonas to scan.

Jonas nodded grimly. "Let's see what Nan thinks."

When Jonas covered the grisly showcase with a plastic sheet, the group expelled a collective breath.

"Aden," Jonas turned to his second. She stood a pace back, her wire scarf covering her nose and mouth and the ends of her red hair. "Call the Mort Guild. Shame to waste flash on this piece of shit, but we can't leave him to rot."

Tossing the "piece of shit" in the dumpster would be poetic justice.

Jonas studied the plastic shroud. "Wish you hadn't taken him out, Tam."

"The doc was there. I had to neutralize him quickly." The Boss had pushed him into this gig—not Tam's fault there was a growing trail of bodies.

The milling NG pricked their ears at this exchange. No doubt the flap would transform Tam from a sell-skin into a blood-drinking psycho.

"You get anything, Tam?"

"They were told to toss the girl's body to be found."

"By whom?" Jonas frowned.

"Not sure, but someone wanted the girl found as a symbol." Tam considered. The woman had said *this warren hub*. "They may be out-warren."

"We establish a net. Call up volunteers as we go. Start from the Den's perimeter and move in." Jonas's boom sent NG scrambling.

"Jonas," Tam said quietly as the others filed out. "That kid. Same skittish girl who slipped in to see Del before she set up." Del had recognized her—and said nothing.

Jonas's mouth compressed. "We'll sort that later. Let's find the dull-knife."

Tam sighed, rolled his neck. Odds of finding the butcher seemed a thread shy of bare. Then the obvious occurred to him.

"Boss, I've got a place to start."

Umar's Body Shop. Bright, blunt letters tracked across a white panel, the crispness suggesting fresh paint.

Tam stared at the sign, sure he'd come to the right place, wondering if he was seeing it wrong. Too snarky to be for real.

The "shop" was a two-story prefab. If Balter's Den had a toff sector, Tinker Town was it. Tidy prefabs like this stood in neat rows around a centerpiece of three tall pod complexes, salvaged and reassembled from a failed Fring construction project. Proper streetlights stood sentry at every corner, giving the impression day lingered here, fighting off the night sky that pressed from above.

The door had a ringer. Within seconds of Tam pressing it, Umar appeared. He fished his NG pendant from under his shirt, held it up.

Umar's dark, flat eyes scoured him head-to-toe. "What can I do for the Boss's sneak?"

"A word, if you will."

Umar shrugged, swung her door wide, and marched back inside. Tam hesitated, reluctant to enclose himself with her acrid aura. Duty was duty. He stepped through the entry, sensing only Umar there.

The shadows inside the doorway shifted, a warped, disjointed movement. Tam sprang back. A figure lurked there, aura-less.

Umar's harsh humor scraped over him. "Stand down, EmA."

The figure stiff-limbed backward to brace itself against the wall.

An android. Tam stared at it with queasy fascination. One of its arms ended in a barbed hook. Its face was tan mesh with silver bones glinting beneath. Torn synthetic skin hung from its jaw in peels. A cracked brown eye glared at Tam, light flickering in its pupil. The other eye socket gaped empty.

"You greet patients with that thing?"

"Wards off thieves and other trash."

Shit. Even if Del's services weren't free, patients would flock to her to avoid that horror.

Tam edged into the room, taking in the space. The floor was divided —not by walls but by function. On one side lay an exam table like Del's. The wall behind it was covered in cubby-shelves, stocked with implements that looked more like oddments in a sundries shop than medical equipment. A deep-basin sink affixed to one wall. A work bench dominated the other side of the floor. Tools of a different nature scattered over its surface; a grease-smudged metal cabinet braced its back. The air stank of solvent.

"What is all this?"

Umar propped a hip against her exam table. "I fix things, boy. Fixing equipment an't that different from fixing a body."

"So … folk bring you their busted vid-screens and their busted bones?"

"Your off-world high-nose might consider those things on opposite sides of a divide, but I'm Maze born and raised. I do what folk need. Docs here need to dev their own med supplies. An't unusual." Umar's aura dimmed like a private memory bubble formed around her. "My man was doc before me, but he taught me what he knew."

Tam skimmed his gaze over the divided space. "You were the machinist. You kept shop together."

Umar's eyes narrowed with amusement. "That was years ago. Guess you never broke a bone, boy?"

"No." And he'd sure as hell never sought a doc. As a child, he'd had Golalya to heal his hurts. As a man, he'd had to heal his own.

"He was *also* warren chief before Valerian. But I expect you know that," Umar said with an edge.

"Before my time."

Umar straightened, folded her arms. "What's amiss that brings you to my door?"

This sour-bit was shrewd. No point trying to maneuver her.

"We found a kid. Near death, face mangled. Wondered if you know of anyone in the area into the darker stuff."

Umar's brows raised. "I an't hurting for business. Even with your toff giving it away for free. Working on bodies, working on tools. Pays the same."

"That an't what I asked you."

"I *fix* things, pretty. Mangling an't in my charter. If a patient of mine suffers, an't because I set out to hurt them."

Her emotional signature grated, rough with annoyance, but no trace of a lie. "Know anything about exotic alterations?"

Umar grimaced. "I an't cozy with any dull-knives if that's what you mean. Only a fool would step outside Pell Mahr to get that work done."

Umar's expression grew smug. "I'd think *you*'d know more about all that than me."

Tam frowned around him. No visible evidence. No hint of blood.

He glanced between the mech-tools and the exam table. That was too clear a link to ignore—if not for this case. "Ever do patchwork?"

A laugh like a dry cough burst from her. "Patch is against the rules here now, an't it?"

Tidy sidestep.

"So, no patchwork?"

Umar stalked across the room, flung open her cabinet. "Go on, search the place. If that'll get Valerian out of my hair." Her voice flattened over Jonas's name. Resentment crouched in her aura.

"You got no love for the Boss, eh?"

Her metallic teeth bared. "If I hated him, couldn't live here, could I?"

Now *that* screamed of a lie—but it was no secret Umar resented Jonas, and she wasn't the only Denner to reap the warren's benefits while chafing at its rules.

Tam searched the pod, not expecting to find anything. The only interesting discovery was an ancient image displayer, hung on her bedroom wall, flipping through anatomy diagrams like a grisly art collage. Watching the full image loop turned Tam's stomach but didn't reveal anything incriminating.

"Satisfied?" Umar hit him with thick irony when he returned to the entrance.

"Had to rule it out." Then he tested, "Can't imagine you're happy with the warren for securing a proper doctor."

Umar's lip curled. "Yeah, I an't thrilled Valerian lured some off-worlder here to syphon my business." She flung her hands wide. "But I an't hurting for flash." Nothing lurked beneath her words to suggest deception.

The block-mama here despised Umar, gossiped to Jonas like an ear. Someone would have seen the patchworks go in and out in *this* neighborhood, but Tam couldn't rule it out. Another line of investigation. When would he find time for *Emere*? Weariness weighed Tam's shoulders.

Umar studied him with arms folded. "If you hocked your soul for those alterations, boy, you got played a cruel joke." She blinked her focus toward the floor. "I was only five when those ghouls plagued us, but I'll *never* forget. Landed their ships outside OBMG's net, slithered close on hov-bikes, then crept through the warrens on foot. Made sport of hunting us. My mam would hide me under the water heater, hoping the heat would fool their scanners." Tam's limbs locked, his heart hammering harder against his ribs with each word. "Guess the OBMG hoped they'd wipe us out for them. We're *still here*." Umar refocused slitted eyes on Tam's face. "You're pretty enough, I suppose. Not ashy blue. Lack the ghouls' pointy bones and odd-spaced eyes."

"Thanks for your cooperation," he managed through set teeth, feeling as if Umar's slurs against Rynet had spattered slime over his mother's spirit.

As he left, he imagined Umar's eyes boring into his back.

The creepy android lurked at her shoulder.

27

———

Tam clutched the disk Interface had given him, the locator that led Tam to the southernmost dregs of the Maze—a dangerous, two-hour truck ride through the roughest warrens, past the gates of gang burrows. Tam had hired the ride from Taber, paid a full week's wages to convince the driver to chance it. Tam had hoofed it for over an hour to secure that ride, but he couldn't risk hiring from Balter's Den. Too many flap-tongues.

Jonas had closed The Bar to prep for a warren meeting, and Del was overseeing the girl Pepar's care, granting Tam a full day to focus on himself—which currently consisted of staring stupidly at mounds of rock demarcating the wasteland's border.

Tam opened his gloved hand, studied the disk. Was he supposed to wait for someone?

Sighing, Tam moved closer to the rock. Its surface blurred—another holo-image—exposing an opening. Stairs cut a steep path down. His surprise lasted an eyeblink. This was *exactly* the sort of place smugglers might nest.

He needed to erase the Trenabic *ssura-ri's* ugly suggestion *Emere* "took flight" with smugglers. Just the idea she might have abandoned him left a restless ache inside him, and Umar's ugly slurs had piled on, spurred his need to reach *Emere* somehow.

Tam steeled himself and braved the stairs, keeping one hand on the wall to navigate the slick, uneven steps and thickening dark. As he descended, the rock grew smooth, rippling as if formed of ice, its foamy green luminescence lighting the path.

Tam paused and flattened his palms against it, breathed in the wet stone scent.

Pressure charged the air around him.

Tam closed his eyes, hesitated. He must never selfishly reach for *Emere*, but duty demanded he respect her touch. He opened to her wisdom.

———

TAMLN SAT CROSSED-LEGGED BEFORE HIS MOTHER ON THE COMPOUND'S CLAY floor. She knelt, her long, thick twine of black hair over her shoulder, tied off with citrus-grass, its clean scent meant to make him more alert for learning.

"Stones carry stories." The ritual words to kick off a stone-lore lesson. She held a smooth chip of stone on the flat of her palm. "What do you scent from this?"

His nail-sheaths slid back, freeing his sharp nails to prick his palms. He unknotted his hands, placed them flat over his knees. These lessons were painful. His Human blood diluted his fehren; he could not smell as his mother did.

Her free hand curved with the reassurance *ah'nea*. "Subtlety is no less valuable, Tamln."

Her eyes were level with his. At ten, he'd reached her height. Smaller than the smallest of his cousins. They were Trenabic, but his lack still rankled.

"Focus, pup."

He took the stone, rubbed it in his fingers, brought it to his nose. "It … smells like baby Kalala after her bath." He gestured his embarrassment.

Emere captured his fingers in hers to still them and laughed, a rumble low in her throat that revealed true humor. "So, it does. The moisture in the stone shifts its scent."

"Why do we smell stone, *Emere*?" Trenabic didn't. He doubted Humans smelled much over their own stink.

"Much of Vlera, our homeworld, is shelled in stone—beautiful, marbled swirls of color, bleak jags of dullness. Some perilous, some inviting. Our ancestors subsisted on mossy vegetation and subterranean springs. They survived by sensing the stone." She brushed the tip of his nose.

He never tired of her tales of Vlera, despite the confusing mix of sadness and joy she radiated. "So only Vleran Rynet smell stone?"

"Yes. That is why our geoscientists are sought after. We understand the earth by gift of blood, not only with intellect and tools."

Tamln's fingers worked an anxious *ah'nea* before he could stop them. "That's why the mine wants to cage you."

Anger ribbed her aura, making him lean away. "Yet Vlerens bound me to the OBMG."

"I don't understand." Vlerens were good. Mine Humans were the enemy.

"I became *namere*, without family. That made me a child of the province, though I was grown. A child of the province serves the province. They traded me to OBMG in exchange for access to a jumpship pathway."

Tamln felt like she'd slapped him. "But why were you *namere*?"

She flicked a gesture of reluctance. "My family wished to align with another prominent house. I was bonded to a son of that house. A false bond. The falsehood was discovered. He and I were cast from our clan."

"That's not fair!"

She tilted her head side to side, a Rynet shrug that swished her hair over her tunic. "What society is free from snares? I should have resisted the pressure, honored the *ela* of our clan, not the ambitions of my parents. We foolishly hoped the bond would follow the ceremony."

"I don't understand. Why didn't you bond? Why bond with—" A Human. If she'd bonded with that Vleren, Tamln would have been full-blood, happy on Vlera!

Amusement sparked in Emere's aura. "One cannot bond for willing it. I did not wish to bond with your father, but the heart is wiser than the will."

Tamln glowered at his folded feet. "You hate him."

An awful sadness wrenched her. "Oh, pup. I loved him beyond life. His loss has lined every beautiful memory with thorns."

Hot denial pulsed in Tamln's head. "He betrayed you!"

"He gave up everything to fight for my freedom. We escaped the mine. He arranged for us to leave the planet on a smuggler vessel. He was betrayed."

Tamln couldn't endure her pain. He patted her knees in contrition.

She didn't react, caught in her thorns.

THE *ELA* RELEASED TAM; HE BLINKED HIMSELF BACK TO THE PRESENT. HE stood alone surrounded by eerie, silent stone. His forehead was pressed to its cool dampness. It smelled like little Kalala after a bath. He fought an awful press of tears.

Emere had never spoken so of his father again, and that one positive story couldn't overwrite the years of her anguished silence.

Unthinking, he continued down the stairs toward where they bent from view.

If the *ela* memory gift signified a warning, he didn't sense the warning in his bones.

A FIELD-TECH BARRIER HUMMED AT THE LANDING. WHEN TAM FACED IT, HIS hair stood on end. He drew the locator from his pocket. The barrier vanished, releasing a chorus of voices and bewildering mix of auras. The landing led to a cavern as wide as Jonas's taproom. Stalactites decorated the high ceiling, looking like drizzled wet sand. The walls and ceiling were shaped from the same luminescent stone as the passageway. Two dark archways hinted of adjoining caverns. Large knobs of rock rose from the floor, used by the occupants as makeshift tables. No chairs, everyone stood. Two Trenabic clustered around a table with a Human.

Some dozen heads twisted to scan Tam, then turned as if uninterested.

The "tables" each had a round device set atop, privacy filters, by the faint whir.

Smugglers arranged business here. It wasn't their main hub. Vague disappointment stirred Tam. He'd only glimpsed starships in the distant sky.

"You've the look of your father."

The hair rose on Tam's nape. He whipped around to find a small, wiry man standing at his shoulder. Tam had been so absorbed by the strange space, he'd missed the man approach.

"Didn't mean to lift your fur." Excitement and anxiety transmitted through the man's emotional signature. "I served with Laurent when we were inservice to Cartor."

Tam studied the man, carefully blank. "I think you have the wrong person."

A layer of clear bumps textured the man's pink skin. His hair was white, each strand thick and transparent as if made of nylon. Otherwise, he looked Human. He didn't smell Human. An elusive musk clung to him.

The man inclined his head. "Doohran."

His name?

"A divergent species of Human." A thick accent stretched the vowels of each word.

Heat prickled Tam's face. "Sorry."

The man laughed, a cheery cackle. "I'm used to it. And your people do have sensitive noses."

My people … Tam had tinted his skin, worn a cap over his hair.

A warmth radiated from the man's aura, shaded by regret. Tam struggled to resist letting it lull him.

"Come, have conference with me. Name's Kuranev, Nev for short."

"You knew I was coming." Too impossible a coincidence.

"Yes." Nev winced, his skin flipping between pale pink and dark rust, eyeblink fast.

A camouflage reflex evolved on his homeworld, Tam guessed.

Nev said, "You're safe here. This place is neutral territory. Anyone who breaks that rule is blacklisted."

Tam warily followed Nev to the only free table, against the wall. A soft-teal stalagmite rose beside the table like a permanent guest. Nev and Tam took positions on either side.

Nev's lashless, violet-gray eyes fixed on Tam, curious. "Laurent and I stayed in touch after we got out. He took a job with the OBMG. I engaged in less aboveboard work."

"I know nothing about him," Tam said through a stiff jaw. "Never met the man."

"Ah." Nev averted his gaze. "He always found trouble, never could endure injustice. I fled it, while he fought it. Landed us in the same place, kicked out of the Corp without prospects on Cartor." Nev ran a clear fingernail over his cuticles like a nervous habit. "He contacted me for help, so I took a run to the Outer Rim here. The plan was to deliver my load and pick up your parents. At the rendezvous point, my crew mutinied. I warned Laurent—too late, but he fought to protect your mother. They dumped me in the wasteland so they could nab Laurent and collect OBMG's bounty on him.

Nev swallowed hard. A strange veil clouded Tam's read of his emotions. A shield? "A formidable man. I always imagined … he'd escaped."

Tam's mouth had gone dry. Still like a child—desperate for a shred of information about his father while recoiling from it. "You haven't explained why you're here."

"I got stuck here, but found the Shadow Warren. I put feelers out with them—any word of my ship, Laurent, your mother. When you queried Gate, I got a ping."

"I was promised anonymity," Tam said, hard.

"This was in-warren business, and my query pre-dated yours by twenty years. Interface gave you the locator. If you'd never used it, that would have been that."

"What do you want?"

Embarrassment flushed through Nev's aura. "I owe Laurent." His chin lifted. "Doohrans don't take debts lightly."

No hint of deception in his emotional signature. His aura radiated earnestness—the strongest Human aura Tam had encountered outside of Del's. "My mother told me my father was a telepath."

"As am I." Nev grinned, closed-lipped as if to harness it. "But my gift is like a lightbulb to Laurent's star." His humor fled. "If I'd been stronger, I could have warned him in time."

Tam braced against the table, the solidity of rock soothing. "My mother, she disappeared from the Maze nine years ago."

Nev's hairless brow furrowed. "I guessed it from your query. You want to know if she came through here."

Yes, Tam mouthed.

"No way. I'd have known, with the feelers out."

"What if she was … disguised?"

"Difficult to conceal the sharper bone structure. I'd have been alerted if a masked woman tried to hire passage. Smugglers do nest outside our warren. The real sharks, who bring in the dark stuff and deal with top-tier gangs. Can't imagine your mother would go there."

Tremors waved over Tam, a strangely deflating relief. "Not smugglers, not OBMG."

"The AI, Gate, is overconfident. It can tap Inside, yes, but the OBMG keeps information about its sensitive operations behind stronger firewalls."

"So, I can't rule them out." Tam pinched the bridge of his nose. Why was everything so fucking hard?

"I can't believe I'm going to tell you this," Nev muttered, winced toward the table. "Get yourself caught."

"Sorry?"

"I've been nabbed by the MS three times for being in the wrong place. Even they aren't draconian enough to hold a body without more cause."

"There's no way I want them poking into my DNA."

"Never took mine. Used facial recognition. Complies with interplanetary beings' rights standards."

Tam crinkled his face. "What would getting caught buy me?"

"If they suspect a link to your parents, they'll ask questions. You may find answers through the questions they choose—or don't choose—to ask. Of course, this suggestion assumes you haven't actually committed a crime they'd bury you for."

All Seven Hells would freeze over before Tam willingly flung himself into MS hands.

"I … should go."

Nev dipped his head, whispered, "Laurent was a good man. Come back when you're ready to hear about him."

Tam covered his mouth with his hand. He'd come for *Emere*, not the bondmate who'd left her brokenhearted.

"Here." Nev handed Tam a disk, this one red. "Across from here, there's a brown shack with a red door. Give them this. It'll get you a ride home."

"Thanks." Tam took it mechanically.

"Young man." Nev studied Tam with a grave face. "I will get space-borne again. You'll have a way off, then, if you want."

Kuranev had held the hope of regaining a ship for *twenty* years? All sane Maze-dwellers accepted that death was the only way off. Tam couldn't take his offer seriously.

Tam hurried away, feeling like he fled.

You've the look of your father. The man with the electric blue eyes. Tam resembled his mother. Too late to ask what Nev meant.

Emere's memory-gift, Nev's story—Tam's father had won their devotion. For so long, Tam had dismissed his father as a creep. That he might be wrong spun his head, left a weird, shaky sensation in his stomach.

Tam knew Emere would never have abandoned him. Sheer, useless curiosity about her bondmate had drawn him to the smugglers nest. He'd gleaned more information than he'd imagined possible.

So why was he running from it?

28

Sponsor Vinn,

I've found a solution for obtaining a nurse. I'll train one of the
mayor's employees who's expressed an interest. If successful,
I'll train others. This could be crucial to the mission's sustain-
ability. I hope you will approve my request for three trainee
diagnoses. For the first time, I'm optimistic we can make a
real difference here.

Tam hated warren meetings—too many people, far too many stares. The tavern was choked to twice its capacity, milling bodies decked in everything from scrubby coveralls to lamé unitards. The air vibrated with the shrill emotions of people desperate for a festival atmosphere, ready to fake it if they had to.

Tam couldn't bother pretending. With Del flitting around "connecting," it had turned into a bigger headache than usual.

Del and Jonas had hashed it out over her attending. Del won.

Jonas figured he'd take the opportunity to map any unhealthy interest in Del under his watch. Not that Del knew about that little sidebar.

Tam leaned against the bar, scanning for her. Jonas had NG peppered through the crowd. Tam was supposed to keep his eyes peeled from a distance. If he trailed Del like a leash, they'd never draw anyone out. But her slight form got swallowed by the crowd. Short of standing on the bar to watch, he was doomed to failure.

Unless she had pity on him.

As if to punctuate his thought, Del materialized from the dense wall of bodies—with an eager shadow at her heels.

From behind the bar, Nan signaled Tam. "You gonna do something about that?"

He didn't bother pretending to misunderstand. Del—she of the high-collared, loose-fitting jumpsuits—was slinking around in black leggings and a clingy shirt that bared most of her back. The glossy ringlets spilling from her ponytail drew his eyes straight to her naked spine.

Del's new look lured attention like a beacon in a blackout. He'd assumed her usual frumpy uniform was camouflage to keep Maze-rats from getting ideas. He'd have to rethink that idea.

"Tam?" Nan pressed through his distraction.

Tam scratched his brow to hide a grimace. Since Nan had started training as Del's nurse, she'd gotten bossier than Jonas about Del.

"You gonna let some slag take her home?" Nan continued as if he intended to hand Del over to flesh-traders.

He spun to face Nan. "None of my stuff as long as she's safe."

Of course, he couldn't let Del wander off, and the idea of standing guard-post outside while some guy threw down his moves on her was … creepy. The ale he'd chugged earlier suddenly churned like acid.

Nan watched him with skeptical disapproval.

"I an't letting anyone take her home. Okay?"

Nan nodded without dropping her frown.

Del excused herself as the crater-faced scrub chatting her up tried to sneak an arm around her. The man dropped the appendage sheepishly. Oblivious, Del glided up to the bar, pleasure frothing her aura.

Nan shot her a blue concoction.

Del took a swig. "Gods, it's hot."

Tam didn't trust himself to say anything.

Del studied his face. "Don't you look grim."

A customer hollered for service. Nan moved off, shooting Tam a significant glare.

Del leaned closer, lowering her eyelids. "Now you can clue me into what you've been too embarrassed to tell me all evening."

"Huh?" Playing the clothead was his only defense.

"I'm starting to think I've a neon 'S' emblazoned on my forehead." At his carefully blank stare, her eyes grew steely. "Out with it."

No escape. He reached over and gingerly undid the ribbon that bound her hair, clumsy with the intimacy. The ribbon slid free, releasing her curls over her back.

"My hair?" Del blinked, then sighed as understanding dawned. She gestured airily. "Explain. That woman over there is practically bare to the navel. How is exposing my spine more indecorous? Is there some sexual significance to the back here?"

Whoa. "Maybe you should ask Nan."

Amusement glimmered through Del. "I'll chalk it up to another Maze-culture mystery."

If she'd laugh at him…"It's not exactly—um—indecorous." Exposing the back signified sensual vulnerability. "But it sends the message that you want to score."

"Is that all?" She blinked at him. "In that case …" She grabbed for the ribbon.

He flinched, hand clenching over the cloth, heat singeing his cheeks.

"Don't scowl like an old flora. I'm joking, of course." Her manner flipped to genuine ire. "You might have told me straight off, instead of letting me run around looking like a tart. I need people to take me seriously!"

Tam stroked the satiny strand with his fingers as she flounced off. Catching himself, he stuffed the ribbon into his pocket.

His father came from Cartor, like Del. Had he spoken with that same clipped accent? Hours after his encounter with Kuranev, Tam still felt raw, exhausted.

He'd decided the party offered opportunity to ask for Del's help. He'd tell her he wanted help finding a missing friend. He wouldn't say anything about a Rynet—not yet—but would get a sense of whether Del could help. If so, he'd risk revealing more. If not, he'd bury the idea, find another angle.

His eyes tracked to where Del stood smiling at Caleb Freth. A strange burning agitated his chest. This evening hadn't gone like he'd imagined. He'd figured she'd be relaxed, less obsessed with work, easier to talk to. But she was busier than ever.

And she was annoyed with him.

Freth leaned close, his face inches from hers. Tam gritted his teeth. He'd lose his chance if she took some charming's lure.

He took a gulp of the sweat-spiced air that he immediately regretted. This night couldn't end soon enough.

THE BAR HAD TIPPED PAST THE POINT OF EVENING CHEER INTO ROWDY NIGHT. Caleb only had to stand near the serving counter to sense it—a routineness that rubbed his already roughened temper. The Boss had better give his speech soon, or the crowd would be too drunk to listen. Like many NG, Caleb had been assigned to running crowd control.

He scanned the press of bodies. Familiar faces, all. He relaxed his spine against the wall outside the meal-nook's beaded curtain.

An unmistakable voice, filled with hypermanly bluster, scraped Caleb like sandpaper—Aden's scuzzy ex. Caleb should duck into the backroom before he had to witness what followed. Instead, he stood and waited.

Aden sidled up to Caleb, cocking her hip on the wall beside him. "Why don't you go talk to her?" She jerked her chin toward Del, standing at the other end of the bar.

Convenient diversion.

He didn't need to *actively* watch Del. The Bar might as well be AI-webbed the way folk marked her every breath.

"An't in the mood to make nice." Caleb scowled, shoving his thumbs into his waistband. He narrow-eyed the gilt winking in Aden's right earlobe—a bright contrast to the tarnished silver one that lay like soot on her left. "You want something sparkly, Addie? I'll finally trade that piece of shit I gave you for something nicer."

"Thanks, but I'll wear this 'piece of shit' 'til you pry it outta my ear." Her mouth twisted down.

As an idiot kid, Caleb had caught Addie red-faced, ringed by girls teasing her for not having a single line of gilt. He'd run errands for block roughs for weeks to scrape enough flash to buy her that cheap silver line.

Caleb fingered the matching one on his left ear. Just as tarnished. Just as precious.

They'd been too poor to do better by each other.

He jabbed a finger at the gold glint on her ear. "You know that line's been in another woman's ear."

Mean, but Aden needed mean to shake her out. Too many times he'd had to pick up the pieces when her shithead layboy took his gilt back.

Aden tensed, her shoulders swelling. "I know your folks were a bitter pair. Don't mean you should let it rule your life."

As if her putting up with losers didn't stem from her own struggle with the past.

"Fine. But if that creep breaks your heart again, I'll shove the gilt so far up his nose it'll hit his brainpan."

Aden gave him a wrenching look, shifted as if she'd stomp off, then averted her face and said, "Go talk to the doc."

Caleb jerked his chin. "Scuzzy's waiting for you."

"Now that's just childish." The annoyance puckering Aden's face was her brand of forgiveness. "You don't get to insult him 'til he makes me cry again."

She sauntered away, flipping a hand toward the ruddy-faced chunk at the bar who kept hooking her heart, past all sense. His sloshy stance revealed how pickled he'd gotten already.

Caleb turned away.

Movement alerted him, Del approaching. "Hello."

He scanned her. The warm yellow of her silky top enhanced the golden cast to her skin. Del never dressed snooty, but tidiness shaped her every line—even in this casual rig.

Made him a sloppy contrast. He resisted the irrational urge to check his fly.

"Hey." His forced his body into a relaxed posture. "How're things?"

Del was too delicate, but her green eyes glowed with gradient shades, like he imagined real leaves might look in the light.

"Rather busier now."

"Yeah." Beyond *busy*, forcing Caleb to glue himself to The Bar every spare moment. Then again, minding Del's safety was the only part of his sidebar that didn't chafe.

Del's slim fingers traced her ear, tucking back her hair. "I wanted to thank you again for your kindness in those first weeks."

He cocked his head.

She smiled. "The blackout and loan of your light?"

Caleb cast for something to say. "Doc, I'd offer up a hundred wrist lights for you helping folk here."

"Thank you, then."

A slur of bass words passed close behind Caleb. "… on, baby, let's get …"

He twisted around.

Scully sleazed past with Aden tucked like she'd sprouted beneath his armpit.

"Everything all right?" Del studied him with concern.

"Don't care much for drunks," he said, too tightly. He swallowed, managed a weak smile. "Guess that's funny, considering the hours I post here."

Del tipped up her face to meet his gaze. "This place is a great deal more than a bar."

He wondered if he imagined the edge to her tone. "I expect where you're from, there's a pill or something that keeps folk from getting stupid drunk like that."

Her gaze intensified, hard to hold. "I'm afraid people poison their minds and bodies despite the wonders of medical science."

He shoved his hands in his pockets. "Didn't mean to sound prickly."

"It's hard to witness those we care about succumb to addiction," Del said softly.

A frown pinched his face before he could stop it. Had he exposed so much?

Del said, "Addiction robbed everything from my mother, finally her life."

Caleb met Del's gaze, startled.

"Privilege isn't protection against weakness. In fact, it may invite it." She winced. "I apologize. I didn't mean to push a confidence on you."

His heart tripped like she'd offered flirtation instead of honesty. "I lost someone to drink. My father. You guessed that, huh?"

"It's a distinctive kind of grief."

Caleb couldn't think of a damned thing to say. *You're right* seemed inadequate.

Movement caught his attention—Lyn clearing a spot to sit on the serving counter. No doubt people melted from the sneak's path. His face twisted their way.

How could the Boss trust such a *blank* with Del? How could he guess what went on behind that resin surface?

Lyn's lips warped in a smirk as if Caleb's thoughts had scrolled across his face.

One scrap of proof from Dugan, a single clear angle, and Caleb would shut Lyn down.

Del excused herself, disappearing into the crowd like a curtain closed behind her—leaving Caleb standing like a bumble. Making eyes at Del was wasted time, anyway. He needed to case Lyn.

A firm grip on Caleb's arm made him jump. "You okay, there?"

Caleb lifted startled eyes to Jonas. "Yeah, thanks, Boss."

Beneath Jonas's concerned gaze, words primed to tumble free from Caleb, warnings about Dugan, Belek, a plea for help, for forgiveness.

"Hey Boss, it's time!" A shout carried over the crowd.

As Jonas turned away, his big hand ducked Caleb's head—the same distracted affection he'd offered since Caleb was a little knee-biter.

Caleb wiped sweaty palms on his pants. *Impossible to tell Jonas, risk Addie. Watching Del, neutralizing Lyn's threat—there was nothing evil in that.*

Blinking away his distraction, he shoved through the press of bodies to find a better angle to observe. Mistrust of Lyn already existed. Caleb only needed to find a way to fan it.

DEL'S ENJOYMENT HAD SHRIVELED BENEATH TAM'S REMINDER OF HER cultural ignorance. By some miracle, she discovered an empty stool at the bar and perched on it gratefully. If nothing else, the evening evidenced

Jonas's cleverness. He encouraged people to engage in this civic duty by offering participants free drinks.

Jonas's head and shoulders appeared over the crowd; he'd stood on a platform set in the taproom's center. "Yo, Denners! Your attention for a few." He didn't need a microphone. His bass carried. "We got an opportunity to take to vote."

The room hushed with remarkable speed.

"As you folk know, the OBMG's pumping out their trailings—their watery waste—on our western border. Crap even salvagers don't want."

A round of boos rolled through the tavern.

Jonas nodded gravely, kept going. "I've found someone who does want it. Thing is, we need to convert it, sift the material for reuse. The profit margin is too thin to interest the salvage companies, but it sure could give us a boost—in real credits."

He paused.

A woman raised her hand. "Those Pell Mahr pricks in the Currency Guild gonna convert it for us?"

Jonas smiled, wide. Del stared, transfixed. She'd never witnessed joy on his face before. It transformed him. "Won't need Pell Mahr. I've negotiated with a Fring bank. They're willing to set up a kiosk in our Fring gate square."

Astonishment rippled through the crowd.

Jonas raised his hands for silence. The furor died. "No more hoofing to Pell Mahr to exchange Maze credits for G4 gelts. No more letting them bottleneck our progress. We can exchange at our own doorstep. That'll open us to better trade with the Fring and others."

Excitement charged the air—disbelief, anxious hope.

Del was mesmerized, wrenched with ire and awe. She'd had no idea that challenge faced Balter's Den. Little wonder residents practically worshipped Jonas.

"Now, this salvage opportunity. It's big. But I won't lie to you. It means sacrifice. We'd need to keep schedules. We'd need solid commitments from workers. We'd need folk to spend months skilling up. The work will be messy, and there are risks."

"Shit, Boss, that mess is already poisoning us, squatting close," a drunken man slurred.

"That's true. But living next to it and handling it are two different things. We'll take every precaution. I have a source for protective gear, but I an't lying about the risks. I'm willing to take them myself. I'll put in as many hours as I can."

Del drew a slow breath. She'd need to prepare for a contamination scenario.

The room burbled as people conferred. Jonas let it simmer, then swept the room with a grave gaze. "Here's the other thing. We'd need to manage operations solely in barter until we rake our first profit. Profits will be split; twenty-five percent goes back into the business, twenty-five to the warren. The bulletin will reveal exactly how it's spent. The remaining fifty will be divided among workers—as always, effort-in equals flash received."

"You sure you an't overreaching, Valerian?" Scratchy dissent rose from the crowd. Del's neck tightened. She recognized the voice, the "doc" Paela Umar. "Seems like you're trying to twist us into Pell Mahr's mold."

A few rumbles of agreement followed.

"I appreciate that concern, but we an't looking to become Pell Mahr. We're looking to become a prosperous Balter's Den that can support its people."

"*Prosperity* attracts gangs like sugar lures cril," a quavering male voice chimed in.

"Ha! You lot just don't like that you an't holding the sugar bag anymore!" Someone called from the back, followed by hoots of agreement.

Jonas waved the room silent. "Every voice is heard here."

"You gonna build your fences even taller to protect this new prosperity, Valerian?" Umar's voice rose, a querulous sneer. "Fancy walls and a fancy militia all in tidy uniform?"

Annoyance flickered over Jonas's face. "Right now, we're beholden to Pell Mahr for too many key services needed to survive. I aim to change that for our protection." His frown cleared, and his gaze skimmed the crowd. "We'll be taking votes throughout the week. Job roles are listed on the ballot, and I need volunteers to fill them—solid commitments. If we don't deliver, the customer will lose interest." He flapped a hand. "Pass the word."

That signaled the meeting's end. Jonas stepped off the platform.

A small hive of figures cut through the crowd to the door, Umar among them. Umar's eyes slashed toward Del as she passed.

Del studied her hands, knotted in her lap.

Nan had said Jonas transformed the warren. He truly was its heart— and brain. So much rested on a single person ….

A petite, round-bodied woman slumped up to Del. "I got some advice for you, doc."

"And you are?" Del arched a brow, too tired to pretend to politeness.

"Lettie. An old *friend* of Tam's."

Del blinked, unable to connect the woman to her meaning. Not wanting to. "I wonder why you'd be interested in dispensing advice to a stranger."

"You help people here, so I want to warn you." Lettie's face puckered with an attempt to appear concerned. "I got some history with your boy."

Del shuddered like Lettie had screeched her nails down grimy glass. "Unless you have something civil to say, I'll thank you to let me enjoy my evening." Del glared pointedly away.

"I wouldn't trust Tam Lyn if I was you."

How predictable. "You'll forgive me if I question your motives."

Lettie gave her a befuddled look, as if she'd prepared a script and Del kept throwing off her lines. "Toss-outs like him don't turn out good."

Del's repressive manner didn't silence the creature.

"Parents sold him to an alteration hack. You know. Made him a freak, and pimped him out to toffs who like freaks."

Del flinched, unable to help it.

"I'd watch your back. He's—"

"Enough!" Del slashed a warding hand.

Behind the bar, Nan edged closer.

Del glared at Lettie. "Take your spite elsewhere."

Lettie turned away with a smirk, and Del sagged in her chair, nauseated. What a cruel lie.

Lettie cursed, and Del's heart flipped. Tam stood paces away, his irises leeched of color. He radiated a chill that sucked the heat from the tight-packed room.

———

When Tam spotted Lettie, a sulky splotch beside Del, threat prickled over him. He hadn't glimpsed the nasty-bit in four years, but she was unmistakable. "What do you want?"

She smirked. "Just talking to the doc here."

Del leaped to her feet.

Tam's mind whited. He grabbed Lettie's arm, dragging her from Del, toward the door. Gape-faces craned after him until cold air and the sealed door blocked them.

"What the fuck do you want?" For an awful instant, Tam could barely breathe, remembering the slaver's garrote pinching his neck.

"Just curious how you been." Lettie tried running a finger down his chest.

He flinched away. Revulsion crawled over him. Those marshmallow cheeks and surly eyes … "Your latest scam run dry, so you're trying an old trick?"

She glared; his distaste mirrored in her eyes. "Don't worry. Your ghoul look an't in fashion anymore."

He narrowed his eyes. "This is about the doc."

"After what I told your precious doc, she won't be so keen on you anymore."

Humiliation flashed through Tam. Time had only been ticking until Del heard that rumor. He'd expected it, not from Lettie. "Who are you working for?"

Her eyes hardened, but her lips quivered, betraying her. She was scared—not of Tam. "I don't work like that."

"Right. You only make deals with flesh-traders." Surreal that his rage burned after so much time.

Poisonous envy spiked into him. "You should be *thanking* me. 'Cuz of me, you're all *cozied* up to the Boss." Lettie grinned with sly enjoyment. "Too bad I felt sorry for you. Should've left you for a gang-bitch."

Left him naked beneath leering eyes, his Rynet features catalogued and measured for sale.

"Stay the fuck away from Del." He pushed fury into his eyes, warping the shape of his pupils.

Lettie gaped as if a creature she'd considered toothless suddenly bared fangs. "What? You all juiced up over that snooty stick? She a kink into ghouls?"

He shoved his hand over Lettie's mouth to cover it. "Del is worth a *thousand* of you."

Needles of salacious curiosity alerted him, people gawking from across the street. A gold gleam of hair. Freth lurked there, his stare avid ... *eager*.

Tam jerked his hand from Lettie.

Lettie spat. "Toff-chaser!"

He should pressure Lettie to reveal her game, who she worked for—duty demanded it—but Tam couldn't endure the ugliness.

Lettie stomped away.

Tam pushed back into The Bar, walked to the serving counter, gripping its edge so hard, his trimmed nail sheaths swelled under his cuticles. Crackles of laughter and hissing whispers thickened the air. He wanted to disappear.

"Tam." Del approached, her aura, always such a clear signal, hushed now.

He straightened, wiping his palm on his pants, the imprint of Lettie's mouth corrosion on his skin.

His intention to ask for Del's help with his mother shriveled beneath the heat of humiliation. The gulf between their life experiences stretched like a chasm. He meant to say nothing, but words rose like bile, "What did she want?"

"To be ugly." Del didn't react to the bite in his tone.

"What did she say?"

"Nothing I cared to mark." The intensity in Del's eyes made them impossible to hold.

Tension strung his shoulders. "She doesn't know anything about me. Not remotely." Unbearable if Del believed he'd been sold as a fancy-boy by his own parents.

"All right." Her gaze flicked away from him, and the smooth skin of her forehead creased. Her expression cleared. "Will you walk me home now?" Her soft voice barely carried over the din.

He shifted his attention to the crowd, tried to smile, but his face wouldn't cooperate. "Seems you're having fun, doc. I can wait."

"I'd rather you walk me home," she replied in the same quiet tone.

He didn't want to look at her, couldn't help it. "Okay," he said, through a tight throat.

Her answering smile caressed, burning away the icy sensation freezing his face as if she'd touched him with the warmth of her hand. "I'll get my coat."

CALEB WATCHED LETTIE STOMP AWAY FROM LYN. SHE PAUSED MID-STRIDE, pivoted to watch Lyn disappear back into The Bar.

Seeing them together sparked Caleb's memory. She had some old connection to Lyn. Gossip was gold here, yet that thread had vanished years ago—which meant both Lettie and Jonas wanted it forgotten.

Aden had deflected Caleb's most circular approaches to Lyn's story. She didn't care about Lyn, only about Jonas—a stone wall of loyalty Caleb had no heart to test.

But Lettie? Caleb's role smoothing things for Jonas in the warren threw her into his path now and again. No longtime resident got by without leaving footprints—hers walking the short path to trouble.

Caleb approached her.

"Already got a lark." She crossed her arms. "An't interested."

He repressed a grimace. "NG." Which she had to know. "Just making sure you're okay."

Her blue-bead eyes brightened. "Got a tip for you."

"What'll it cost?"

She opened her mouth.

"Make it reasonable. Boss won't pay for intel, and I can't afford more than a nip." He flared his coat in a theatrical gesture. "As you can see."

"I'll take twenty."

"Ten."

Face wrinkling, Lettie caught the credit he tossed. "Got a friend with links to the Shadow Warren. She swears that glitter ghoul met with the patchwork gang there *before* they tried to jack the toff's shit."

He drew a slow breath. "Who's the friend?"

"Can't tell you that."

"What's the proof?"

She rolled her eyes. "You're an NG slick. Check it out yourself."

He turned away in disgust. Hesitated.

Gossip is gold.

29

Tam had returned to The Bar to calibrate Del's equipment after escorting her to the Fring early so she could work on a proposal for OBMG—the political crap that always roughened her temper. The Bar buzzed when Tam stepped through the doors—too many folk juiced with toxic excitement. The presence of the warren's worst flap-tongues added another clue. Something had happened. Bad news made good business.

The harshness made him itch to back out again.

As he crossed the tavern, more eyes tracked him than usual, gleaming with malicious speculation.

Tam's stride hitched. The treat they chewed related to him.

On stiffening limbs, he pivoted toward the backroom. A woman, puffed with pious cruelty, shoved her chair out to block him. Her ugly glare clawed into him.

He darted around her.

The air charged with hostility. He shrunk against it, unable to breathe until he reached Jonas's office.

Jonas frowned from behind his desk. "Lettie's boyfriend came in, all white-eyed, claiming she's gone missing."

Tam froze inside the doorway. "Maybe she found another lark?"

"Up and left all her stuff, her flash." Jonas's expression was too level.

Shock rippled through Tam. "You think I—"

"Give me some credit." Jonas waved his hand as if warding away a foul smell. "But folk are talking. Someone's spreading rumors."

Tam relaxed, only to clench up again. Jonas knew she'd approached Del at the warren meeting to cause trouble. "Why?"

"Lettie made some claims about you."

A troublemaker with a history of running cons "made claims" and the warren turned against him. Why did that *hurt*? They already called him a ghoul to his face.

Jonas gave him a level look. "Said you hired the patchworks through the Shadow Warren."

Tam held utterly still. Close to the truth and miles off. Lettie knew the patchwork's client. "Do you believe that?"

"No." Jonas's mouth flattened then he said, "Someone either paid or forced Lettie to disappear. I got no doubt she was put up to approaching Del at the warren meeting."

A tic fluttered under Tam's eye. "I'll find her."

"No. Rushing off half-cocked only plays into the enemy's hands." Jonas spoke implacably. "I put Aden on it. Lettie's from Aden's old block."

Why hadn't Tam pressed Lettie when he had the chance? "They made an example of her because of me."

Jonas's pale eyes grounded him. "*If* they made an example of her, it's because she agreed and then failed to do something to hurt you, or Del, or God knows who else. My guess is they meant to use Lettie to separate you from Del. When that failed, they left a blunter message."

Tam's throat convulsed over a reply.

"That girl was never going to come to a good end," Jonas said.

The truth hinged on who the patchworks were hooked to—the Surge? Umar? Brutal nights of stealth-work, spread thin between the two, had led to nothing. Jonas's ears hadn't done any better. "Do you think it's revenge for the mess at the recycling pit?"

But the Surge—their patron—had wanted to strike Tam down before that. *Let's kill him and send his head.* Fet scrutiny may have stayed their hand, but the threat lingered. And Tam had never told Jonas.

Jonas squinted at his desktop. "The Surge backed down the second I threatened to pull in Belek. I paid compensation, and we're officially calling it a wash. But, yeah. They an't happy with you. They won't make a flashy strike that might draw Belek's notice."

"Lettie's body will turn up to ratchet the fuss." Tam's stomach knotted.

"That's likely, so I need you to lie low for a while."

The knot tightened as Tam met Jonas's eyes. "Del needs me. I won't hide in a hole."

"It's just for a little while."

Was Jonas being upfront with him? Tam had failed to push Lettie for intel. Failed to catch the patchwork infiltration before it threatened Del. She'd flung herself into danger over Tam's mess with the Surge. Jonas wouldn't tolerate a chain of mistakes when it came to Del.

Tam knotted the fabric inside his pockets. "Me 'lying low' only gives our enemies what they want."

Separate Tam from Del? Or from Jonas.

"Sometimes giving in is necessary to keep the peace." Jonas pinned Tam with a gaze grown flinty.

Jonas's deeper meaning sank in, cold and hard. "You're reassigning me?"

"Folk may get ugly about this."

"*May* or already have?" *Even Jonas …*

"There's clack about bringing you to a questioning over Lettie's disappearance. I don't want anything to fuel it."

Arguments burned through Tam. He desperately needed to make them but couldn't speak.

He pushed from the doorframe. "You *wanted* me to care about this. About Del."

Jonas spoke. Tam couldn't hear it over a ringing in his ears.

It's over. He rushed from the tavern through the backdoor.

CLOSED WITHIN HIS OWN WALLS, TAM FLOPPED FACEDOWN ON HIS PALLET and roared into the cushion until his throat couldn't bear the strain.

Stupid … so stupid to get this involved with Humans.

Even Jonas. Why the hell did Tam endure so much for Balter's Den … any of it?

Tam sought his mother's spirit as he did whenever despair bit deepest—inexcusable, selfish clinging. Emptiness answered, and he bit his lip against it, hard enough to hurt. Then a soft tickle of warmth teased his extra senses, Del's aura as though she were near. Imagination, yet he closed his eyes, grasped that trace of her. Released it like an expelled breath. Del was no more his to hold than *Emere's* spirit.

Tam staggered to his feet. If it was over, he had little to lose—and little time left to take advantage of his Fring access.

30

Lights glowed over G4's crown, like a fancy hat above a wince-worthy face, marking the presence of a light-flier landing pad. G4 was uglier up close than at a distance. Below the pad hulked a gigantic lump of rock—not much to differentiate it from the planet's other homely formations.

A tram had taken Tam to the Fring's northern edge. There, the highway to the mine-city rolled out like a paved tongue—a low bridge strung above the dips and juts of the terrain. Towering light posts lined the road, casting a daylike glow over it, making the night sky overhead denser.

The need for action had driven him—escape from the awful, restless helplessness.

He hiked to the roadside and perched on the guardrail. Crisp air spiked through his sinuses as if some chemical had washed it clean. He raked a hand through his hair. *Get yourself caught* the smuggler Kuranev had suggested. *Be somewhere you shouldn't.*

Tam's heart drummed.

Putting himself in MS hands would be an irrevocable act.

Tam rose to his feet as if unwound by a rusty crank.

A truck whipped past, tossing his hair like an icy wind, and disappeared from view.

With a slow-drawn breath, Tam crossed the road to the far side—hesitated—hopped the guardrail, and half-descended the smooth embankment. His fingers traced the ocular in his pocket. A spy's tool.

He slipped it on.

Tam couldn't detect much through the magnification. The entrances' blankness revealed enough. Vehicles materialized or disappeared like magic on the highway—G4 was gated by field-tech.

A vehicle hum snatched Tam's attention. He flipped up his ocular, spun around. A tandem hov-bike settled into idle on the roadside above him. The faceless, helmeted heads of two Mine Security stiffs twisted his way.

Tam sank to a crouch.

"Come up with your hands raised," came a tinny voice.

A stiff climbed from the tandem, hefted a huge rifle. "You have no clearance to be here." The inflectionless voice warned an android lay beneath the carapace of armor.

Tam lurched to the side, helpless against the urge to flee. Force slammed against his back, zapping his nerves, sending him plunging down the incline. He sprawled at the bottom, eyes skyward, unseeing. Stun blasted, if not to unconsciousness. He twitched beneath a war of numbness and pain.

A dark shape loomed over him, cuffs gleaming in its gloved hands.

LIKE MOST DAYS, ENTERING THE VACUUM-SEALED SILENCE OF HER QUARTERS lifted a layer of stress. Like most days, the quiet grew oppressive.

Del had never lived so isolated. Until now, she'd always belonged to a community, if a disapproving one. How she'd despised its artifice yet had taken for granted an essential sense of belonging that came from understanding the rules. She'd fled from pretense but feared the tentative relationships she'd formed in the Maze were as hollow. They accepted her, insofar as she made herself useful, buffed her edges to fit the narrow slot they allotted her.

'They'll drain you dry.' Paela Umar's cruel warning kept ambushing Del in low moments.

Del rubbed her temples.

Go away. It's not the same.

She only needed rest.

Oppressed by her self-pity, Del tossed her vid aside and stretched up from the sofa, every joint crackling. A glance at the time showed it was only 22:10. She should finish her overdue proposal to expand hospital access. Her head ached with the attempt to find words that might move bureaucrats, to advocate for *real* lives via the sterile format. So much simpler to reach patients with her own hands.

Isa prodded her to find allies outside government, influencers in G4 who might lobby for her, because IWA's remote efforts had failed. *'Get into G4, build connections face-to-face.'* Easier said than done, and just the thought of playing politics made Del's stomach hurt. Too like the world she'd left behind. And with so many patients—an endless flood—how could she justify the time?

Del's stiff joints warned exercise was as overdue as her activism. Some movement might help unblock her. She'd changed into a fitness bodysuit when her door comm buzzed.

Frowning, she flipped up her wrist-vid, activated the comm. "Yes?"

"Del Marks?" an unfamiliar voice came through.

"Yes."

"I'm Corporal Brill from Mine Security. May we have a word?"

Del blanked with astonishment, shook herself. "Just a moment."

She flew down the stairs, slapped open the door. Two soldiers stood there, one a domed helmet reflecting a distorted image of her face, the other a young man with close-cropped hair. "Yes?"

"Ma'am, we'd like a word with you about the activities of your employee, Jon Gray."

She gripped the doorframe, too stunned to speak.

"Will you come with us to the station?"

Del's heart and mind went on pause as the two soldiers escorted her to the First Ring security station—not the closest, but one facing G4.

The corporal led her into a beige cube of a reception room, no visible surveillance equipment. But then, it wouldn't be visible.

Her handler, Qalvert, sat there, waiting. She hadn't seen him in person since he'd "arranged" her meeting with Jonas—nearly getting her killed. He lifted his gaze from his wrist-vid. The perpetually hooded eyes within his blandly sculpted features reminded her of a reptile.

Hard to confront that face suspecting he'd hired the Surge to threaten her, keep her from allying with Jonas. Isa Vinn might lament Del's inability to play an activist role, but every interaction with Qalvert warned Del that becoming too loud would hobble her ability to serve as a doctor. Del's laser focus on her practice had made Qalvert more cooperative.

"Administrator."

"Doctor." He gestured across the table. "Please sit."

A resin table and two chairs stood within the otherwise starkly bare space. An interrogation room?

Her stomach tightened. She shot the soldier a questioning look.

His expression softened, but he averted his face, as if harnessing an impulse to reassure her. Ducking out, he left her alone with Qalvert.

Why fetch her to a Mine Security station to meet her handler?

"What is this about?"

Qalvert presented her with his pinched equivalent of a smile. "Perhaps you can tell me?"

"It is quite late, Administrator Qalvert. I put in a twelve-hour workday, so I hope you'll forgive me for begging directness of you."

"Yes." Qalvert flicked his eyes to his wrist vid. "I see you crossed out the west gate at 7:02 and returned at 18:48—well, *nearly* a twelve-hour workday."

She stared at him, her eyes burning with the need to blink.

"Your employee, Jon Gray, crossed in with you at 18:48, back out at 19:00." Qalvert settled a cold look on her. "Then came again less than two hours later. Not to come to *you*, but to tram his way to the G4 highway."

She gripped the chair's armrests, digging her fingers into the foam.

"This is off-cycle for him. What do you suppose he was doing?"

"Taking in the view?" Del clipped back, determined to give nothing away.

"The view?" Qalvert managed to project the impression of raised brows without any movement on his resin-smooth forehead. "Of the security to lower G4?"

"Perhaps he was enjoying the cityscape?" Her retort ticked out. "It is best viewed from there. Is viewing the city's shell illegal?"

Her heart thudded the beats to his response.

"No. Not illegal." His words failed to loosen her tension. He was too smug. "Curious. And you cannot afford curious."

Qalvert's gaze dipped as if he could see her death grip on the chair. Perhaps he could.

Del tucked her hands in her lap, scanning his eyes for signs of lens-wear. "Where is Jon?"

"He's being held for questioning. He compounded the problem by trying to run."

Oh, Tam. Of course, he had.

Qalvert added, "Don't imagine we aren't aware of everything you do, doctor."

"Truly?" Del cocked her head. "And here I assumed you had no interest in my work for the people of the Maze."

"We know this Jon Gray goes by a different name in your *Maze*. Tam Lyn. We know your security situation is *less* than ideal."

She felt as if she'd swum too deep in a pool and surfaced in a dangerous place, unable to draw a full breath. Everything was slipping away—just when she'd believed she might make it stick.

Qalvert met her reaction with a wire-thin smile.

Del said, "Most Maze folk forgo last names." True enough.

"That's not an explanation."

"Jon is formal. He prefers to be called Tam." Her voice came out too breathy.

What the *hells* was she doing? She didn't know the first thing about Tam's past. Qalvert might have his entire history plotted. What if they checked her lie against Tam's statement?

Her linked fingers tightened. Foolish to allow Qalvert's intimidation to warp her judgment.

"And what do you call him in your private moments?" Qalvert's tongue lingered over "private."

"Tam," Del said flatly. Qalvert's pettiness freed the constriction in her lungs; pettiness was the tool of a bully. "The Maze lacks a registration system. He can hardly be accused of using a false name when he has no legal one. As I understand it, Mine Security uses facial recognition, not names, as primary identification."

"Hmm."

Taking a long, silent breath, she leaned back in her chair, crossed her legs. "So, the OBMG has kept tabs on me? I confess I'm grateful for this silent protection. If that's what it is."

Qalvert blinked.

After a strained pause, he spoke like she'd triggered playback on a recording, "You are aware of the position of our government. We do not acknowledge the squatters and cannot provide you any protection. You signed waivers—"

"I am aware of the risks I've assumed. However, it did seem alarming that the OBMG might be completely disconnected from the situation."

"We have a nest of thugs and thieves at our gates. You may be sure we *keep tabs* on every aspect of the situation."

Surveillance via technological or human tools? Both. So, she'd assumed. Qalvert's openness about it made it feel worlds more sinister. "I serve *people*, not nests of anything."

"Let me guess." Qalvert gestured expansively. "You're enacting the middle's rebellion?"

"Pardon?"

"Perhaps you don't have that saying on your home world? The middle child. Runs away with musicians, gets body-brands—anything to gray her parents' hair."

Del found herself staring again. He'd struck too close to the mark. "I'm an only child."

"My apologies. I might know that if your background weren't sealed."

"Privacy protections can be necessary in some posts." This one more than most.

"I'm sure your Allied connections find that excuse convenient."

He's only throwing barbs to see what makes me flinch.

Del shifted into the carefully correct posture drilled in from childhood —knees aligned, hands laced, chin up—a protective instinct she'd never shed. "May I be frank? It's quite late, and I imagine you have more important concerns."

"Certainly." His focus grew diffuse, like his mind rushed elsewhere.

"I've no interest in politics. I only wish to continue my work." A slice of flattery couldn't hurt. "What would you suggest I do to make that happen?"

"Keep tighter rein on your man, for starters."

Not *fire your man*.

Her fingers relaxed against her thighs. "I was only told G4 is restricted to us. If you could provide clear guidelines about other off-limits areas, I would be grateful."

"I'll have something patched to you."

"Thank you."

He stood, then paused as if considering. "I think it would be wise if we touched base on a biweekly basis. To align on any other issues that might arise."

As if she had the time to waste! This had been an empty, sign-off exercise. Taking advantage of Tam's blunder to remind her the OBMG had the power to kill her mission? Why bother? And Qalvert had done more than that. He'd revealed they were spying on her.

"If you think it necessary." She gritted another smile. "Now, will you release Jon—Tam, if you will—to me?"

Qalvert studied his wrist-vid. "It seems he's been identified as a person of interest. You may wait here until next steps are determined."

He strode from the room.

"Just a moment!" Jerking to her feet, she stalked after him, but the soldier stood outside the door, barring her way.

31

———

HEAT SEEPED THROUGH THE CELL'S FLOOR. TAM STOPPED PACING. IT ONLY made it hotter. Maybe the temperature felt cozy to Fring toffs put in the box, but the MS stiffs had found an ideal way to torment a half-Rynet— not that he was sure they knew. Yet.

Kuranev was wrong. They'd taken his DNA. He'd spent his whole life stressing over what would happen if his mixed blood got exposed in the Maze, and he'd just handed it over to the MS.

Get yourself caught to figure out what the MS knows. Genius plan.

Tam plunked onto the cell's low plastic stool, chaining his thoughts to his physical discomfort. Thinking about anything else made the glue holding him together crack.

He stared at his hands. A thick, black coating rimmed his cuticles, his sheaths growing in again. The nailbeds were inflamed. He couldn't bear to keep yanking the sheaths out—but then, he wouldn't have to, now.

That realization dragged Tam back to his reckless stupidity, like his thoughts were magnetized to it. He groaned, bit his thumb—a habit of frustration since childhood. *Emere* always clicked her teeth to scold him for it.

Sighing, he draped his arms across his knees. How many times had he lit a flame in the darkness for her this way? Beckoned trouble to himself?

Choice made, pointless to regret it.

A beep outside his cell startled him. The door slid open, revealing an expressionless stiff.

Tam straightened on the stool as the woman moved inside. When another, helmeted solider followed her, Tam pressed his back against the wall. Their dark uniforms made the blank white walls seem lit from within. He blinked until his vision adjusted.

With a single stride, the woman stood before Tam's boot tips.

The other soldier blocked the door.

"Relax, Mr. Gray," the woman said. "This is only an interview."

He studied her silently.

She was all harsh lines—curveless brows, severe mouth, iron-straight bangs. She focused on a card-sized device in her hand. By the smear of color above it, its screen holoprojected but had a security filter. "I'm your detainee liaison."

A bullshit name for an interrogator?

"What am I being held for?" he asked, low. They'd already grilled him about his misguided sightseeing. This was something else.

The woman shifted aside, fingers flying over the device. Tam startled as an image flashed up on the cell wall. Jon Laurent. *'You've the look of your father.'* The large image forced Tam to see what he'd missed: the jaw, the cheek bones—like blunter versions of Tam's.

"You recognize him." Not a question.

Lying was pointless. "Yes."

"Who is he?"

"My gene doner."

"Your father."

"Never met him."

"Do you know where he is?"

"I barely know *who* he is."

The woman kept her gaze fixed on the device even while she spoke.

Tam's skin crawled. This whole cell must be webbed, feeding her an analysis of his reactions. "What does my father have to do with why I'm here?"

Her eyes lifted, her aura as chill and emotionless as her stare. "There is a process, Mr. Gray—or Lyn—or whoever you really are."

"Seems like you know more about who I am than *I* do."

"Clever." A weird smirk twisted her face. She fixed back on her device, waited.

What did it matter what he revealed? His father decades gone, his mother a decade lost, he could only damage himself.

Tam kept himself blank-faced—futile if she read his spiking vitals through the webbed walls. "I know he did something to piss your bosses off, then got kidnapped by smugglers."

The woman held silent until time stretched to snapping.

Questions bubbled like hot oil inside him, but he needed to draw her out, not expose himself.

"You are an anomaly, Mr. Gray. If there are *twenty* Human-Rynet mules in all the universe, I should be surprised."

His stilled, skin crawling with threat.

"And *those* tend to come from test-labs—parents more eager than able to commingle. You are a mystery. Your Human father, Jon Laurent, kidnapped a Vleran Rynet from our stable, fled to the Outer Rim. The investigators kept the case open but surmised he'd killed her."

'He gave up everything to fight for my freedom.' For the first time in his life, Tam burned to defend his father.

"You are a problem, Mr. Gray. You see that, of course? The investigators' theory doesn't explain you."

His pulse tripped as it struck him. The MS didn't know what happened to *Emere*. Get to the truth by the questions they ask, or don't ask. In that, Kuranev had been right.

Which left Tam a step closer to nowhere if the MS never released him.

Expelling a breath through flared nostrils, Tam glared into the woman's face until she finally met his eyes. "You want the sordid story so you can solve that cold case?"

Another weird smirk. "My organization dislikes such loose threads."

Tam probed, "You have another reason for caring."

"Perhaps her people finally demanded her back." Words too smug to gauge their truth.

The nagging heat, the scrutiny, grew unbearable. He only wanted out. "My parents made me and figured I might not go down well in *the stable.*

They planned to escape on a smuggler ship. Got betrayed. My father drew the smugglers off. My mother fled into the Maze."

A hint of ire rippled through the woman's emotional signature. "You're saying she's been here, in the Outer Rim, all this time?"

"She's dead. Otherwise, I'd let you grill me a thousand years without telling you squat."

"You're telling me, Flepa Ke Ali got *accidentally* impregnated by her Human handler, *willingly* fled with him, bore you in the wild, and *chose* to stay there."

"Truth flies freer than fiction."

"And then you just happen to materialize among us with this IWA activist?"

His anger cracked beneath the needle of new threat. "I've been kicking around Balter's Den for years. Shouldn't be hard to verify."

The woman slapped off the holo on her device, snuffing Jon Laurent's image. She pivoted sharply toward the soldier.

Panic broke Tam's surface calm. "You can't hold me just for being an *anomaly*. I've cooperated."

The woman spoke without turning back. "The problem is the difficulty in assessing the veracity of your statement. Half-Human. Half-Rynet. Which behavior algorithm should we use?"

The door hissed shut behind her.

Tam sank over his knees. Despair gripped him as it hadn't when the Surge captured him.

A fate worse than beheading—to be sealed in this featureless box forever.

Hours passed. It must have been hours. Tam couldn't be sure. They'd taken all his equipment.

"You're free to go, Mr. Gray."

Tam blinked against a startled contraction of his pupils. A stiff stood in the doorway. Tam hadn't heard it open.

Before the stiff moved aside, Del's aura flared nearby, barbed with agitation. For a moment, he couldn't unlock his legs to leave the cell.

Del stood beside the stiff, her hands crimping the edges of her coat. Face averted, she handed him a plastic sack, his things, then turned and strode down the corridor.

He followed like a scolded child.

Curious stares tracked them through the station lobby. He'd given the stiffs a nip of excitement.

Del swiftened her pace when they crossed through the exit.

The night air's cool relief didn't penetrate past Tam's skin.

Del flagged a light-tram and stepped on. Tam awkwardly followed. They were the only passengers, but he couldn't speak. Del clearly wouldn't.

They reached her quarters in silence.

So tempting to take off, never have to face her. Muzzy-headed, wobbly, he longed for the safety of his pod. His heart wrenched. Had the MS told her?

Biting the inside of his lip, Tam forced himself to step inside after her.

Del didn't face him. "I wonder if you consider that you owe me an explanation?" The foreign clip he'd hardly realized had softened, now re-honed her voice.

"I've never gotten a good look at G4. I was curious."

"Do you think I'm stupid enough to swallow that?"

"Would it be so strange? This is my world, and I've never seen more than a sad blip of it."

"You are the most *incurious* person I know."

He inhaled slowly. "What the hell does that mean?"

"I have never witnessed you asking an idle question—not once in all these weeks." She spun to look at him, and he wished she hadn't. Her face was an unfamiliar mask of anger. "I don't suppose you were thinking of getting *inside* G4? Even I don't have clearance for that."

"I just wanted to check out its shell."

"You'd jeopardize my mission for mere curiosity?" Her lips pressed white. "They are itching for an excuse to kick me out. You know that, Tam! They've been tracking our every movement in and out of the gate."

He blinked at her. *Stupid, stupid ...* He'd been stunned brainless by Jonas's rejection, had hardly given Del's risk a thought.

"They took my DNA." His words slipped dully out. "What will they do with it?"

Del's eyes flashed. "How the hells would I know? This rock doesn't exactly follow CP Human rights conventions."

He sucked in a breath, her cutting sarcasm a shock, though her anger already saturated his senses. He'd never witnessed her be cruel.

"Why are you worried? Is there some trouble they can link your genetic signature to?"

The MS hadn't leaked his heritage. Del's punishing aura drowned his ability to react.

"They already know the name on the ID I secured for you is false—I suppose *I* was insane to agree to that in the first place."

Tam's hand closed over his ID pin. Numbly, he removed it, thrust his hand toward her.

Her anger only boiled higher. "What's this, Tam? You wanted to sabotage me or yourself?"

"I don't know what you mean."

"You never wanted this job, only took it because Jonas pressed you."

Unable to speak, he opened his palm to her.

"That's rich. You're quitting now?"

"I'm not quitting, I'm being fired," he said hollowly.

His throat knotted so fiercely, he blinked against the pain. He dropped the pin, watching it clink over the floor. Then he turned and fled from Del's furious reaction.

<hr>

Del stared at the pin, Tam's tiny holo flickering. She raised her foot to smash it to dust. He'd wanted to be fired! He hadn't even given her the courtesy of the truth.

Gnashing her teeth, she drew her foot away, pinched up the pin. Tam's acting a child was no excuse for her following suit. She shrugged off her coat, slumped onto her desk chair, and tossed the pin down.

Tam's image glared with accusation. *'I'm not quitting, I'm being fired.'*

Could she even manage without him? Jonas could find her another guard, but Tam did so much more for Del. She rubbed her eyes and groaned. Too much. He worked as hard as she did—harder—because he trekked twice the distance every day. He calibrated her equipment, managed her supplies, guarded her on outcalls, kept rowdy patients in line. Not to mention the "stealth-work" on her behalf, the constant danger.

Little wonder if he'd forced her hand.

Del knew perfectly well Tam had some reason for his choices tonight that he'd never share. He deserved her outrage for risking her mission over some secret scheme. But she wasn't blameless.

Her anger caved, leaving a horrible ache in its place.

"I always ruin everything," she whispered.

Enacting the middle's rebellion.

Her family's chill love, her grandfather's autocratic behavior, made it easy to justify running from them. Yet she'd never found anyone to replace the hole they left.

'I doubt you care a whit about the populations you devote yourself to. It's not about them at all. It's about congratulating yourself for your own piety.' Mario-Johns's poisonous words thrust home now as they hadn't when he'd spoken them.

Did Del see her patients as individuals or as numbers she stacked up to prove her effectiveness? She'd been heartsore when Pepar first came to her but had forgotten her until they'd found her mutilated and near-death—and Del had considered leaving her blinded and disfigured to save a voucher.

Did Del appreciate each NG who helped protect her? She didn't know half their names. And Tam? She hadn't offered him a regular day off since he started.

Del could be as cruelly selfish as the rest of her pampered clan.

She spun Tam's pin with her finger.

The digital on the desk interface blinked midnight.

Del shot to her feet, sending her chair spinning backwards. Dashing across the office, she palmed open the door, nearly stumbled over him. Tam sat beside the entrance, arms knotted around his knees, head tucked down. A ripple moved over his shoulders as he processed her presence.

"Come inside, Tam. It's bitter cold."

She held her breath until he uncurled and rose. His gaze shifted, landing anywhere but on her. She stepped into her office, resisting the urge to grab his hand and tug him with her. He followed, hovering inside the doorway.

He looked remote, so miserable.

"You might have told me if you wanted to quit," she said softly.

He focused on her, direct and intense, as if peeling away her expression. Del resisted the urge to drop her eyes. He seldom looked at her so squarely.

How vividly sketched his features seemed—as though projected there by something brighter than flesh and blood. Del seldom looked at him that directly either, afraid she would look too long.

She swallowed against a stinging in her throat. "I can't imagine how you've tolerated me."

He watched her silently until her cheeks began to heat. Hard-edged alertness transformed his manner. "You paid me a shit ton of money to trail your boots, doc."

She winced. "Yes. Twelve, fourteen, even sixteen hours a day. Tiring, tedious … dangerous."

"Danger came with the territory, or didn't you consider that when you hired me?"

His words struck like a slap. She'd been so eager to begin her work, she'd scarcely spared a thought for the danger she would place him in.

As if he'd lured her thoughts into a snare, Tam said, "This is my home. I've seen the suffering here *all my life*. I have more right to risk myself for this than you do."

Tears built behind Del's eyelids as he continued, "Life's short here. It's not like I lived in a safe little bubble. Dying for a cause beats dying because some flesh-trader nabs me."

He was manipulating her, but his words still hurt. Her tears spilled over.

Tam made an odd, slashing gesture with his hand.

Glaring through blurry vision, Del whirled away.

He caught her shoulder and tucked her against his chest. The rough fabric of his jacket pressed against her cheek. She registered the lean, muscled length of his body.

"You need me, angel," he whispered. "You still need me to keep you safe."

Del ached to sink against him and savor the delicious contact, his softened manner, but his breathing was too careful, too compressed. "What's wrong that you don't want to tell me?"

His hands dropped away.

She leaned back to meet his eyes, but his face tilted toward the floor.

"Jonas is assigning someone else to you."

Her breath whooshed from her, a strange, dizzy relief. *That* was what had set this off!

"*Jonas* doesn't pay your salary. Why would he presume to do that?"

"Lettie disappeared."

"And?" Her voice thinned.

"They're saying … someone's spreading rumors that I …" Tam lifted his eyes to hers. His words leaked through immobile lips. "They're trying to make you get rid of me."

A strange buzzing in Del's mind made her sway. Fierce protectiveness roared inside her. Tam flinched as though she'd shouted aloud. His gaze scoured her face, hunting furiously for her response.

Del closed her eyes. The evening's events had proven how easily her new life could crumble, how easily the OBMG could use Tam to make it crumble. Del had won Isa's cautious support. If Isa found out—

"Del," Tam whispered.

She opened her eyes.

He stood as if braced for a blow, his eyelids crimped, his hands clenched.

"That will never happen." Tam mattered too much. "Not unless you want it."

His chest gave a deep swell. "I'm sorry I … fucked up tonight."

"Please take a few days to decide what you want."

"I don't need a few days." His voice hardened. "I'm not quitting."

'*They took my DNA. What will they do with it?*' She'd callously considered his words only as they impacted her. Tam's fear must link to the past he so fiercely guarded. Genetic manipulation was as illegal on Galta 4 as on more civilized worlds, but not even the OBMG could blame a fetus for its birth. Perhaps Tam was protecting someone.

"You're not quitting, but you want to." Perhaps needed to.

His eyelids dipped. She sensed how deliberately he erased all trace of vulnerability. "You need me, and you know it."

"That's my problem, not yours. If you continue with me, I must have your promise never to jeopardize my mission again." He opened his mouth, but Del spoke over him. "Take the time off—for me, if not yourself."

Tam's brows pinched. He scanned her face, nodded, edged back. "I should go."

Del knew Tam needed comfort and reassurance but was unable to ask for those things. When he turned, she caught his forearm. The corded muscles clenched beneath her grip. "Keep me company a while."

"It's late." He edged toward the door, hesitated.

"I've a fine bottle of Cartoran wine." She added, singsong, "Nan would be upset with you for leaving me to drink it alone. I'm quite cranky when hung over."

"You could take an enzyme pill." His gaze flickered over her body, making her conscious of her form-hugging workout clothes.

"Where's the fun in that?" She covered her sore heart with a mischievous smile. "Come. I promise to stick to vapid subjects. I'll even change into one of those charming jumpsuits you seem to prefer."

"Is that supposed to be an incentive?" His lips twitched.

"I'm certain they're the height of fashion … somewhere in the universe."

He shook his head, the tension in his shoulders easing. "You keep telling yourself that."

Tam couldn't bear to leave. The hum of Del's aura, the quiet of her quarters, soothed his agitation. Crushing desolation would return without her.

He sat in her plush, deep-bellied chair, boots off, knees tucked, guarding her sleep. She lay on the sofa, curled into fetal position, her hair fanning from its queue to cover her shoulders. The wine had dropped her quickly. Or more likely stress and exhaustion.

What *was* it about Del's aura?

He couldn't help but suspect she had psychic gifts, too, that the irresistible pull of her aura signified connection. It went deeper than auras and emotions. Sometimes he read her will like she planted it in his mind.

Del might be unaware of it herself.

Tam's fingers, curved over his kneecap, absently sketched an *ah'nea*. The gesture expressed something difficult to fit into Human terms—equal measures warmth and gratitude. Catching himself doing it, he contracted his hand.

Tam found himself using *ah'nea* with Del more and more—as if she had a prayer of understanding Rynet emotion symbols. He probably looked like an android with a tic to her.

Yet, Del increasingly saw beyond his frozen face. Despite the ugliness surrounding him, despite his spiny nature, she hadn't cast him off. Tonight, over the wine, she'd spun words that transported him from the Maze, off Galta 4, totally engaging, touching nothing personal.

She'd sheltered him again.

Del stirred, her fingers flexing, threading through the hair beside her cheek. He glanced at his hand; his skin tickled as if it were his fingers twining through her hair.

Her grace period chaffed like a punishment. She'd promised Tam the choice to continue, but she'd be upset once she connected the dots, realized Lettie's disappearance represented a personal strike against him. Jonas would no doubt help her connect them.

Del could have—probably should have—fired him for his stupidity tonight. Just considering his action could have handed the OBMG an excuse to kick her out hurt his stomach.

Tam rubbed the heels of his hands against his brow as if that could erase his mistakes. Fixated on the past, he rarely considered his future. Crouching outside Del's office, loss sapping his limbs, he'd realized he had a future to risk, after all.

Rising soundlessly, Tam knelt beside Del.

His search for his mother was exactly the cause to fire Del's compassion. If she saw through his cover story, she wouldn't push him. She'd never use her diagnose on him for curiosity. If he woke her now and asked, she'd do what she could for him.

Tam's hand hovered over her cheek to brush away the hair. He lowered it without touching her.

He'd withered thinking Del might pity him based on a lie; it would grind him to powder if she pitied him based on the truth. *Hide, hide,* the litany of his childhood, whispered from *ver'ela* still ...

Del sighed, curled tighter in sleep. He retrieved her coat from the sofa arm where she'd flung it and spread it over her.

Protecting Del meant never jeopardizing her mission. It meant never poking his nose anywhere near the OBMG's Rynet program. It meant steering clear of the Shadow Warren.

He needed a different path to truth about *Emere*. Maybe a different kind of truth. He could think of only one place to try. Home. If he could get in. If they didn't kill him first.

Tam would risk it. He couldn't risk Del again.

32

The Xeno warren's outer walls stood six stories high, made of a sandy, unscalable material and crowned with barbed wire. Light-tubes flickered at intervals to illuminate intruders. The Maze's non-Humans had learned to mistrust their Human neighbors.

Bleakness filled Tam as he studied the barrier. The Arnec gate guards would never allow Human-looking Tam through.

A storm-battered notch lipped the No Man's Land side, just below the top, flat enough to secure a grappling cable. Tam shot his cable. The connector clipped the lip and arced back down. He tried again—over and over—until he swallowed a shriek of frustration.

Tam closed his eyes to reset his nerves, tried again. It struck and held, at last.

He hooked the base to his belt then retracted the cable, walking his feet up the wall as he rose. At the summit, he flipped on top. The barbed wire scratched the leather clothing he'd worn for protection. He released a ragged sigh.

A huge shadow surged toward him, bolting him against the wire. Bumpy hands clamped around his throat—iron strength that could easily crush his windpipe.

"Not so easy, Human!"

"Wait!" Tam wheezed in Trenabic.

The being dragged Tam toward a light, snagging his body over the barbed wire.

"Tamalan!" The strangle-hold released.

Flecks of beige dappled the matriarch's glossy gray forehead. Distinctive brow ridges shaded her bead-round eyes. Her hairless head was covered by a sheer blue mourner's scarf.

Easing off wire that cut into his nape, Tam sat and tucked in his rubbery limbs. "Peace, *ssura-ri* Yoranya."

Yoranya belonged to the cluster neighboring Golalya's. Lucky she'd recognized him, or she'd have tossed him from the wall like a toxic threat.

A Trenabic watcher *atop* the wall. Something had happened.

"Tamalan, why are you here? The cluster is closed to you. You are grown now." She used the slow clicking cadence reserved for children.

"I seek ... knowing." Tam cringed at his clumsy words. He'd grown up with Trenabic, would never forget their language, but was years out of practice forming its sounds.

"Information?" Yoranya interpreted. Her smooth cheeks puffed with unease.

"My mother."

Golalya had told him that his mother left for a job to help the cluster before she disappeared—a lie, but one she'd clung to like a sacred truth. The informant Hana's story about a Human incursion into the Xeno around the time his *emere* vanished niggled at him, made Tam want to test Golalya's truth again.

Yoranya dipped her chin, the equivalent of a headshake. "You live as a Human now. You cannot seek the cluster for any reason."

"Cluster sought *me*. Two weeks ago." Golalya's visit was the only reason he'd dared this.

Yoranya blinked rapidly. Surprise or distress.

He switched to Common. She'd prefer it to his garbled Trenabic. "They asked for my help. I gave it. Now I ask for help in return."

"I cannot let you inside." He opened his mouth to argue, but she dipped her chin again. "You would not survive. Humans killed an Arnec outside the walls last week. For sport."

I'm not a fucking Human, he burned to shout. No point. "Please speak with me."

She pressed her abdomen, the equivalent of a sigh. "Your mother's fate, only rumors. Rumors sting worse than ignorance."

Trenabic possessed memories as fierce as their frames. Tam considered how to sway her. "What about truth? Events around that time? Anything you can remember."

She hesitated, then began in Common. "Big push then for rellium. Mine borders expanded. OBMG believed illegal mining a security threat."

"What kind of threat?"

"Unclear. Gang mining is like flea bites. So much planet. So much ore. But, if they get close, OBMG worry. Big salvage that year. OBMG retired fleet of diggers, gave to Freshay." Freshay, slang for Free Space Salvage Handling, an OBMG-sanctioned company that carted away rough material and chemical waste for repurposing.

Yoranya slid her upper bony mouth-plate over the bottom in concentration. "One digger exploded underground. MS swarmed site like dumpster cril. Then we dismantled for recycling."

Mine Security had investigated the wreckage before allowing Freshay and its Trenabic workers access.

Digger explosions must be rare. Anticipation tugged at Tam. Could it have been the Fet digger from Hana's story? Jacking a digger from OBMG strained plausibility, but from Freshay? And Hana's Fet lover had claimed they'd enslaved a female Rynet for their illegal mining.

"Did they … find anyone?"

"Bodies gone before we arrived. Bad damage to craft." Yoranya's small eyes blinked rapidly with distress.

"Do you remember where?"

"West." She spread her hand flat, sketched a map over her broad, leathery palm. "Here G4 City walls. Small crater west of Fring. Maybe, visible still."

How could Tam reach the site? OBMG monitored the wastes outside the Fring. *Stupid idea, anyway.* Security would have stripped any evidence of his mother if it existed; Freshay scrounged every scrap of wreckage; and after nine years, whatever remained would have corroded away.

"Tamalan," Yoranya said as if to signal the interview's end.

Tam swallowed, looking away.

He tried to pierce the dark shrouding the Xeno below but only made out weak blobs of light, wavering in smog-dense air, hinting at the lumpy shapes of buildings. For a blink, he imagined diving down, as if the gloom could cushion his fall.

"You have no cluster?" Yoranya's voice quavered with pained disbelief. To Trenabic, it was unthinkable for a male to leave the household with no new family to join.

Tam dipped his chin. "My mother was all I had."

Yoranya flared her double-thumbed hands in a wide, helpless gesture.

He couldn't help pressing. "Whatever truth remains of her is here."

Yoranya switched to Trenabic. "Golalya vowed to keep you safe."

"Humans took my mother." Tam tested, though reading Trenabic with his gift was tricky.

Yoranya sighed. "That is all we know."

"Gangsters?" He managed through a squeeze of his heart.

She made another helpless gesture. "Humans all dressed alike. Some thought them OBMG. Others a gang. To us, there is little difference."

"No one fought for her," Tam whispered, hollow. So hollow.

"I cannot know what she intended, but she went willingly."

Tam flinched, a cold, remote reaction—too small.

Yoranya reached out and knuckled his chin higher. "Your mother was tiny, but she was a matriarch. She would never allow her cluster to die for her."

He couldn't speak.

"Before you go, share dorepa with me," Yoranya insisted softly, unhooking a canteen from her belt.

As a child, he'd hated dorepa, a tea Trenabic consumed with as much enthusiasm as Humans did ale. Yet as the tart, syrupy liquid slid down his throat, it tasted so much like home his vision blurred with tears.

"Tamalan, to our people, no one ever leaves family. Always here." Yoranya's hand thumped against his chest.

He licked dryness from his lips. "I am holding her. It's hurting her." *Hurting us both.*

Yoranya's head bobbled. He thought he'd confused her. Then she brushed his temple with her leathery finger. "Release here." She patted his chest again. "Hold only here."

Tam breathed sharply, at the edge of an awareness at once obvious and elusive.

Yoranya's face quirked in the equivalent of a smile.

He mimed the expression, braced himself to leave. "*Ssura-ri,* why are you here watching?"

"Things are stirring outside our walls in Human spaces."

"What do you mean?"

"I mean … danger." Yoranya blinked down at the lights of Human habitation as if struggling to read the threat in the patterns they formed.

33

―――――――

Dear Rhemy,

It grieves me to worry you, but this place, these people, are real to
me now. Giving up is impossible.

—Del

DEL FACED YET ANOTHER QUERULOUS ELDERLY PATIENT, EYEING EVERY STEP OF the exam with squinty suspicion. It still daunted her to encounter such mistrust after months of grinding success.

Considering Umar, they'd no doubt a right to hold misgivings toward "docs."

Del watched Nan usher the patient out the exam room door with a soft-voiced word of reassurance. Gusting out a breath, Del propped her hip against the exam table, gave a thin laugh. "You're a godsend, Nan."

Nan winced. "I'm sorry. I busted that syringe."

Ignoring the protest in her weary back, Del straightened. "Nan, you *do* realize you've flown through months of prework in mere weeks." Astonishing, really.

Nan shrugged. "Don't need much sleep." Her mouth gave a wry twist. "We an't total rock-heads here. Jonas smuggled in workstations, set up a school on Meyar block—everything from basics to advanced. Folk log there when they can."

Del studied Nan's tense shoulders. "I know that. It's appalling that education must be *smuggled*, but the ingenuity here quite takes my breath."

A rap on the door alerted them before Caleb poked in his blond head. He spared Del a tight smile before fixing his gaze on Nan. "Belek's called a questioning. We need to escort Del home."

Del swallowed a protest. Cutting her hours short for safety had become a familiar drill.

Nan quickly stowed the loose supplies and locked the closet while Del fetched her outcall pack. They followed Caleb down the hall. Aden met them at the base of the stairs. Jonas's second maintained a friendly reserve with Del, her brash dress and manner like a shield.

The entrance burst open. Del flinched as Torx strutted inside wearing her tasseled visor and high-stacked black wig. Her tonsured partner followed behind, head and shoulders framing her.

Aden and Caleb gated the path before Del.

Nan stood, iron stiff, and Del reached for her hand.

The two Surge gangsters strode across the taproom, swallowing the space with their presence. An NG waiting by the backroom door waved them over. It had grown so quiet, Del detected the clinking of Torx's tassels against her high-necked jacket.

Torx paused, whipped her head toward Del. "I owe your freak for Fuse. We'll demand Valerian give him over like a present."

The grief in Torx's rough voice struck Del harder than the threat. Del trusted Jonas would never allow that demand.

Aden and Caleb didn't relax until the gangsters disappeared into the backroom.

"I should have killed that bitch when I had the chance." The violence crouched in Nan's voice slackened Del's grip on her hand.

"I hope you never have to," Del managed weakly.

Dear lords, it still shifted the ground beneath Del to see her friends morph from caring warmth to hard hostility. It shook her belief that she could ever embrace the life here.

Tam studied the steel column embedded in the Fring's western wall, an overlook facing No Man's Land. Hard to imagine what toffs wanted to view here. Maybe they needed a window out of their fenced-in world, even to a wasteland.

Hard to imagine what *he* wanted to view here. Yoranya's tale of the exploded digger made too thin a thread to call a lead. Yet he found himself compelled to try and view the site.

Del's "handler" had sent a list of Tam's boundaries. He wasn't risking her mission with this trip, but his skin prickled with awareness that the MS could cage him again anytime they decided the *anomaly* warranted it.

An android manned the overlook's base to screen visitors. Shuddering under the android's dead stare, Tam hopped into the enclosed car. He'd never been in an elevator before. It raised him to the top in seconds, leaving a weird sensation in his stomach.

The elevator opened to a narrow chamber with a shallowly out-curving window. Tam stepped close to the glass, staring down. The taupe-and-purple-washed stone field that formed No Man's Land looked eerier from this vantage. Even the sky appeared different, rusty-cast and clashing against the cold-tinted ground.

He drew his ocular, slow-scanned the terrain. *There.* An odd-shaped divot marked the landscape's center. The right area for the exploded digger.

Tam studied the depression, gooseflesh misting his skin. Could this be *Emere's* grave?

He stared until the sealed silence, the alien atmosphere, wore on him. No certainty awoke; no stirring from *ver'ela* offered a clue.

With a sigh, he pushed off the glass. Hesitated. Peered deeper through. In its stillness, the desolation held a kind of peace.

Tam felt Yoranya's phantom touch at his temple. He curled his hand over his heart, absorbed her wisdom, the wisdom of her people.

He'd been chasing rumors and smoke for four years, not truth. The belief he must learn *Emere's* fate to free her reflected *his* need, not her spirit's imperative. His weakness. An excuse to cling. Another reason to stay focused on the past, ignore the bleakness of his future. For years, he'd had no one to hurt by the obsession but himself. Del had changed that. His denial of that change had threatened her, nearly cost him everything.

Emere, with her matriarch's courage...Tam would find his own courage.

"Goodbye," he whispered through a knotting throat and sketched the *ah'nea* for filial respect, limitless love. He pressed his forehead and fingertips to the cool glass, sensed a tingle of her presence against his skin. It dissipated, mingling with his expelled breath.

Tam flexed his fingers against the window, then wrenched himself from the view and strode to the elevator.

He'd hung back like Del asked, taken two days off. He wasn't giving her a third.

CALEB STEPPED OUT THE BAR'S FRONT DOOR, BUMPED STRAIGHT INTO BELEK. Freezing like he faced a blade, Caleb blocked the rest of Del's escort. He waved them back and let the door close.

Belek eyed him like some incomprehensible, ridiculous thing. "Don't wet your pants, Freth. I an't here about you."

Caleb expelled a shaky breath.

"Convenient, that mess about the toff's exotic." Belek spoke close, an odorless puff against Caleb's cheek. "Don't suppose you'd know anything about it?"

Caleb stiffened. The flap that Lyn had offed Lettie. The flap that might land Caleb in Lyn's job—that Caleb had planted to ensure it did.

Checking for watching eyes, Caleb said, "What the hells could I know?"

"Can't help thinking it has Dugan's stamp all over it."

Belek shouldered past him into The Bar. His train of stimps shoved harder, leaving Caleb trembling with hate.

'*We want the same thing as Dugan,*' Belek had said when he'd force-recruited him. Caleb had assumed Belek meant the Fet wanted to spy on Del, but he could interpret the enforcer's words another way—they also worked for Dugan.

Aden poked her bright head out the door. Caleb stiffened with the irrational fear she'd overheard.

She frowned at him. "Okay?"

"Just had to make way for that Fet slick." Caleb managed a wry grimace.

The smile half forming on Aden's face wilted. She spoke behind her then squeezed out the door. "What's going on with you, Goldie?"

He folded his arms, cocked his head. "Aside from running into that snake? Not a thing."

She studied him beneath a wrinkled brow. "That restless prickle in you lately worries me. You an't done something foolish, have you?"

"Come on, now." He held her gaze by force of will. "Plenty to be restless about these days."

"You can always talk to me." Her brow smoothed but her scrutiny didn't relent. "You know that, right?"

Gods, in that instant, he longed to. His throat grew tight with it. Unload to Aden. Cry his shame. Let her fix it. But he wasn't a rag-nosed kid anymore. He'd flipped the Trickster's Coin—his future to win or lose.

"I know, Addie." He squeezed her arm, tense beneath his fingers.

Before she could say more, Caleb yanked the door open. "All clear."

Grimm, the third in their escort team, poked his shaved head out, then ushered Del onto the street.

Caleb turned concerned eyes on Del. "Okay?"

"Perfectly fine." Del lifted her chin.

Aden widened her copper scarf, as if the wire accessory could ward the chill. "Don't worry. That enforcer's all business when he comes here."

Del's lips pursed. "It's my canceled appointments I'm worried about."

Aden crinkled her eyes like she held in a laugh. "You should take advantage of the break and fluff out your skirts."

Del blinked. "Pardon?"

"She means have some fun, doc," Caleb translated.

"You *do* have your colorful sayings here."

They set off with Caleb and Aden flanking Del, Grimm taking the rear.

The Boss hadn't said anything about Lyn, only told them they'd be running escort a few days. Caleb should be pleased.

He was pleased.

Just edgy.

The Lettie situation had unfolded like Belek said, *convenient*. But assuming Dugan had the means, he wouldn't have bothered arranging Lettie's disappearance. He'd been confident in the power of gossip. *'A sound plan, at last, if a bit messy.'*

Messy. The shades of that word rippled through Caleb.

The Boss suspected the Surge. Just a sick, ill-timed coincidence. Convenient. Ill-timed. Caleb's stomach wouldn't settle enough for him to decide which held sway. He *needed* it to be coincidence.

The streets grew crowded as they neared the Fring gate. Migrant season had started, so more folk crossed into the Fring than usual. Block-sentries manned their route but wouldn't be much help once they descended into the square. Crime rarely happened close to the secured gate, but more bodies increased its potential.

A trike-cart whipped past in an acrid cloud of overheated fuel cell, nearly clipping Caleb's shoulder. He glanced at Del, resisted the urge to cuss the cyclist.

Lean forms peeled away from a building and twined through the commuters to encircle them. Punks bent on trouble.

"Be ready." Aden flipped open her jacket to access her weapons harness.

Caleb tugged Del behind him. Grimm and Aden closed around her.

A teen with a buck-toothed grin sidled up to Caleb. "Don't be like that. We just want a word with the pretty fem."

Six kids formed the pack. Caleb didn't recognize any, which put him on further alert.

Aden flashed her blade. "Get your handouts elsewhere."

The boys danced away, eyes comically wide, hands raised. Caleb started to relax his guard when a slouched figure surged through the teens, flung an object between him and Grimm. "Toff bitch!"

Caleb twisted his body to shield Del, catching a flash of the attacker's red-glazed eyes as he turned. A splash against his jacket hem. A clatter under his feet. The stench of acid seared his nose. Then Del's scream consumed him.

Del sagged in his hands. He kicked aside the metal container the assailant had thrown, sank to his knees, easing Del down with an arm around her back. He stared into her eyes, stunned, before regaining his wits and yanking off her coat—smoking at the collar.

"Aden!" He glared around, but she'd torn after the assailant.

The kids had vanished.

Grimm remained to stand guard, and a block-sentry rushed toward them.

Angry welts covered one side of Del's neck. She clawed at her jump-suit's clasp, the acid a dark corrosion soaking her collar. Caleb covered her hand with his, helping her draw down the zipper and ease the cloth away. Del panted with agony. Swallowing hard against the sight of bubbling flesh, Caleb drew a knife from his belt, cut away the fabric, and tossed it.

"What should I do?" he said, unsteadily.

Her eyes swam to meet his. "Were you hit?"

"I'm good." Her concern made him flinch his gaze away. "Let's get you to The Bar."

He shrugged out of his jacket, hacked off its corrupted hem, and tucked the fabric around Del. His hand trembled, concern for her warring with the awful significance of this failure.

Wasted chance …

An image of Lettie's round, eager face flashed through him.

Wasted …

Caleb got control and swung Del's limp body into his arms. He jogged toward The Bar, heart pounding with his footfalls, Grimm and the sentry guarding his heels.

34

Tam took in the sparsely occupied tavern, the sullen air, and stopped short, drawn up in his eagerness to reach Del like he'd been yanked.

Nan, weaving her way between the tables, waved him over. "Belek called a questioning. He and his pack are here talking to Jonas. Surge already cut out, long-fanged mad."

Her strained manner heightened his tension. "You mean Belek found out about the recycling pit."

"Jonas'll do what he can to protect us." Nan glanced toward the stairs. "If you're looking for Del, Jonas sent her home."

"What?" Tam stiffened. "*Who* with?"

"Aden, Grimm, and ... Caleb."

Tam dipped his head mechanically, stalked to the stairs. Caleb Freth— who always moon-eyed Del, who Jonas had considered assigning to Del at the start.

When Tam reached the exam room, he stood before the door, staring blankly.

How hard would Jonas push Del? She'd clashed with Jonas over Tam after the Surge fight, but this was more serious.

He unlocked the door, shoved so hard it struck the wall. Unoccupied, the room lay gray and grim, like an empty cell. Tam had spent many painful hours here, punished by the attention of strangers. *Ghoul. Glitter boy. Freak show.*

Tam sagged against the doorframe. God he was tired, like the past few days' emotional toll had hit his body more than his heart.

He stepped back and reset the locks.

A disturbance below pricked his ears along with something he shouldn't sense—Del's aura.

Imagination?

Tam dashed to the landing. Froze. Freth wove through the taproom, around jabbering NGs streaming in from the backroom, his yellow head bent over a form draped in his arms.

Del.

Tam sprang down the stairs in two bounds. Jonas appeared from nowhere, catching his arm with a forceful yank. Tam whirled, stopping shy of striking him.

"Easy, Tam. Let him report."

"A woman threw acid at her out of the blue. Aden went after the bitch." Freth's voice shook—anger, distress, a hint of fear.

Tam's eyes locked onto Del. Freth had covered her with his jacket, but her torso was clearly bare. Her neck bubbled with red, angry skin. A sickly-sweet smell reached Tam through the usual choke of ale, grease, and male sweat.

His lip peeled back, a challenge hiss forming low in his throat. Jonas tightened his grip, releasing Tam from his Rynet reflex.

"Get Nan!" Jonas roared to Kimber who manned the bar, watching with alarm-goggled eyes.

"Give her to me!" Tam glared at Freth like he could crush him with his gaze.

"The handoff will hurt her," Jonas warned. "Caleb needs to get her upstairs."

Tam took a shuddering breath; forced himself to let Freth pass ahead. He shook Jonas off, stalked after.

The tavern exploded with gossiping voices and spiky emotions.

The instant Freth laid Del on the exam table—removed his hands from her—Tam was beside her. Leery gaze on Tam, Freth backed from the room.

Del's eyes were closed. She breathed with shallow hitches. The rage drained from Tam, replaced by a sick, gnawing sensation.

"Del?" He touched her cheek, found it clammy.

With nothing else to do, Tam tugged a blanket off a cot and covered as much of her as he safely could.

Nan burst in, emanating such a thick steam of anxiety that he flinched back. "Tam, the diagnose!"

He stumbled to the closet. The whites of Nan's eyes flashed as she accepted the tool. She initiated a scan with shaking fingers. He tried to read over her shoulder.

Muttering, Nan leapt to the supply shelf, knocking over items in her haste.

Tam's breathing kept tempo with the rapid rise and fall of Del's chest.

Nan returned clutching two syringes. Teeth rooting into her lower lip, she pressed them against Del's arm. Del twitched with each stick. A syringe clattered to the floor.

Nan jerked her attention to Tam as if recalling he stood there. "She'll be okay."

Her words weren't confident enough to unknot Tam's stomach. She held out the diagnose, but Tam didn't shift his focus from Del's face.

Del's eyelashes fluttered, lifted. She blinked at them as if clearing her eyes. "I've ... caused a commotion."

"You scared *the hells* out of us." Tam's relief twisted in on itself.

Her subtle smile flipped his heart, made him feel foolish.

He retreated onto a cot, tucking up his knees to prop his chin.

Nan applied healing gel with Del's guidance. Del's calm soothed Tam. She never looked at him, but he knew she was aware of him, just as he knew her serenity was crafted for his sake.

Before long, Jonas burst in, refilling the well of tension in the room.

Tam swallowed a snarl. Not the time for blame.

"We have the woman. She's connected to that kid you rescued."

Del's aura spiked with alarm. "We won't have to return Pepar, surely? She's still in the hospital."

"Hells, no. We need to root out who hurt her and stop them." Jonas turned to Tam. "I'll need you."

The urge to act, take down the enemy, fired Tam's nerves—a more comfortably familiar sensation than his ache of concern for Del.

35

TAM HAD TO SWITCH OFF THE CONNECTION BETWEEN THE CREATURE shivering on the backroom floor and the brutal burns on Del's body. He didn't trust himself. Bound and gagged, the woman lay like a pile of rags and twigs—too lost to addiction to care about food. He covered his nose against the miasma of puke and unwashed body.

"That's her," Tam told Jonas, standing at his shoulder. Jonas must have weighed the need for Tam to identify the woman over his *laying low*.

Tam ignored Del's worthless escorts, who hovered behind Jonas.

Jonas squatted beside the prisoner. "You have broken Balter's Den law and been placed under NG justice."

Her eyes burned defiance as Jonas ripped off the gag. "Fuckin' toff chasers!" The force of her curse spewed foam from her mouth.

Tam recoiled. Jonas held like iron against both the ferocity and the spit.

The woman arched up. "Toff bitch deserved it. She killed my man!"

"No." Tam inched closer. "*I* killed your man." He was only spicing the flap about himself. He didn't care.

Jonas shot him a quelling look.

The woman gaped at Tam. Her flat, dirt-colored eyes jerked to Jonas. "Keep your ghoul away from me!"

"Who put you up to this?" Jonas demanded.

"Put me up to it? What, Boss? You think folk want that toff spreading her off-world stink here?" Whatever she saw in Jonas's face straightened her sneer.

Tam swallowed his rage. "Did anyone put you up to burning our doc?" He needed the woman to answer directly.

She smirked. "That bitch took my kid and my man, so I gave her some payback."

"You an't that girl's mother." Jonas glared with icy revulsion. "What mother tosses her child like trash?"

Her ruined cheeks twitched. "I thought she was dead! I swear! And she's mine. Ask around."

"Either way, we don't tolerate mutilating children in this warren." Anger stamped each word. Jonas leaned down. "Give us the dull-knife's location, and we'll let you off with exile."

"Don't know." Fear coarsened her aura. "That hack just gave me some lush now and then. Didn't realize what happened to my kid 'til too late."

"She's lying," Tam snapped. She was in it up to her lush-doused eyeballs.

"Start talking or face in-kind justice. Never mind what you did to our doc, you left that child mangled and suffering." Jonas unsheathed a knife.

The woman's lips quivered around her gap-toothed maw.

Tam shifted closer, struggling not to gag on her sour stench. "You sent Pepar to our doc two months ago. Why?"

The woman wobbled backward, a jitter of bone and fabric. "To jack stuff for the dull-knife. What else? But she fucked that up."

Of course. That's why Pepar had been so skittish.

"Where's the butcher's nest?" Jonas growled, grabbing the woman's filth-matted hair, wielding the knife.

"L-let me go, and…I'll tell you. I swear!"

Tam narrowed his eyes. "Why'd you have Pepar after you handed her to the dull-knife?"

"Only got a nip for the brat. Be more if she lived. I fed her, wiped up after her—all the stuff the dull-knife was too high-nosed to do."

"*Right*, like tossing her when she died," Aden said with soft-voiced horror.

"Too scrawny to start. Dull-knife said she was ... unworthy." The junkie squinted with concentration over the last word, ending in a hysterical hiccup.

"How many 'unworthy' were there?" Jonas smacked a fist against his knee.

"No others ..." She jerked her head left and right. "My kid, she was a ... test."

Tam sensed an anemic trickle of grief, as if beneath the hespar lust that had swallowed her soul, she was capable of regret.

Jonas snatched the woman's chin, held her still. "You've given us nothing, so you better focus and think."

She blinked. "The Surge. Dull-knife talked like they were the customer?" Impossible to judge her honesty now. She'd burnt through her wits.

"You'd muck with that knowing what the Fet will do if they find out?" Jonas asked. The Fet considered trading in exotics their turf.

"An't *me*. Just the dull-knife."

"You were leaving Pepar as a symbol. For what?" Tam interjected. Time was running out.

The woman squinted at Jonas like he'd asked the question. "Eh?"

"*Who's* the dull-knife?" Jonas pressed. "A name, description. We need details."

She choked on her saliva, her poisoned blood pulping her mind, shredding her aura.

Tam's anger curdled. Whatever evil this creature had committed, she'd get a dose of justice. Hespar made a cruel killer. "Jonas, you'd better get the location *now*."

Jonas met Tam's eyes, lifted a hand in signal.

THE DULL-KNIFE'S NEST LOOKED AS ROTTEN AS THE JUNKIE'S TEETH. It sulked between two pod complexes, like a slump-shouldered vagrant, its narrow frame unequal to the weight of its tiled roof. A second-floor window gaped open, unlit. The first-floor windows were boarded up.

Tam trailed Freth and three other NGs as they burst inside, wrist-lights flaring. The militiamen's commotion stirred the musty stillness like a current. Tam paused in the doorway, needing to expel a hostile breath before dealing with Freth. *Golden boy* stiffened beneath Tam's narrow glare and edged deeper into the space.

Jonas shouldered around Tam. "Abandoned."

He'd insisted on joining the operation. The target lay in the Taber warren, just inside its border with Balter's Den. Protocol demanded the warren chief arrange the NG's passage through the gate—a boundary that had been disputed until Jonas negotiated a settlement and built the fence.

Jonas crossed the cramped entryway to the only visible interior door, kicked it open, and shone his light.

"This is it, all right." Jonas flipped on a string of ceiling lights.

Cold illumination gleamed over a raised metal slab in the room's center—the operating table. One shelf-lined wall was jammed with oddments Tam had no desire to close-eye. A chemical stench oozed from a small sink.

Unwilling to cozy with Freth, Tam left to search the upper level. The junkie had been too far gone to give a name or description of the dull-knife. They needed clues.

Tam recoiled at the filth. The floor crawled with clothes, bottles, and other trash, the air fetid with traces of reefer, rotten food … fouler things.

Yet the lab showed a pretense of hygiene. Maybe the junkies had lived up here, minding the girl in this filthy space. Covering his nose, he crouched over blankets littering the floor. Bloodstained. Tucked in one corner lay a lump of cloth. When he probed it with his boot, he found a face clumsily painted on, a makeshift toy. Tam whirled away with a sharp-drawn breath.

He stalked back down the ramp joining the two stories and checked the remaining spaces. There was a meal nook, fouler than the upstairs, and one other room, its door lurking beneath the ramp. Tam kicked it open. Another workroom, mechanical parts scattered over a workbench, the air thick with a solvent smell—cluttered, but not squalid like the living areas.

A glass tank on a shelf drew him. Inside, a small creature writhed; a cril with a metal plate grafted to its head. The ugly, furless creatures plagued the Maze, but this was too cruel. A second tank squirmed with roaches, live ones crawling over the dead. Experiments.

The dull-knife had started with vermin and worked his way bigger— until he'd turned his butchery on a Human child.

It wouldn't end there.

Tam straightened, whirling his focus around the room. *This* was both the patchwork's augmentation source and their shadow partner. After Pepar failed to jack Del's stuff, the dull-knife tried with the patchworks. And when they failed …

Gritting his teeth, Tam drew a knife and ended the cril's misery. As he wiped his blade clean on a rag, his neck prickled with warning.

Tam expanded his senses, perceived no one close. He crossed to the lab. Jonas and the others were searching the room, revulsion churning their emotional signatures.

Tam stepped toward a boarded-up window. A noise scraped from outside. Through a slit between the planks, a presence flickered. Tam narrowed his focus.

As if noticing Tam's wary preoccupation, Freth frowned at him.

Tam spun to go outside and investigate. His gaze landed on a screen shoved against a dim corner. A strange outline, just visible in the play of light at his angle …

An NG closed to investigate that corner.

"Ogranta, get back!" Freth leapt toward his teammate.

A form burst through the screen with a whirring and a flash of silver. A curved blade thrust into Ogranta's chest.

Shouting erupted through the room.

The android's blade yanked free.

Freth surged forward to grab Ogranta as he collapsed with a gurgle. The blade slashed toward Freth's head.

Tam leapt to the operating table, shoved it against the android's torso, pinning it to the wall. Its bladed arm snapped up, hammering the table with a spritz of blood. The table bucked, shoving against Tam's gut.

"Some help here." He wheezed.

Jonas came, thrusting the table so hard, metal ground against metal.

Tam blindly groped for his crossbow, nearly dropping it as he drew it. Biting his lip, he aimed it at the sensory eye in the android's fraying mesh face. The bolt missed. He gnashed his teeth as the table shook. His second bolt struck home.

The android's limbs spasmed. It flailed blindly.

With a growl, Jonas grabbed a stool, bashed the android's head until it whined and curled over the table, its mesh face caved in.

Behind Tam, a soft click sounded through the window slit, barely audible over layers of heaving breaths. A buzzing followed—*inside the room.*

Gooseflesh crackled over Tam.

"Everyone out!" Tam shoved Jonas and dove through the door. A pop punished his ears, shouts, a pelting noise. He tripped, striking the entryway floor hard on his forearms.

With a stunned gasp, he pushed onto his knees. "Jonas?"

"Here." A heavy rasp came from behind him.

"You okay?"

"I'll do. What the hell?"

"Android self-destructed."

Triggered from outside.

Cursing, Tam pushed to his feet. "Umar. It's fucking Umar." *Of course,* it was.

"Guard the Boss," Tam snapped at Freth, who had rolled up against the wall.

Tam staggered out the front door, chased by Jonas's bark of inquiry.

For a breath, the night air was cold static. Then Tam detected the scuff of retreating footfalls. He followed the sound around the building. There, he made out a bulky shadow in the alley, swift-striding away. Tam pursued on the balls of his feet to muffle the sound, but his quarry caught his scent, began running in earnest with a lumbering, uneven gait.

Tam closed the distance.

His target whirled to face him. Tam was confronted with Thuron's distorted features and lopsided bulk.

The patchwork's small mouth twisted. *"Lyn."*

Thuron's aura was unrecognizable, as if his soul had curdled. Hatred blazed, invasive, personal. It drew Tam up short.

Thuron hunched his massive shoulders, twisting his bulky prosthetic. The blade released with a snick. The prosthetic appeared cruder than the one they'd removed, but the blade's gleam was unmistakable.

"I've been waiting for the chance to kill you."

Tam crouched into a fighting stance, leveling his crossbow while wielding a knife in his other hand. "Come try it."

Thuron closed the gap between them in two long bounds, his muscles bunched like a large beast's. Tam's crossbow bolt met its mark on Thuron's shoulder. Pinged off. Then the bandit was on him.

Tam dodged Thuron's powerful swing, ducking under the blade. He whipped his knife across the bandit's torso. The blade met flesh. Thuron grunted. His metal plating didn't extend below the upper chest.

Tam darted behind Thuron, squeezed off another crossbow shot.

Thuron pivoted, making the shot go wide.

Twisting, Tam avoided a slash from Thuron's blade. A metal-gloved fist slammed into Tam's shoulder. Pain exploded down his arm. His crossbow went flying. He barely held onto his knife and leapt away from Thuron's follow-up swing.

They circled each other, breathing harshly.

"Why are you blowing up dull-knife digs, patchwork?"

Thuron's hatred crested over Tam. "Wouldn't you like to know, jack-bait? Maybe I'll tell you after I separate that pretty head from your body."

Thuron lunged with wild, hard swings of the club. Tam dodged each blow. The bandit had him in brute strength, not speed. Flesh and metal didn't meld well.

"Umar add more rust to your body, but you an't happy with the result?" Tam probed Thuron's anger. Its acid spike showed Tam hit close to the mark.

Thuron lurched with a powerful swing that would have taken Tam's head off had it connected. Tam darted away but slipped on loose pavement. Thuron's gauntleted hand grazed the side of Tam's head, dropping him hard on his tail bone. Tam kicked out, knocking aside a strike that would have split him down the middle.

Thuron raised his blade, using his hand to support the heavy appendage.

Tam rolled, sprang to his feet, and scrambled back—clumsy from Thuron's blow.

"You're a slippery little bastard," Thuron snarled. "You fight as fem as you look."

"Yet you still can't best me."

"Tam!" Jonas's bellow echoed from the dull-knife's lair.

Tam startled. Thuron snatched something from his belt and flung it. The dart burned a slice across the side of Tam's neck.

"Here, Boss!" Tam called, clamping a hand over his wound.

Thuron sprinted away, down the alley.

Cursing, Tam dashed after him. Slowed by the punishment he'd taken, he couldn't close the distance.

The cramped wall of buildings opened, exposing a sheet of blackness ahead, the border with No Man's Land. With a grunt and a scuttle of stone, Thuron disappeared.

Tam halted, peered down. Thuron was skidding down a steep incline leading to the wasteland. Adjusting his pupils to find a purchase in the dark, Tam leaped down and landed behind Thuron. The bandit whipped around. Tam smashed his shoulder into Thuron's chest, sending Thuron tumbling with a roar.

Thuron smacked flat on his back and slid against a boulder.

Tam surged after, pinning Thuron's club arm with his knee, pressing his knife to his jugular. "Move and I'll slice you open like a tin of hash."

Thuron bucked. Tam dug his blade in a fraction, and Thuron froze.

"You got a grudge against Umar, but you knew she abandoned her digs." Why lurk there? Why the flashy strike at the NG? "You making war on Balter's Den?"

"You can cut me and kill me, but I an't telling you anything." Hard determination shaped each word. The frustration and rage in Thuron's emotional signature gave no clues.

Tam couldn't imagine the patchworks willingly becoming leashed to anyone. "Umar got to you lot, didn't she? What does she have over you?"

A blast of light blinded Tam.

Thuron took advantage, flung Tam on his back. Tam caught the club's sides with his boots, countering by instinct. The blade sliced into one of his soles. Gripping with his feet and jerking with all his strength, Tam unbalanced Thuron, sent him tumbling—cursing and scrambling to the bottom of the slope.

Tam spotted the light's source. A truck, waiting below.

"Go after him?" a voice called from the cab.

"The little shit's quick. Next time." Thuron called, "You better hold onto that sweet piece of yours, Lyn!"

Tam sagged against the rocky ground. The hov-truck glided away. He stared after the lights as though lashed in place.

36

Since meeting Del Marks, Tam had made too many grueling treks. By the time he got back to Umar's dump, Jonas and the NG had cleared out.

"Stupid," Tam spat.

Umar had kept two places, two identities. Part of the old guard, in control when no fence partitioned Taber and Balter's Den, Umar could easily have assets in both warrens.

Jonas's ears had failed to track Umar here. Tam could clone himself twice over and still be stretched too thin to case all their enemies.

He tapped his ear only to find his audio clip missing; lost in the fight.

Swearing, Tam retrieved his crossbow and jag-footed back to The Bar, half sheeted with exhaustion by the time he opened the tavern's door.

Del was there, crouched between two men stretched out on pallets. Anxiety shaded her aura. A plastic-like substance covered her neck and shoulder, exposed by the tank top she sported. Light rippled over her arms as she moved. Her hair tangled down her back.

Del turned, gaze clicking to his. He felt relief bloom inside her, at once warm and sharp. She stood as he limped across the taproom.

"What the *hells* are you doing, Del?"

She jabbed her pointy chin at him. "My job."

"You should be resting."

Tam frowned at Nan, who knelt by a patient, flustered. No use blaming her.

He sighed, shifting to the wounded men. "Everyone make it out?"

One turned wary eyes toward Tam. "Ogranta didn't make it."

Of course, he didn't. The bloody spatter from the android's curved blade … Tam dragged a hand through his hair. A loss like this would hit Jonas hard.

"Boss and the other boys are checking your tip about Umar," the man said.

Good. "You guys gonna be okay?" Tam asked mechanically.

"Thanks to the doc … and you. Without your warning …" The man shuddered, as uneasy giving Tam thanks as Tam was receiving it.

Tam could prove his value a *thousand* ways, and these Humans would never see past his surface. He glowered at his mangled boot, drew a slow breath.

"They'll recover in a few days," Del said low, studying him. "You're hurt." An accusation.

"It's nothing."

"How can I put you at risk if you won't accept care when you're wounded?" Her eyes were weighted with a question, *a test.*

Days of stacked stress bore down, but Tam forced himself to answer calmly. "I will. I promise. When it's serious. It's not."

"Your face is black and blue, and you're covered in blood!" She pressed her fist against her temple like raising her voice pained her.

"Go lie down and take care of *yourself* for once."

"Not until I ensure these men are settled."

"You *will* go if I have to carry you. Nan can watch over them." Del's stubborn stoicism was more than he could handle.

Nan's leery gaze shifted between them. "I'll do, doc. You need to rest."

Del seamed her lips, propped her hip against a table—trying to hide how crown-to-toes wilted she was.

"I'll go if Tam agrees to let me treat him."

He padded closer. "I'm not negotiating."

"Don't test me, Tam Lyn. I've been waiting for *hours* not knowing what the bloody hells happened to you. Jonas is worried sick. NGs are combing the streets for you as we speak. Why does it always have to be *you*?" Her voice frayed.

He glanced at her patients. Better not make their precious doc cry. "Fine. No big deal." Tam stomped to the stairs.

Del minced after him. Tam stalked back and swung her into his arms, disoriented as her aura surged into him—or maybe Thuron had knocked his brains loose.

"I can walk," she said through her teeth. "I don't need you dropping me on the stairs."

"I'm not watching you hobble like a gnarl-jointed granny. And, if I had two broken arms, I could still haul a little-bit like you up these stairs."

"Bloody Maze machismo."

He steadied himself, carried her to the exam room, and gingerly set her down.

She scowled, patted the exam table. "All right. Up you go."

He shrugged off his jacket, wincing at the singe mark on the collar. "It's just a scratch and some bruises. I can deal with it myself." His heart drummed jaggedly. He couldn't let her turn the diagnose on him.

"I can't imagine what you think you must hide from me. Your medical history would be confidential. You know that." Her gentle rebuke covered a well of hurt.

He knotted his hands to hide their shaking. "I'm tired. I can't … get into this now."

Her gaze flicked to his hands. "Very well. We'll discuss it later."

"You need to rest." He swayed with a relief that seemed to lighten his brain.

He helped her to a cot, settled her against the pillow.

"What happened tonight? I heard some of it … Umar …" Her eyes glazed with fatigue.

"Rest first. Please."

He stepped to the closet, grabbed healing sealant, and dabbed it over the slash on his neck. When he turned back, Del lay staring at the ceiling like she'd been clobbered and left stunned where she'd fallen.

"You don't have anything to prove to us anymore," he whispered.

"No? Perhaps I have something to prove to myself."

"Why?"

After a pregnant pause, she said, "I come from a place of hollow privilege, hypocrisy, and blindness to the suffering of others. I won't live that way."

Whatever drove Del was far more painful and personal than that. "You can't undo it all yourself."

She closed her eyes.

He studied her finely sketched profile, the movement of her eyes beneath the lids, the flare of her nostrils as she breathed. *'Better hold onto that piece of yours.'* Thuron's parting threat replayed in his mind.

37

———

THE LOUNGE WAS NESTED INSIDE A CLEAR BLISTER ON THE SPACE STATION'S side. The absolute vastness threatened to swallow Delmara whole. She huddled in a chair, hugging her updrawn legs.

Her father loomed before her. "This is the premier space resort in *all the civilized worlds*. It's beautiful! Like floating in the stars."

Angry impatience. Like she usually got from her floras, not from him —not from his words, anyway. Her lip trembled.

"Stay here for now. I must secure our rooms and go … find your mother." *Mother.* His tone carried burrs of meaning, too painful for Delmara to grasp. "Flora Tepith will watch you."

Tepith hated Delmara most. Why didn't her father realize?

He walked away with angry steps.

The plush seats scattered through the lounge seemed like dollhouse furniture set in a jar, drifting through space. Tepith stood by the lounge entrance, arms folded, scowling down at her wrist-vid.

Delmara bit her lips. She mustn't cry. Not even in her head.

She tried. Truly tried. She sealed herself shut—mouth, eyes, fists—no sound escaped, but Tepith's head jerked up. *Be still! You unnatural child!*

Why did Delmara *hear* the poisonous thoughts? Surely, she was far enough away? She squeezed her eyes shut, rolled her forehead against the knobs of her knees.

"You can't fall in, you know."

Delmara nearly toppled from her seat. The chair beside hers, facing outward, spun toward her, revealing a small figure inside. Another child. His appearance startled her more than his voice: pointy bones, a sparsely lipped mouth, and blue skin—not jewel-bright shades like from stories, more like a wash of watercolor, a mist-grayed sky.

"You're a Rynet," she blurted, swiping the tears from her eyes.

"And you're a Human," he shot back. His fingers lifted, a ripple of meaning she didn't understand.

He was about her size, but his manner made her think him older.

"Please excuse my rudeness," she stammered.

"You're the first Human I've met who cared about being rude to a Rynet." His accented words danced, making it impossible to guess if he laughed at her.

"Why should Humans be rude to Rynet?"

He flashed his narrow teeth, purple-glossed—a protective coating, she recalled from lessons.

"Humans are rude because they fear us."

She lifted her chin. "I'm not afraid of you."

"Yes. The stars are much scarier."

"I don't like them around me." She frowned. "It's like you could send your thoughts out there and they would be swallowed up."

"You're one of those moody, poetical children." He leaned toward her, expectant. "Perhaps we shall get along. I'm Jenl."

She squinted at him. "Delmara. You don't mind I'm Human?"

As if he hadn't heard her, Jenl said, "In a way, the stars *can* carry thoughts away—from people like *us*."

"Um?" *People like us.* Warmth lightened her belly.

Jenl rested his head on his knees. "Thoughts can pass through natural energy pathways as voices transmit across communication pathways."

She wrinkled her nose. "What do you mean?"

He twirled his fingers. She somehow knew it meant he couldn't say. His dark eyes faded, his eyes bleaching to a dull gray.

"What's wrong?"

"I'm only tired. So many...don't understand."

"I will try." Delmara leaned forward to show she meant it.

His thin lips curved. "That makes me feel better."

They sat together, eating sticky, dried fruit he'd pulled from his pocket when a shrill bleat startled them apart. "Delmara! What are you about? You are not to play with … strangers. Are you eating with your *fingers*?!"

"Here comes the graytle herder." Jenl, sighed.

"A what?"

"A domesticator of animals." His eyes sparkled, lightening from black to gray.

She smiled with grim challenge. "I will not be a graytle. Ever."

Jenl took her hands in his cool, dry ones. Delmara stiffened. She wasn't used to such contact, though it felt nice. "If I teach you to reach me, no one can keep us apart," Jenl said.

She trusted he was serious. "Teach me."

He smiled, tightening his grip on her hands. "I'll show you."

A froth of sensation fizzed through her brain—painful and pleasant at once.

***

DEL STIRRED FROM SLEEP, THE BASE OF HER SKULL SORE, A NOW FAMILIAR pain.

The Rynet boy again. Real memory or dream-muddled? Snippets of memory stitched into a dream. Del was cold and agitated as if faced with a forgotten keepsake trove, both frightened and eager to discover what it contained.

Her mind swam with images: Jenl's mood-stone eyes, his lilting voice, the glossy black fronds of his hair, the flicker of his fingers ….

So like Tam …

Del's thoughts and dreams muddled and mixed as she pulled back into sleep.

***

DLMARA

Jenl's voice, at last. Delmara's skull ached from calling for hours.

Unimaginable physical distance separated them, but reaching him had never strained her so before.

You wouldn't answer so long. I was worried.

Forgive me. I'm only tired.

His feeble presence frightened her, yet she spilled her fear for herself. *They think I'm mad. They want to take me to some horrible place.*

Then you must stop talking to me.

Never! I'd be alone again.

Ett'eren, it grieves me to leave you.

He didn't mean her situation. He never spoke of his, but she sensed things beyond the thoughts he shared.

Take my energy to get stronger. She poured all her will through their connection.

Pain spread over Delmara, snapping her into her body. Her cheeks stung as if lashed with nettles.

"Your father is here! Wake up, girl!" Tepith's hateful eyes raked her.

"Don't strike her." Her father's voice came, breathless, disturbed. "We'll take her to that specialist as my father demands, after all."

A babble of voices kept her from Jenl. She fought them. He needed her! A sting on her arm flooded cold into her veins.

She swam in and out of darkness before she made out voices.

"… extraordinarily rare condition, Mr. Fedelo. Growing research indicates it may be a mutation—n-not *ill*ness, but a rare neurological—"

"Quackery," her father said, as if deflecting a horror. "I can't have my child made a spectacle."

Heavy silence. A deep, scratchy breath. "All we know for certain is that abnormal brain development causes this activity on the scan, a static in the mind."

"How do you *fix* it?"

"Neurotherapy…might repress it. We could try antipsychotics. But there are side effects."

"Worse than her fading from us? Do what is necessary, doctor."

Jenl! They mean to make me a graytle! Jenl?!

Blankness, as if he were wiped from existence.

TAM CRACKED HIS EYES OPEN, REGISTERING NAN AND DEL'S VOICES, TOO groggy to grasp meaning. Playing guard, Tam had crashed on the cot beside Del's. That her distress hadn't woken him was a measure of his exhaustion.

When his head cleared, he peered at them.

"Only a nightmare," Del rasped. "Truly."

"You need meds?" Nan asked.

"Thank you, no." Embarrassment steeped Del's aura. "Please rest. You're exhausted."

Nan met Tam's eyes. "Okay. I'll be down the hall if you need me."

After Nan left, Tam sat up. His body creaked in protest. Facing away, Del didn't notice him until he perched on her cot. She tried to twist around, winced, and lapsed back as if her wound protested the movement.

"Easy, angel," he chided.

"I'm sorry I woke you."

He couldn't resist stroking the hair from her face. It curtained her pillow, silky against his fingers. "You okay?"

"Fine. It's … childish nonsense." Her aura-shade rippled with distress, maybe grief?

"You're cold."

She closed her eyes, thin brows pinching over her nose. "A little."

"If you're hurting, you should take meds."

Her hand cupped her nape. "I have already. I've a stubborn soreness here."

He tucked her blanket around her and gingerly stretched out beside her, propping himself on his elbow. She stilled with surprise, then relaxed against him with a sigh. Sinking his fingers into her hair, he massaged her neck. Her shivering faded. He felt her emotions soften with her body.

"Thank you. That's much better," she breathed.

His fingers paused in their work. "You're not getting rid of me, okay? I won't screw up again."

Her eyes opened, sheened with tears. "Please don't make that decision now—after what just happened."

"The only decision was in your mind." He resumed the massage. "I didn't need an hour, never mind three days."

Her eyes slid toward him, unable to connect. "All right," she whispered, sinking her cheek back against the pillow.

He dipped his head closer to hear her breath, and a strange sensation tingled through his mind, like restricted airways opening. Her aura touched him, not with emotion but with sensation, a soothing hum.

Sighing, he sank against the mattress alongside her, her hair a satiny pillow beneath his cheek. He wondered drowsily why she always smelled so good, salty sweetness that teased him whenever he got too close.

38

WHEN TAM WOKE THE NEXT MORNING, HE DETECTED JONAS'S SUBTLE signature pass the exam room. Much as he wanted to ignore it, he dragged himself up, careful not to wake Del. Swiping his face with a towelette and tugging his rumpled clothes straight had to serve for grooming.

He swung open the door, bumped into Freth lurking there.

Tam curled his lip. "What do you want?"

Freth flinched then recovered his swagger. "Just checking on Del."

"She's fine, no thanks to you."

"You think you could have stopped it?"

"I don't *think* it."

Freth had the nerve to smile, a shabby cover for the frustration shredding his aura.

"Yeah, guess we fucked up. But I can't help wondering whether that skank would have been there if *you'd* done your job. An't you supposed to be the Boss's super-sneak? These patchworks, the Surge, the dull-knife. An't it your job to untangle their schemes?"

Tam saw white, a strange, disconnected rage. Freth edged back.

"All right, boys. Take it down a notch. That crap an't helping Del." Kimber's wary voice rose from the stairwell.

With a deep-drawn breath, Tam eased away from Freth, itching to go for his throat. He forced himself to turn to Kimber. Her pale hair looked unbrushed and her cheeks were splotchy pink over her arrow tattoos—she'd taken on warren tasks to free Nan for nursing.

He said, "Can you watch over her? I need to talk to the Boss."

Kimber almost touched Tam's arm as he passed. Her golden fingers dropped away, but she had his attention. "Don't do anything rash."

"Don't worry." *Rash* would be to linger and give into the impulse to rework Freth's smug, pudding face. "She's sleeping, Freth. Let her rest."

Tam continued down the hall, trusting Kimber would take the hint and keep Freth out. Either way, he couldn't put off talking to Jonas.

He descended the stairs to find Jonas slouched over the serving counter, attention on Nan. She knelt by the wounded men's pallets with her trainee diagnose. For a blink, Jonas's heart was in his eyes. Then his habitual stoicism clamped over him. He'd noticed Tam approaching.

"Pull a stunt like that again, and I'll throttle you myself." The lines etched deeper in Jonas's face; dark circles overwhelmed his pale eyes.

Tam perched on a stool, arms binding his ribs. He frowned at the print-smeared counter. The staff had other things to worry about now.

Jonas heaved a sigh. "You can be sure I caught the knife-edge of Del's tongue for reassigning you."

Tam compressed his lips to keep from firing back. Before Del, Tam had believed Jonas the only Human who gave a shit about him. Compensation for the loyalty Tam seemed hardwired to offer his rescuer. He'd conveniently forgotten that Jonas cared for people in the *plural*. His heart held no space for individuals who didn't fit into that greater good.

"I wish you'd both reconsider," Jonas said.

"After yesterday? I don't think so." Tam didn't bother keeping the chill from his voice.

Jonas's gaze settled heavily on him. "Now explain what the hells you were about last night."

Tam gave a clipped, abbreviated account of his clash with Thuron.

When he finished, Jonas said, "We found Umar's Den digs empty. Equipment gone. How'd you know?"

"The android. Saw it at Umar's shop." Tam bit his thumb, scowling.

"You think that explosion was meant for us or Umar?"

"Thuron was casing the place. Triggered the self-destruct. He knew we were there."

"Couldn't have known we were coming."

"With all the gossips, it wouldn't be hard for Umar to learn we caught the junkie. Umar vacated in case her lackey ratted her out, had the patchworks case her nests to see if it was safe to go back."

"Why the android?" Jonas's jaw flexed. He was thinking of Ogranta.

Tam shook his head.

Thuron hated Tam, but there were easier ways to get at him. Jonas spent most of his time holed up in The Bar. Umar would know Jonas had to negotiate the NG's entry into Taber.

Jonas's gaze grew unfocused, inward. "It sits strange, Umar's involvement. The old guard dished corruption, not this twisted stuff."

"You've been chief a while now, Boss."

Jonas waved a hand as if to erase the topic. "Think there's anything to the junkie's claim the Surge are involved?"

"They focus on mechanics, not medicine. Doesn't sit right." Or maybe Tam only wanted to think that.

A frown of comprehension deepened the creases on Jonas's face. "*Lettie.* Umar paid her to link you to the patchworks. Umar wants you gone to make Del's equipment an easier target."

Yeah, and thanks for tossing me for her.

Jonas scratched his stubbled jaw. "My ears reported Surge recruiters hanging around the Threader and Tiller blocks. If the Surge keep stretching their scope, Belek will shut them down." He spoke with hard confidence, as if to convince himself that was a positive.

An image of sly Torx and her thuggish partner squaring off against coldly cunning Belek flicked through Tam's mind. Raw as Tam felt toward Jonas, the possibility of a gang war waged in Balter's Den struck his weary body like a stimulant.

CALEB DIDN'T KNOW WHERE TO LOOK. JONAS'S GAZE SEEMED TO STRIP BARE his failure, his faults—part of the warren chief's power, a steely talent for wringing confessions before he opened his mouth.

Aden stood beside Caleb, lined up before Jonas's desk, her brashness undimmed, though tension radiated to Caleb through the brush of her shoulder.

"I'm sorry, Boss. Got no excuse," Aden said.

Jonas flapped a hand. "I didn't call you here to apologize. Something was bound to happen. Just glad you caught the woman and Del's okay."

Aden cocked her head. They'd been on-roster to join the hunt for Umar.

Jonas looked wrecked, shirt rumpled, hair slicked to his head like it needed a washing. "I want you to keep digging into the Lettie case. We can't afford to be short a man over hearsay."

Heat prickled Caleb's neck. One failure, and it was right back to Lyn.

Jonas tapped his thumbs together over laced fingers like he'd prop himself up with them. His eyes hadn't lost their sharpness. "You got something to say, Caleb?"

The heat rushed Caleb's cheeks. He averted his face as he spoke, low. "Are you sure, Boss? About Lyn? I saw him arguing with Lettie outside The Bar night of the warren meeting."

"I'd stake my life on it. On him."

The calm certainty, the patience in Jonas's voice drew Caleb's gaze back to him.

Jonas said, "But I won't run this place like mine is the only opinion that matters. That's why I'm asking you to investigate."

"Body hasn't turned up," Aden said. "It's looking likely someone paid her to stir trouble then vacate."

Caleb shot her a frown.

Lettie alive … would keep her face from haunting him … but let Lyn oil free.

Dugan's pressure would redouble.

"Umar's a suspect, but we need proof to calm the clack over it." Jonas shifted pointedly toward Caleb. "Can you tackle this with an open mind?"

Caleb clenched his fists inside his jacket pockets. "Yeah, Boss."

"Good, then." Jonas turned to Aden. "You got a notion where to start?"

Aden whipped her purple jacket over her shoulders, stuffed her arms inside. "Where I left off. If there's a trail, we'll find it."

Caleb followed her out, stomach stone-weighted, raw and heavy. *Too late for confessions.* He straightened his spine, not wanting Jonas to read his reaction.

WITH EACH STOP, THE ARGUMENT BUILT.

Aden was a master at flipping modes, chatting with block-mamas, accepting sweets with thanks and a smile, then shredding Caleb the second the mama's door closed behind them.

After the third stop, Aden finally reached the point. "I know you don't like Lyn, but shit and shivers, you're stubborn."

"'t fuck, Addie?" He trotted to keep up with her hard-heeled pace. "You don't like that sneak any more than I do."

She stopped mid stride. "He don't give me a warm 'n cozy, but I an't condemning him for being unlikeable."

Caleb didn't want to think about Lyn, about the possibility of his innocence—the *consequence* of his innocence. "Come on! His old enemy stirs trouble, churns folk against him, then conveniently disappears?"

Aden looked like she'd spit. "Lyn don't give a shit about gossip." She stalked forward. "If he cared, he might just be a bit more *likeable*."

"With so many folk against him? Pressuring Jonas over his role with Del?" Caleb bounded to catch up with Aden, getting a dirty look from a street vendor whose foot he nearly trod. "An' all the shit with the Surge? Too convenient. Saving Del from them like some vid-drama hero. *Twice.* And the instant he's out of the picture, some junkie hurts Del—linked to Umar and those patchworks?" His voice spiked its pitch, and he swallowed for cool.

Aden whirled on him. "God knows I'd like to release myself from responsibility, but I an't scraping up a conspiracy to do it."

He crossed his arms to hold his ground. "He had dealings with Thuron. We saw evidence of it with our own eyes." It *was* suspicious.

"Lyn offered that up himself, and one thing he an't is stupid."

"What? You've converted now because the Boss buys his holo-games?"

Aden peered into Caleb's face as if squinting through a haze, then sighed. "Nan."

"Huh?"

She shook her head like she could shake off his denseness. "Nan witnessed Lyn take down Torx's crew. How he risked himself for her and for Del. Nan don't lie, not to herself or anyone. And her trust is harder won than Jonas's."

When Aden strode forward again, Caleb gaped after her.

Deflated. Sick. Memory of Lyn's quick action against Umar's android sunk him further.

The glare Aden tossed over her shoulder spurred him forward on rubbery legs.

Their investigation had taken them to Nerin block, as seedy as seedy got in the Den. Crumbling pavement, fixtures stolen from streetlights so often no one bothered replacing them. A sullen, shadowy realm two blocks from where Aden and Caleb grew up.

Aden blazed through it like she owned the place. People cleared her path.

She reached the block-mama's sooty storefront, Maf's Stuff.

Most mamas were women, but not all. Maf had held the role long as Caleb could remember. Maf walked the right side of warren rules—except when taking bribes to keep folk off the census and free of barter duty. Jonas tolerated him, preferring the devil he knew.

Caleb followed Aden into the shelf-crammed space. It stank of reefer and fried meat.

"Yo, Maf," Aden called.

A figure hunched over a clear bucket, sorting objects that were either flashlights or sex toys—could be either, amid this bric-a-brac. He didn't pause his work. "Yo, girlie. Only late on the barter 'cause my block folk are late."

"An't here to hassle you about that. Just need some info."

Maf twisted around, his puckered face as sooty as his shopfront. "About?"

"You know that fem, Lettie? She reefer baited for your cousin."

"I heard the flap. All I can say is, I saw that nasty bit once after the warren meeting. Came in here more sullen and snappish than usual. Scared probably. Who knows why?"

"You ever seen the Boss's sneak around here?" Caleb cut in, earning Aden's glare.

"No," Maf snorted. "But then I wouldn't, would I?"

Despite the nothing they got, Aden rewarded Maf with sweet-chew and a cheery wave as they left.

"You're something," Caleb muttered.

Aden grabbed his jacket flaps and shoved him into the alley, making him choke with surprise. Her face flamed redder than her hair. "Getting passed over for Del's guard an't the end-all, be-all. You only want it—*her* —because she's the new, sparkly thing. Like a window out."

Caleb shook her off, feeling exposed. "I an't that childish."

"I'm sorry I ever encouraged you." Aden folded her arms like she pinned her fists with them.

"I'm so sick of everything! Nothing changes here. We're wearing grooves over the same old paths. The harder we work the less we see— whether Jonas pats our heads or not."

He flinched, expecting a cuff to the ear, but sadness, not anger, lined Aden's face. "You don't remember our childhood if you can say that. Jonas has been transforming this place for years, tiny strings of miracles you're too impatient to see."

Caleb's throat knotted too hard for him to retort.

Poetry from Addie. She'd mulled over those words a while.

A chug-bike sputtered past, coughing exhaust on them.

He didn't react.

Aden didn't relent. "Your jealousy of Lyn is a kind of cruelty. You have so much more than he does without even trying."

"It an't jealousy," Caleb said between teeth gritted hard enough to crack.

Aden studied him with an indulgent softening in her expression that only swelled the pressure in his jaws.

"So many contradictions fight inside you," she said. "It scares me. Running from your pap's path an't the same as running from this life."

He glared away from her. "Stop being melodramatic."

"Then, tell me what's wrong! You're family to me. About all I've got."

That snapped his gaze to hers. "We an't family, Addie."

She blanched, her arms loosening to shield her middle.

He unleashed his own stored words. "Family can slap you around, stammer excuses later. Family can shove you onto the street for hours in the cold so they can bang the neighbor. *We* are *better* than family."

The wind whistled through gaps in Maf's awning, flapping the edges of Aden's jacket against her legs.

She leaned in, cupped his cheek with her calloused palm. "I wish to hells I could ground you here." Her voice shook. "I get my heart broken, lose folk, scrape bottom—over and over—but *here* is what I'm fighting for. Always."

The awful need to cry burned Caleb's eyeballs. He scowled the sensation away. "You think it's so different for me? I wear my soles as thin as yours for this place."

"You can't defend something when you're running from it." Aden sounded defeated.

The shadows sketched a mask of grief over her face. She swiped her hair behind her ear. And then he noticed like a thump to the chest. Her bare right lobe.

When she turned from Caleb, it had an awful sense of finality.

"I'm sorry." He stretched out his hand, dropped it to his side. "I was an ass. Not noticing ..." The gilt her scuzzy lover had taken back, yet again.

Aden spun to Caleb, hands on hips. "Idiot. You think I care about *that* when I got you acting crack-brained?"

He expelled a shaky breath.

Aden marched down the street. He trailed after her, his limbs loose with reprieve. But certainty numbed his core. If Aden knew what he'd done, she'd never forgive him.

39

"Humans can love, Tamln, but they love differently. Bond differently. I cannot understand, yet I pray you quicken as a Human, for someday you must live among them."

THE NGS WERE COMBING THE WARREN FOR UMAR. KNOWING THAT AWFUL woman used tools of medicine to mutilate a child lit a constant, simmering anger in Del—impossible to vent.

She wanted to ask Tam to help with the investigation, but he'd slipped from The Bar that morning without a word. More bloody stealthwork.

Del worked in the backroom, nursing the injured NGs who rested on pallets there. She'd judged it pointless to risk moving them upstairs.

Her head throbbed over things she needed quiet contemplation to work through, including Tam and the resurrection of disturbing childhood memories. A luxury time disallowed. Or cowardice, more like. But too much depended on her. Cracking open her past, dissecting her connection to Tam … She couldn't allow herself to become *unreliable*.

Pressing her palms against the table, she scrunched and released her face to recapture her focus. Then she prepped the men's pain meds from the supplies she'd arranged on the table.

As she knelt administering them, Caleb entered the room and approached, his saunter too casually crafted. Her patient closed his eyes, as if to give them privacy.

"You look good, Del." Caleb's gaze flickered over her neck. "I mean, it's amazing how you healed up."

The patient's lips twitched.

Del packed away her press-syringe. "I'm fine now, truly."

"Look." Caleb crouched beside her, tickling a breeze across her arm. "I wanted to say I'm sorry for letting that bitch get you."

"It wasn't your fault."

His smile wavered, but his gaze intensified like he'd dialed up the blue of his eyes, a blend of confidence and uncertainty Del couldn't interpret.

"Need some help?"

She sighed gratefully. "Thank you." The stiffness of her healing skin nagged, and meds made her languid.

Caleb flashed a crooked-toothed grin. "I'm at your service, doc."

She blushed. Clearly, she'd gone too long without enjoying a little flirtation. "Perhaps you could fetch a nutrient pack?"

He moved to the table, then froze with his face downturned, his shoulders bowed as if beneath an invisible weight.

Del creaked to her feet and crossed to him. "Everything all right?"

She expected him to apologize again, but he said, "Do you ever feel like what happened … to your mother follows you? Like a curse sucking you down."

"More often than I should." She hadn't forgotten what he'd confessed about his father. It hung between them whenever they spoke privately.

"How do you deal?" He grabbed a nutrient pack, tracing its edge with a thumbnail.

She groped for an answer—something neither false nor too personal. "By keeping on, I suppose. Movement toward something better helps banish the ghosts. Sorry. That sounds clichéd."

Caleb met her eyes, revived her blush. "No. That sounds about right." He winced a grin. "And I'm supposed to be helping."

He handed the pack to her, stiffened, staring behind her.

She whirled to find Tam there, radiating chill. His hostility—fists clenched, eyes slitted—startled.

"You should be resting, doc." His words were void of inflection.

Caleb frowned. "I'm helping her finish up, so she *can* rest."

"Nan can take over." The skin beneath Tam's eyes twitched.

"Nan will be helping Mr. Ogranta's family." Del glared. "I'll be done here shortly. Then I'll take a break."

A muscle flexed in Tam's jaw, the only reaction on his stony face. "You're the boss."

He stalked from the room.

Impossible man! You'd think after his near-disastrous arrest he'd feel less free to infuriate her. He was entirely too sure of her.

"Del."

She turned.

Nan stood in the doorway of Jonas's office. "Kimber will do condolence duty, so I can take over."

Nan's grim expression locked Del's protest behind her teeth. Nan tilted her chin toward the door where Tam had disappeared.

Del hesitated. Nan had undertaken far more than IWA protocols permitted. But Del couldn't be everywhere all the time, and what Nan could do with her trainee's diagnose was worlds better than the nothing patients would have without it.

"Thank you, then. Both of you."

Tossing an apologetic smile toward Caleb's tense face, she hurried after Tam.

As Del crossed the tavern, she spotted him on the stairs. A press of curious eyes followed her as if she provided some exotic entertainment, *still*.

Del caught Tam at the exam room door. "What was that about?"

"I'm tired, and I'd like to get you home. Or maybe you'd rather go home with him?" Tam's eyes had paled so dramatically that his irises were indistinguishable from the whites.

"I'm staying here another night." She fought to keep her tone level. "You're welcome to go home, if you need."

"That would leave things open for Freth, huh?" Tam's hard gaze shifted to the stairs. "He's NG. Might be safe to score with him, but wasn't he supposed to protect you when you got acid thrown at your face?"

"I don't know *what* you're on about."

His cold mask slipped, the corners of his mouth turning down. "Don't let me stand between you and a good fuck." He shoved into the exam room.

Del stomped after him. His back was to her, his jacket bunched in one hand. She slammed the door. The jacket slipped to the floor.

"Caleb helped me with patients, his injured friends." She spun Tam to face her. "Now, stop being an idiot!"

A tremor rippled over his face. "If you're needing action, it's less complicated if you look in the Fring."

Del breathed through the urge to shout. "You needn't take being my *body*guard so bloody literally."

His eyelids clenched as if he resisted the impulse to look away. "You can't ever go unguarded in the Maze."

"Then you needn't worry, because I'd become an avowed celibate before putting either of us through *that* humiliation." This place could crush the life from you.

Tam absorbed her reaction, ran a cool finger along her collar. "Hells, doc, if it's that much of a sacrifice, we could arrange something."

"Is that a personal offer?" she flashed back.

His finger twitched away. "That might beat lurking like a perv while some creep throws down his moves on you."

She glared, frustrated by his Maze-rat act, unable to see past it. "Take the mask off. You don't need it with me."

Del expected him to retreat, but he averted his eyes, his fingers fanning to shield the lower half of his face. "I can't."

She refused to let his bleak confession derail her. "What is this? You don't want me friendly with Caleb, or you don't want …" *me friendly with any man?*

"I'm sorry," he said, more plea than apology. "I shouldn't have talked to you like that."

With him a breath from her yet in helpless isolation, Del's own loneliness surged. She stared past his shoulder. "That apology is a cop-out."

"Not him. Not anyone." The words leaked through Tam's lips like a whispered accident.

She shut her eyes, unsure she understood.

A touch on the back of her head made her start, then his mouth was on hers, rough with clumsiness. She recoiled in astonishment. The awful expression on his face made her wish she hadn't.

The look wiped away. His lips twisted. "Sorry. Of course, that wouldn't work … with me."

She couldn't think past the startled squeezing in her chest.

"Guess I'd need to have a wandering eye and a few warts or something." His face clenched, his eyes widening, as if he had no idea how to handle his mortification.

He flicked his fingers over his heart—a curious, painful gesture—and spun away.

Heart tripping, she caught his hand. He swallowed hard and tugged back, but she curled her fingers around his to hold him there. "Tam, you only surprised me."

Purple flared over his cheeks, the first time she'd seen him blush.

Stepping into him, she twined her good arm around his neck. The hair at his nape brushed her fingers, a silky tickle. A tremor rippled through him as she tugged his face to hers and kissed him. Del meant it to be brief, but he melted into softness, his breath misting her skin as he explored her mouth, tentative, tender.

She couldn't bear to end it. Teasing his lips apart, she deepened the kiss, let her tongue slide against his, tasting a nutty hint of fretha.

His fingers feathered over her hips, as though she were something delicate and precious that might break beneath his touch. His restraint sent a rush of heat through her. She melded her body to his, letting the kiss build until their mouths slanted against each other, combative with need.

They broke for air, their jagged breaths mingling. Their eyes met. His irises had re-faded to unnerving, white-washed gray.

He stumbled back, a smile twitching unsuccessfully over his mouth. "Here I thought you were so prim and proper."

"You lit the match. Don't be surprised your fingers got singed." Fresh confusion roiled inside her, but she forced her manner steady. She was tired of Tam manipulating her whenever he wanted to run from some deeper feeling.

He stared at her, painfully long. "I didn't hurt you—your neck?"

"It's nearly healed."

His shoulders eased. "I … should go … take care of something."

She nodded. He needed to flee, and this time she would let him.

He raked his hair with trembling fingers, and she caught a flash of bright color on his palm before he closed it into a fist. He shot her a startled look.

"I'll be back later." He staggered out the door.

Del unpent a sigh, sagging against the wall.

She wasn't foolish enough to read Tam's possessiveness as a sign of undying passion. Tam was complicated—every glimpse of his true self proved that more.

Past his own upset, he'd read her loneliness and tried to ease it. The innocence his clumsiness revealed wrenched her heart.

So beautiful. So closed.

What had happened to make him utterly alone? She'd burned to understand. Now, she feared she couldn't bear to know.

Hurt, thwarted desire, and regret jumbled inside her. *I should have played it off as a joke like he wanted. What possessed me to kiss him that way?*

She closed her eyes, and her heart betrayed her, beating triumphant, like the voice of a distant, half-forgotten self.

⁂

Tam seethed, frantic to reach the shelter of his pod, but he had no energy to run.

A few blocks from The Bar, his limbs gave way. He backed against an alley wall, slid down, rested his head on his knees.

What insanity made him *kiss* her?

Finding that slick Freth chatting up Del had been a sick shock—that she'd *responded.* Tam had sensed her pleasure like a vicious blow. Through the jealousy knifing him, a powerful instinct awoke. *Remove the threat, draw her closer, secure her.*

He groaned, rocking on his heels. *Stupid, impossible shit!*

The sense of closeness he'd built with Del was an illusion. She hadn't comprehended his jealousy, and his passion had shocked her. When they kissed, he'd felt her desire, but his reaction afterward snuffed it—his childish words, his blanked irises.

What Del needed to ease her loneliness wasn't a twisted thing like Tam. She needed someone normal, who could touch her without bolting into a hole afterwards.

Tam had fooled himself that Del needed him, that only *he* was qualified to protect her. He hadn't kept her from being hurt, had blamed Freth, even Jonas, for what was his own fault. Freth had been there when Del got burned because Tam hadn't.

He leapt to his feet, sprinted for the only place in Balter's Den uncluttered with presences. The abandoned transmission tower—a rickety set of stilts with a platform on top, long since stripped of equipment.

Sitting atop its chill metal deck, he tucked up his legs, ground his forehead against his kneecaps. Activity pulsed below like noise muffled by walls. Wind whipped up, carrying it away.

Pressure built inside his mind. He clawed his knees, lifted his head with awful disbelief.

Emere?! His mouth gaped in a soundless denial. He'd been so certain at the overlook! As if he'd crossed a threshold, lighter, stronger.

What true-hearted Rynet clung to their loved one's spirit until it frayed?

Selfish, pathetic mongrel. Unable to let his mama go. Blindly, ignorantly, clinging in his utter aloneness ...

"*Emere*, you should have *killed* me rather than leave me alone here."

When sobs took him, he was too stunned to do anything but surrender to them.

40

TAM STARED DOWN FROM THE TOWER, DETACHED FROM HIS TREMORING BODY, from the Human spaces below. Trouble brewed there even if he couldn't penetrate the darkness to parse its nature.

Why should he care? He was nothing to this place. *Ghoul. Glitter-boy. Useless sneak.*

Strain wrenched Tam. He'd convinced Jonas to put him on-roster to investigate a new Surge nest in Nerin block tonight. Umar's mess dangerously diverted focus from their threat, and Tam wouldn't trust Jonas's ears after their failure with her.

A violent spat of rain had left Tam drenched, drained, and chilled to the core. He ached to return to his pod to sleep to stave off thinking.

Instead, he let duty hijack his limbs—without understanding why. He clambered down the tower, made his way to Nerin at a shuffling jog.

The block lay along the warren's southeastern border. Tension cloaked the area like a mist, silent and unstirring. The Surge's nest occupied an unmarked two-story structure. Only one first-floor window, painted black and barred over.

Jonas had given strict orders not to engage, no matter what went down. More pressing, Tam couldn't break inside unequipped and unmasked. He squinted around for a vantage point.

Across the street from the entrance stood a shoe-repair booth with a wobbling holo of a boot above. Tam tucked himself behind the booth and waited, wanting to collapse against the bitter cold. He'd forgotten his jacket in his humiliated flight from The Bar. *Idiot all around.*

After an eternity of chill nothing, a flock of black-garbed figures approached over the wetly gleaming pavement. Fet. He recognized Belek by the efficiently compacted menace of his movements. Tam's skin crawled with his instinct to slink away.

Belek signaled to his men with a slash of his hand. Three peeled off and disappeared behind the building—blocking the exit. The rest clustered around the entrance, Belek and four others. If they knocked, Tam didn't hear it, but the front sentry's muffled voice came through the door, words Tam couldn't pick up.

"Send your topper out," Belek snapped. After a beat, the enforcer added, "Do it or we include the whole lot of you. Topper's choice."

The door creaked open, leaking a babble of protest from the Surge crew.

Belek's escort aimed lethals as Torx's thuggish partner pushed through the doorway. Boxed in by black forms, only the shiny dome of his head was visible.

"Stay inside," Torx's voice came from behind him. "I've got this." She sharply cut through his protest. He hesitated, then vanished behind the door.

Tam didn't dare angle for a better view with his pale skin exposed.

Belek shifted, his hair like black oil beneath a streetlight. "Your org's been testing its leash since you blood-signed treaty with us."

"That what Valerian told you?" A trace of mockery rippled through Torx's words.

That's what Jonas met Belek about yesterday, convincing the enforcer the Surge had broken treaty—protecting Tam and Nan. Otherwise, it might have been Tam waking to the chill shock of Belek on his doorstep. Tam coiled his body tighter.

"I don't rely on Valerian to watch my little treaty sibs." Belek's coldly clipped words should have intimidated Torx, but no telltale fear spiked her aura.

Tam squinted at the Surge nest. What made Torx so confident?

"I an't a trusting sort," Belek added. "I suggest you hold that in your pointy head."

Torx's anger seared through the Fet pack's psy-haze of anticipation.

Tam shrunk down, braced for violence.

"Clear as that gun in my face." Torx's voice stayed level.

Tam peered back around the kiosk.

Tension radiated like dark energy from Belek's rigid posture. "What'd you lot want with Valerian's toff? What was worth twisting Valerian's tail and losing crew?"

Tam narrowed his eyes. Why bring up Del?

"Didn't we cover that, enforcer? Valerian's sneak busted into our digs." Torx's gruff simplicity rang false—playing foil for Belek's bladed cunning by blunting her own.

"You wanted to stir things up, no?" Belek said. "Bleed Valerian by striking close to home, kill his exotic and jack his woman?"

Tam rolled his lips to seal in a hiss; by "woman" Belek meant Nan, not Del.

"The sneak made the first strike. We only followed up on the opportunity."

"And the toff?"

"Came looking for the exotic, like we said. Valerian didn't deny it, eh?"

"A little toff commando?" Belek sneered. "Or maybe you figured you'd use her skill to muscle into our exotics trade?"

"Exotics?" Surprise dented Torx's calm. "We deal in machines, not glitter. We know you lot got a claim."

Tam rocked back. Claim? On the exotics trade or *Del*?

"An' the lethals?" Belek pressed.

"Valerian's word against ours. His sneak lied to protect himself from punishment for risking your wrath. He thought he had a line on us. He was wrong."

'Leave my treaty-brothers to me.'

Tam knotted numb fingers in his shirt. If Belek bought Torx's lie …

"This will be your only warning, Torx. Rein it in, or we will shut you down. No more lethals. No more jerking Valerian's chain. Nothing outside the treaty without my leave."

Venom foamed Torx's aura, but her voice grew as toneless as Belek's. "I know what's expected, enforcer."

"You're breathing on sufferance already."

Tam couldn't decipher the reply.

Torx's fist thudded on the door, making Tam jump. Then she slammed back inside.

The Fet pack retreated, drawing near the kiosk, lighting Tam's nerves.

"You believe the sneak lied about the lethal?" a man asked, low.

"Can't afford to," Belek said. "We keep sharp on this."

"Stinks of a holo-game. The Surge are weak now but building ranks, fast."

"We honor the treaty," Belek snapped. "Until we have proof they betrayed it."

Tam curled into himself like a clenching fist as the Fet pack disappeared down the street.

Doubt sickened him. The possibility the Fet enslaved and killed his mother for their illegal mining churned inside him. Did they mean to take Del for her skill, too?

Murderous rage pulsed through him for two strangled breaths, impossible to act on.

He shoved to his feet, driven by irrational fear for Del, and rushed to The Bar, pushing his strained body to its limits. Fumbling through the lock-down security, he hurried across the darkened tavern.

As he levered himself up the steps, Del's aura swept over him like a rush of relief.

He stumbled to a halt outside the exam room.

Waves of nausea staggered him. He was beyond exhausted. His skin flamed on one side. He pulled up his sleeve. The red splotch on his hand had crawled up his arm.

No way he could let Del see him in this state.

Collapsing against the wall, he stared at the closed door. Agitation shaded Del's aura.

Don't fret about me, Del. Just rest.

He closed his eyes, his body trembling as if it struggled to shake something loose.

Pressure built—the odd sensation in Del's head that plagued her more and more—left her vibrating with restlessness, pacing tight circles through the exam room.

Strain upon strain.

"What are you trying to tell me?" she whispered then rubbed her eyes, expelling a laugh-threaded groan.

She'd scanned herself four times in the past hour, but the diagnose detected no signs of illness or disorder. Only a strange brain activity. Unexplained. Undiagnosable—which meant untreatable. *I can't afford to become unreliable now!*

"Enough." She thrust her hands to her sides. "It's only stress." The diagnose needed recalibration.

Del flipped up her wrist-vid, stared at the message flashing for attention. A vid-message. From Rhemy. With the spotty connection it was taking *excruciating* hours to download.

Pacing snatched her up again, driving her through countless passes of the tiny chamber until dizziness swamped her.

What did she fear from *Rhemy*? Betrayal, after all? A warning that Mario-Johns would snap her up, wrench her freedom away by proving her unfit?

Her vid hummed over the sensitized skin of her wrist. She stared at it. Stupidly. Dazedly.

Flicked it open.

Rhemy appeared. More angular than she remembered in his last vid, as if he'd lost weight. A kinetic energy radiated through his eyes, despite the smallness of the visual.

His mouth twitched in a nervous smile. "I must confess, Mara love, that this is the seventh attempt to record this message. So bloody difficult with the file restrictions."

He blinked then averted his gaze from the camera's eye. "Heart sister. I know how abominably I've neglected you. But I've never stopped adoring you. You ran from the family. I hid among them but retreated inside. I ..." His gaze flashed back up. "I've been a coward, yet I've tried to turn it to advantage. The privilege. The wealth. And ..." A grin twitched into a bloom of pure joy, lighting her heart with an echo of that exhilaration, a visceral gladness for him. "I've succeeded. *At last.* Legal Em. My brainchild, with support from far more sagacious intellects than mine, advocates for vulnerable populations, an interplanetary operation. Still small, but I've plans to grow."

He sighed. She couldn't hear it, but it struck her across the impossible distance, the time differential. "I want you to be a part of it."

Her heart began thudding. Her fingers spasmed, an impulse to switch off the message.

"I've a thought … we could create a medical aid branch. You'd lead, of course. Or farm the admin tasks, practice as you desire. Your own team, or *teams*, sent to serve vulnerable populations. My staff could handle the diplomacy and such." He leaned toward the camera. "Don't you see. It's *perfect*. Both our passions and strengths. Pure *good*." He gnawed his lip, a rare show of insecurity, but one that evoked an elusive sense of their shared childhood. "I'm not authorized to operate in the frontier yet. We need proof of concept, to build our base. I wish to all hells I could rush to you now, cape unfurled, to help your Maze folk. But please consider. We can build. Together, we can make it happen someday, more nimbly and effectively than your IWA."

She couldn't breathe, temptation and the longing to please him squeezed so tightly.

"Take time. Think on it. I know I've flung myself on you unawares again." His gaze flicked away. "Damnation. Out of space again."

The message cut off, a black blankness replacing Rhemy's heart-wrenching vulnerability.

Dear gods. To see him again. To be loved. To share a vision. To off-load the tedious, awful weight of activism onto more capable shoulders. *Damn you, Rhemy.* To be sucked in by *family* again.

Del ached for Tam with sudden, fierce intensity. Her talisman of shelter, her silent ally.

For all their kiss had hurt him, tangled things between them …

She sighed, pressing her forehead against the door's cool metal.

Where are you, Tam?

A familiar prickle in her head had her straightening.

She stared without focus, slowly opened the door.

He was there, flopped against the corridor wall, quaking, his clothes slicked to his body, his skin bleached to a shocking pallor.

Del dove for her diagnose then rushed back. She tripped over his sprawled legs, landed on her knees beside him, nearly braining herself on the wall.

"Tam?"

He didn't stir.

Swearing, she booted up the diagnose, counting the seconds for the menu to load.

Clammy fingers looped around her wrist.

She jumped, met Tam's eyes.

"You didn't use that on me, did you?"

"You promised, when it's critical."

"I'm fine. Just tired."

"You're shaking apart!"

"No diagnose." His desperation hit her hard.

"Tam." She placed her hand on his chest. His heart bucked through the contact. "I would never judge you for what's in here."

He pushed her hand away.

"Let me think." She tapped her fingers against her thigh. "There's a setting ...." Her fingers darted over the device. "A critical analysis setting. It will only provide treatment options for injury or illness. It won't reveal other information."

"I'm not *injured or ill*. I'm just a freak. So that won't work."

She rocked back with a choked breath.

The pressure in her head flared, bearing down like an outside force, spreading blackness with it. The diagnose clattered from her fingers, and she crumpled face forward.

41

____

"WHAT'S WRONG, NAN?" TAM'S VOICE HOVERED CLOSE.

Del couldn't open her eyes.

"The diagnose shows some odd brain activity. It an't setting off alerts, but there's no explanation. Except that she's sleeping."

Warm breath tickled Del's ear. "Please wake up, angel. Sorry I was such an asshole."

Del stirred to reassure Tam, but a thick drowse made the effort too heavy, sleep too welcome. She let herself be drawn down again.

Her head so heavy ... thoughts, foreign and strange, closing like a neural net ...

____

"WAKE, CHILD. YOU ARE NEEDED." HIS FATHER'S VOICE, HELPLESS, scolding, confused.

Meaningless compared to Dlmara's plea. His *ett'eren*. She had begged Jenl not to leave her, and it anguished him. He cared nothing for his father's baffled grief.

Medication had killed Jenl's pain, yet it haunted like a phantom. He convulsed in a ball.

Beeps of equipment. Murmurs of concerned voices, not truly for him, but for his gift, the thing they coveted.

He would keep it from them through the end. His gift was only for his *ett'eren*.

"What is he saying?" someone hissed.

Jenl's lips silently formed the ritual chant for *ver'ela*—so easy. *Ver'ela* was love, and his love was breath. His connection with Dlmara was already strong, even if she couldn't respond. It was like touching one who slept.

I know you cannot hear me anymore, but I shall hold you until my last breath. I promise. Those awful ones who do not love you as they should, as I do.... I will not leave you alone with them. I promise. I will be with you, protecting you. Forever.

"ARE YOU HURTING? YOU'RE CRYING, ANGEL."

Cool fingers brushed the skin beneath her eyes.

"Wake up. You haven't eaten in hours, and I've got Nan's turnip hash for you."

A crisp smell of food. She couldn't open her mouth to receive it.

"Fair enough. I wouldn't wake up for that, either. How about I promise to get you something from the bakery if you'll open your eyes?"

A whisper against her cheek. "I need you. Please wake up."

IT WAS HOT AND EVERYTHING HURT . THE HARSH-SPICED MUSK OF HUMAN male chafed her nose. She lay on the digger's gritty, rattling deck, searching for Tamln with grasping desperation.

Her son needed her, but how could she know if she reached him? She acted to protect him, but would he understand? With every path closed, this was all she could do for him.

Closing her eyes, she distanced herself from the discomfort, the sounds of her captors struggling to free the digger from the OBMG's trap. She traced her thoughts over forms her grandmother had taught her; layers of meditation, opening the mind to *ver'ela.*

Instinctively, she shifted to words she'd crafted for Tamln, a game to teach him Common that had grown into their own private world of myth and fact. "Bring me a stone and give me its story. Bring me a story baked from the earth…." She mouthed the poem until calm enveloped her. Her mind expanded outward. She felt the distant stirring of quizzical, drowsily yearning thoughts. Tamln, at last.

A helpless smile shaped her lips. She clung to a memory of him tucked against her, his feathery hair tickling her lips.

She let the memory go as pain frayed her from him.

DEL'S EYES SNAPPED OPEN. THE ABRUPTNESS MADE TAM JUMP. HER GAZE WAS unfocused.

"You must be safe," she whispered like someone else.

Her eyes shut again, moving erratically behind closed lids.

Sitting beside her in a chair that had fused to his spine, Tam touched her shoulder. His hand shook with worry and the queasiness that hadn't loosened its grip. He'd spent most of his vigil in a restless doze.

"Come on, wake up."

After a painful beat, she reopened her eyes.

"Hey." He was too wrecked to savor his relief. "You scared us."

She glanced around the exam room, as if trying to orient herself.

He brushed her cheek with his fingers. "You there?"

She turned her face into his palm, her breath fanning his skin. The unintentional caress sent a tingle up his arm.

Finally, she met his eyes. "Sorry. I'm not sure what happened."

"You fainted, wouldn't pull out of it."

"I was dreaming." She rubbed her arms. "Such vivid dreams."

"Are you cold?"

"I just feel so odd."

"You should eat something."

He studied her. If he closed his eyes, he could sketch each curve and line of her face—her left brow, arched the slightest bit higher than the right, the peaked bridge of her nose, the deep divot in her upper lip—but something made her strange to his eyes now.

She sat up, sliding her legs off the cot. She lifted one hand, staring at it with pinched brows. "I dreamt I was … your mother."

"Um." He blinked at her, shifting back in his chair.

She rolled her hands over his and examined his nails. "I was Rynet."

An eerie sensation assailed him, like every pore in his body opened. She hadn't simply used the word *Rynet*, she'd pronounced it perfectly, keying him into something he'd been too crushed with weariness to process. She'd spoken in Vleren when she woke. *Th jeh ina en. You must be safe.*

Del snapped her attention to him. "Gods, I'm so stupid!" she breathed. "Of course." Her eyes scoured his face.

His irises betrayed him, a pulse of pressure, paling as though on cue. "You know what I am, don't you?"

She fixed on his eyes as if mesmerized. "Yes."

How? "You used your toy on me, didn't you?"

Through thick confusion, she said, "Yes."

A small word to wound so deeply.

"Del." He crouched in front of her. "Did you find out using that diagnose?"

Her brow crinkled. "Yes."

It was a lie. As a lie, her *yes* struck more viciously than it would have as truth. Deeper than a betrayal, a rejection.

"Why?! *You*, I trusted over anyone."

Ignoring the limp hand she held out to him, Tam spun away.

His control cracked, and he fled the room.

42

Pounding on the door earned Del nothing but bruised knuckles.

"Let me in! I will camp out here as long as need be and annoy all your neighbors!"

She'd vid-called Tam with push-button compulsion until worry overtook her. She snuck from The Bar to find him—a trial that involved wandering in circles to locate his nest, endurance jumping until she hooked the release to his ladder, then dangling off it until her body-weight dragged it to climbable height.

Del was in no mood to be ignored.

The door cracked. "I'm fine. Go away."

It slammed shut.

"Let me in to talk this o—"

The door burst open. Tam's hands snatched her inside. "What the hell are you doing here alone?!"

"I was worried," she managed through the launch in her pulse.

He was a dark outline in the unlit room, the dimness more intimate than the clasp of his hands. The space settled over her, the closeness of the walls, the dim static of the warren's bustle below. Tam's breath, a warm tickle against her forehead ...

"You came here *unguarded* for worry?" His voice dripped sarcasm, but his fingers transmitted tremors to her arm.

"You can't imagine I'd leave things like that." She refused to apologize. He was testing her again.

Tam laughed scornfully, releasing her.

They stood in silence, in the near-dark. It occurred to Del that he could see her—Rynet had night vision. "You might turn on the lights."

"I *might* not."

She reached a hand toward him—a feint. As he shifted to avoid her touch, she slapped out with her other hand, scrabbling her fingers over the wall for the light-button. He caught her intention too late. His face flashed into view—one cheek splotched with an angry, reddish-purple rash. He wore a robe over loose pants, open at the throat, revealing that the rash purpled his clavicle.

She sucked in a breath. "Why didn't you send for me?" Sweat sheened his skin, and she'd never seen him perspire before, had half thought him incapable. "You promised, when it was serious."

"I think the fact that *you* broke your promise negates mine."

Not bothering to respond, she whipped her diagnose from her pocket.

He pushed her hand away. "You don't know what this is, do you?" His deliberate manner made her pause.

She looked at him blankly, warily. "Why would I?"

"Because I've had it since yesterday. It just hadn't hit my face." He leaned a shoulder against the wall, crossing his arms. "Why did you lie to me? If you'd used that diagnose like you said, you'd have found this."

"But—"

"Want to check the log?"

She jerked her attention to the diagnose. When she reviewed the logs with clumsy fingers, she found nothing about Rynet. She shook the device as if that could change the result.

"Del."

She drew a silent breath, lifted her eyes.

"Why did you lie?" Tam's flat expression muted the pain roughening his voice.

She couldn't speak. Of course, Tam had taken her excuse for a lie—reading her in that uncanny way he had.

"Tidy way to get rid of me."

"Of course not!" she stammered. The diagnose flopped to her side.

"You let me believe something you knew would kill my trust." His throat worked, a hard swallow that didn't clear the rasp from his voice. "What am I supposed to think?"

"It made sense." Del couldn't look at him. He was absorbing her reaction, watching her self-assurance fray.

Tam lifted his hand as if to touch her, dropped it. His palm was as inflamed as his cheek. He tucked his hands under folded arms. "What really gave me away?"

"Your eyes, hair. Gestures." The gestures should have given him away. Genetic manipulation could explain Rynet-inspired features, but gestures were learned behavior. Human-Rynet children were so *impossibly*, extraordinarily rare it had never crossed her mind.

"That's not it." He glared away from her.

What could she say when she didn't understand herself?

'You, I trusted over anyone.' He would never trust her again.

Tam hissed between his teeth. *Rynet* teeth.

She blenched—a cruel mistake that he leapt on. "What a shock to realize the poor, glitter-faced exotic isn't a Human-made thing, but something more disturbing." He leaned toward her, lips sliding back to bare his narrow, mauve-tinged teeth. "Go find another case to save."

"*Don't.* You know damned-well how much I care about you."

"You care about everyone, *doc.* Much harder to trust though, isn't it?"

"And you've trusted me? Truly?" The absurdity of it bristled over her.

His mouth curved, too bleak for a smile. "In ways you can't imagine. But I can never escape from what I am, can I?"

"And what is that?" Del clutched the diagnose so hard her fingers ached.

"An accidental thing that doesn't belong anywhere."

Anger choked her—awful, misplaced—because she was terrified that he meant it. "Don't dare spew that nonsense at me."

"You're afraid of me now. That's what you felt today. That's what made you put the pieces together. You could feel the wrongness!"

"That was fear of *myself,* not you. Don't play this game with me. It's the same sort of manipulation you use whenever I touch anything personal. I've been more open with you than you ever have with me."

"You need a demonstration?" He snatched the hand that held the diagnose. "Do your worst."

She didn't move.

"No? Okay." He jerked the device from her, held it against himself until the beep signaled the scan's success. Taking her resisting hand, he slapped the diagnose into her palm. "Look at it, doc. You wanted to treat me."

Her focus dipped to the screen, her mind buzzing as she processed what private space she'd invaded. "Side effect of a Rynet sexual response." Rynet pheromones had triggered an autoimmune reaction on his skin, likely a result of his mixed heritage.

Tam's lip curled. "I'd call it the *side effect* of your tongue in my mouth."

She blinked, her thoughts going to the red spot she'd glimpsed on his hand after she'd kissed him. "That was hours ago."

"Yeah, well, I guess that's how it works with Rynet." His sarcasm cracked, exposing raw confusion. "I wouldn't know."

Her lips parted as the significance settled. He'd experienced the *rush*, the Rynet sexual quickening. For her. And Rynet were monogamous, absolutely.

She swept back a loose strand of hair with agitated fingers. With Tam's mixed heritage, there was no telling what it meant.

His eyelids dipped, and he lightly traced her jaw with his knuckles. "Still want to help me?"

She struggled to sound like a professional instead of a breathless twit. "The pheromone causing the issue should only be present at the first sexual quickening. You won't likely experience this again." Heat crept up her neck. "I'm certain there's something I could do to ease your symptoms now," she added weakly.

He shifted closer, placing his palms on the wall on either side of her head. His body emanated a light, clean scent like air after a rain. "There's something you could do, all right."

She couldn't help the flutter in her pulse, though he meant to drive her away. She sensed his pain as though it radiated through the heat of his skin. "Tam, I see you so easily now," she whispered.

He twisted his face away, straining against the wall like he wanted to push it over. *"Please!* Don't you get it? I can't stand for you to see me like this."

"Why? You're still beautiful. You must know that." The words slipped out on a sigh. Her palm curled against his chest.

His breath caught, and he stilled. Then his arm twined around her waist. She felt the heat of his body before she was pulled against it. The diagnose slipped from her fingers. She clutched the fabric over his ribs, registering the delicious pressure of his body against hers, his warmth.

He cupped her nape, pressed his brow to hers, furrowed. "You should go."

Sanity demanded she pull back, get him talking again. She nudged his mouth with hers instead. Then he was kissing her feverishly, holding her so tightly, she lifted off the floor. She couldn't draw breath to kiss him back.

He eased her down, arced his body away, but laid his heated cheek against hers. "You can't know what you're doing."

"How could you imagine it would matter to me?" she whispered, hurt pressing in.

He pulled back and lowered his face.

"Look at me, Tam." *Then tell me you want me to leave.*

His breath teased her skin as he sighed. He lifted his head, and his eyes locked on hers, threaded with silver. The vulnerability she longed to shield him from shifted to her through that gaze. *"Rehe al,* Del." Then, "stay with me."

As if she could move with him looking at her like that.

He bent to kiss her again. Melting into the caress, she molded against him, twined her arms around his neck, slid her fingers through the feathery softness of his hair, kneaded his nape—tried to show with her body how completely she accepted him. She let his passion carry her, the swift current of her blood washing away the feeble warning from her mind.

43

Forgive my grief, Tamln. I spent so many years with my heart blissfully untouched, coolly sheltered. How miraculous to have that protection shattered and to experience the warmth of contact. How brutal to have the exposed part broken, to have to patch together those protections again.

TAM STARED AT THE CEILING, HIS BODY LANGUID WITH WELL-BEING, HIS MIND restless. He and Del lay tangled together on his pallet. Her breath misted his neck, and her dark russet hair ribboned over his chest, a strange contrast with his cold-colored skin.

Surreal that they'd landed here.

He'd been consumed with anguish, his body on fire with that traitorous Rynet reaction he didn't understand. When she'd shown up at his door, every instinct demanded he *secure her, draw her closer.* All his snarling, only smoke. The second she'd turned those warm, green eyes on him, he'd been lost.

The lights were on.

Del's aura hummed with contentment. He ached to snuggle deeper, but that light niggled. A lifetime of hiding chained him to fear. Yet he felt like he'd touched with his bare skin for the first time.

He shifted, and Del stirred, curling into him, sending a tingle through his body. With a snuffling noise, she lifted her head.

"Hello," she whispered, the corners of her mouth curving.

"Hello," he echoed stupidly.

She arched up and slid her feet to the floor. Her warm hip pressed against his. "You're looking better."

Like he'd had a case of the sniffles, instead of a disgusting condition caused by his split nature. How she'd stood touching him …

He compressed into a seated position, drawing up his knees. "Yeah, you fixed me, all right," he muttered, like a jackass had stolen his tongue.

Her face blanked. She shot to her feet. "I should go."

Cringing, he caught her hand. "Don't."

Her chin pointed toward the door. "I didn't sleep with you for that."

"I know. I'm sorry." He tugged her down, his mind desperately casting for something to patch his mistake. He bit the pad of his thumb. "I don't know … how to do this."

"It's not complicated."

He almost laughed. *She* sure as hell didn't believe that.

"It is for me. I never … I can't tell anyone what I am, but keeping it a secret …" He sketched the *ah'nea* for dishonor. His throat tightened.

She softened. "Anyone who's worth anything won't care."

Then you may be the only person who's worth anything.

He felt clumsier, conscious of their nine-year age difference as he never had been.

"Don't fret, Tam. Nothing need change between us." Del sighed, resting a hand over her stomach.

"Hungry?" He latched onto the possibility like a lifeline. "I can scrounge something."

Del rewarded him with a thin smile. "Famished."

Once they were wrapped in robes, settled at the table over eggs and thickly brewed tea, awkwardness clamped back over him. He'd shared countless meals with Del. This seemed very different.

She paused over her fork, lifting skeptical eyes. "That I can see, we're none the worse for a little sexual release." Her laughter sparked at his startled expression. "Now, eat. This looks delicious and I'm about to expire."

Tam shoveled eggs into his mouth, barely tasting them. Del ate with more enthusiasm.

As they finished and sat sipping the tea, Del's focus sank inward. Anxiety crept into her aura. She pinched the bridge of her nose. "I haven't explained."

He drew her hand from her face, stroking his thumb over her palm. "I was being an ass. You're a doctor. Of course you put the clues together. I accepted that risk by taking this job."

It truly didn't matter to Del. The fear knot he'd carried since they met, primally irrational, unbound with dizzying intensity.

"While I was unconscious, the diagnose detected unusual activity in my brain. It was *that* activity which locked me in dreams, though the meds I'd taken contributed."

He braced for what she'd tell him.

"My dreams were like hallucinations. I believed them utterly as if I were living in someone else's skin." She spoke steadily through the tension webbing the air between them.

"You spoke to me in Vleren," he said quietly. "A Rynet language." The language of a small Aran province. His mother's language. The impossibility of that coincidence sank in.

Del rubbed her arms. "I don't speak it."

That eerie sense of Del's aura layered with another's … The power of what Del had experienced left him stunned—so stunned it took a moment to fit the last piece in place. His breath thinned, making words difficult. "You dreamed you were my mother."

She hesitated. "Yes."

The other aura was his mother's. The tenacious instinct Del might lead him to the truth wasn't her toff connections, but something far more fundamental.

Could *Emere* live? His head spun. He'd been so sure he sensed her spirit. But how could *Del* sense it? More than sense, *connect*, and more intimately than Tam ever had.

"What did you see?" He managed through lips gone numb.

Her fingers worried the rim of her mug. "Nothing coherent."

"She disappeared when I was twelve, and my adoptive family either couldn't or wouldn't say what happened to her. I've spent years searching for answers."

Del's green eyes were intense beneath the skylight's diffuse, silvery glow. Her lashes swept down to cover them. Cold pebbled her forearms.

He rose and moved to her, shedding his robe to drape over her shoulders. Her bare feet were tucked against the chair legs. He turned her and knelt before her, drawing her icy feet into his hands to rub them. "Sorry. I should have cranked the heat. Cold doesn't affect me much."

"Rynet adapt to temperature better than Humans," Del said, mechanically.

Tam stroked her arches until her body softened. "Please tell me what you can."

He pressed through Del's silence, forced his tone level. "Where was she? In the dreams?"

Del shrugged helplessly. "Once, here in the Maze, I think. Once, in a rough vehicle."

"With?"

"I'm not sure. Humans." Del averted her eyes as she spoke. "She tried to reach you—um—with her mind. To protect you."

"How?" His churning emotions left him no room to read hers, but her legs shook.

"The dreams were fragmented, only moments when she reached for you."

"How did she try to protect me?"

"Spirit gift." Del swallowed, pushed through her reluctance. "Um— *ver'ela.*"

Tam's fingers went slack, and her feet slipped from his grasp.

Ver'ela signified death.

"Tam." Del lifted her eyes, startlingly strong. "As a child, I heard voices in my head. I believed I was communicating with another child telepathically. My father took me to a neuropsychiatrist until it stopped. These dreams, the strange headaches I've been experiencing, might be signs of the condition returning. That's why I couldn't bear to tell you."

"You said you don't speak Vleren. How could you know *ver'ela*? Or anything?" His voice faltered. That *anything* shredded his understanding.

Del's gaze stayed carefully steady. "The child I 'spoke' to was Rynet."

"*Rynet?*"

"We spent weeks together at a space resort when I was around seven. My treatment blocked the memory. I'd forgotten him entirely until …"

"You met me," Tam breathed, putting it together. His brow pulled tightly. "Who was he?"

"I don't know, really. He traveled with his father who I believed was testing his telepathic gift." Del's hands knotted in her lap. "It … hurt him."

Nothing to do with Tam's mother, a bizarre coincidence.

"Do you know my mother's name?"

Del shook her head.

"Tell me. Anything." He'd *felt* the layered auras.

"She sang, trying to reach you. A kind of nursery rhyme." Del's voice thinned to a whisper, turning singsong. *"Bring me a stone and give me its story. Bring me a story baked from the earth. Bring me a story carved by the ages."*

Gooseflesh rippled over him as if her words brushed across his skin.

Del's throat convulsed, and she fell silent.

"Bring me a story of worth," he finished, clenching his hands over his knees.

Del knuckled her lips, twisting away.

"You're not crazy, angel," Tam whispered brokenly, absorbing her grief, a distraction from his own. "My mother made that up for me."

A long exhale stuttered from her. No easing in her—as if she feared her psychic gift as much as she feared madness. He echoed her anguished sigh as he processed her reaction. To Del, psy-gifts represented a threat to her calling, a distraction.

Because they carried a cost.

44

An address chalked on a slip of cloth. Caleb clenched his hand over it. He had no idea how it had gotten in his jacket pocket but had no doubt who it came from. The address led him to a freestanding pod in the Taber, a gray box of a building, cramped between two others just like it. Only a short trek from Balter's Den, but weariness weighted him after his stressful, futile duty with Aden—he felt heartsore from disappointing her.

A man stood before the pod, smoking a stim-stick. Belek's sentry.

"Evening," Caleb said, sick, as the significance of this act struck him. Betrayal of Jonas. Of Balter's Den.

There would be no turning back.

The stimp squinted at him, opened the door.

Caleb hesitated.

The stimp parted his jacket to reveal the dark gleam of a lethal.

Choice had already abandoned Caleb.

He stepped inside, feeling like tiny roach legs tracked down his spine. The space was empty, bright lit, with an antiseptic smell. The stimp crowded behind him, pointed to an adjoining doorway.

Caleb crossed into a spare room with a sofa and low table.

Belek sat on the sofa, studying clutter spread over the table. Alone. Clearly, he didn't consider Caleb a threat. The enforcer ignored him, freeing Caleb to glare. The gangster had shed his long org jacket, but was still tip-to-toes in black. The outline of Belek's ribs showed through his shirt. His unnatural leanness had to be self-inflicted. Not like any Fet enforcer was hurting for food.

Caleb blinked, noticing what absorbed Belek's attention, a stars' set, a simple kids' game played in the poorest blocks. Each game piece was formed of three tiny metal rods, fused into an x shape. Belek twirled a small, red ball through his long-boned fingers as he stared at the scattered pieces.

Caleb bit his tongue; any reaction would be a snare.

Belek's hand flicked out. In three bounces of the ball, he nicked all the stars. He rescattered them then lifted his face to Caleb. His brows raised, questioning.

"You wanted to see me, enforcer?"

Belek's expression didn't alter. "You know why you're here. So, talk."

"Here's the thing. I an't sure what I'm expected to report on. Can't imagine what could interest the Fet." His words ticked forward, too fast, stuttering over the possibility Belek would ask about Lettie. "You can't jack Del's shit without busting treaty with Balter's Den. That'd be less of a score than slags like those patchworks think. The sweet stuff can only be charged from the Fring. Del don't keep a full stash of meds Maze-side either. Jonas an't crazy, after all."

Belek smiled, the skin stretching over his cheekbones. That gauntness made his even-featured face repellent. Maybe the point.

"A hit, NG." The enforcer bounced the ball, scooped up a handful of stars. "We got no interest in the good doc's shit."

"Look, I just need to know what I'm supposed to be marking. Dugan wants to make sure she an't an Allied ear—which she an't. Can't even imagine what the Allies would want to grub up here anyway." He tested, "And he wants to make sure she don't get into too much trouble."

Belek leaned back, his black eyes unblinking on Caleb. "Dugan tell you that?"

"Much as admitted he's watching her for his links behind the Wall."

"An' what do you suppose his links want?" For once, no mockery edged Belek's tone.

Caleb found himself answering like he gave a shit what the enforcer thought of his wits. "Those ore-diggers don't like the Allies helping us. They won't make it easy for Del, but letting her get killed would be bad for business."

Belek plucked up a single star, twirled it in his fingers. "IWA demanded a mission. OBMG allowed one crusader in. Only one. What do you suppose the value of that *one* life is compared to all that sweet ore the Allies need?"

Those words, spoken so blandly, struck like a threat. The far-off, civilized universe of Caleb's imagination warped and crowded close.

"How do you think a lazy slick like Dugan got himself such a tidy setup?" Belek asked through Caleb's silence.

"He's their spymaster here," Caleb whispered.

"I wouldn't assume Dugan's agenda matches theirs. Dugan runs his own games. If he churns things here, he can raise the price of his services." Belek tossed the piece down, watching it ping across the table. "Have you ever played stars, NG?"

"Time or two as a kid." Playing stars showed a kid for a seedy ragnose. The enforcer's skill was telling, but then the Fet liked to recruit kids young, from places they wouldn't be missed.

"Were you good?"

Caleb shrugged, wondering if Belek meant to trick him into revealing his scorn.

"An inexperienced player scatters his stars before making his first move." Belek demonstrated, flinging the pieces over the table. He played the ball, only nicking up two stars in the move. "An experienced player learns to concentrate the pieces in the center." Belek gathered the pieces, tossed again. This time they clustered together. He bounced the ball, caught them all in a single sweep.

Caleb got the direction of the enforcer's little lesson but couldn't pinpoint it.

"A more familiar example?" Belek's voice flexed with irony. "What do you do when something's been nibbling your bread stash, and you want to know if it's cril or rats? Put a wedge of that bread in a trap and see what takes the lure."

"Okay." Caleb flattened his mouth against impatience. "Del's bait. For what?"

"Those Inside pricks made her off-limits to their so-called Maze allies, demanded her protection. Less to do with the toff than with a test of how capable their pawns and *her* allies here prove."

A test of Dugan and Jonas? Where did Belek fit? "So, you want me to keep tabs on who's interested?"

"I want you to keep tabs on everything about the woman—who she's cozy with, who's hot-eyeing her, who tries to jack her shit." Belek's gaze bored into Caleb. "You'll also tell me what questions Dugan asks and mark his reaction to your answers."

Caleb absorbed Belek's words, struggling to smooth his breath. Spy on Dugan. No doubt of Belek's intention now. And pincered between three opposing interests, Caleb had small chance of not getting crushed.

Belek narrow-eyed the table's surface. "Imagine stars were a true game of strategy. What would you do first? Mark all the players in the game." Belek began grouping the pieces. "This place might seem like chaos to your off-worlder, but nothing moves here without getting hooked to something else. As if the pieces are magnetized. Messy, but there's a pattern. Those Inside pricks like to know that pattern, to shift it, when it amuses them."

Belek's hand whipped across the table.

Caleb jumped as the stars flew, pinging across the floor.

Belek's nostrils flared. "An' they can so easily clear the game."

Silence stretched. The enforcer studied the blank table as if a map lay there.

"Now." His tone flattened. "Tell me what the little doc has been up to."

Caleb gave his report as flatly, but when he finally escaped the pod, his knees were trembling.

No surprise Inside would use Del to stir things. The Fet's stake remained murky. Their being part of Dugan's spy network could explain their interest. Yet Belek didn't trust Dugan, planned to use Caleb for intel on him. To what end?

No doubt Jonas could unwind the enforcer's meaning. Caleb held a key piece for exposing the source of unrest in the warren but couldn't place it without cutting his own throat.

'*You an't done something foolish, have you?*' Aden's words punished him.

Not as punishing as the fear his foolishness might bleed her, too.

His mind tripped uselessly between wrenching thoughts as he long-strode for the Balter's Den gate. He burned to run, reach shelter. Pointless. He couldn't escape himself.

45

———————

"Tam?"

Del's voice startled him from a doze.

Tam blinked up at her. She stood beside his pallet, twining up her hair. The grainy skylight teased out the russet in her dark curls.

Right. He'd been waiting for her to finish in the washroom. He must have drifted off.

The enormity of what happened between them kept scattering his thoughts. He'd never imagined it possible to share that with anyone ... ever.

And her gift. Its significance for them both.

Del laughed with a flash of white teeth. "Are you awake?"

"Um." He rubbed his eyes, stretched up from the pallet, and gave her a squinty scan. She'd suited up, zipped her vulnerability behind work mode.

Too bad. He'd hoped to lure her back to bed, to snuggle against the salty-sweet warmth of her skin. He fought a yawn.

"I've a request for an outcall. Can we go?"

Tam drew a sharp breath. "It's not a good idea. Jonas wants you to stagger your schedule for security, no more outcalls."

"Jonas isn't *forbidding* it. He knows the good of the community comes first."

In other words, she'd do what she liked. "It's too dangerous now."

"Why? The woman who attacked me is dead."

"Things are ugly between the Fet and the Surge. If they make Balter's Den their battle ground—"

"I'll be needed all the more."

"That's not the point. And we still don't know the patchworks' game."

Her jaw set. "There's nothing to indicate it's anything to do with me."

Except Thuron's sly threats and Umar's involvement. "Del—"

"*If* there is a threat, we'll never uncover it by me hiding in a hole."

"I won't dangle you as bait." Pain flared in his chest.

"There's a little girl who needs—"

"No." They stood nose-to-nose, voices hushed and sharp, arguing about more than one out-call. She'd rejected her gift—acted as if last night had never happened—just as he feared.

"The child needs me."

He groaned with sudden understanding. "Del, sweetheart, that kid isn't Pepar."

She flinched and a flush deepened her golden skin. "I know that," she said between her teeth. He'd pinched too close to the nerve. "I won't weigh my safety over patients' lives. I *can't*."

"But I can."

She studied him, uncomfortably long. Then her eyes hardened, and she said with quiet dignity, "It's always dangerous here. If I give in to fear and intimidation, I may as well give up."

Her words clawed into his chest so hard he couldn't breathe. A reply leaked through his teeth. "All right, then."

She blinked as if disbelieving he'd crumbled so abruptly.

"Let's go." He stalked to the door to keep her from seeing the tremor in his face.

She was sabotaging herself. Again. Ruining things when someone grew close.

Del slid Tam's profile a glance. Expressionless.

Tam's stoicism made so much sense now. Rynet emoted with gesture as much as expression. Not that she had the cypher to interpret emotion signals.

His pointer finger curled and uncurled as he walked. *That* she didn't need a cypher to understand. He was angry. He had every right to be. She'd promised herself never to put him in this situation again. Yet the thought of failing another child had shoved an unrelenting compulsion inside her.

Del bit her lip. Tam was too perceptive, too young, too innocent. He worked for her.

None of that had mattered last night.

She flushed through a swoop in her stomach, and he shot her a frowning glance. He seemed to detect her emotions as easily as he breathed.

Get it together.

She was a professional … *had* to be.

Willfully, repeatedly ignoring danger, bending protocols, sleeping with her assistant—she'd left herself a great deal to hide from her sponsor.

Morning hung damp and gloomy over the Maze. The sun struggled to penetrate the smog, setting the thick air aglow without doing much to illuminate the ground. Any time Del fell back, Tam caught her arm and drew her a pace behind him. He glared through the mist, too alert.

She opened her mouth to call out to him, tell him she'd changed her mind and wouldn't put him at risk this way. She didn't. Instead, she kept trundling behind him.

Tam stopped, flicked a finger for silence. Without looking, he grabbed her arm, shifted her under a building's awning.

Please let it only be rain!

It wasn't. Even she could discern a stirring ahead. Muffled voices, a whir of wheels.

Tam pressed his mouth to her ear. "Move silently." He snatched her hand, began leading her back the way they'd come, crossbow drawn.

A burly figure whizzed out from an alley on a scooter. She caught a flash of wild eyes beneath a plumed helmet. Tam's crossbow whipped up. He squeezed several shots straight into the man's chest. Del's head swum as Tam yanked her away. The man's fish-mouthed surprise left a residual image, the sound of his crash rang in her ears.

"Sprint," Tam hissed.

They tore back toward Tam's place.

He jerked to a halt. Del staggered into him. His face twisted, turning her stomach with it. Sounds of struggle came from ahead. Before she made sense of it, Tam dragged her into an alleyway.

They plunged through barren early morning streets, Tam's grip tight enough to numb her fingers. Their path opened into a concrete glade with a massive metal structure in the center, an abandoned transmission tower. Its metal scaffolding rose like the bones of some long-dead beast and appeared about as sturdy.

"Up, Del," Tam panted. "Ladder, over there."

A narrow, warped apparatus clung to the tower's side.

Tam allowed her a split second to gape before he dragged her to it. "Go!"

She cursed as she tackled the uneven rungs. The ladder swayed, vertigo perhaps.

Tam crowded her heels. "Hurry!"

"I *am* hurrying."

"That old tip-flask who begs outside The Bar could go faster."

Del had no spare breath to retort. She craned her neck to see the top. Not halfway there.

Their pursuers burst into the square. A quick glance showed three figures, two unmistakable: Thuron and Paln.

The unknown, his face concealed by a hood, began scaling the tower's frame with terrifying speed. From Del's dizzying position, his body looked elongated, eerily thin and long-limbed. He used the clawed hooks that extended past his hands as if they were part of his flesh.

Tam drew his crossbow, reholstered it. The patchwork's quick, erratic movements defied a clear shot. Tam leapt to a support beam to intercept the enemy, slashed with his knife.

The patchwork sprang away, not fleeing, trying to get past Tam.

Del clutched her taser, a pitiful weapon against that menace.

"Come down, pretties," Thuron called from the ladder's base. "We got business!"

Tam chased the unknown patchwork with an aerialist's ease.

Each movement iced Del's stomach with terror that he'd fall.

Like a mechanical thing, stiff-jointed and deadly swift, the enemy got around Tam. He perched meters above Del. His hood slid off. Shock numbed her limbs. He was Arnec—the leathery skin and round eyes of a Trenabic but larger, anvil-skulled.

Her gaze jerked to Tam; her mouth slackened with the need to cry out. She snapped it shut. Reckless to distract him.

Two powerful strikes of the Arnec's claw at a rail over Del's head, and one side of the ladder bowed out. Del shrieked, clinging harder to the connected rail.

Parting his mouth, the Arnec bared his bony plate at her, extended a claw toward the other rail. "You go down."

Palsied with height-fear, she clambered onto a horizontal beam and crawled lock-jointed toward a support post.

The Arnec surged after her.

Tam jumped onto her beam, imposing himself between them. "Up, Del!"

He dodged a swing of the Arnec's metallic claw.

She lifted onto her toes but couldn't reach the beam above. Gritting her teeth, she glanced back.

A claw connected with Tam's side. He cried out. Del echoed the sound, braced for him to fall. He pitched sideways, caught the ladder rail, and clung on. No blood. Only the tip of the Arnec's claw was bladed.

Del gripped the support post with trembling fingers.

Tam leapt onto the Arnec's back, snaked an arm around his neck.

The bandit swung his claw wildly but couldn't reach Tam.

Gripping the Arnec's torso with his legs, Tam whipped his knife across his neck. Tam dove off, caught the beam beside him.

The Arnec tumbled backwards with a nerve-jangling howl. He grabbed hold of a pillar, sliding down. A metallic claw gave way. He dropped like a stone. The thump of impact was followed by Thuron's roar of rage.

Del's gaze connected with Tam's. He gasped for breath, crossing the distance between them, his movements rusty with caution.

"Gods, are you alright?" She took his arm, found it steadier than hers.

"I'll do."

Del glanced down. Paln was scaling the ladder, barely hindered by its damaged side.

Tam gestured upwards. "We need to get to the top."

Del tipped her head. The platform tilted dizzyingly far above them.

"You won't have to climb." Tam pulled a cylindrical device from his belt, squinting up.

A cable shot out and attached to the platform's bottom edge.

Del turned incredulous eyes on him. "You might have spared me the heart failure."

"Out of range from the bottom." He clipped the device to his belt. Bracing on a beam, he wrapped an arm around her waist, drew her to him. "Hold onto me, good and tight." His breath steamed in short bursts over her face, belying the calm of his voice.

"You're wounded," she managed thinly. Of course he was.

"I'm fine. Just go easy on my ribs."

She locked her arms around his neck.

Tam lifted her, and she clung to him. His arms bound her as they rose, the cable device retracting with a shrill whirring. Del sealed her eyelids, pressed her face against his shoulder.

The motion halted. She cracked open her eyes. They hung right beneath the platform. *Now what?*

"You'll need to climb up."

"I was afraid you'd say that." Her lips had gone numb.

"I won't let you fall. Let's twist you around. I'll boost you up."

She struggled to unlock her legs, which felt fused to him. He levered her torso onto the platform. An awkward shove propelled her the rest of the way. She crawled onto the chill surface, limbs quaking with fatigue. Her fear-bittered saliva had dried in her mouth.

Tam sprang up beside her. "You okay?"

"Yes," she croaked, flopping onto her back. "Did I neglect to mention I'm deathly afraid of heights?"

"You did fine." His gaze darted around them.

"The struggle we heard on the street?"

"The Surge and the patchworks."

Her swimming head couldn't make sense of that. "Um?"

"Patchworks must've known about the trap the Surge set for us. Can't be a coincidence. They decided to nab us first."

And the patchworks worked with the butcher Umar.

Two enemies at once. Del had flung herself and Tam straight in their path. "I'm sorry." Easy to say. Pitifully inadequate.

Tam focused on checking his weapons harness. "If we'd been coming from our usual direction, we'd have stumbled right into the Surge's snare." His lips quirked. "At least the patchworks wiped them from our tail."

Before his smile could form, it morphed into a frown. He cocked his head.

"Paln is working her way up," Del said.

Tam nodded, reached below the ledge to draw up his cord. He jerked back. Del shrieked as a metallic claw lashed, narrowly missing his face. He scrambled back. The Arnec rose like a disjointed mech over the platform, black blood oozing from his neck, one metal claw bent at an odd angle.

Tam crouched, childlike, before the Arnec's bulk. "Back, Del!"

She scurried to the platform's far end, gained a few body-lengths of safety.

"We go again, Sly One," the Arnec said, a gravely rumble in his chest.

Tam's head snapped up. He growled throaty, sibilant words, gibberish to Del.

The Arnec's shoulders twitched back. Tam spoke his language. The Arnec's eyes rolled. His mouth gaped to expose his bony plates, which clacked together like a piston—what seemed an instinctive answer to Tam's challenge. It freed Tam to draw his crossbow.

Face twisting with anguish, Tam fired the bolt into the being's neck. The Arnec pitched backward with a gurgle. His claw flung up, grazing Tam's temple, as he fell.

Del jerked as if struck herself. Tam toppled, blood welling. Denial keening in her throat, she rushed to him. She unslung her outcall bag from her back, whipped out the diagnose. Tam lay, eyes closed, mouth slack. Blood soaked his hair from the laceration on his forehead, skin cut to the bone.

With desperate, gulping breaths, Del whirled a look around. The Arnec was surely dead and Thuron lurked below, but Paln ...

Gods! She had to hurry.

A scan revealed a concussion, and his ribs ... Despite the dire situation, her breath whooshed from her in awe—the gleaming image on the scan, dense and tensile tissue—Rynet. After that fierce blow from the Arnec, Tam's ribs were only contused.

Del shook herself. Concussion first. She covered his laceration with healing sealant; no time to properly knit the wound. With the surgical, she eased the damaged tissue in his brain. She didn't dare administer pain meds, a realization like a whomp to the chest. The diagnose had no information on drug safety for a half-Rynet.

Reaction set in, palsying her hands. She managed on autopilot. *Selfish, so selfish. So stupid.* Looking at Tam's beautiful, bloodied face, her sickness surged. "I've pushed you so hard, love."

He could have been killed. *Could* be killed, she reminded herself.

A scraping sound alerted her. Del twisted around, reached for Tam's crossbow seconds before an object whizzed by her ear. It clattered against the deck and bounced over the side.

A silver head popped over the platform.

Del's hand closed over the crossbow. A stinging shock tentacled around her ankle. She was dragged facedown. She kicked wildly, flipped herself onto her back.

Paln knelt on the platform, her side propped against a pillar, bracing herself as the whip manacling Del's ankle retracted into the mechanism on her forearm. Paln's eyes fixed on the crossbow in Del's grip. She slapped her forearm, and the whip stopped winding. "You shoot me, we're both going down."

"I don't want to shoot you. I want you to go away and leave us alone."

"That an't a choice." Bland features sharpening with calculation, Paln yanked her arm, sending Del sliding toward her.

Del dug in her heels, crunched to seated, raised the crossbow. Her shoe tips rested inches from Paln's knees.

Paln shoved her free hand forward to block Del's shot.

Del swung the weapon like a club instead, whacking Paln's head. The impact almost jarred the weapon from Del's hand.

Paln yelped, twisted to the side.

Del redirected the crossbow at Paln's face.

The bandit narrowed her flat gray eyes.

Del forced steadiness into her voice. "Release me and climb down from here. I don't want to shoot you, but I will if I must."

Paln's lip curled. "How do I know that you won't shoot me once you're free?"

"Killing isn't in my purview."

Glaring hatred, Paln unwound the whip from Del's ankle with jerky movements.

Del shoved herself backwards.

Paln grabbed her shin.

As Del kicked free, her finger squeezed the crossbow trigger by reflex. The shot went wide, grazing Paln's arm.

Paln lunged for the weapon.

Del flinched away, scrambling to a crouch, taking aim. Nothing happened.

Out of bolts.

Paln smirked, her body bunched to pounce.

Del swung the crossbow like a club.

Paln swatted it away.

Del's arms felt anesthetized. Struggling to her feet, Del groped for her stunner.

Paln oiled her way to standing, her whip trailing the deck, a triumphant grin warping her bland features. "Now you're just insulting me."

"What the hells do you want with me?"

"*I* don't want anything but your corpse under my boots. Client wants a word with you first." Paln flipped her hand, revealing a small device strapped to the underside of her wrist. A syringe.

"You stick me with that, how do you expect to get me down?"

"It would be a *shame* if I dropped you." Paln smirked. Her eyes flicked toward Tam. "*Shame* if I had to strangle him where he lies."

Paln's menace shadowed the platform—too close to Tam's helpless body. Resignation crushed over Del. "Leave him alone, and I'll go without resisting."

Paln's grin bent, and she glared from Del to Tam.

Del clutched her stunner. "I can cause enough trouble to tumble us both over the edge."

With a mocking bow, Paln slashed a hand toward the ladder. "After you, then."

"We go together."

Del wouldn't trust this violent creature alone with Tam for a heartbeat. Del risked a glance at him. His hands curled limply at his sides. His blood was a crimson shock against his pale skin.

Her fear drained, leaving an ache of anger. No more skulking threats. No more getting Tam hurt over her. Whatever the cost to herself, she had to end it.

46

TAM PROWLED AROUND THE BACKROOM, HARNESSING THE URGE TO KICK THE stacks of folding chairs, twined cords, and other clutter from his path. Perched on the table, booted feet planted on a chair, Nan avoided his gaze as he circled—probably not wanting to see her desperate worry reflected in his eyes. They were alone in the space, only the flap of his jacket as he turned and the hiss of a faulty vid-panel breaking the silence.

The need to act was shredding him, but he had nothing to do, no way to find Del if they couldn't root out the patchworks' location. God knew how long he'd lain unconscious on that tower before waking to the sick shock of Del's absence. Bitterness coated his throat like a manifestation of his failure.

"Leave off," Nan snapped. "You're wounded, and you an't doing Del any good wearing tracks in Jonas's floor."

"I won't hide here like a toothless cril while—"

"Running rough through the Den with Jonas and the rest won't help her. We need to think, work this mess out. *Sit* while you think. That glue on your lid won't hold if you keep wiggling it."

He flopped into a chair, unwilling to test the tension beneath Nan's surface calm.

She flipped him a water vial that he nicked from the air. "Drink. You're dehydrated."

342

"I know who has her." Tam swallowed a draught, tepid and tinny. "What we need is to find their lair."

"Are you *sure*? The Surge are playing their hand now, too."

The gang had taken out three block-sentries in the attempt on Del, a blatant act that split Jonas's focus and left him braced for worse. The NGs had started their hunt before Tam returned. With the comm down, he had no easy way to report the patchwork threat.

Tam shook his head, punished with uncertainty.

Thuron and Paln had been the more formidable threat, but he had no idea how many men the Surge had mustered or if any were lethal-armed. He'd weakened the patchworks by taking down the Arnec.

The Arnec's face, twisted in shock as Tam's bolt struck home, flashed in Tam's mind. *'Xeno never betray their own.'* But Tam had been left with no choice.

He winced the memories away, refocused. It was possible the Surge had wrested Del from the patchworks.

"You think the Surge are working with the patchworks?" Nan asked.

That Tam could answer. "No. I saw one of those patchwork roaches at The Backhand. Didn't know what to make of it until after we found Umar's nest in Taber." And the male junkie Tam killed rescuing Pepar from the dumpster had lurked outside The Back Hand—too seedy for a Surge recruit, he'd been Umar's resource, spying on the Surge.

"You sure Del was the Surge's target this morning? Not you?"

I'm not sure of anything. He swallowed down a boil of frustration.

Nan drew her knee up, drummed her fingers over it. "We've been zigzagging over shifting theories the past few days, conflicting intel. Those thugs could be linked in too many ways. Or in none." She slowly met his eyes. "What links *Del* to them?"

Tam expelled a breath. "But—"

"Patchworks rely on docs to install their patch. Jonas's ears got wind the Surge might be poking into the exotics business. The Fet buy exotics for the flesh trade. What if it's Del's skill they're all after?"

"Too tidy. Thuron threw us that bone from the start. I don't trust it." Tam met Nan's eyes, cautious of treading on wounds. "Do you think Torx would be drawn to that?"

Nan grimaced, gestured to her temple. "Step me through it. Just to totally kill the idea."

"Umar used the Surge as a smokescreen, first through Thuron's hinting they were his client, then when Pepar's 'mam' claimed they were the dull-knife's customers."

Tam rapped his fingers over his thigh, glanced at Nan and stilled them.

"All a holo-game. Considering how I met Del, the Surge made a convenient hole to lead us down." Tam had jumped headfirst when he triggered the disaster at the recycling pit.

"And the Fet?"

"—have a stranglehold on the exotic trade already, via Pell Mahr." Torx's comment about a Fet "claim" had terrified Tam, but he'd had no context for it. His fear the gang wanted her for their exotic trade didn't tie with what he knew of the enforcer. "Belek an't stupid. He'd know jacking Del to enslave her is a poor gamble." *Del would die first.*

Tam swallowed against a fresh knot of fear.

Nan raked a hand through her dark sweep of hair. "Back to needing to find the bastards."

Umar had abandoned her digs, and they had no clue where the patchworks nested.

Cursing, Tam stalked into Jonas's empty office, wrestled the gang-activity vid-tile from a warped desk drawer.

Nan stood at his shoulder.

Tam waved up the screen, and the warren map spread over its surface.

He pointed. "The patchworks approached from the west—southwest, I'd wager, because Del and I came from northwest. They weren't behind us."

Nan pointedly kept her focus on the vid. Tam sketched a warding *ah'nea* over his thigh. The clever woman was piecing together the reason for his and Del's unorthodox path.

"They could have been hiding, no?"

No. He'd have sensed Thuron's poisoned aura. "Patchworks an't exactly inconspicuous. Plus, I doubt they cozy too close the Wall." He pointed again. "The Surge were lurking north of The Bar—near the outcall request. They must've called it in."

Nan tapped her lip, studying the pins on the map. "The Boss thinks the Surge are revving to take on the Fet. Maybe so. But that map don't look right."

Another pin had been added since Tam last studied it, at the Waterflow block. The pin pulsed red, indicating suspected Surge activity. "What were they doing at Waterflow?"

"Don't know." Nan traced the map with her finger.

Tam bit his thumb as he studied the image. "No pattern with Fet nests. Some close, some not."

"They wouldn't need to squat close to the Fet to engage them, but … look at our blocks they're lurking around."

"I see it," Tam said, breathless. "Tiller, Waterflow, Yanear."

Nan's eyes locked on his. "Food, water, energy grid—and our security scattered."

They stared like there was nothing else to do.

"That's crack-brained." A gang—a freshly minted *mid-tier* gang— taking on a warren? Even if they had lethals, it was suicide. Taking on the Fet was suicide. And if things got out of control, OBMG would smash Balter's Den, hard.

As if sharing his thought, Nan expelled a breath. "Yeah, crack-brained."

Back to having no idea what the Surge, or their shadow patron, were after.

Back to Del.

He closed his eyes against the press of panic. *Son of a bitch.*

"I can help you."

Tam whirled. A kid hovered outside the doorway, Pepar. Kimber stood beside her, supporting her arm and streaming anxiety.

He frowned a question at Nan.

"Got released from that Fring hospital today. When Del didn't show, I met the med-techs at the gate and picked her up."

Tam glared in disbelief. They should have questioned the kid straight away!

Nan's lips thinned. "Jonas already tried," she whispered. "She was trauma-shocked, incoherent."

The kid looked pitiful, her face covered in a plastic protective mask, her hazel irises glowing against reddened whites. Her skinny arms wrapped around her ribs. "I'm sorry. I felt weird."

The kid's fear seeped through Tam's guard, cooling his outrage.

"What are you doing out of bed?" Nan demanded.

The girl looked like she wanted to melt into the floor, but her hands fisted with determination. "I want to help."

Kimber winced. "She nearly had a fit. I was afraid to not help her down."

"Before she … messed me up, the dull-knife flapped about there being someone she knew could do it right. Maybe she meant your doc."

"Who was it? What did she look like?" Tam asked, just to hammer in certainty.

"D-doc Umar." The girl's arms tightened over her ribs. "I can show you to her digs."

"I'm sorry, little bit," Nan said. "Umar cleared out of her lair already."

"Oh." The girl's frail hands bunched in her tunic. "Wait. I think … I heard stuff about No Man's Land. A … launch point there."

Tam's gaze impacted against Nan's. "Get hold of the Boss."

Her face pinched. "Comm's still down."

"Try," was all he could say before he tore out the door.

***

DEL WOKE SPRAWLED ON A COLD, PITTED SURFACE—A CORRODED METAL floor. Skin crawling, she pushed to her elbows and twitched her fingers away from the sticky residue beneath them. The chemical odor reminded her of spacer utility areas.

The wall across from her shifted.

She froze.

"Wakey, wakey, doc." Thuron sat with his huge, leather-clad form wedged in the empty doorframe of the cramped enclosure.

Del slowly pushed to a seat. A dripping sound drew her attention to a crack in the ceiling, oozing fluid that congealed on the floor. *Lovely. Toxic, no doubt.*

Her head swam. The patchworks had drugged her once she'd made it off the tower. "Where am I?"

"Her lair," Thuron replied, staring vacantly at the doorframe.

He didn't mean his whip-wielding partner. "So, you do work for Umar."

"Thanks to you." His tone was limp, as if he couldn't bother to muster anger.

That mild reaction only made Del warier. "How can that be?"

"Simple." Thuron shrugged. "We got a job. Test the new doc's defenses and take what loot we could to split with the client."

His body creaked with the rise and fall of his chest. The odd, sharp-chunked outline of his torso revealed he was armored under his leather jacket. She wrinkled her nose. Some of the acrid odor came from him.

"I caused your problem by not allowing you to rob me?"

"The *problem* was that your glitter-boy took our patch. Had to get replacements. Lucky us, client could do the work." The creak of his breathing quickened. "Too bad she overreached."

Del pressed her back against the slimy wall, sensing anger rise like heat from beneath his flat demeanor. Her eyes hunted for his blade, but it lay on the side facing away from her.

"Umar's augments an't the best." Thuron fingered a metal disk imbedded in his temple. A crude attempt at a neural implant? He glanced at Del. "But she's promised us upgrades."

Promised to make Del provide the upgrades. She curled her fingertips against the wall, grounding herself against a dizzy disconnect. *How did I get myself here?* "Why ever did you risk it?"

"Umar did right for us in the past." He traced the reddened flesh around the implant with a palsied finger. "Nerves an't healing properly, so the implant's useless." More than useless, *painful*.

"You *all* let her experiment on you?" Utterly mad.

"Just Callet and me. He ripped his out." Thuron flinched his finger from the implant. "Didn't survive it."

The floor's residue seeped dampness through Del's pants, and she shifted to a crouch. "You might have *asked* for help." Gall gripped harder than the discomfort. "I could have removed them for you."

Thuron's gaze snapped to hers. "Yeah? You'd have helped misfits who'd threatened you?"

"Yes."

His lip curled.

"It's not a lie. The idea of *anyone* stumbling around in that state makes me cringe."

Face contorting, Thuron swelled inside his heavy casing as though he'd burst from it. His prosthetic blade clunked to the floor. It scraped over the metal as he crawled jaggedly toward her. She flattened herself against the wall—head, back, hands—like she could escape through it. He swallowed the space between them until she choked on his thick, sickly odor. His eyes were crusted at the corners with discharge, his unwashed hair slicked to his head, the cords of his neck stood out from under red, inflamed skin. Furrows cut deep and ferocious in his brow, around his mouth, as he glared.

He was hideous, terrifying—pitiful.

"Don't," she whispered through rigid lips.

Thuron sagged onto his haunches. For a strained moment, the only sound was the creak of his breathing. Del's legs trembled, desperate to collapse under her. She held them by force of will, afraid to move.

Thuron's mouth spasmed and he looked away, eyes flared wide, unseeing. "You were a fool to ever come to this place."

Her eyelids convulsed with the urge to close. Thuron was right. *Fool* to imagine she could meet the need here, navigate the menace … Del had enjoyed a level of protection few Maze-dwellers had, yet she hadn't escaped threat. No one here could. They fought just to live free. What tools did she possess for *that*? Instead of squandering her life on pride— the arrogant belief *she* could shift the tide of suffering—she should have seized Rhemy's generous offer.

Any rational person would have. Del pressed her finger pads to her temples; their clammy chill felt like neural-therapy nodes. She flinched them away.

Thuron slid back, cradling his sword arm in his lap, his brow crabbed with pain.

"I'll help you if I can." Nothing could trap those words behind her teeth.

An odd, pained humor reset his expression. "Between that quack and your glitter-boy, there's only Paln and me left."

"I didn't invite you to attack us," she braved thinly.

He raked a gloved hand through his greasy hair. "We weren't gonna kill you."

"You tried to kill Tam with that booby-trapped android, or was Jonas your target?"

"Maybe I don't like androids." Thuron smirked with feral satisfaction. "Don't worry. We're under orders to get glitter-boy alive. Umar wants him *bad*. Figures if she opens him up, she can learn how to make one like him."

Del stared an awful moment then her legs gave way, and she sank against the slimy floor.

"Don't this look cozy. Hope you an't falling in love there, Thuron." A raspy voice from behind Thuron's bulk broke the cell's silence.

Thuron groaned to his feet and shifted, bringing Del face-to-face with Paela Umar. Umar's cynical, knowing stare had lurked in Del's conscience—the stare, the smug warning. Umar wore a blue velveteen slacksuit, her sleek white cap of hair exposing the gold lining her ears.

"Why did you bring me here?" Del snapped, bracing against the cold, slimy wall to stand.

"To help me, of course."

Pepar's small, mangled face flashed through Del's mind. "Why would I *ever* help a butcher of children?"

Umar jabbed an arthritically knobbed finger at Del. "The practice of alteration hasn't done you any harm, has it? I'm sure you've made use of your lovely 'assistant.'"

Del hardened her mouth.

"You'll teach me to do alterations." Umar folded her arms. One hand fisted a pistol. "Then, I might let you go."

"Why do this?" The quality cut of Umar's clothing, her relative health … "You have so much." So much more than most Maze-dwellers.

"Wrong, toff! I *had* so much—a respected practice—until Valerian brought you with your fancy toys to give it away for free."

"So, this is about revenge?"

"Too easy," Umar snorted. "You attracted attention from all the players here like a fresh fancy-girl. One was bound to get rid of you for me." She smiled, a reptilian curve of her lips. "But why waste a resource? You shrank my flash. I've worked a way to make you replace it."

Such cruel, selfish rationalization! Del swallowed the urge to shout. "There's so much *need* in the Maze. My practice can't begin to touch it."

"Why should I let a damned off-worlder push me from my nest?" Umar unbound her arms, pointing the gun at Del, her eyes crimped with fury. "Valerian's wanted me out for years, and you suddenly appear? *Just the one* to help him do it."

Too numb, Del didn't react to the threat.

She opened her mouth to argue. Snapped it shut. Jonas's advocacy had drawn IWA to him, and he was clever enough to use Del's practice to solve multiple problems.

Umar gulped a breath. "Either way, I'm sick of bending to *the Boss's* rules. Sick of listening to sniveling about my fees. Alterations pay better. More interesting." She slashed a look at Thuron. "My boy there's a sample of my work, but I'm aiming higher. Putting metal to flesh is easy. Shaping the flesh itself? That's a whole other realm."

Del couldn't help shuddering. "I'm a general practitioner, not a plastic surgeon."

"And I was once a machinist who watched her man heal folk. Now I create human works of art." Umar gestured to Thuron. His face creased with furious mortification, but Umar didn't bother with his reaction. "You got fancy equipment and fancy training. You'll do."

Del bound her arms across her chest. "I won't help you harm anyone."

"Look at her, Thuron, judging us." Umar cocked an elbow as if nudging him remotely. "Skinny as she is, I bet she never went hungry a day in her life. Never knew a second of pain 'til she got here."

A tic worked in Thuron's lantern jaw. He glowered at his boots.

"Go ahead and judge, toff." Umar's focus grew diffuse. "I spent more years helping folk here than you been alive. And you know what? Makes no difference. They still die. Still kill each other. Still starve." Umar's tone flattened with something akin to despair—the afterimage of an emotion long since burned away.

Del knew the endless pool of patients, the crushing need. The helplessness. Despair.

Umar blinked, expelling an impatient breath. "You keep your nose high for now. Once I lure your pet here, you'll jump to my will right enough."

'Umar figures if she opens him up …'

Del dug her fingers into the fabric over her ribs, tightening the bind of her crossed arms. "These odds won't work for him."

"Flap has it he's *all* juiced over you." Umar bared her tarnished metal dentures.

Del laughed, a stilted failure. "Rumormongers have nothing better to do."

Umar moved closer, and Del got a whiff of her cloying perfume. "Once we've gotten him good and worried, we'll set a snare for your lovely, and he'll fall right in." Umar's manner shifted, growing tautly expectant. "Let's go." She slashed a hand at Thuron. "Come make sure the toff behaves."

Thuron steered Del into a low-ceilinged corridor, its gloom relieved at intervals by portable lights fused onto the walls. The floor slanted, a shade of the surreal, as if Del were experiencing the nightmare room in a fantasy virtual. Thuron's massive shoulders brushed the narrow walls. Not a thread of fresh air that might reveal an exit to escape from.

"What is this place?"

"My digs." Umar smirked. "If I tell you more, can't ever let you go, can I?"

They wound through a chain of corridors until Del couldn't have found her way back to her cell if she wanted. The air grew increasingly stale.

Umar stopped before a closed entryway. A crude metal lever had been welded on as a handle, compensation for failed automation. Umar gestured to Thuron, and he yanked the hatchway open. Umar avoided drawing close to him.

The chamber was large, lined with cabinets—no, instrument panels—

covered in rusty silt and clutter. Two seats squatted at warped angles before a massive, dead screen. A derelict spacecraft? She'd never heard of such a thing in the Maze. *Where the hells am I?*

A flimsy fold-up table, covered by a scattering of tools, stood in the center of the space. Del's outcall pack rested there.

Umar ran a finger over the table's edge. "You're gonna teach me to use this stuff."

"Why would I do that?"

Umar shrugged. "Imagine the damage I can do with this junk—" She hooked the bag's flap with one finger, pulled it closer with three short tugs. Her gaze clicked to Del. "—not knowing how it works."

Del blanked her thoughts to keep her expression impassive.

"I could say please," Umar continued. "Or I could let Thuron convince you."

Thuron expelled a breath. He loomed at Umar's shoulder, watching.

Let's see what she knows—what danger lurks in her knowledge. "Very well. Shall we start with the diagnose?"

Umar shoved the bag toward Del.

As Del fished out the device, Thuron's focus latched onto her movements. Perhaps her tranquilizer trick had taught him to be wary.

Like his reaction was contagious, Umar said, "Keep it pointed away from me. Wouldn't want you getting any ideas."

"I'll need to scan *someone* to demonstrate how it works."

"Use him." Umar jabbed her thumb toward Thuron.

Del smiled with grim humor at his alarmed expression. "This won't hurt a bit."

He edged back, glanced at Umar, and stilled.

Del scanned him. "Your minion eats too much fatty food," she said to Umar, then to Thuron, "You have high cholesterol, Mr. Thuron."

"Can't see how it matters. I an't likely to live to a ripe old age."

"And?" Umar twitched her hands, as if repressing the urge to snatch the diagnose.

Del gave a staccato overview, spicing her explanation with jargon.

Umar frowned at the screen, flicking her fingers against her thumbs. She reached into her pocket, pulled out a pair of goggles, and slipped them over her head. Del recalled she was nearsighted.

"Show me again."

Del repeated the process, no slower. The diagnose couldn't harm, but if Umar figured it out, deciphering the surgical would be easier.

Umar squinted and scowled. "Show me the other toy."

As if it was that easy! As if any *toy* could replace grueling years of study.

"I wouldn't waste the charge. Surgical tools drain power quickly," Del lied.

Umar's head contracted into her shoulders, and her lips peeled over her metal teeth. "Think you're clever, you high-nosed bitch? Outsmarting me with your big-credit words? Well, you've locked the door to your own prison. If *I* can't use this junk, you'll have to use it for me."

Del stared stonily, shuttering her reaction. She hadn't fully considered how dangerous her equipment would be in ignorant hands. Whatever the cost, she must ensure Umar never got the chance to use it.

Umar's eyes slitted. "Keep in mind, the longer you're missing, the more churned your precious warren will get. Valerian'll blame the Surge; the Surge'll blame the Fet. And the Fet?" She snatched up Del's pack and shook it. "You'll return to a pretty little war. If you return at all."

Del swayed, flattening her palms against the table. It shifted beneath her weight.

Umar spat to Thuron. "Chuck her back in her cell."

"Yikes, doc," Thuron muttered, steering Del into the hallway. "I think you just made it personal."

"It already *was* personal."

Thuron returned to using his bulk as her cell's door. Del tried to ignore him, but his scrutiny dragged her from her thoughts like annoying ambient noise.

She turned a glare on him.

"What'd you see in that scan of yours?" He met her gaze steadily. "You meant for Umar to test it on me."

So, he wasn't a complete moron.

"Besides the fact that the machinery you've grafted to your body is poisoning you?"

He didn't react. "Besides that."

"Why do that to yourself?" She stalled.

"Lost the arm in a fight." He traced his sword arm's blade-release with a jagged fingernail. "Figured I'd make it work for me."

Naturally, a transplant or decent prosthetic wouldn't be available.

Thuron's small mouth twitched. "You an't feeling sorry for me, are you?"

She slitted her eyes. "Certainly not."

"Good. 'Cause I strode down this path long before I got my patch. Now tell me. Please."

The awkward addition of "please" swayed her. "You have no neural implant. Umar lied to trick you."

"Figured you'd say that. Why should I believe you?"

"Believe me or not. Makes little difference to me."

"Why?" Several questions twined within that one, thickly voiced word.

Del shrank from his emotion. "A neural implant, capable of sending pulses from the brain to control artificial components, is extraordinarily complex. As complex as organ or limb regeneration. Impossible for Umar to fashion one." She drew a deep, silent breath. "Also impossible for me."

He held stock still.

"If that disk in your head causes you pain, it's because it was *designed* to. You need it removed. Umar may believe I can upgrade it to a real neural implant. I don't know. But she ensured you'd do anything to force me to try."

"You're wasting your breath." Thuron studied his palm, upturned on his knee. The fingers tremored.

"Why?" Her turn to keep it simple.

"Nah, doc? What's my life expectancy? Aging. Losing allies." His mouth pressed grimly. "I needed an edge. For me. For Paln. Still do."

He knew no other way to live. Pity pressed on her. "It's information. Do with it what you will."

He gave her a sidelong look but didn't speak again.

47

———

Tam sat on the fence, hands clawed over his kneecaps, glaring into the blackness of No Man's Land.

Pepar's words had drawn Tam to the edge of the wasteland where he'd chased Thuron from Umar's nest. The bandits' hov-truck had headed straight west then, but they could have gone anywhere.

Tam blindly hoped to catch the scent of Del's aura but faced bleak emptiness.

He jumped off the fence and climbed down the incline. At the bottom, he faced a sheet of darkness, no ambient light to allow his vision to adjust.

Where are you, angel? As if she'd answer.

The thought prickled.

Tam's father was a telepath. Del must have a similar ability. That was how her aura projected so clearly. Maybe how she'd experienced "visions" of his mother?

His anxiety over *Emere* lay buried beneath his awful fear for Del. Those fears melded, threatened to undo him. He sucked a gasping breath against a swell of panic.

Think, fool.

Emere had been clear that *ela* was spirit, not ghost—a remnant, not a whole. Her *ela* was a static thing, stronger than mundane memories but still rooted in Tam *as a boy*.

Del couldn't pluck *Emere's* memories like a clairvoyant. *Emere* had telepathically transferred a psychic imprint—thoughts, memories?—to Tam. Del could only have drawn it from his mind. Burning with curiosity about his past, Del might have subconsciously hunted for answers with her gift.

Tam ploughed his hands through his hair, dug his nails into his scalp. "You're a fucking genius." He'd let passion rule him for days, landing him here—everything too little, too late.

He squeezed his eyes shut, helplessness threatening to jack his reason. *Get it together*.

The Rynet boy Del had mind-spoken with … She'd labeled it illness, but the evidence of her gift made that unlikely.

What if Tam could reach her the same way? The thought captured him, stole his breath.

After she'd been burned, he'd lain beside her, experienced that sensation of opening, touching her aura with his. And those times he'd read her will … not with empathic perception alone because *will* linked as strongly with thought as emotion.

Tam had already connected with Del's mind. He could do it again.

Standing straighter, he scanned for Del—sent thoughts to her until his head throbbed—but got only aching cold and silence.

He started walking, stumbling over stones and ruts, the nothingness of the wasteland a void crawling over his skin.

Sense returned. He'd do Del no good by breaking his leg in a hole.

Tam sank to his knees on the chill ground. The wind was a sly hiss in his ears, the only break in the stillness. He imagined himself petrifying there, a worthless sentry left to erode away.

Love was *loss*. The cruel lesson of his boyhood. How had he been fool enough to repeat it?

A rumble under his knees startled him; a boreworm passing deep below. Closing his eyes, Tam pressed his palms to the ground. Gooseflesh rippled over him until the vibration faded. He'd never encountered a boreworm before, but then he'd never listened for one.

Never listened …

Tam snapped open his eyes. He'd gone about it wrong! His gift wasn't centered in intellect but instinct, rooted in senses not thoughts.

Don't think *at her*, reach *for her*.

He sank into his perceptions of Del—her richly faceted aura, her lithe, passionate body, her quick, complex mind—then stretched out with his longing, groping through the emptiness.

A tickle inside his head jolted him. He flinched. Lost it.

Heart pounding, he sucked in a breath and tried again. Easy now, as though he'd been groping for a path and discovered he need only open his eyes to find it.

The contact slid through him, a silken twining between the synapses of his brain. Its intensity made him shudder before the connection solidi-fied. Pure warmth.

She was there. *Tam.*

His mouth relaxed into a smile. He responded wordlessly, a light touch.

I miss you. Hers the barest shapes of words, misty but real.

He tried adding words of his own. *I'm here.*

It's so cold here. So … wrong. Her message devolved into emotions, affection, concern.

Show me.

Disorienting sensations—chill, disgust, stench—a blur of dark things, not quite images, not quite thoughts.

Where are you? He pressed.

I don't know. It's like a jump-ship but drearier.

Jump-ship? He couldn't repress his alarm.

A mistake to react so strongly.

Her mind sharpened like a blinding brightness. Her voice rang as clear as if she stood with him. *It's truly you? No! It's a trap. You mustn't come.*

The contact severed. She was gone.

Tam leaped to his feet, a wild, elated grin splitting his mouth. The line might have gone dead, but he had a bead on the signal. He detected the distant static of her mind, shying away from him, afraid for him, longing for him.

48

Caleb hardly understood his panic, the itch of impatience to act, keep moving. The Boss had them fanned throughout the Den, patrolling, searching for Del. Caleb had split from his partner, too revved to deal with the plodding indifference of Aden's stand-in.

Caleb moved through a tunnel-like section of cramped pods and low-hanging smog. The streets had emptied. Folk hunkered in their pods, afraid Surge violence would spill onto them. His eyes scanned his surroundings as if he might find something—anything—to erase the awful weight of dread.

When a line of shadows materialized before Caleb, he didn't startle. Drawing his stunner, he whirled to run, found himself boxed in.

Belek appeared, arms crossed, watching with that infuriating condescension. "How nice. We were about to hunt down our ear, and here he is."

Caleb tensed against Belek's scathing humor, lowered his stunner.

"What's Valerian stirring with all this activity?" Belek demanded.

Caleb struggled to hold Belek's gaze.

"Spill," Belek snapped. "Unless you want him to know about our arrangement."

"Surge hit a few blocks."

"And?"

"Doc's missing." Caleb thinned his mouth at Belek's lack of reaction. Like maybe Belek already knew. "What's your interest?"

"I see." Belek laughed. "The saint has another convert."

Caleb held stock-still, studying Belek—the amusement shaping the narrow lips, the emotionless black eyes.

Belek sneered. "Did you really think Dugan believed *you'd* protect the toff better than her uncanny exotic?"

Caleb clenched his teeth over a retort.

"You're the worst breed of turn-skin, fooling yourself that profiting off Del Marks served her protection. Dugan was never her friend. Who do you imagine hired the Surge to menace her at The Back Hand in the first place?"

Belek's words squeezed Caleb, though they only confirmed his suspicion. He burned to spit a denial.

"Dugan sell you on his good will? He an't an ally to Balter's Den. In Valerian, he sees a rival. An't much flash to leech from the Maze. He wants it *all* for Pell Mahr."

Caleb fought to quiet his breath. He hadn't been stupid enough to trust Dugan. Not ever. Yet the enforcer's words bit deep, stripped Caleb's stupidity bare.

"What a catch for Dugan, corrupting Valerian's golden boy, using him as the tool to eliminate Valerian's prized sneak."

"I didn't give him *shit*." Caleb's throat muscles spasmed with the force of his words. Never loyalty. Only failure.

Belek narrowed his eyes. "Your self-deception makes you an unreliable source."

He moved so fast, Caleb didn't register what happened until the blade's hilt jutted from his side. The dagger inched free, dripping red. Caleb dropped to his knees, crimson splashing down his body.

A flurry of movement. Belek's gaze bored into him. "That stick shouldn't be fatal if you get medical care. You want your doc back to patch you up, you'll tell me what I need to know."

Agony blotted Caleb's thoughts. Fear burned worse than the pain. "Taken … the Surge."

Belek's expression morphed—a fierce, feral tightening. Belek flowed to his feet like a black mist in Caleb's wavering vision.

"You won't hurt her?" Caleb rasped, unable to help it.

Belek's head turned, the white oval of his face disembodied against the darkness. "I never said that."

Caleb collapsed against the ground, his cheek scraping the hard, gritty pavement, his hand pinned beneath his chest. He thought of Del as he'd so often seen her, giving him a warm, distracted smile while she followed Lyn from The Bar.

49

WATERY HINTS OF DAWN STREAKED THE SKY AS TAM HUNKERED BEHIND A boulder to case the hideout, a grounded aircraft. No Man's Land was littered with debris like this—junk salvagers wanted to pitch, wrecked smuggler ships downed by Mine Security, and other mess. As the sky paled to a gutter-runoff gray, Tam could see the aircraft was a junker, listing to one side, corrosion mottling its insect-like shell with rusty splotches.

The hideout lay at the planetscaping's edges, thinner air making Tam breathless—or maybe his injuries. After crossing the inky plain at a slow lope for over an hour, he swayed with dizziness and his head throbbed.

No word from Nan. The comm was still blocked, or Tam was out of range.

A low buzz betrayed the existence of a power generator. With his ocular, Tam spotted it, clumsily fused beneath a bent fin where a fuel cell should have been. No hint of movement.

Del was close, her aura like a bright stroke of color on a blank screen. He could locate her as though she wore a tracer.

He crouched lower, widening his ocular's field to hunt for the best way in.

DEL PACED THE CELL UNTIL THE SOUND OF HER FOOTFALLS DROVE HER MAD. A teen guarded her now. The boy rocked and stared at the wall as if a film were projected there. When she inched toward the doorway, he blinked to alertness, glaring at her, and flashing his stunner.

Her stomach was raw with worry, but her nerves sang with restless elation. The lingering thrill of Tam's touch. Its significance.

Del stopped pacing.

Her *whole life* she'd feared this—let it chase her halfway across the galaxy—as if, real or unreal, it carried the power to undo her. Somehow, on this bleak planet, in that primitive slum, she'd found herself. Let herself be found again.

She traced her temples and cheekbones with her fingertips, thinking of Jenl with a half-formed smile. Perhaps his spirit had stayed with her as he'd promised, and buried awareness of his love, their shared gift, had helped shield her from her unloving family.

Yet that gift might have led Tam straight here. She could try to re-open the link, warn him again. Foolish idea. That would draw, not deter, him.

Del bit her lip, resuming her pacing.

Her gift hadn't burst forth upon her need. Contact with Tam had slowly unlocked it. The headaches, the vivid dreams, her heightened awareness of his presence ... The illusive recognition she'd experienced the night they met had been resonance between their minds. So many mysteries she'd simply accepted—how he sensed danger before it broke over them, how he knew people's intentions, how he sensed presences through closed doors.

How he always seems to know how I feel ...

She stopped, thumped her fist against the slimy wall. A flicker of weakness bumped her thoughts against his.

Del gasped. He was close. *No, Tam!*

"Shit, stop shouting. I can hear you just fine."

She whirled around. He stood in the doorway, a lean shadow outlined in the flimsy light.

"It's a trap," she steamed through set teeth. "I didn't warn you off on a whim."

He grinned. "Good to see you, too, angel. It may be a trap, but they don't know it's been sprung yet."

She rushed to him, failing to douse her selfish joy as he took her hand and drew her into the passageway. His skin was icy against hers.

Anxiously, she scanned his forehead. Spotting a healing patch beneath his bangs, she expelled a breath. He'd gotten to Nan.

Del kept her eyes up as she passed her young guard's body.

Tam gave her hand an impatient tug. "Tased, Del."

He led her down the crooked, tunnel-like passageway. Only the creak of the vessel's settling bones disturbed the silence.

Tam jerked to a halt and nudged her back. A jolt weakened her limbs as she spotted the huge shadow blocking the passageway. Whipping up his crossbow, Tam fired.

The shot pinged off, and Thuron grunted with satisfaction, releasing his blade with a snick.

"That'll do, Thuron."

Del spun. Umar lurked behind her, smug face formed from the shadows, a gun gleaming in her hand.

"Drop your toy, or I'll blow off something vital, see if she can fix herself."

Tam didn't take his attention off Thuron as he threw down his crossbow. He flattened against the bulkhead, tugging Del against his side.

"You didn't figure he'd show, Thuron, but look how *juiced* he is over the toff." Umar leaned a hip on the bulkhead opposite, giving Tam a sneering scan. "The Boss's super-sneak. We had better in my day."

"Bugs and cril?" Tam curled his lip.

"Tools match the need. Your mistake was looking for something *new*. I've always been here. First watching for my man, then for myself."

Tam dipped his chin, tense, thoughtful. "You were old Umar's stealth-worker. Or was it secret police?"

Old Umar? Tam meant the former warren chief.

Baring her metal teeth, Umar held up a syringe in her free hand. "Stay still boy, or I'll let Thuron play with your lover a bit."

Del curled against Tam as if that could shield him. Her throat knotted with the memory of Umar's threat to *open him up.*

50

THEY LED DEL INTO THE VESSEL'S INNARDS. THE HULK GROANED BENEATH ITS own weight—eerie, echoing creaks and clicks that made her imagine oceanic depths. Umar's teen minion slumped along ahead of her. Thuron lumbered behind, a far more convincing menace.

Umar had separated Tam from Del, and something fogged their psychic link, nagging like a numbed limb.

Thuron prodded her into a wider passageway where they were brought up short by a set of massive doors, affixed with makeshift handles. The teen wrestled them open to reveal a chasm of a compartment: a cargo bay cluttered with tipped crates spilling dubious contents onto the deck. The grime-streaked bulkheads looked spongy, as though they swelled into the compartment—warped. Pressure oppressed her, an odd claustrophobia within such a vast space.

In the center, light shone over a rickety platform, level flooring that balanced the ship's tilt. Umar stood there like the captain of an ancient sailing vessel, legs braced apart, arms akimbo. Her eyes blazed irony. Umar was enjoying her own act. Behind her, Paln squatted, arms draped over her knees in a posture of indifference. A metal table stood on the platform. Tam lay on top, motionless.

I've always been here, Umar claimed. A malignancy lurking beneath all Jonas achieved.

Turning medicine into twisted satire for greed.

Narrowing her eyes, Del stepped onto the stage.

TAM'S AWARENESS SEEPED FROM UNDER UMAR'S DRUG. A CLUTTER OF presences ringed him, one of them Del's. Her agitation sent a frisson over him, bringing him further awake. He blinked up at a cavernous ceiling. A slurry of strange odors pitched his stomach. Coarse straps pinned Tam across his thighs and torso to a metal surface. His chest was bare. He flexed against his bonds, tight and chafing.

Rolling his eyes, he spotted Umar, facing away. Two teens perched near him, sitting on a crate, swaying listlessly. Outside of blurred murmurs from that apathetic audience, it was silent. He tried to touch Del with his thoughts, but his focus scattered. He brushed by her, some fierce emotion arcing through the contact.

Del's light footfalls approached, layered with heavier ones, Thuron's. Tam craned his neck toward her. Her lips curved for him, but her eyes were charged with outrage.

"Time to make yourself useful, toff," Umar said.

"You served the warren's people for years. Don't you care anymore? Is revenge so important?" Del's limp tone showed she knew her words were futile.

Hatred soured Umar's aura. "You think I give a *shit* about hurting you? You're a blip, a useful tool. And the warren? Let it burn. Valerian's twisted my home into something I don't recognize. Constructing a cage like he's taming an animal. Animals are better off free."

Umar drew closer, and Tam swallowed against the gag reflex. She studied him with eyes misshapen through a pair of lenses goggled to her head. "Time to work, Dr. Marks. I need you to teach me how to make *this*." Her stubby, gnarled fingers hovered over his chest.

Tam's muscles contracted away from her touch. His head spun. His secret was about to be gutted open in deadly company.

"Tam is unique," Del replied. "Unless you can clone him, you're out of luck."

Umar snapped her hand back and forth. "Yes. The base material is good. I need to know how to make this skin, those eyes, that hair. But no *ghoul's* blue. A pretty violet or green."

Like the dirty dull-knife could flip skin color from a decorators' pallet.

Del's ribs swelled as if her denial built beneath them.

"If you're no use to me, doctor, I'll return you both to Valerian in bits." Umar hacked a laugh. "Now map the exotic for me."

Tam strained against the straps.

Del stilled, a strange, flat expression transforming her face. With narrowed eyes, she skimmed the room, the teens, the patchworks. Then her gaze settled on Tam.

Del? He tried, but her mind was closed to him. "Del?" he whispered, irresistibly.

Jaw set, she faced Umar. "I'll do what I can, but I'll need my equipment." Del's voice shook, but Tam couldn't penetrate her emotion.

Del? he pressed again, useless.

"Hand over the toff's bag," Umar ordered Paln as if initiating a ritual.

Del stepped up to Tam. He expected to find her diagnose in her hand, but she held her portable surgery tool—similar in size, worlds different in purpose. His gaze shot to her face. What was she up to?

"Thuron," Umar barked. "Cut off the toff's head if she makes a false move."

Thuron grunted, anger seething through his emotional signature. His focus dipped to the gun strapped to Umar's waist, then away.

"You wanna outlive the patch on your body, you need me alive and cooperative," Umar added.

Thuron shifted closer to Del, slid open the sheath to his sword. Tam sensed his mental shudder.

Tam fought his restraints until they seared his skin, a challenge-hiss forming in his throat.

Del touched Tam's shoulder to still him—warm, impersonal. Her fingers ticked over her device, a cool confidence enveloping her as if this were her exam room and Tam just another twitchy Maze-rat from her patient queue.

She glanced at Thuron. Something passed between the two that hollowed Tam's gut.

Del leaned over Tam. She had the surgical tool pointed in the wrong direction, at herself. That wouldn't fool Umar for long.

What are you doing?

Hush. The force of her mental voice stunned him flat.

"There are traces of varium under the top layers of skin. I can only assume that's what gives it that color, but I couldn't tell you how to achieve it."

What was Del planning? Her dismissiveness made Tam feel more exposed.

"You feeding me a load of dung, Dr. Marks? I'll have Thuron slice off a piece of you."

"See for yourself," Del said, voice colorless.

Umar hesitated. "You read it." She jerked her chin at Thuron.

Thuron shrugged. "Can't read for a rat." He was lying.

Umar muttered, stretching her head like a carrion bird to peer at the device.

Del tilted the active end toward Umar. "See here?"

Umar squinted at the screen, cringed back. Her face contorted, and she clutched her chest, eyes bulging. Confusion dizzied Tam until he remembered Umar bragging about her heart valve. Had Del dislodged it?

"Thu-ron," Umar choked, one hand clawing her breast, the other fumbling up her gun.

The huge man hefted his sword arm, sending Tam jackknifing against his bonds.

Del leapt back.

Thuron whirled on Umar.

Tam was trapped between relief and panic.

A sickening thunk.

Del recoiled, slapped her hands over her mouth. She spun, thrusting herself between Tam and Thuron.

"Get out of the way, Del!" Tam thrashed, helpless.

Thuron glowered at Del, his breastplate heaving. Paln's aura spiked with cruel anticipation. Del squared her shoulders, held Thuron's stare.

The bloodlust melted from Thuron's face. He glowered toward Umar's teen minions. "I suggest you vacate. Your hespar-mama is gone."

The kids gaped with clone-like blankness.

"You wanna test my blade?" Thuron leered, monstrous with his distorted features and bloodied blade.

The teens plunged into the darkness, shoving and sniping.

Del ducked by Umar's body, scrabbled up the gun, and staggered from Thuron's reach.

Thuron lanced her an amused look.

"I thought killing wasn't your thing, toff?" Paln stalked forward, coiling her whip around her gloved hand.

Hostility frosted Del's aura. "I saw a disease. I eradicated it."

Tam sucked in a breath. *Del?*

Her head tilted toward him, the only acknowledgement.

He clawed the strap over his chest, the sheaths he'd neglected trimming retracted over nails impotently blunted.

"Just ax the bitch, Thuron." Paln flicked her whip, fixing her gaze on the gun. "She don't have the balls for *honest* murder."

Del's vulnerability raked Tam. Digging with his heels, he fought to wriggle under the straps. He gained an inch but felt like it cost some skin.

Thuron clamped a hand over Paln's shoulder. "Umar lied. Used us. It's over."

Paln glared furious defiance at Thuron.

"Back away!" Del's voice thinned, betraying her strain.

Thuron wheezed a laugh but stepped back. Without lowering her guard, Del groped under the table with her free hand until Tam's bonds sprang loose. He shoved to a crouch on trembling limbs.

Thuron leveled a dismissive sneer at Tam before turning to Paln. "We're cutting out." He leapt from the platform, tossing over his shoulder, "Don't get lost scurrying home, Lyn."

Tam squinted into the gloom until the patchworks disappeared through the bay door. He sucked in a shuddery breath for calm.

Del stared at Umar's corpse, white-knuckling the gun, her lips pressed bloodless.

Easing behind Del, Tam slid his arms around her and steadied her tremoring hands with his. He rubbed his cheek against hers in *ah'lir*. "Easy, angel."

She caved against him with a broken sigh.

He stroked his thumb over her fingers to unlock her grip on the gun, shifted it to his hand, and thrust it into his belt. "We need to get back, fast."

"I killed her," Del said tonelessly. "With my surgical."

"I know." He turned her in his arms.

She lifted unfocused eyes; her aura so faint that he tugged her closer to feel her breath. "There's ... something dark inside me."

"Yeah. I drink it all in, the dark with the light." He traced her jaw with his thumb. "Let's go home."

Del blinked, frowning at the deck. "Home ..."

"Jonas, Nan, the whole warren needs you." Her hair had come loose, and he sank his fingers through the snarls. "They need you, because I'd let it all burn to keep you safe." He shuddered against a dramatic paling of his irises.

Her breath whooshed out, tickling his neck. Her eyes locked on his, startled. He kissed her, resenting the foreign scents that had seeped into her skin. She kissed him back, her chill fingers digging into his bare back.

They broke apart, and he brushed his lips across her forehead in wordless apology. "We can work this shit out later, okay?"

Del stared at the hollow of his throat, intensifying his pulse there, then she blinked as if to reset herself, seal away feelings she couldn't face. "Will we return in time?"

He stepped back, drew the gun. "If we're quick, we might just hitch a ride."

51

Del crouched close to Tam inside the patchworks' hov-truck. Her mind kept wandering from their dire situation to Umar's headless corpse, the arterial spray—less grotesque than imagining how Umar's heartvalve drove into her ribcage as if Del had fired a bullet from inside the body.

Umar deserves it. The cold thought snaked to the surface. Del knuckled her lips with a shaky hand. Her chin quivered beneath her fingers. *I'm not the person I thought I was.*

She couldn't think about it now, or she'd break apart.

The cab reeked of sweat and old vinyl—and Thuron. They'd left Paln behind, spitting with rage, vowing to choke Del blue. Neither Tam nor Del knew how to pilot a hov, so they'd been forced to bring Thuron, who seemed unsurprised and unmoved.

Without touching Tam, Del sensed the tension wiring his body. He stood behind Thuron's pilot seat, pistol aimed. "Don't get any ideas about tossing us. I might accidentally blow your brains out."

Del studied Thuron's profile, the faux neural implant, the inflamed skin around it, his pain-wrinkled brow.

"Tam," she said quietly. "You don't need that."

He shot her a scowl.

"Get us safely to Balter's Den, Mr. Thuron, and I'll do as I promised once things settle."

What the fuck, Del?

She winced. Tam had learned to fling his thoughts with his telepathic voice.

I promised to undo the damage Umar inflicted. A small price for a little peace.

Tam hissed, his characteristic expression of disgust, a mannerism she might have recognized as Rynet. But then only snippets of her Jenl memories had returned, and she'd never trusted media depictions of alien races.

"If I didn't think you'd keep your promise, I'd have let the old psycho have your boy," Thuron snarled without heat.

"You figured out the bitch tricked you. That's why you chopped off her head." Tam's snarl, on the other hand, hadn't lost any teeth.

"I'll keep my promise," Del said with careful calm.

"Just don't die before I can collect."

Del stroked Tam's sensitive nape to startle away a rumble forming low in his throat. In these cramped quarters, Thuron wouldn't fail to notice the alienness in the sound.

Tam shuddered, shot her an incredulous look.

They reached the Maze border in silence. Thuron grounded the hov, its systems groaning over the uneven surface. When the hatch opened, Tam grabbed Del's arm, steered her toward it. Thuron twisted around. Del found herself meeting his eyes. He lifted his chin in a gesture she couldn't interpret. "Doc, stay clear of Valerian, if you mean to keep your promise."

"What do you mean?"

"No more'n I said." He turned away.

Tam tugged her into the fresher air, hustled her up the incline. Apparently, he didn't trust Thuron wouldn't run them over. The hov-truck spun around and disappeared.

52

Each step fought him. Caleb clutched the alley wall, shuffling, shuffling inch by inch. The streets lay empty. He could try calling out. He didn't. Just clamped one hand over his wound and fought his wobbly feet forward. Belek's accusations looped through his mind, spiraling tighter and tighter.

Dugan had played Caleb as the fool's jape in his sharp game from the start.

How will Valerian react?

I heard Valerian's breaking ground on a new project—you'll tell me what it is?

Get Valerian to off-load his sneak.

Valerian, Valerian, Valerian …

Dugan didn't give a shit about Del except as Jonas's asset to destroy the moment his Inside patron looked the other way. Dugan didn't care about the Fet or the Surge—only cheap little stars on his gameboard.

Dugan's real target was Jonas.

Belek's stars lesson, only an illustration of how much Dugan enjoyed twisty games. Kill Jonas. Blame the Surge. Throw the warren into chaos to undo Jonas's hard-won progress.

And Caleb was the only one who knew.

He desperately wanted to curl against the cold, crumbly pavement, let his guilt gush away with his blood. Instead, he kept staggering forward.

Hands seized Caleb. He struggled to shake them off.

"Easy, now. I'm trying to help you."

More words ticked around him, incoherent.

His knees buckled, his thread of strength snapping. Arms bound his shoulders, eased his fall.

"What happened?" A man. Hovering, too close.

A whirl of movement and someone crouched beside Caleb with a gaudy purple jacket. Aden's. The cloth pressed to his side, making his vision white with agony.

"Hey, Goldie." Aden's voice, forced gentle. "What've you gone and done to yourself?"

Not Addie. He winced his eyes shut. *Anyone but Addie.*

He wilted against her shoulder as she slid her arm around him. The thick, perfumy scent she'd worn too many years goosebumped his skin. His hand groped for hers.

"Get Nan. *Sprint.*" Aden barked to the man. Caleb wished she'd used his name. His muzzy mind couldn't place him.

Didn't matter.

"The Boss, Addie" he rasped against her neck. "… after … Jonas …"

Her hand cupped his nape. She pulled back, forced him to meet her eyes. Her mouth pressed into a white line, corners trembling. "You tell me now, damn you."

His eyes stung. He clenched them shut to block her out. "I fucked up … all went … tumbling … wrong."

"I know that, you shit." Her voice shook; her grip on his hand tightened. "I've seen it building in you for weeks. *How* is what I'm asking."

"Don't … matter now." He panted through a wave of pain. "Pell Mahr … It's Pell Mahr … Dugan."

"You an't making sense. Who the fuck is Dugan?"

"Pell Mahr toff. His game. Controlling the Surge. Maybe the Fet. Target's the Boss."

"You sold out." Cold and flat words, but her awful grief crushed him anyway.

Caleb didn't answer. Didn't have to.

"You're stuck clean through," she said between her teeth. "Like from the kind of dagger that enforcer carries."

"Go. Warn Jonas." *Get away.*

"I an't moving one step 'til Nan gets here."

Aden would fight it as long as she could. Stubborn as ever.

Love—unwanted, undeserved—squeezed him so hard, he couldn't breathe.

"Lemme go. I ... earned this. Like my fucking father." Those bitter words mingled with the bile souring his tongue.

Pap staggering into The Bar, tripping into Caleb and his fellow scrapers' table, knocking over their drinks before he crashed to the floor. His clothes puke-caked, his lips blue. Slurring nonsense, pissing his pants as he died, one filthy hand stretched toward Caleb. Disgusting.

Yet Caleb had poisoned himself with something worse than alcohol. Betrayal. Something no one forgave.

"*Go,* Addie."

Aden's mouth pressed to his ear, too hot against his skin. "Here's the thing, Goldie. I an't getting you out of this scrape. You an't dying. Too easy."

"Please ..." Caleb struggled in her hold, head throbbing, nausea cramping his stomach.

Aden kept her cheek pressed to his, too firm, as if she couldn't let go.

Caleb whimpered, and she relented.

He met her furious eyes. Moisture gleamed in them. He couldn't remember ever seeing Addie cry before.

"Let go ... for Jonas."

Shame was swift corrosion. It ashed his anxiety for Jonas, for Del. His lips went numb—the only thing that kept him from begging Addie not to expose him.

Voices and movement whipped the air around him—Nan and Kimber rushing up, panting with exertion.

"I need to triage him." Nan tugged at his clothing. She ignored his feeble resistance. Her hands poked and pressed, spiking his anguish.

A sharp stick to his arm and relief flooded him like a reefer high, weighting and numbing his body. He didn't want it, but the intense contrast tear-blurred his vision.

Grimm appeared beside Nan. Caleb couldn't bear the worry in his face.

"What the hell happened?" Kimber asked, shifting anxiously at Nan's back.

The muscles of Caleb's throat spasmed. "All this mess … target's the Boss …"

Nan sat up straighter, her eyes unfocused. "The gang map … They *are* hitting the warren." She bent over Caleb. "How do you know this?"

Caleb turned toward Aden; her gaze bored into his, daring him to lie.

Turnskin. Coward. Fool.

"Belek … much as told me."

Nan bared her teeth like maybe she'd bite him; she rummaged in her medical pack instead. "Grimm, fetch Jonas's cart."

Grimm ran, ignoring Caleb's moan of denial.

No one gave a shit what he wanted.

"We'll get him to the Fring gate," Nan said to Kimber, pulling a vid-card from her pack.

"What then? Without Del—"

"Show this voucher, and they'll call the emergency in."

"No!" Panic pressed on Caleb. "We … lock down the hub. Now."

He was worse than useless. But the hells he'd leave!

"I an't a doc," Nan said. "All I did was slap on a patch to keep you from bleeding out."

He contorted his face in a failed grin. "Belek wasn't aiming for my vitals."

"Belek?" Nan snapped up straighter.

Caleb wanted her to understand. And didn't. "Fet are hunting Del. It's all gone to shit."

"You sure?" she said quietly, with layers of meaning.

"I'm sure." He looked at Aden, irresistibly.

Her lips twisted in a double-edged smile.

"Comm's still down. We're being blocked." She frowned at Nan. "I'm running for Jonas. I know which patrol he routed with."

Aden pressed close to Caleb, kissed his cheek, and whispered, "You *fight*, Goldie. In this pit, death is the only fuck-up too bad for a restart."

Then she was gone, cool air stinging in her wake.

Her boot-falls pounded swift, distant.

Kimber and Nan's gazes were locked over Caleb, an intensity meant to be private.

"Lock down The Bar." Nan tossed the voucher at Kimber. "Things settle, and you cart Caleb to the Fring."

"An' what are you doing through all this?" Kimber fisted the voucher, snapped her hands to her hips.

Nan's face warped into a ferocious mask. "Warning everyone I can. It's war."

53

———

ABOVE THE ROCKY INCLINE, A JAGGED LINE OF SHAPES ROSE LIKE BLUNT, uneven teeth. The low cloud cover glowed a rusty orange, reflecting the tepid streetlights. Balter's Den.

"What I wouldn't give for a vid now," Del muttered when they topped the incline. "Better yet, transport." Reaching the border was a far cry from reaching The Bar. She felt she'd climbed a massive staircase, only to find another stretching above.

"Are you cold?"

Del clenched her jaw to control her chattering teeth. "I'm fine."

Short of offering his pants, Tam could do little about her chill. They hadn't risked the time to hunt up their jackets. She regretted it now.

"Those kids will have run off with anything they could carry."

Del slanted Tam a look. "Are you reading my mind, Mr. Lyn?"

He smiled, a warm, subtle curve of his lips. "No. Your face."

If he kept smiling like that, she might not need a jacket.

She sobered as she considered the gun he fisted. "What will happen if the wrong person sees you with that?"

He averted his eyes. "It's our only weapon."

Biting her lip, she studied his bare chest. Now that she knew, he looked *so very* Rynet. She closed her eyes. It was a toss-up which would flatten her first, anxiety or exhaustion.

Tam's hand closed over hers. "We'll try the first block-sentry we see. If the comm's working, they'll get a message to Jonas."

Early evening gloom lay unnaturally thick, padding their path. No light shone from windows, yet the streets were deserted.

"What's going on?" Del trotted after Tam, struggling to match his pace.

He frowned. "Folk may be hiding to avoid any Surge trouble."

No block-sentries. Del wanted to cry.

They shuffled on until Del's whole being went numb. She longed to lean on Tam, refused to allow herself. He had to be more exhausted than she, and he'd been wounded.

Tam grasped her arm, making her trip when he sped up.

All right? she sent.

Brow furrowed, he didn't respond.

Del winced. She shouldn't have taxed him. Her slapdash triage had prevented serious concussion from the Arnec's blow, but without rest ...

Tam dragged her into a trot. She nearly rebelled when the wall rose before them. He was leading her to the gate! She opened her mouth to protest, but he broke into a jog. It was all she could do to keep pace. Her ankle buckled as they took the stairs into the square. Tam steadied her, rushed onward. He halted before the pedestrian gate.

"Followed," he panted.

Panic bubbled inside her. "I'm not leaving."

Tam faced her, urgently. "The Surge are after you."

She folded her arms. "Or you."

"Someone needs to let the warren know you're safe before things really tank. I'm better equipped for that if I don't have you to protect."

The hells! Bare and bruised, he appeared worse for wear than she. "I've learned to do my own protecting."

That startled a smile from him. "This job calls for muscle, not brains." He shot a look over his shoulder. "Hurry."

Was he maneuvering her? No one pursued them into the square. Squinting at the structures that crowded against it, she caught movement in the shadows. Real or imagination? *There are always people moving in shadow here.* But her skull prickled with warning.

She glared at Tam. "Come with me."

He tapped his bare chest. "Kind of lost my pass."

"Your face is on file."

"Would you respect me if I did?" he whispered with a pained expression. He cut off her protest. "Time here stacks the risk."

"Tam, *please*." Injured and exposed, how could she let him go?

He brushed her cheek with his knuckles. "I have to, angel. You know that."

"Don't you *dare* get hurt." Her throat grew tight.

"I won't."

Right. Swearing, she whirled away. She glimpsed elation bloom on Tam's face as though seeing her safe brought him joy—no matter the danger he flung himself into.

Del stalked through the gate as Tam sprinted away behind her.

She froze.

Ahead, the First Ring gleamed with early evening. Behind her, the Maze flickered with shadows. The First Ring square lay empty, the city like a panoramic projection at its edges, blurs of movement, the rhythms of the evening rush.

Her perspective shifted, disorienting, as if she'd passed into another dimension.

She sagged against the wall, limbs rubbery, and closed her eyes. The air hung heavy and silent behind her. The hum of vehicles woke like an insect chorus before her. A familiar soundtrack of civilization.

Reality rushed in, and Del pressed her palms against the wall's slick surface to keep from collapsing. Disbelieving. Sick. She'd *killed*. With a tool of healing.

To save Tam.

To save herself.

How great a distance truly lay between Del and Umar's twisted self-indulgence?

Del's extremities numbed as she imagined Isa Vinn, or anyone outside the Maze, discovering her actions. She curled into herself, her fisted hands pressing against her breastbone.

What could Del do against the Maze's chaos? What *would* she do? Carve out more of her soul, corrupt herself further? If Balter's Den crumbled, she would lose the life she'd established. But if she continued to bend her morals, she would lose her purpose, herself ... everything.

Going Where the Need is Greatest ...

Need isn't unique to the Maze.

Del flinched as if a stranger had hissed the words in her ear.

Her cold rationality formed a cruel juxtaposition against Tam's smile, his selfless joy in her safety. Yet if Del followed Tam, she'd undo what he'd risked himself for.

Rhemy's offer welled in her thoughts, his passion and plea. Achieving greater good together. No more pressure to advocate. No finding herself mired amidst incomprehensible cruelty. No compromising with her *own* darkness.

She closed her eyes, swayed forward as if she could sink against Rhemy's vision, let it comfort and envelop her. The elation on Tam's face flashed across her closed lids.

Del snapped her eyes back open. People had to matter more than visions, more than her own weaknesses.

Del straightened. Crossed back into the Maze.

Tam had lost his bloody mind if he imagined she'd cower in cushioned security with everyone and everything she cared about at stake.

KIMBER PEERED OUT THE BAR door then slammed it shut, jabbing the security panel, white-eyed. Metal gates cranked down before doors and windows, a buzz signaled their electrification. Kimber shoved the heavy bar across the entrance for good measure.

Caleb lay on the taproom floor, propped up with pillows, the pilly fabric of an old blanket scratchy beneath his palms. Kimber's alarm reached him, remote, as through a vid recording. His body pooled, languid and weak, like after a night of partying. The crimson painting his clothes shrieked the difference.

Kimber swore a hot stream. "Surge heading this way. Whole mess of them."

Dugan's plan, bearing its rotten fruit.

"Nan was right." Kimber stared blankly, then fixed her gaze on Caleb.

There was no one else. "I can't fucking believe it. They're making war on us. The whole warren."

"Yeah," he rasped.

"Nan promised," Kimber whispered, stroking the gold lacework decorating her mechanical hand. "She'd add stars to this."

Caleb swallowed hard.

She frowned at him, vibrating with uncertainty. "Wish I could get you upstairs."

"Get me my knives." He pushed himself straighter, ignoring the weird tug in his side. "I can at least throw them."

Kimber studied him, too long.

"I'm all you got." His mouth twisted with bitter irony.

Muttering about "dumbass swagger," she ducked behind the bar. Pressed his weapons belt into his hands without meeting his eyes.

His fingers clenched over the familiar, worn vinyl sheaths.

Commotion erupted outside The Bar. Kimber dashed for the backroom. Caleb squinted at the security monitor beside the door. Three flashy wheeled cars pulled in front, helmed men on their extended grills, flag-decorated motorcycles at their extended bumpers. Twice the number as had been recorded rolling parade-style through town.

The toppers unfolded from the lead car, Torx and her beefy partner. Stimps ranged around them like a human wall. Scorning the protection, the toppers climbed onto the car's hood.

"Come out, Valerian!" The man's voice roared like a giant's, making Caleb jump—voice-amped.

Kimber stomped back into the room, bat in hand, a weapons belt draped over each shoulder. "Only Grimm in back. He'll batten down. I'm sealing the door to the backroom in case they get past him."

"They're lethal-armed."

"Yeah. I'll shutter the windows upstairs." Kimber turned away. Hesitated. "They're really after the Boss?"

Hollow disbelief, not a real question, so Caleb didn't reply.

"We've got a knife to your warren's throat," the man boomed. "Can make all your fancy plans crumble!"

Caleb clenched the blanket in his fists, hatred of Dugan surging past his self-hate.

Torx's laugh shrilled with a screech of static over the amp. "You warren grubs got a choice. Turn over Valerian, or we smash you. Poison your water. Burn your new business on the border. Kill your doc and anyone who crosses us."

Addie was out there. Planning how to take *that* on.

Caleb couldn't think of her now.

"Where is Jonas?" Caleb muttered, unable to believe he'd stay away long.

Kimber's mouth pressed whitely. "Far away, I hope."

Caleb let his gaze unfocus. When he next met Jonas—if they survived—he'd face the Boss. Caleb knew the warren chief's justice; he'd helped dish it out often enough.

Banishment.

Caleb would be dead to anyone who mattered. Even Addie.

How long had he fantasized about escaping this place? Never like this.

'I get my heart broken, scrape bottom, but here is what I'm fighting for.' Addie's words came back to him. He understood now. Too late.

Caleb closed his eyes, bit his lip against a spasm in his throat. He wished he could crawl out, let the Surge crush what was left of him.

***

TAM'S LUNGS BURNED AND HIS SOLES HAD BLISTERED. HE TUNNELED HIS focus on putting one foot in front of the other, as fast as his abused body allowed. Wind iced his exposed skin, whistled in his ears.

An amped voice carried on the wind—*smash … poison … burn*—just as a clamor of presences struck his psy-awareness, people gathering in numbers around The Bar.

His pace dragged as if the turbulence thickened the air like a physical storm.

Idiot. He might be safely tucked up with Del now! What the hells did he owe Humans who punished his sacrifices with scorn? Even Jonas … shoving Tam into hiding over their cruel ignorance.

Tam slowed further, turned toward the path behind him.

'Your mother was a matriarch.' Yoranya's reminder froze him. *Emere* had

sacrificed herself to protect Tam, but also the Trenabic cluster she'd never truly integrated with. A lesson more starkly, painfully profound than any *ver'ela* gift.

Del pushed herself every day without reward. Sharing her life meant sharing her path.

If Balter's Den fell to chaos, IWA might yank her home.

Tam stumbled, wheezing for air through a constricting chest. Gulping a deep draught, he spun toward the warren's heart and ran.

54

DEL HESITATED IN THE DESOLATE SQUARE. BACKLIT BY THE GATE'S LIGHT, HER shadow stretched like a charcoal slash through the center. Commotion churned, distant.

She squinted into the warren's gloom, awareness prickling. More than awareness. *Instinct.* A tug on her gift. Like the instinct that had led her to Tam that first day.

Del shook her head, swiftly strode toward The Bar. The commotion swelled, and a deep, amplified voice snarled Jonas's name. Del tripped, Thuron's parting comment twisting through her mind. *'Stay clear of Valerian if you mean to keep your promise.'* Thuron had warned her, but not in the way she'd thought.

Dear gods. Tam would be there, tangled in the chaos. *'This calls for muscle, not brains.'* Muscle couldn't shield him from anarchy. Half-naked. Carrying a banned weapon. Awful helplessness burned in her chest. Del had no power to calm a mob, neutralize a gang.

She frowned toward the darkly pulling presence.

Exhaustion had muddled her brain. Instinct would have to do. She ran toward the source of the mental itch.

Figures stirred down the street ahead, blending into the shadows. Del ran, tracking them with her extra sense, fighting for balance as if images layered her vision. Exertion heated her torso, dragged at her legs.

Del slowed as she drew close. Deadly to approach them unawares.

The center figure halted, whirled to face her. The others whipped around a moment behind with guns raised.

"Hold!" Belek snapped to his men.

Del's breath stuttered. A split second had divided her from a riddling of bullets.

Belek's shrewd gaze bored into Del.

Realization tipped her into vertigo. *Those eyes.* From her dream, the strange Human boy who'd entered her cell. She'd believed it a simple nightmare then, but if the visions of Tam's mother were real … If Belek was that boy …

This gang had captured Tam's mother. Caused her death.

Del tensed to keep from swaying. *Tam must never know.*

Belek stepped close. The back of her skull prickled madly. She shuddered but faced him squarely.

"You've managed to surprise me, toff."

"Myself, too," she murmured through numb lips. What the hells was she doing? Taking a lunatic gamble to save her home. "You were following us before. Why?"

His head cocked. "You can't be crack-brained enough to fling yourself into our hands for that slice of curiosity."

"No. But knowing the answer might help me feel a bit less crack-brained."

He laughed, a flash of white teeth, then narrowed his eyes. "You an't foolish enough to imagine privilege protects you?"

Del recalled the dream, the blanket the boy spread over Tam's mother, the glimmer of compassion beneath his coldness. "I've no reason to expect anything, but I hope you'll speak with me."

Belek's fingers pinched her chin, a warm shock against her chill skin. He tilted her head up. "You could've been safe through that gate."

She hardened her gaze. "There's nothing I want through that gate."

"Well, then. We'll talk."

She startled when he took her arm, steered her down the alley. Her questions sealed in her throat as he led her through the streets—away from the warren's center.

Fight fire with fire. The only idea she had. The Fet were more powerful than the Surge. Little as she understood deadly warren politics, that was clear.

Her teeth chattered, conspicuous in the stillness. They crossed onto a wider thoroughfare. Still late afternoon, but streetlights glowed, and miner-sticks colored the windows of structures lining their path.

Belek thrust her into the mouth of an alley, releasing her.

She went rigid as he shrugged off his coat, but he swirled it over her shoulders, settling warmth and a clean scent over her. It had draped to his knees but brushed her ankles. His face creased with irony, almost a smile.

"Thank you," she stammered.

"Now, Dr. Marks, what do you want to discuss?"

"It's Jonas." Her voice rode a thinly gusted breath. "The Surge mean to kill him." Umar had known. Had lurked in the waste like a spider, waiting until she could return to Balter's Den.

Belek shrugged. "Yeah."

"Will you stop them?" Her fingers dug into the coat's heavy fabric.

His head twitched back. He laughed. "Just like that?"

"You can't want the Surge to take over."

Smugness warped his face. "I want the Surge to overreach like the gullible fools they are. Either warren folk or the OBMG will crush them eventually with no effort from my organization."

"Eventually ..." Awful images of chaos—lost friends—flashed through her mind. "You'd let them kill Jonas?"

"You might've seen Valerian and I cozy up a few times, but we an't friends."

"Jonas is this warren's heart. A body can't survive without one."

He leaned against the corner of a building, folding his arms. "Mildly poetic."

This was going as well as she might have expected.

She knotted her hands more tightly in the scratchy fabric of his coat. "He's what keeps this warren thriving. His leadership. His ideas. His funds."

Belek sighed. "And?"

She sensed his men's stares, their menace at her back, but held her focus on Belek. "You once told me your organization only survives when its host does. What happens if Balter's Den falls into chaos? Sinks deeper into poverty?"

Belek prowled forward.

She stumbled back, bumping into the man behind her.

Tension creased Belek's eyes and mouth. Not indifferent, after all. "What will you offer me to save it? Eh, toff?"

Her head spun, not a single idea forming.

"So *easy* to ask for things when it costs you nothing." His fingers braced her neck, his thumb stroking her jaw hard enough to hurt.

She swallowed. "I'll do anything in m-my … means."

Belek's thin lip curled. "What do you have that we'd want?"

"You called me a symbol," she whispered like a gambler tossing a weak hand.

His eyes grew heavy-lidded. "Go back to the Fring where you belong." He released her with a shove, turned his back.

The synthetically amplified voice growled in the distance, "… out … Valerian … start dying." Protesting voices filled the background like a news scroll on low volume.

Dizziness swept her, and she flailed her hand against the wall to steady herself.

She'd squandered her strength on desperate, stupid futility.

55

Tam found himself trapped by a crush of others. Denners clogged the streets around the warren-hub, punishing Tam's extra sense with their anger, disbelief, fear.

A roar overhead rattled windows and sent people ducking. Wind sucked up then released their clothing. Tam jerked his eyes skyward. A dark shape hovered, like the underbelly of a marine beast. A Mine Security gunship—flying too low. Its spotlight swept over them before it blasted away, its engine vibrating through the air like an insect buzzing over a sonic amp.

Tam shoved ahead. The gunship roared by, circling Balter's Den, churning the air into tiny, localized squalls as it passed. Churning the people more. Tam froze, dug his nails into his palms. If the MS stood on alert, things were already coming apart.

Just move. Do what you can.

He pushed onward.

———

"Valerian! Valerian! Valerian!"

Del's stomach was raw, her limbs leaden. Her teeth chattered despite the warmth of Belek's coat. An airship blew by overhead, whipping up the coat's hem. She was too miserable to react. She longed to reach for Tam, reassure herself of his safety, but he might realize she was Maze-side. *I'm a fool.*

Valerian! Valerian! The cries had faded but echoed inside her mind.

Memory flashed through her—Jonas on the podium in The Bar, his face glowing over the improvements he'd offered his people. Too cruel for it to end this way. Jonas, Tam, Nan—so many devoted their lives to this place. So easily broken …

Valerian! Valerian! The people's cries rose again, seeming more distant now.

"Please." The word slipped out, brittle and low, directed toward Belek's retreating back.

Belek stopped.

She stumbled backward as he spun to her.

He gripped her shoulders and shoved her against a building. A miner's-stick over the awning reflected red on his pale skin, glittered in his black eyes. "I choose the time and manner."

She couldn't breathe to respond. Fatigue tremored her legs like they'd give way.

"That clear?"

She dipped her chin, too dizzy with defeat to think.

He released her and flipped up his wrist-vid. "Make ready. We move."

Belek snatched Del's arm, dragged her so swiftly that her head snapped back. "You might live to regret this deal, toff."

56

A BIZARRE STANDOFF. THE CROWD SURROUNDED TORX AND HER CREW, A seethe of outrage. Torx stood atop a car roof like a sinister idol on a stage, her shaved skull painted with crimson stripes, her visor over her face, a rapier in one fist, a long-nosed pistol in the other. Her hulking partner stood at her shoulder. Their helmeted entourage bristled around them, staggered over the cars' hoods. The Bar formed the backdrop—the dented door and broken windows signs its fortress-sturdy exterior had weakened.

Wedged against a building, Tam absorbed the situation, despair soaking in. Too late. No one to warn. No point.

Umar's gun hung heavy in his cramping fingers. He'd never shot one before.

Eleven Surge stimps on the car tops. How many were lethal-armed?

Enough to decimate the crowd. Denners might crush the enemy with sheer numbers if they grew enraged enough to suffer the losses. Tam couldn't risk firing with such grim odds.

He thunked his head against the wall behind him.

The airship blasted over, but Torx held her cocky posture. When the noise settled, she glowered around. "You folk ready to die for Valerian? He's just one man to your many."

The Surge had been spewing threats too long. They were building the crowd to raise the drama and the stakes. Leaving Jonas without a choice.

Tam snatched a glimpse of Nan moving in from the alley beside The Bar, Aden and other NGs around her. His heart soared, sank.

They'd be no less helpless than the rest.

"You want me? Here I am!" a voice boomed, equal to Torx's synthetically amped one.

Tam's chest caved as a burly figure stepped from a side street, paces away—Jonas, looking bizarre, his torso covered by a black armored vest so tight it seemed rooted into the muscle below his ribs. On his head, a shiny black helmet. In his hand a massive gun, bigger than his brawny arm, like an MS rifle.

Shock rippled through the crowd. Tam swayed with its force.

"You've gone too far!" Torx shrilled. "The gangs will unite to spike your head on a stick."

"Mine beside yours," Jonas said. "Make war on our warren, we make it back."

Nan shoved through people to reach Jonas, her face pure heartbreak. "Jonas, no."

Jonas squeezed her shoulder. "The Bar goes to you." He turned from her horrified reaction as Aden flanked his other side.

"Boss, we've resecured water and grid." Aden's customary bluster hung limp around her.

"Aden, you ready to stand for me?" Jonas's attention dropped heavily on her.

Her mouth pressed into a hard line. "Yeah, Boss. Always."

"The warren's on you now."

Aden's chin squared as if to counter its tremor.

"None of it matters without you." Nan's voice quavered like she'd aged fifty years.

"Del matters," Jonas said with unrelenting calm. "All of it does."

Nan covered her mouth, bowed her head.

"Make your choice, *Boss*," Torx gloated. "You fire that murder-stick, and we start killing whoever we can reach."

Jonas handed Aden the rifle, end-up. Tam twitched forward, but

Aden shouldered him back. She took the gun without hesitation, though it might mean her death sentence.

Jonas stripped off the helmet and armor, handed it to Nan. "Wear it," he snapped when she made to refuse. "We need you fit to nurse the wounded."

Then he turned to Aden. "If the Surge break the deal, or turn on this crowd, you use that gun."

Aden's free hand hooked the wire scarf at her throat. Her *yessir* was silent.

Tam edged around her to face Jonas.

Jonas's eyes widened, taking in Tam's bare chest and blood-spattered neck, then crinkled with grim irony. He approached the Surge, firmly shifting people from his path.

Unbearable, despite the hurt Jonas had dealt him. "Wait!" Tam cried, futilely.

Hands loose at his sides, face expressionless, Jonas stepped up to Torx's car.

Crazed elation slashed over her mouth.

Her partner's expression held grimmer satisfaction. "Come on up."

Tam twined through bodies to reach Jonas. "Don't, Boss! They don't have Del. Never had her. Don't—" He sounded like a kid yapping for his pap's attention. Helplessness choked his words. No words could sway Jonas. He wouldn't let a single Denner die for him.

Torx slashed her blade toward Tam. "Tame your freak, or I'll blow its brains out." Her rancorous words were white noise.

Jonas met Tam's eyes, such weight there, impossible to read.

"I didn't do right by you." Jonas tugged the gun from Tam's hand, dropped it, and kicked it under the car. With a boost from the fender, he stepped easily onto the hood.

From the roof, Torx aimed her pistol at Jonas's head.

The crowd howled, surged forward, crushing Tam against the side panel.

"Valerian, Valerian, Valerian!" The chant rose.

Torx fired a warning shot into the air, flinching the masses silent.

Murmuring voices waved through the crowd from the periphery. Tam wrenched back to breathe, craned his neck to see. Black figures appeared on rooftops around them. High overhead, the MS gunship hovered, predator-patient.

A pack of black-garbed men sliced through the crowd.

Del's aura blazed, close, making Tam's muscles seize and his head swim. *How is she here?!*

A Fet pack strode through the parting crowd, Belek at its point. And Del. She stood at the enforcer's shoulder, swallowed in his black coat. Tam was too bludgeoned with horror to reach for her with his mind, and she didn't reach for him.

Tam dropped to his knees, biting his tongue as he struck the ground. His hands hung boneless at his sides.

All for nothing.

Like his mother … the vicious cost of caring too much …

Cramped against the car's fender, Tam kept his front-row view. Folk made way for Belek as though too stunned to react any differently.

Belek drew before the car with empty hands fanned by his sides. The Surge's lethals snapped toward him—Del vulnerable at his side.

"Did you really mean to take what's ours?" Belek's snipped off words carried over the dumbstruck crowd. "Did you think we wouldn't notice?"

"This an't about you lot." Torx's amped bluster slurred with static. "But we can make it, if you want."

"It's about *all* of us, no?" Belek cocked his head. "Dugan ensured it would be."

Torx's mic switched off with a scree. "Dugan sent you?" A dent in her swagger.

Curling his abused tongue inside his teeth, Tam groped the car's side, dragged himself to a crouch. Jonas's booted feet stood a hand's breadth from Tam's face. Torx's lethal still threatened Jonas's head.

"You might've reported in and spared us this drama," Belek said.

"We got it under control," Torx said.

Tam clawed his hand against the car's unyielding metal, dizzy, sick. Not a war between the deadly gangs, an *alliance* against the warren.

Tam's gaze sought Jonas, helpless. The tendon's stood out on Jonas's thick neck, but his face stayed stony.

"You lost a piece, though didn't you, *topper*?" Belek thrust Del before him.

She rag-dolled against the aggression. Anguish charged her aura, searing through Tam, palsying his limbs. Tam hunted her gaze, but her face twisted toward Belek.

"We got no further use for that bit of bait." The shrug in Torx's voice mismatched her predator's alertness.

Belek seized Del's hair, baring her throat. "Valerian is attached to this piece."

Tam crouched lower, vibrating with the desperate need to spring.

The near crowd surged, unmuted.

The Surge stimps fired into the air, but it only spiked the clamor.

On one knee, Tam scanned dazedly around him. Too many rough-shod legs caging him. Dirt and crumbling pavement under his hand. An object snagged his attention. Umar's gun, beneath the car's undercarriage. He ducked down, stretched until he felt his arm would pull from its socket, then his fingertips hooked the grip. Scrabbling the gun up, he jammed it into the waistband at his back.

A touch on his shoulder made him jump. He met Nan's urgent eyes. She thrust a wad of cloth at him, jerking her chin toward his back. A jacket. To hide the gun. Sparing her a nod, he slipped it on—warm, stinking of spray-clean and sweat. Not Nan's.

Tam pushed behind the first row of spectators, hunting an angle on Belek.

Atop Torx's twisted stage, Jonas extended his hand to the crowd, a simple gesture, a powerful entreaty. Stillness waved outward, startling and swift.

Jonas pivoted to face Belek. "The MS has their eye on Dr. Marks," he said with hard dignity. "You risk more than warren wrath."

Belek smiled like a cadaver and jerked his coat from Del's shoulders.

Tam watched through a gap between gawkers' heads, his pulse throbbing at his temples, his nail sheaths drawn back. His vision narrowed on Belek's hand, clamped over Del's arm. *Touching her.*

No, Tam! Del's voice sliced through his skull, staggering him.

Hands bit into Tam's arms, a pair on each side, shoving him to his knees. His tunneled vision expanded. Without awareness, he'd prowled toward Belek. Fet stimps flanked him. Tam tensed to fling them off.

"Easy, Tam," Jonas called with forced calm. "Let's hear the enforcer's terms."

"The Surge may have *you*, Valerian. But we might keep this piece awhile." Belek stroked Del's cheek with his knuckles.

Pressure in his irises signaling their fade, Tam thrashed in the gangsters' grip. A knee jabbed into his spine, inches above the hard outline of Umar's gun. Tam froze. Death if they found it.

Belek studied Tam, mild distaste shifting his flat expression. "Our freak-peddler's been hot-eyeing you for years. Wants you for one of his jonnys. *I* think you're too feral to be broken. You remind me of a creature we once possessed, one we should've killed before trying to declaw."

'A creature we once possessed …'

Shock iced Tam's rage.

Hana's words swept his mind. *'The enforcer bragged how they'd captured a Rynet … made her a slave to pull ore …'* Belek was too young to have been that enforcer but old enough to have been a conscript.

Alarm pierced Tam—Del's reaction, not his. She flinched her gaze to his eyes.

She knows. She fucking knows.

Tam?

Just tell me! Tell me that these bastards killed her.

"You look even more like a ghoul, snarling like that." Belek strummed his fingers over the lethal at his hip.

Tam twisted from the stimps' hold.

One leapt to shield Belek, drawing his gun.

Tam crouched an arm's length away, his slitted eyes fixed on the weapon's bore, his hand clenched at his hip, a thwarted attempt to reach his own.

Belek leveled a rancorous glare on his stimp, then released Del hard enough to make her stagger. "I suggest you leash the exotic, and quickly!"

Del tripped forward, clutched Tam's arm, feeding him her horror through her touch.

The pulse at the base of Tam's throat beat savagely. Belek's stimp had holstered his gun. Two moves. All Tam needed. Shove Del down, draw Umar's gun. At this range, he couldn't miss Belek.

Del's palms braced Tam's sides, and she butted her forehead against his collarbone. *Please. If they kill you, I'll be lost here.*

His breath hitched; his heart lurched with confusion. Del's small body propped him up, the mingling scents of her hair and her fear a dizzying mix.

The blind wrath drained from him, his tension dissolving into tremors.

Del locked her arms around his ribs. *I'm sorry, love. I'm so sorry!*

God. He'd been a heartbeat from throwing his life away. If he'd triggered the Surge, then Del …

Tam clutched her with hands gone nerveless, now too lost in his own horror to sense hers.

DEL CLUNG TO TAM, SLUMPING BENEATH HIS TREMORING WEIGHT, BENEATH the awareness of how close she'd come to getting him killed.

And all for nothing.

'The Surge may have you, Valerian.' Del couldn't cry betrayal. Only fools made deals with devils.

What madness had robbed her reason? Trying to play savior. Interfering with what she didn't understand—earning the accusations her friends here had leveled at her. She was a healer. Violating that mandate warped it. Warped her. Brought disaster.

Tam's bare skin cold-slicked her cheek, his pulse rioted against her ear, his breath gusted jaggedly against her brow—close to hyperventilating.

Breathe, love. Deep, easy. As if she'd the right to play that role now.

Hands dug into her arms, tore her from Tam.

Another gangster at Tam's back wrestled off the strange jacket he wore and tossed it. "Well, look at this." He shoved Tam to his knees, holding up Umar's gun.

The blood drained from Del's head.

Belek's eyes narrowed on Tam. "Toss him up with Valerian. Let the sneak die with his master."

"No!" Del whipped toward Belek. A choking grip on her collar snapped her back, a gangster behind her.

"Come on, Belek!" Torx snarled above them. "Let's get this done."

Del glanced up, snared Jonas's gaze. Past his stony expression, across the distance, she read the heartbreak in his eyes.

Belek slashed a hand. "You wanted a carnival. I'm supplying it."

He stalked to Del. She wheezed through the garrote at her throat. He shot a poisonous glare over her shoulder, and the choke hold released.

"Please." A tired line now. Hope drained, she had nothing else.

"It's time, toff." Belek's spindly fingers pincered her chin, forced it up. "What will you give me to save him?" His hard gaze drilled in the reality —the "him" on auction had changed from Jonas to Tam.

"*Any*thing." She meant it.

"Think, Del," Belek said, low, only to her. "It's your show now."

Uncertainty raced through her, incomprehension. The vice of his fingers kept her upright.

"Let it unfold," he whispered, a slither of words that didn't reshape his hard mouth. "You can still crawl home. I'll allow you that."

"Or …?"

He didn't reply, only held her with his relentless stare.

The warren folk simmered around them. Ready to boil. Jonas waited, a willing sacrifice.

And Tam … She'd left her heart on the ground with him.

What use was her calling, her life, with no one to center it? She might save a thousand lives in some saner haven and never make up for that precious *one*.

Del steadied beneath Belek's grip. "What would you ask for any of them?"

His eyelids crimped, a frown ghosting his face. His gaze averted for two excruciating breaths before clicking back to hers. "A marking."

Her breath stuttered out. A mark. Like Nan's.

Belek released her chin.

She jerked her head in affirmation.

"You understand?" Cynicism creased his mouth. "While you stay, *it stays.*"

No healing herself, he meant. Her throat convulsed. To agree would appear irrational to anyone beyond the wall.

Cold logic had no place now. "Yes."

Belek's starkly outlined ribcage rippled in a sigh. Then he faced the hostile line of warren folk. "Keep your doc. But know it's on *our* sufferance."

Two of his sepulchral men flanked Del, seized her arms.

Her attention flew to Tam. His arms were wrenched behind him, forcing his head toward the ground. He fought the manacle-grip.

Please, Tam.

Tam stilled, panting. He craned his neck, lifted his eyes. *I'm trusting you.*

Belek stepped between them, pressing a ringed finger against a device in his palm.

Above, Torx's laughter peeled, a cruel delight, irony-edged.

Tiny tremors sensitized Del's face. She compressed her mouth against the urge to cringe. Movement caught her attention—Nan, pacing at the crowd's edge like a fenced animal.

I must be strong. For all of us.

Belek's eyes bored into hers. "I know you can't understand, but this is necessary for all of us." His echo of her thoughts chilled.

Overhead, the gunship whirred, tossing the air.

Belek's long-fingered hand wrapped around the base of her skull, shooting a frisson through her, tightening her neck.

She squeezed her eyes shut as the brand closed. Her heart thumped off-kilter. She strained against the hand pinning her head. Searing pressure ripped a scream from her. Instinctively, she fled, her mind expanding like particles through the air, her awareness dispersing with it. She absorbed the scene—a small woman dangling from Belek's hands; Tam wrestled to the ground; the writhing, howling throng; the whirr of the gunship, its blare of warning.

The clamp over her nape whipped away. Belek's hand blurred up, fisting a gun. An angry retort and the sky erupted with its echoes while people shrieked.

Her people.

Del's fury swelled—all she had left to her, distilled to a pure ferocity —a force that burst from her as one obliterating command. *Leave us alone!*

Belek recoiled from her with a noise like steam escaping a valve. Tam's tormented mental groan threaded through distant shouts and scuffling.

Strength gushed from her, blanking her senses.

Her awareness seeped back into her limp body like liquid soaking a rag. Sprawled on the ground, Del cracked open her eyelids.

Belek crouched there, close enough to mist her cheek with his breath. "Now you've *really* surprised me." The visceral interest in his eyes flipped her creeping suspicion to certainty; Belek was gifted, like them.

"Too bad I have to let you go," he murmured like a cool, impersonal touch.

He stood. "Consider this a marker of debt. You'll pay when I call it in."

The gunship circled overhead. "This crowd must disperse, imme-diately!"

Del's focus centered on Tam, anguish she imagined more than perceived. The fire branding her cheek watered her eyes, but it wasn't as vicious as the fire in her mind.

Leave us alone!

Del's mental roar stunned Tam flat, ricocheting through his head like a sonic blast. He gasped, helpless against its force until the ringing eased enough for him to breathe. He lay dazed. A hysterical laugh peeled from him. *So strong.* She'd fair cracked his skull.

Del's agony shrieked through Tam. He wrestled free of the stimp pinning him.

Belek released Del, flowed in front of her, and drew his gun, flicker-fast.

Followed the direction of Belek's weapon, Tam sprang. He plowed into Jonas, sending him tumbling from the car.

Torx's weapon barked as she collapsed backwards, her partner knocking her over and tumbling with her.

Gunfire erupted through the street. Panicked cries and screams.

Tam scraped himself off the pavement, squinting up to find Jonas supported by a dozen arms. Unbloodied.

Fire woke in his arm. Blood inked an angry line where Torx's bullet—meant for Jonas—had grazed him.

Death and fear and gunpowder fouled the air. The press of auras, the dense-packed psy-noise, consumed his awareness like a physical pressure over his body.

A pair of black-clad legs lined Tam's vision. Belek stood, pistol poised, before the car's blood-smeared hood. Torx crouched beside her partner, where he sprawled on the hood, her visor knocked off, blood spatter lurid over her cheek.

Tam scanned wildly around. The Surge crew was down, gunfire silenced. *How?*

He sucked in a breath—the drama with Del had been a holo-game to distract the Surge, enable the Fet to box them in.

Torx glared baffled hate at Belek. "Stay back, you bastard!" she snarled, her lethal gripped in one shaking hand, her other pressed to her partner's gory chest.

"You the topper, then?" Belek faced her weapon's bore, unflinching. He knew damned well that Torx led this crew. The bald goon was only her bodyguard and proxy.

Torx's chest heaved. Her grief, fear, rage seared across the space.

"I'm topper." Her proxy's gurgling voice carried. "Go, Tia."

Her head twisted toward him. Whatever look they exchanged had her sliding as if boneless from the hood. When Aden yanked away her gun and jerked her by the arm, she didn't struggle.

The proxy's tremoring chin lifted, and he repeated, "I'm topper."

Belek's lips twisted in a weirdly pitying smile. "Did Dugan promise you lot immunity?" The expression wiped. "He lied."

The gunshot flinched Tam lower.

Gore spewed from the proxy's head.

Belek turned away, his face wrenched with an emotion unreadable through his dead aura, unnerving Tam more than the violence.

Eerie silence blanketed the crowd, disturbed only by the muffled cries of the wounded.

The wind whipped, and a tinny voice pelted them from above. "Cease the unrest and disperse." The airship's massive guns pointed down. "This is your final warning!"

Aden's fiery head appeared, as she climbed atop a battle-scarred car. "You heard the MS. Move out!" Aden fought to be heard over the gunship's whir.

People flowed in conflicting directions, some toward the center, others away.

"Boss, you okay?!"

"Jonas alive?!"

"Where's the Boss?!"

Hoisted to his feet, Jonas bellowed, "Settle down! I'm here."

Tam sagged, every ache and strain flaring to life. The residual buzz of Del's psychic scream punished him. Her distress drew him. He lifted his sore head. She lay paces away, limbs sprawled at haphazard angles.

Jonas crossed, stiff-jointed, to face Belek, and propped a hip against the car's hood as if Topper's pulped remains didn't lie there. "What's the price?" His voice was level, but his chest kept a ragged rhythm.

Belek holstered his gun in a fluid motion. "You have your toff to thank for your life, Valerian."

"You haven't answered my question."

Belek's mouth stretched with his cadaver's grin. "The chip is hers to pay."

"I'll take her debt." Jonas hard-stared Belek. "It's really mine, an't it?"

"Initiative should be rewarded, don't you think?" Belek smirked toward Del. "An' her offer is more appealing."

Rage flushed over Jonas's face.

A rumble formed in Tam's throat—as feeble as his limbs. He scramble-crawled to Del, tugged her up by the shoulders, shielding her with his body.

People churned around them, their cries raking air already sharpened by smoke and sour sweat, but a bubble of tension sealed Belek and Jonas inside.

"This is a bargain, Valerian. It's a numbers game, an't it? You, the toff's exotic, NG there." Belek stabbed a finger toward Aden, who stood at crowd's edge, rifle in her hands.

Belek didn't give a shit about rules. The Fet's interference with the Surge had given him an excuse to flex his power.

Del wobbled to her knees, braced within Tam's arms. "It's okay, Jonas. I agreed," she said as if her quiet conviction might tame the stubborn fury in Jonas's face.

"Take this calmly, Valerian, and she gets away with that marking."

Jonas's mouth compressed.

"In exchange for the lethals." Belek pressed. "As for saving your life? That's between me and the toff. I'll choose my price … when I see a need."

Del had taken a demon's bargain, open-ended, perilous. Tam panted, useless with exhaustion.

Del's hands captured his, small, cold, fierce.

He met her eyes as if compelled.

"One problem at a time, all right?" she whispered. A smile tugged the corner her mouth toward her unmarred cheek. Tam whimpered at the brutal mark seared in the other, an angry round blister.

"Del?" Jonas's frowning voice reached them.

She squared her chin as if too exhausted to lift anything else. "The enforcer and I have an accord." Her gaze shifted between Jonas and Belek, equally hard.

Belek sneered, a futile attempt to hide his amusement. He spun from Jonas. "You'd better put all this back in the box before we meet next, Valerian."

Retreating footsteps marked the gangsters' withdrawal.

The gunship whipped another circle overhead. "Continue to disperse in orderly fashion."

Tam shifted Del's grip, so their fingers threaded together. They knelt, knees touching. He pressed his forehead to hers.

Curiosity needled into him, people watching. He blocked them out.

"You gave me the worst scare, angel."

She scanned him, her focus landing on his bleeding arm. "You broke your promise again."

"We're quite a scuffed pair." He cupped his hand over her wounded cheek.

"My head hurts," she croaked.

He puffed a laugh. "I'll bet." His hand flopped to his side. "Let's get you inside." Not that he could imagine lifting an eyebrow, let alone Del.

Jonas strode to them, scooping Del into his arms.

Nan materialized at his shoulder, strange in Jonas's armored gear.

Held between two NGs, Torx glowered from paces away, fierce despite the blood and defeat wilting her frame. Why had Belek spared her? Respect for Topper's sacrifice? Reluctance to deal double punishment? *We might all regret that slice of mercy.*

Nan studied Torx a hard beat then turned to peer anxiously at Del's face. "Okay, Del?"

Del didn't answer, curling into Jonas's chest and closing her eyes.

Aden thumped Jonas's shoulder to signal she'd manage the cleanup, then spun away. "You all heard the Boss! Clear out and fast!"

In a few long strides, Jonas had Del inside The Bar. He took the stairs two at a time with Nan at his heels. Tam limped behind, winded and weak. By the time he scaled the stairs to the exam room, Del was settled in a cot with sealant over her wounded cheek. The mark seared indistinctly but was meant to represent a snake.

Tam closed his eyes, reminded himself that Del came before revenge. Always.

He knew his mother's fate, after years of searching, of grinding frustration. Its abrupt end settled, anticlimactic. The knowledge might come to matter more someday, but he'd made his peace with *Emere's* loss.

Nan closed on Tam with a healing strip in her hands. He submitted with a murmured thanks.

She shot Jonas a scowl. "Where the hell did you get that mega-lethal?"

"Another life." Jonas's grim irony didn't invite further questions.

Rumor claimed Jonas came from G4, but Tam never dreamed he'd been MS.

Jonas turned from their astonishment. "You okay awhile, Del? I need Nan."

"Yes. There were injured, surely?" Del rasped.

"Aden and Nan will manage. Anyone critical we'll send through the gate with a voucher. With that airship monitoring, the gate sentries will be expecting it."

"Not … enough left."

"We'll make do."

Del only nodded, a clear sign of her wrecked state. She watched Nan and Jonas exit with pain-slitted eyes.

Jonas paused in the doorway, giving Tam a searching look that re-fired Tam's tension.

57

Del woke to a shiver of threat—not from gangsters, or patchworks, or a madwoman—only friends ringed around her. Her head ached with disorienting ferocity. Judging by the rough-grained sheets beneath her skin, she lay on an exam room cot.

"—too dangerous for her now," Jonas was saying.

"She won't thank you to make her decisions for her," Nan said.

"I'm responsible for her safety, and—"

"It's over for now," Nan cut him off. "No call to push Del out."

Push her out? Del fought to open her eyes.

"We can't wait for Belek to call in her debt. I won't put Del in that danger, no matter how much good she's doing here." Jonas's firm tone wilted. "No matter how much I want it for the Den."

Nan said, "Del's one of us now. Accept it and stop playing her pap."

"Do you think our martyr will go find a civilized nook to snuggle into?" Tam's voice sliced in.

"Don't. You've known all along we can't keep her forever. How are you *both* going to feel if she gets killed?"

"I'd half feel like dying myself," Nan said. "But Del has a right to her own choices."

"Tam?"

"Like Nan said, an't my choice." Tam sounded emotionless, but Del detected the desolation in that void.

She cracked open her eyes. Nan and Jonas stood shoulder to shoulder beside her cot. Tam paced at its foot. He froze, turned his face to her. Dark smudges shadowed his eyes, and his lips were thinned colorless.

Del couldn't shout through her sore head, but her feeble croak commanded the room. "I'm a grown woman. I don't need machos to make decisions for me."

"Your practice takes more than your effort," Jonas said.

"I'm well aware of that. But do you think this," she pointed to her scarred face, "was a victim's gesture? I did what was necessary to protect *my home*—just like *any* of you would have." Del stared at Jonas, remembering how he'd carried her here, his heart thudding beneath her cheek, his grip firm and protective. Now he wanted her gone.

"Damn it, Del. Don't look at me like that. I want this place to deserve your devotion more than anything."

"I want it to deserve yours, too."

"I can't let you die for this."

"Like Nan said, it's my choice."

"That's the pinch for me. It's actually mine."

Del let her eyelids close. Her temples throbbed. In that moment, she wished Tam had left her in the wasteland. Tam sighed, and she imagined it tickling her skin.

"I don't know what to say to you, Del," Jonas's whispered. "I don't think I can bear to know how you swung that miracle today. I'm scared for you."

The raw honesty in his voice hurt.

"You seem to think I have some cushy place to return to. I don't. I have no home if not here." She glared at the ceiling, beneath the weight of unspoken questions.

Maze-dweller reticence left them unspoken.

Del studied Jonas, the grief wrecking his face, his soot and blood-spattered clothes, his wild gray halo of hair. "Big as your heart is, it can't shelter everyone. My choices aren't your burden."

He swallowed with a bob of his larynx.

She continued before he could speak. "If I'm hurting more than helping, I'm on the first jump-ship out. Otherwise, I'm not leaving."

Jonas swore softly.

Tam crossed his arms, inscrutable.

Nan smiled and rose. "I'll bring up a tray, doc. You must be hungry."

"You win, Del." A smile ghosted Jonas's expression. "But becoming a real Denner means you have to listen to me."

"I always *listen* to you." Del bit her lip over an answering smile. Her heart thudded, absurdly fast. A real Denner. A simple sentiment to make her giddy. Not the effervescent joy she'd felt receiving her IWA acceptance, something deeper, rooted in its cost. More precious.

Footsteps shuffled. The door clicked closed, Jonas following Nan out.

Del sagged against the mattress.

Tam prowled to the cot and squatted to her level. He stroked cool fingers across her brow, feather light. She closed her eyes, soothed despite herself. The meds hadn't relieved her throbbing head—the price for straining her psychic ability.

"Headache?" His smoky voice shivered over her.

He chuckled when she cracked open her eyes suspiciously, but his fingers trembled.

Her heart squeezed with her awareness that they had difficult things to discuss. "I need to explain."

"No, you need to rest." His touch slid to her nape, spreading relief with it.

She took his free hand, drew it against her chest. Her heart drummed a reassuring rhythm against the comfort of his touch.

"When you're feeling better," he added, "I'll tell you *exactly* what I think about your martyr complex."

"It wasn't that." She tensed. "You understand, don't you?"

His fingers paused. "Yeah. I do."

She sighed, pressed his palm to her unmarred cheek, relaxing into his touch, letting him soothe her.

58

———————

THE INJURED CRAMMED THE BARROOM FLOOR, LAID OUT ON MAKESHIFT pallets—piled blankets, cushions, inflatable mattresses—whatever volunteers had scraped up. The Bar's chairs and tables were shoved under the stairwell like unwanted company.

Caleb had lost count of the people shuffling inside. Bruises. Broken limbs. Head wounds. Bullet grazes.

He'd overheard more than he wanted from NGs rushing through to the backroom. Three dead. Two critical and ushered through the Fring gate with the last of Del's vouchers.

Nan and a cadre of block-mamas played nurse to the less injured, Nan leading with Del's fancy gadgets and her own customary calm.

All unbearable.

Caleb fought his way to his feet, using the wall for support. Pain flared. The drugs had worn off, but he refused more. Others needed them. Unlike him, they didn't deserve to hurt.

Aden was still out in the warren, steadying folk, supervising cleanup. The wrenching words already spoken would have to stand for goodbye.

The space stank of terror's aftermath, bitter sweat, alcohol, the astringent scents of home remedies. Not every injury warranted the off-world meds. Del's Maze-side stock wasn't equipped for this crush.

Paces away, binding a man's arm, Nan lifted her gaze to Caleb. Her mouth thinned and she jerked her chin in a gesture he didn't understand. She looked pointedly toward the exit, then toward the backroom. He got the message. He could sneak out or face the Boss.

Caleb was done sneaking.

He limped toward Jonas's office, a pulling sensation in his side hitching each step. The bustle blurred around him as if he were a ghost passing through it. No one reacted to him. He supposed the gossip hadn't hit yet. *Gossip is gold.* His mouth twisted with irony.

Jonas's door lay open, warren folk packed inside. Standing behind his desk, towering over everyone, Jonas spotted Caleb in the doorway. By his hard, heavy look, Jonas knew already.

Caleb held his side protectively as Jonas shooed the others out. For a few awful breaths, Caleb couldn't move, couldn't lift his eyes to meet Jonas's.

Jonas rose, startling Caleb. His big hand clamped over Caleb's arm and steered him into a chair before his desk. He shut the door and plunked into his own seat.

"Aden told me."

Caleb nodded, limp, pathetic—like he was a young scrapper again, facing Jonas's disappointment. But the stakes had advanced with his age. He fixed his gaze on the worn knees of his pants. *He* was worn, shabby, in ways that went deeper and more vital than that surface.

"Tell me, then." Jonas's echo of Aden's words almost made Caleb smile. The Boss had rubbed off on her.

He bit the inside of his lip. Thought through his bleary exhaustion. What did Jonas need to know to protect the Den? Caleb spoke, until his throat grew raw. What he knew or guessed of Dugan. Belek's words, as close as he could remember them.

Jonas listened in silence.

Then he said, "Why'd you come back?"

Caleb managed, "Tried a shortcut, Boss. Figured I'd slick myself up, play the hero here."

Impatience and weariness weighted Jonas's sigh. "Don't dare lie to me now."

Shame flushed over Caleb's whole body. "I came back because Belek gutted me with the truth. My stupidity. I'd figured I could play Dugan, pad my pockets, bring you intel. Never meant to be ..." His throat spasmed. "... a turnskin."

"You should have come to me. I can't afford to lose someone I ..." Jonas's voice thickened, smothered the last word.

Caleb shrank beneath awful, heavy silence.

"One year."

Caleb's gaze jerked to Jonas. He was startled by Jonas's reddened eyes. "What?"

"One year, banished. Then, you decide if you're ready to commit, all-in next time."

Weakness washed over Caleb, relaxed him in the chair. *But.* "Boss, if you want me strung up, I'll take that punishment now." Denners would never forgive betrayal.

Jonas's lips whited. The creases deepened in his face. "Nan and Aden. My most trusted. No one else knows why you got stuck, and *they* don't gossip."

Tears rushed Caleb's eyes, so abruptly he couldn't blink them away. They dripped down his cheeks. "I don't understand."

"I've known you since you were no higher than my knees. I know your limits and your strengths—likely better than you do."

Caleb bit his lip. It tremored beneath his teeth.

Jonas spoke on. "Since your father passed, you've had both feet in the warren but your eyes to the sky. One year. Then decide if you can turn both eyes to this rough life and *choose* it."

Jonas's chair squeaked as he shifted his bulk. Caleb read the dismissal.

Struggling up on watery legs, Caleb dashed the tears from his eyes. He needed a last look at Jonas before he left. He absorbed the pain compressing the strong, scarred jaw, the condemnation and forgiveness warring in Jonas's eyes.

He'd gotten off easy.

As if reading Caleb's mind, Jonas said, "An't easy starting over. Building a life from nothing. Things are tough outside Balter's Den—unless you take Pell Mahr's lure again."

I'm sorry. Those words couldn't pass Caleb's lips. Jonas already knew, and it didn't matter. Instead, he said, "Take care of Addie for me. She'll be …" His throat convulsed. "…lonely."

Caleb turned away, not waiting for Jonas's response. Being sure Addie was okay meant surviving his banishment. It meant earning his way back.

59

Dearest Rhemy,

> *Your vision is beautiful. Thank you for offering to share it. My*
> *own vision has grown both simpler and more complex.*
> *Protect my home. My people. Perhaps someday, our visions*
> *will converge here. Until then, know that I love and miss you.*
> *Always.*

TAM COULDN'T SLEEP, BUT LYING BESIDE DEL, DRINKING IN HER BREATH, made for a more satisfying rest. He absently stroked her hair as she slept.

Balter's Den survived. Del could stay. Those points for him had become too intertwined to untangle.

His bandage pulled and he glanced at the patched wound.

Tam had given far more to Balter's Den than to his birth home. It had never been mutual, but his role here had filled a bleakly simple need: to keep emptiness from devouring him.

Now, not emptiness but connection consumed him. Del had slipped through his guard to fill his entire life.

To fill … fulfill.

Del sighed, pulling from sleep. She lay on her side, her hand curved beneath her chin, her scarred cheek upturned. Her eyelids fluttered open. She stretched, half propping herself on an elbow. Studying him, she laid her palm against his chest, stirring his pulse beneath it.

"Tell me truly, love. How are you?" she said, drowsy and earnest at once.

Fine, the nonanswer primed on his lips. He swallowed it. To stand any chance with Del, he needed to learn to share himself. "My mother used to say you can never cast a shadow chasing only moonlight. A Rynet saying. I never really understood it until now."

Del blinked as if clear her drowse. "Tell me," she whispered.

"To Vleren, sunlight is action, future-facing. Moonlight symbolizes reflection—the past in a sense. Both are needed, but ..." He struggled to express meaning in Human terms. "I got lost in reflection, not seeing beyond myself. *Emere* loved me. She lived with courage. It's enough—however she died."

Peace born of certainty melted Tam deeper against the mattress. He had released his mother to Serenity at the overlook. The pressure he'd felt at the tower afterward, the memory fragments Del had read, all telepathic imprints—things of the *mind*, not the spirit, not *ver'ela*.

Del sought his hand, brushed her lips over his abused nailbeds. "I'm glad." Tucking his hand to her chest she relaxed down.

"And you?" He brushed his fingertips across her forehead.

"I must learn to manage."

Her gift, she meant.

"Untreatable headaches, distraction ... those don't mesh well with my calling." A tiny line formed between her brows.

He stroked it away. "We'll figure it out, angel."

Yes. The barest glimmer of a thought, but a soft smile captured her lips as her eyelids succumbed again to sleep.

After everything, she still wanted to stay.

Del was better off away from this pit, yet Tam couldn't let her go. She'd become his home, as Balter's Den never could. He'd do whatever it took to keep her.

"*Rehe al*, Del," he whispered against her hair. "Stay with me."

Del woke, her pain reduced to a dull throb, exhaustion still sapping her limbs. Tam was stretched out beside her, his breath stirring her hair. His lashes lay an inky fringe against his pale skin. His pulse fluttered at his throat, too swift for sleep. Too weary and sore for sleep, perhaps. Tam's body was a collage of hurts. Through all the dangers, he'd made it her shield.

Her own weariness sank her impulse to explore and ease his injuries.

How novel to lie beside someone whose physical essence she couldn't map by rote. Mystery lay beneath the pumping of his lungs, the beating of his heart. And yet she was more certain of Tam than anyone she'd ever been with.

Her arms were folded by her chest, and she absently fixed on the winking of her wrist-vid. The time and date pricked her memory. Something about it …

With a gasp, Del pushed onto her elbow. Her handler! She was supposed to meet him today—in less than an hour.

Tam twitched, sat bolt upright.

She twisted toward him, blinking through pain-watered eyes. "I need your help."

The Office of External Affairs stuck like a barnacle to the Central Security Station's side. Del stepped off the light-tram, clumsy with haste. Beside her, Tam tensed when he spotted the soldier out front, but his bracing hand on Del's arm didn't falter as they passed.

"You sure you can't reschedule this?" he muttered for the third time.

"It would be a mistake."

"Bigger mistake than going looking like you got grated and—?"

"Yes." She'd done her best to primp in the few minutes they'd had— stuck a concealing patch over her cheek, yanked a brush through her snarled hair, scrambled into fresh clothes.

Winded from their rush, Del fought to quiet her breath. She glanced at her wrist-vid, bit her lip. Six minutes late.

The office handled administration for the First Ring's foreign residents. Only a holo-map of the star system over the reception kiosk relieved its sterile, bureaucratic atmosphere.

Del crossed to reception. "I have an appointment with Administrator Qalvert."

"Administrator Qalvert is unavailable, Dr. Del Marks." A smoothly androgynous voice emanated from the kiosk.

Del's frown hurt. She exchanged a tense look with Tam. "I've an appointment with him at 7:30, upon his request."

"No such appointment is on record."

Whipping up her vid, Del hunted for messages from Qalvert. Nothing. An attempt to call him only routed her to his message tab.

She wilted against the kiosk, and a warning chimed.

Tam tsk-ed, drawing her to his side. "Let's go."

He escorted her in silence with a supporting hand on her back.

When they reached her quarters, Tam followed her inside. "Seems like your stiff's ear hasn't gotten around to reporting your miraculous resurrection."

No doubt Qalvert had decided not to bother keeping an appointment with a dead woman—assuming his spies alerted him of events.

"My message should serve for that."

Tam cast a squinty glare around her reception area. "Hold here a minute."

He stalked into her surgery room, then up the stairs. Scanning for threats.

Sighing, Del plopped onto the sofa to wait him out.

They'd connected the dots between enemies in the Maze. The OBMG remained a blank screen. Likely, she would never uncover their strategy unless they decided to reveal it.

Tam swept back into the room. "Until you get better security installed, I'd better crash here. I owe Jonas a report but won't be gone long."

"I'm sure my person is safe here."

He glowered in answer.

"If that will make you more comfortable." She realized her mistake before the words finished tumbling out.

He sprang on them. "Comfortable? Ha. You attract trouble like a drunken game-runner. Not sure I can keep track of all your enemies." His eyes stayed gunmetal gray.

"Quitting so easily?" She arched a brow.

"Sorry, no."

"I can scarcely imagine the trouble you'd find without me."

"Someday he'll pay for this." Tam bent to trace the patch on her cheek, fluttering her pulse with his touch.

More manipulation. Mere banter between them now. They knew each other too well.

"I'm fine, Tam."

"Please get some rest. You're white-eyed flat."

Gods, she needed rest. She'd never muster the strength to care for the wounded without it. For now, they stayed in Nan's hands. Her as-yet unlicensed nurse…

Tam turned away. "I'll come back quietly, so I don't wake you."

He hesitated at the door, still anxious for her.

"Tam." His name spilled softly from her lips. "This is my home. I'm not leaving you."

His fingers hovered over the door release, then he crossed back to her, his irises glinting silver. Threading his fingers through her hair, he brushed it back. "You are walking the knife's edge here." He leaned in, rubbed his cheek against hers, caressed her ear with his lips. "And I'm your shadow."

The delicious contact deepened her sense of certainty.

As Tam spun away, she glimpsed the elation capturing his mouth. She fought to catch her breath as he strode out. A grin burst over her, expanding through her whole body.

She relaxed deeper into the sofa. Vibration rippled through her, heels-to-crown. Galtan's Rumble. The planet's touch, firm and reassuring.

I'm still here.

THE END

DID YOU ENJOY BENEATH A SUN DEPRIVED SKY?

A few sentences on Amazon or Goodreads helps a lot!
E-mail us at murasakipress at gmail dot com with your published review and join our VIP list as thanks for your time!

PLEASE WRITE A BOOK REVIEW!

THANKS FOR SUPPORTING INDEPENDENT ARTISTS!

ACKNOWLEDGMENTS

First and foremost, my heartfelt gratitude to Britta Jensen—editor, mentor, and dear friend—without whom this book would not exist. She championed my story and gave me the courage to put it out there. Thank you to my detailed proofreader Nancy Knight, and to the talented Sarah J. Coleman for the beautiful cover design.

Thanks also to those who supported the novel over its many fits and starts: Jenna Carricut who slogged through my first, awkward draft, yet encouraged me to keep going. Teacher Carrie Jones who understood my vision and helped me stretch to reflect it on the page. My thoughtful beta readers: Skye Alexander, Luke Elliot, Matt Kimbrough, Dan Giard, Isaac Goldstein, Whitely Loyd, Beth O'Conner, and Glenn Williams. Kat Patrick and Amanda Moore—readers, cheerleaders, sounding boards, and givers of laughter when needed most. Deep gratitude to my husband Michael and children Nina and Niklas. I would still be facing a blank page without their patience and support.

ABOUT THE AUTHOR

 Kara Lenore is an alumna of the Viable Paradise Workshop. *Beneath a Sun Deprived Sky* is her first novel. Her short story "Climbing" appeared in the *Mixed Bag of Tricks* anthology under the name Kara Stockinger.

Kara spent part of her youth living in Japan and earned a doctorate in Japanese studies, experiences which influence her work. She now resides in Austin, Texas, with her beloved husband and two children, working in the tech industry and escaping to science-fiction worlds whenever possible. **Join her mailing list at karalenore.com.**

instagram.com/kara.lenore